The No-Kissing Contract

Also by Nicole Lightwood

Cage of the Cursed

A Palm Vista Novel

NICOLE LIGHTWOOD

CALADESI
PRESS

The No-Kissing Contract
A Palm Vista Novel

Copyright © 2026 by Nicole Lightwood

All rights reserved. No part of this book may be reproduced, stored in a retrieval system, or transmitted in any form or by any means without prior written permission from the publisher, except in the case of brief quotations used in reviews.

This is a work of fiction. Names, characters, places, and incidents are products of the author's imagination. Any resemblance to actual persons, living or dead, is purely coincidental.

Caladesi Press LLC supports the right to free expression and the value of copyright. Unauthorized scanning, uploading, or distribution of this book is theft of the author's intellectual property. For permission requests, contact: hello@caladesipress.com

Thank you for supporting the author's rights.

Cover copyright © Caladesi Press
Interior design by Nicole, Caladesi Press
Editing: Reece, Caladesi Press
Proofing: Lightwood Team

Library of Congress Control Number: 2026900853
ISBN 979-8-9881418-6-0 (Paperback)
979-8-9881418-4-6 (ebook)

Published by:
Caladesi Press LLC

To my pre-teen self, whose dream it was to publish a book.

CHAPTER 1
Welcome Home, Awkward

A BACKYARD BARBECUE IS my definition of Saturday torture. But it's Brandon's coming-home party, and the easiest way to corral every relative and family friend they have into one spot—though still not as uncomfortable as what happens next.

October in Palm Vista, Florida, feels like summer's last grasp. Clear blue skies stretch endlessly, the sweet scent of fresh-cut grass mingles with the ocean air drifting in from the Atlantic, and a merciless ninety-eight degrees even in the shade. The humidity wraps around me like wet silk, thick enough to taste.

Destiny wilts beside me in the perfect yellow sundress chosen specifically for meeting Ethan's brother. A gold hairpin from the Starlit Jewel holds her blonde curls back from her face, though they're already beginning their inevitable surrender to the heat. Her hand lifts to nibble at the side of her fresh manicure before she catches herself and drops her hand.

"It'll be fine," I say, trying to sound confident for her sake. Ethan worships his older brother Brandon, and I get the pressure she's feeling.

Even in eighth-grade, it was obvious. That enthusiasm used to infect me too. Sometimes too much. Especially when Brandon could do all these cool skateboard tricks, or knew the hidden beach spots nobody else did.

"I want to make a good first impression," Destiny says softly.

"He'll love you, just like Ethan does." I flash her an encouraging smile.

She shrugs, a slight movement. Before I can reassure her further, a tiny figure barrels into my legs.

"June-bug!"

I catch Lucy, Ethan's nine-year-old sister, before she can knock us both over. "Hey Lucy Goosey."

"Mom said you'd be here early to help with the decorations, but you weren't," Lucy accuses, her arms locking around my waist. Her dark braids are coming undone, probably from running around the yard all morning.

"Sorry, Luce. I had work." I smooth one of her messy braids.

"Did you bring ice cream?"

"No," I laugh, "Your mom got cake, though."

"It's not the same as ice cream," she grumbles, then glances at Destiny. "Right, Desi?"

"Right," Destiny agrees with a warm smile. "Want me to fix your hair?"

Lucy loosens her grip to ask, "Can you French braid it, June? I like the way you do it."

"Sure." I flash Destiny an apologetic smile as I pull out Lucy's hair tie and comb my fingers through her hair.

Destiny shakes her head, letting me know it's fine, but her smile has lost some of its luster. "I'm terrible at French braids."

"Maybe June can teach you," Lucy offers generously, the way only a nine-year-old can when trying to be helpful while also making someone feel inadequate.

"Destiny does a fine job," I tell Lucy, giving her hair a playful tug. "You need to let her style it more often."

"I don't know..." Lucy says doubtfully, swinging her arms as I move to the second braid. "Last time Destiny did my hair for soccer, it all fell out before halftime."

"That's because someone—" Ethan appears, balancing three plastic cups of lavender lemonade—"did cartwheels during warm-up."

Lucy sticks her tongue out at him. "Mom said my cartwheel was perfect."

"Here," Destiny says, taking two of the cups from him while I finish Lucy's hair.

Ethan sips from his cup. The afternoon sun catches his tousled brown hair, bringing out the warmth in his tan skin, a testament to all the hours we spend at the beach. I'm so used to seeing him in board shorts and faded T-shirts that the khaki shorts and polo almost make him look formal.

"Mom wants to know if you're staying after the party? For dinner?" he asks Destiny.

"Oh, yes please, June—you have to!" Lucy pleads. "Brandon's back, and he'll have stories, and Mom won't care if I stay up late. Please."

"I was talking to Destiny," Ethan says with an apologetic smile, but then adds, "But, uh, yeah, I'm sure Mom won't mind if June stays too." He shrugs the question toward Destiny.

"Of course. June's like family," Destiny says brightly, but I can tell she's being polite.

We've been spending a lot of time together—the three of us—going to movies, hanging out at the beach, studying at

Ethan's. And while we always have fun together, I've wondered if I'm becoming the third wheel.

"Uh, no. I've got some homework to do," I say.

"Aww." Lucy whines.

"You see me all the time, Luce." I secure the last braid with an elastic. "Now go show your mom before you mess it up again."

Lucy bounces on her toes. "Thanks June! Bye Desi!"

"What about me?" Ethan calls after her, but she's already darted off.

"Guess you're old news. She likes Destiny and me more."

Destiny laughs, tucking a strand of hair behind her ear. "She might like June more."

Ethan wraps an arm around Destiny's waist, pulling her closer. "Don't be ridiculous, Desi. Luce is just jealous you'll steal me away."

I take the extra cup Destiny holds out, grateful for the distraction. The humidity presses against my skin, making my throat feel parched. The lemonade goes down fast, the tart sweetness a welcome relief from the heat.

"Thirsty?" Ethan's voice carries a familiar note of amusement. It's so quintessentially him—from the way his blue eyes crinkle at the corners to how his tall frame shifts into that familiar, casual stance.

"I'm *dying* out here," I say, pressing the cup to each cheek.

Ethan watches me wearing a smirk, one hand tucked in the pocket of his khaki shorts, the other gesturing with his cup. "I reminded Mom you melt in the sun, but since it's *Brandon's* party..." He trails off with a teasing grin.

I gesture with my half-empty cup toward the growing crowd, here to welcome Brandon home from his tour of service. "I guess I'll let it slide." I tip my head back to meet his gaze, though I've long stopped being annoyed about the growth spurt that left him half a head taller than me since freshman year.

Destiny adjusts her sundress as she tracks a group of Ethan's relatives moving toward the food table. She tugs on Ethan's arm, lifting her chin as she asks, "Do I look okay?"

Ethan doesn't hesitate. "You look great. Honestly, you'd look amazing in sweatpants." His voice is affectionate and makes her shoulders relax; her smile turns private. When he leans down to kiss her, I turn away, taking another sip of my drink as I scan the crowd.

Most of the guests are Ethan's relatives—laughing and catching up under the harsh rays of the afternoon sun. A few family friends and neighbors from across the street, as well as Brandon's old football coach, who still teaches at Palm Vista Prep.

I offer Destiny a reassuring smile once Ethan leans away. "You look stunning. That color is perfect on you."

Ethan nods. All this talk of appropriate dress attire has him turning to me with a dramatic sweep of his gaze. He stands back as if he needs more room to appreciate my light blue dress, with darker blue peonies spattered all over the fabric. "Wow, Juniper Blake, in a dress. Hell must've frozen over."

"I wish," Destiny groans, fanning herself with her hand. "Today's the hottest day yet."

Ethan nods, his enthusiastic grin still in place. I shoot him a face. He knows I only wore a sundress because it's his favorite brother's welcome home party.

"Wipe that weird smile off your face," I tell him with a laugh, pushing on his chest.

He holds his ground, solid as ever. Destiny shifts beside me, her fingers clenched tight on her lemonade. "Your mom's calling you."

We follow her gaze to where Ethan's mom stands by another woman, around her age. Her brows lift when she catches his eye, waving him over.

"I'll be right back," Ethan says, squeezing Destiny's arm with a reassuring smile. He tips his chin toward me as he tells her, "You should take a picture. It'll probably never happen again." He throws me a wink before he dashes off.

"Ha ha," I call after him, rolling my eyes as he retreats.

Destiny pulls her phone out of the clutch at her side. "He's right," she says with a tight smile, holding up her phone. "That dinosaur profile pic of you at the zoo has been haunting my feed for *months*."

"What's wrong with dinosaurs?" I hold out my hands, blocking her camera from getting a good shot.

"Nothing. When you're six." She flips the camera to take a selfie and gasps. "Oh, no! That's how my hair looks?"

Destiny spent most of the morning curling her hair into beautiful sculpted waves. But no amount of hair spray or gel could compete with this weather. It doesn't help that there's sweat beading on her scalp and down her neck. Most of the people here wear similar evidence of the tropical devastation, but that fact doesn't soothe her.

"It's not that bad," I try to reassure her, but she makes a small noise in the back of her throat, unconvinced.

"It's *horrible*," she says, her voice rising an octave. She scans the party and the obvious lack of Brandon, calculating the time she may have before he gets here. "Do you think I have time to fix it?"

"Um." I glance around the party, my gaze snapping to the side gate as Ethan's dad's sleek sedan pulls up. Most likely with Brandon inside. I'm about to tell Destiny that she's out of time, but she looks on the verge of tears, so I turn her toward the house. "You've got maybe three minutes."

"Okay," she hurries up the patio steps.

She disappears through a set of French doors leading into the living room. I down the rest of my lemonade and head to the punch bowl dripping condensation on the yellow tablecloth. Autumn hues decorate the backyard, fitting for late October, but clashing with the heat.

As I pour myself a drink, a pair of women approach the table. One I recognize immediately: Sophie Thorne. She's the daughter of Mom's business partner and best friend since college, Bonnie Thorne. The Thornes own a chain of luxury hotels across the country, with their newest one set to ost the Starlit Jewels' yearly gala where Mom introduces her exclusive line.

I'm surprised to see Sophie here, but it's possible she knows Brandon from their time at High School together.

Sophie already has a cup in her hand and slips in beside me to refill it, while the other woman grabs a fresh one from the stack. Sophie glances at me, recognition lighting her face.

"June," she acknowledges with a nod, her tone polite but distant. We haven't spoken often since I stopped coming around the Thorne house years ago. Our mom's business partnership means we're perpetually in each other's orbit, but we've mastered the art of cordial avoidance. It was also easy with Sophie away at college most of the time—only back for holidays and summers. "I'm surprised to see you here."

"I'm friends with Ethan," I explain, tucking a strand of dark hair behind my ear. The same stubborn one that always falls forward whenever I wear my hair down.

"Oh, that's right." A small smile tugs at the corner of her mouth, the kind that suggests she knows more than she's saying, making me wonder what she means by that, or how she knows about my friendship with Ethan. Before I can ask, her attention shifts back to her companion as they pick up the thread of an earlier conversation.

I'm already moving away, back toward the French doors to wait for Destiny, when their conversation roots me in place.

"...But Mom's using the gala to force my brother to mingle with society, hoping one of her friend's daughters will catch his interest," Sophie says.

"She's still trying to set him up?" the other woman chimes in, her voice amused.

The snack table makes convenient cover, so I drift to the far end and feign indecision over the veggie plate, spinach puffs or jalapeño poppers.

"She's more determined than ever." Sophie takes a delicate bite of an hors d'oeuvre. Her gold fingernails glitter in the sunshine.

"A little nudge might help." The other woman adds, amusement no longer hidden. "He was always a quiet boy."

Sophie lets out a resigned sigh. "Sebastian is *different*. The more my mother pushes, the further he runs."

Sebastian Thorne was a reserved child, but he was also stubborn, way too serious, hated playing most games, and fiercely overprotective of his toys.

Even now, at eighteen, that intensity hasn't changed; it's just found new outlets.

I snort before I can stop myself.

The sound draws both women's attention, their conversation halting mid-thought. Sophie arches a manicured brow, her gold-painted nails drumming lightly on her cup. There's a hint of amusement on her face, like she can read my thoughts.

I'm saved from fumbling through an apology when Ethan calls my name.

"June! There you are!"

I glance over right as Ethan strides toward me, towing a broad-shouldered man of twenty-three with similar blue eyes beside him.

Brandon is no longer the lanky teenager with shaggy hair he was before he left for the military. Now stands a man carved from discipline and time, his polo shirt tight across his chest, his skin tanner, and his head shaved.

"Brandon, you remember June," Ethan says, his tone proud.

Brandon's gaze sweeps over me, sharp and assessing. For a moment, I think he doesn't recognize me, my cheeks getting even redder in the silence. He takes in my sundress, so different from my usual jean shorts and baggy t-shirts, my dark hair falling in waves past my shoulders. The hair is all Destiny's doing. I would have thrown it up into a messy bun or ponytail.

The last time Brandon saw me, I was a chubby thirteen-year-old who begged him to teach me how to skimboard.

"Well, fu—freaking finally," he says, glancing apologetically at a group of kids running past before grinning wide. He grabs me in a hug as I toss a confused look over his shoulder at Ethan.

Brandon pulls back to give Ethan a pat on the back. "I knew you had a thing for her," he says, rapping his knuckles on Ethan's stomach.

Horror washes over Ethan's face as realization dawns on mine.

"Oh, I'm not—" I begin as Ethan blurts, "June's not—"

Brandon tosses a confused look between us as someone clears her throat. Destiny pops into sight, her hair now tucked up with her gold hairpin into a beautiful chignon.

Ethan moves to Destiny's side, wrapping an arm around her waist. His ears are tinged red. "This is my *girlfriend, Destiny.*"

Brandon's grin slips, but he recovers, tossing out his hand to shake Destiny's. The air suddenly becomes thicker, oppressive, and I wish I still had my cup to pour on my head.

"Destiny," Brandon says, knocking his knuckles into the side of his head, like he's misplaced part of his brain. Maybe he has, if he thinks Ethan and I... "So nice to meet you."

Destiny smiles, but it's as fragile as glass. Tension replaces the nervousness at meeting Ethan's brother. My stomach tightens at the silence that follows the awkward greeting, and I blurt out, "I cannot believe you thought Ethan and I—" I gesture wildly between us, lava flooding my pores as the words rush out.

Ethan shakes his head. "Yeah, June's like a sister," he blurts, with a laugh that trails off.

Brandon tilts his head at Ethan but turns to me. "You look so different since the last time I saw you."

I rock back on my heels, plucking at my dress and hair. "Not too much," I say, though he's right.

Four years feels like forever, especially when those years are from thirteen to seventeen. I cringe at my younger self, who was obsessed with vampires and followed Ethan's older brother around because he was in high school and had cool surfer friends.

Thankfully, Ethan followed him around, too.

The party stumbles forward, but the tension lingers like the sweat beading between my shoulder blades. I stay out of the way, being a supporting presence when Destiny needs it, catching her eye with encouraging smiles when Brandon launches into another story about Ethan's childhood shenanigans—stories that always seem to include me.

I decide to head out early, once Destiny relaxes, though I notice how her hand stays clasped in Ethan's all afternoon.

The drive home gives me time to stew over Brandon's ridiculous assumption. Me and Ethan? The idea is laughable.

I turn up the radio, but Brandon's voice echoes in my head. *"I knew you had a thing for her."* Not possible. I would have known. I would have seen it. Brandon's been gone too long—he clearly doesn't remember how things are between Ethan and me—more like family than anything else.

Some people don't understand that guys and girls can be friends without it turning into a romantic comedy. Ethan and I were friends before I brought Destiny in, and we fell into this comfortable group dynamic with Tori and Jordan, even before they started dating.

But now that Brandon's planted this stupid seed in my head, I'm seeing how it could look to outsiders. Ethan and I's inside jokes, how his mom still invites me over for holidays.

Does it bother Destiny? She's said nothing outright, but I do sometimes catch these moments, like when she changes the subject when Ethan brings up a funny story that doesn't include her.

I shake my head, gripping the steering wheel. This is exactly why Brandon's comment bothers me so much—it makes me second-guess a friendship that's always been uncomplicated. No, I refuse to let it ruin something that's perfectly innocent. If Destiny had a problem, she'd tell me. It's not like I'm always around. They hang out without me plenty.

Besides, I have bigger problems to worry about. Like how I'm going to explain if it gets back to Mom or Mrs. Thorne, I was eavesdropping on Sophie's conversation about her brother. Or why hearing Sebastian's name still makes my blood boil, even after all these years?

Sophie mentioning the gala brings up another problem. The Starlit Jewel Gala. Mom's been pestering me about it for weeks now, dropping not-so-subtle hints about how important it is that I attend this year—not only helping her prepare at home like last year, but as part of the showcase.

"It's your senior year, June," she'd said over the past few weeks. "You'll be too busy with college for the next four years. This might be the last time, and I designed these pieces with you in mind."

Last year I'd convinced her I'd be more useful helping backstage—organizing displays, assisting models, running emergency repairs—anything to stay out of sight. I'd arranged my schedule months in advance, making sure I wasn't part of the rotation of models displaying Mom's creations. I don't think I can get out of it this year.

"This collection tells our story—your story, too. And I need you there," she'd said, her voice gentle but firm.

My fingers drum the steering wheel in time with the music. The gala isn't the problem—it's who might be there. *Sebastian Thorne.* The boy I once considered my friend—maybe even my best friend—until everything changed between us. The boy I've successfully avoided for years despite our mothers' close friendship. The boy whose family is hosting this year's gala at their newest luxury hotel.

If Sophie's correct, her brother will definitely be there, probably being paraded around by his mother like some eligible bachelor prize. The thought sends an uncomfortable chill down my spine. I haven't shared space with Sebastian for more than a few uncomfortable minutes in years. An entire evening of pretending we don't have history? That sounds like torture.

I'd already tried all the usual excuses—volunteering for extra shifts at Sweet Rush, college application deadlines, even a sudden interest in an SAT prep course that only met on that specific evening. None of them worked.

"The applications can wait one weekend," Mom had countered. "And I already talked to Dana at Sweet Rush—she's happy to cover your shift." The way Mom said it made it clear she wasn't suggesting my attendance—she was expecting it.

I sigh, knowing it's pointless. Mom's been clear about this, reminding me again yesterday: "The Starlit Jewel is your legacy too, June. And you can't spend your whole life avoiding Sebastian."

Can't I, though?

I've done a pretty good job of it so far. Ever since that day at the Thornes' house when I was eleven. Skipping dinner invitations, avoiding the boutique when I know he'll be there, sitting across classrooms, and the cafeteria at school. It's worked well enough.

Until now.

I push thoughts of Sebastian from my mind, focusing instead on Brandon's weird assumption about me and Ethan. That's the real issue here. Not the gala and definitely not Sebastian.

CHAPTER 2

Jewelry, Gossip and Other Sharp Objects

MOM IS IN her workshop when I get home, bent over her jeweler's desk with her magnifying glasses perched on her nose. The smell of metal and polish fills the converted sunroom, mixing with the golden afternoon light streaming through the windows.

"How was the party?" She doesn't look up from whatever piece she's working on, but I can hear the smile in her voice. "Was Brandon happy to be home?"

"I think so." I drop onto the padded stool beside her workbench, watching as she manipulates a delicate piece of silver wire. "After thoroughly embarrassing both me and Ethan."

That gets her attention. She pushes her magnifying glasses up onto her forehead, fixing me with that mom-look that always makes me feel like I'm about to confess to something. "Oh?"

"He thought Ethan and I were dating."

Mom's eyebrows shoot up, and I quickly add, "Which is ridiculous."

"Hmm." She returns to her work, but I catch the slight curl of her lips. "Was Destiny there when that happened?"

"Yes. And it was super awkward." I pick up a delicate silver pendant with an iridescent labradorite inlay from her tray. "Oh—speaking of awkward—Sophie Thorne was there."

"Sophie?" Mom's hands go still, her frown returning. "Oh, that's right. She and Brandon must've been friends in school."

I shrug, not really confident in who Sophie or Brandon knew from school. "Yeah, and did you hear that the Starlit Gala is just a cover?" I try to keep my voice casual, like I hadn't eavesdropped on private conversations.

Mom glances up. "A cover?"

"For finding Bash a girlfriend." I fidget with a stray piece of wire on her desk.

"Sebastian," Mom corrects absently, then blinks. "Wait, what?"

"Sebastian. Bash, whatever." I wave my hand dismissively, like I haven't spent years avoiding saying either version of his name. "Apparently, Mrs. Thorne is determined to send him to college engaged or maybe even married. Or at least set him up with someone they approve of."

Mom sets down her tools, giving me her full attention now. "And how do you know all this?"

"I might have overheard Sophie talking about it." I twist my fingers together, avoiding her gaze.

"Hmm, I haven't heard of anything directly. Bonnie has some very A-list people coming," Mom says carefully, "but I know that she and Greg have been having several 'meetings' with old friends who have daughters his age."

I grunt. "Bet he likes that."

"He's a very desirable prospect, I'm sure." Mom tilts her head, going back to her work. "I always kind of thought you—"

"So... are these pieces for the new launch?"

Mom blinks down at the sketches and bits of metal and half-completed pieces. "No, the prototypes have already been sent. I've been experimenting with these."

I pick up a rough piece of paper with a sketch of a ring with stones and gems tangled with branches, another of a hairpin with hopping bunnies.

"That might explain the unusual guest list this year," Mom says slowly, studying my face. "Bonnie added several new families—all with daughters your age." She taps her chin in thought. "I thought it was catering to our younger client base, but a matchmaking agenda makes sense too."

"Well, according to Sophie, Mrs. Thorne wants him matched up, and I guess the gala is the *Reaping of the Debutantes*." I try to sound disinterested, but my voice comes out too high. "Not that I care. I thought it was funny, you know? Remember how he used to be when we were kids?"

Mom makes a low noise in her throat as she settles back to her work. "You two were quite the pair."

I roll my eyes. "I'm pretty sure Mrs. Thorne made him play with me."

Mom tilts her head. A funny look crosses her face. "Oh, I'm not so sure."

I clear my throat. "Anyway, I should go shower. Get this sweat off me. I'll tell Dad you'll be in soon?"

She nods, her brow furrowing as she looks down at her workstation. The overlapping sketches, half-started metalwork, and tiny gemstones in their sorted containers, waiting. I know that look: she's caught between the mess that needs cleaning and the creative momentum she can't afford to lose. She'll be another hour, maybe two.

"I'll tell Dad to come get you when dinner's done," I say, moving toward the door.

"June." Mom's voice stops me at the threshold. "You know, people change. Sometimes the person you think someone is when they are younger isn't who they grow up to be."

She's not wrong—I'm certainly not the person I was at eleven. It's not only my looks that've changed, but the eager-to-belong little girl I once was no longer looks for others' approval.

But Sophie's younger brother?

The serious little boy has become a *very serious*, six-foot-three brute. Sure, he still furrows his brow in the same concentrated way when sketching in study hall, and last week, I'd spotted him gently relocating a frog from the sidewalk to the grass during a downpour when he thought no one was watching—but everything else about him has changed.

Sebastian has become intimidatingly unapproachable, his silence no longer shy but dismissive. When we're forced to interact, his impossible green eyes ghost over mine before sliding away, like I'm not even worth the recognition of our shared past.

Students part for him in the hallways like he's royalty, which at Palm Vista, he practically is. Between his family's wealthy hotel chain, his artistic talent, that even I won't deny is exceptional, and that face that has girls stumbling over their words, he's become exactly the type of person who would crush my eleven-year-old heart with one sentence.

"Yeah, well, some things don't change," I say, and escape before she can say anything else.

CHAPTER 3
The Fictional Type

"THANKS AGAIN FOR driving." I lean back as Destiny's white Jeep Cherokee winds through the sleeping streets of Oceanview Estates. My surfboard rides securely strapped to her roof rack, a definite upgrade from trying to wedge it into my Civic. "I really need to invest in a bigger car."

"Or a roof rack," Destiny suggests, slowly taking a corner. The early morning sun casts long shadows across manicured lawns and wrought-iron gates. "Though I guess you won't need one once you're living out here."

I snort. "Yeah, right."

"I'm serious! Your mom's stuff is everywhere lately. Emma was showing off one of the new pendants at Bryce's party—the one with the Celestite?" She glances at me. "You must be excited about the expansion."

I shift in my seat, still not used to people talking about Mom's jewelry like this. It's strange how quickly things changed—one celebrity wearing her pieces on the red carpet and the Starlit

Jewel is being featured in fashion magazines, with orders flooding in from across the world. "It's not a big deal."

"*June*," Destiny says, chiding. "Your mom's designing for actual celebrities now. The waiting list for her custom pieces is like, months long. Maybe longer."

I press my fingers into the seatbelt strap, debating what to say. I don't know how to feel about it. Mom deserves every bit of success, but the past few months have been... different. I keep catching her and Dad having hushed conversations at the kitchen table, realtor's business cards left sitting out like a silent warning. Selling the house. Uprooting everything for something bigger, something better. I don't know if it's serious or if they're only entertaining ideas, but knowing they're even considering it makes me anxious.

I dig into the strap, twist, let go. "It just feels like... a lot, sometimes."

Destiny hums in agreement, either understanding or allowing me to be vague. I'm not sure which I prefer.

We turn onto Jada's street. The houses here are massive—all clean lines and floor-to-ceiling windows designed to maximize the tropical views. Destiny lets out a low whistle as we pass a fountain bigger than my bedroom.

"It's crazy how some people live," I say, watching a gardener trim and shape hedges.

"It's gorgeous, though." Destiny's voice turns wistful. "Can you imagine waking up to that view every morning?"

Through the gaps between houses, I catch glimpses of the Atlantic stretching toward the horizon, its surface catching the morning light like scattered diamonds.

We pull into Jada's circular drive behind Dante's vintage Land Rover Defender. The wealthy in our area either drive uber-sleek vehicles or really old-looking beaters that cost as much as a sports car. It's a weird sort of playing poor, but Dante's Defender at least shows signs of actual use—mud splattered on the wheel wells, surfboards strapped to the top rack.

Dante is still unloading when we park, unfastening the straps on his surfboards with smooth, practiced movements. He looks up as we step out, his face breaking into an easy smile.

"Hey Desi, hey, June." His voice carries a slight accent from spending his summers in Costa Rica. "Need a hand?" He's already reaching for the straps before I can answer, his movements automatic.

I grab my beach tote from the back seat as Destiny collects two folding chairs. The air still holds a hint of coolness that will soon burn away, but I revel in the breeze as we follow Dante down the path beside Jada's house, past sea grapes growing almost feral along the white lattice fence.

Dante jogs ahead to hold the gate open as we shuffle by. "After you."

"It's okay, I got it," Destiny says quickly, her hand on the white vinyl.

"No, you've got your hands full." He waves us through, that carefree smile seeming to linger on Destiny.

A chair slips from her grip, and when she lunges to catch it, both crash down, directly onto Dante's sandaled foot. He lets out a string of curses in Spanish, hopping back.

"Oh my gosh, I'm so sorry!" Destiny's cheeks flame red as she scrambles to pick up the chairs. "I didn't mean—are you okay?"

"It's fine, it's fine," Dante says through gritted teeth, though he's still favoring his foot. "Give me a minute."

I catch the gate before it can swing closed on them, watching as Destiny fusses over Dante, her usual confidence replaced by a nervous energy I rarely see. Her fingers flutter near his arm like she wants to help steady him, but isn't quite brave enough to touch.

"Really, Des, I'm good." Dante's smile returns, softer now. "Though maybe I should wear steel-toed boots around you."

Destiny's blush deepens. "I'm usually more coordinated than this."

"Eh, I don't know, I've seen you punt a volleyball right into coach's head," he teases.

Destiny lets out an exasperated laugh. "That was one time!"

"Mm, sure it was." Dante grins, and for a moment, they look at each other, the gate forgotten between them.

I clear my throat. "We should probably..." I gesture toward the beach where I can hear the muffled sound of conversation.

"Right!" Destiny jumps, almost dropping the chairs again. "We should—yes. Thanks for holding the gate." The last part comes out in a rush as she hurries past Dante, gaze fixed ahead.

Dante catches my eye as I pass, and I see my own amusement reflected there. I've known Destiny for years, watched her captain the debate team and organize school fundraisers without breaking a sweat, but something about Dante reduces her to this flustered version of herself.

I file that observation away for later as we emerge onto Jada's private stretch of beach, where the others are already taking advantage of the early morning waves.

Jada's already in the water with Jordan—Ethan's other best friend—and Cam, their silhouettes dark against the rose-gold horizon as they wait for the next set. The waves look clean—glassy and well-formed in the early morning light.

Tori has claimed her usual spot in the sand, arranging her towel for optimal sun exposure despite the early hour. Julie—Cam's sister—sits cross-legged beside her, still looking half-asleep as she applies sunscreen. Next to her, Kai lounges in the sand, stretching her legs out in front of her. She's a sophomore like Julie, who drifts in and out of our group when she's not with her skater friends.

"About time," Ethan calls from where he's studying his board near the water's edge. His swim trunks are already damp, hair pushed back from an earlier session. "Did you have to wake her up?"

"No, surprisingly, she was up." Destiny tosses me a smirk on her way to Ethan's side, giving him a quick kiss.

"You're missing the best waves," he says, glancing lovingly at the perfect sets rolling in.

I eye his board. "Why aren't you out there?"

"Forgot my wax," he explains, tilting his board to show us the scraped-clean surface. Not the greatest if you want to stay on your board.

"Of course you did," I say, dropping my bag next to Tori. "How long have you been here?"

"Since dawn." He runs a hand through his damp hair. "I've been trading off with Cam and Jordan, but it's getting old." He waggles his brows. "I could steal yours."

A whoop from the water draws our attention as Jada catches a perfect wave, her form textbook as she rides it into shore. Jordan and Cam follow, their hair slicked back and dripping as they jog up the beach.

"Dude," Cam drops his board in the sand. "You're missing it. The sets are perfect."

"Atlantico should be open today," Jada says, wringing out her long dark hair. Even fresh from surfing, she looks like she stepped out of a magazine. "They're always open early on nice surf days." She tosses a look toward Dante who's setting up his spot a careful distance from where Destiny's arranging her chair. "Though I don't know why Jason would pick up 6 AM shifts."

"Some of us actually have to work," Jordan teases, but there's an edge to it that makes me wonder about the history there.

"Desi, since you're not surfing…" Jordan waggles his brows. "Go grab us some wax."

Ethan smacks him on his bare chest, the crack of skin on skin louder than intended. "You can't boss my girlfriend around, jackass." Ethan tells him.

"I was only suggesting," Jordan shrugs, "June just got here. I'm sure she doesn't want to miss out either."

"Why do you keep volunteering all the women, Jordy? Why don't you take your scrawny butt across the street?" Tori calls, the sunrise reflecting off her mirror sunglasses.

"Scrawny," he says with false indignation. He turns and feigns like he's about to pull down his board shorts and give them an eyeful, to a round of screams and squeals from Julie, Tori and Kai, at which he stops with a laugh. "You wish."

"I'll run over and grab some," I offer, setting down my board.

"I'll come with you," Destiny volunteers. Maybe too quickly. She's already standing, brushing sand from her legs.

"We can walk," I offer when Destiny reaches for her keys. "It's just past those houses with the weird sculptures."

We take off toward Palm Way Drive, and cut across an empty lot toward the main road. Atlantico comes into view as we round the corner. A weathered two-story building with peeling turquoise paint, and a giant resin shark hanging below the round Atlantic Current Surf Co sign. Despite its shabby appearance, it's actually authentic, unlike the chain shop a couple towns over.

Traffic is nonexistent at this hour on a Sunday. There's one car pulling into the gas station on the corner, but we still look both ways before we jog across the road.

A bell chimes as we push through the door into the blessed air conditioning. The shop smells like pineapple, coconut, neoprene, with a hint of coffee, maybe brewing in the back room.

The shop is bigger than it looks from outside, with a wooden staircase leading to the second floor where surfboards, skimboards, and skateboards line the walls in ordered chaos. Downstairs, racks of men's and women's surf wear take up the center floor space—board shorts, rash guards, and the type of casual beachwear that defines Florida coastal style.

A massive tide clock dominates the wall behind the counter, its face showing both high and low tide times. The checkout counter sits to the left, an iPad mounted on weathered wood that matches the shop's laid-back vibe. The glass display case underneath holds sunglasses and watches, while surf stickers cover almost every available surface. Some so old and sun-bleached you can barely make out the logos.

Jason's reorganizing a rack of hoodies, but looks up at the bell. His face breaks into a lazy grin when he sees us, dark eyes crinkling at the corners. The light blue Atlantic Surf Co. shirt hangs neatly on his lean frame.

"If it isn't my favorite Spanish tutor," he says, abandoning the clothes to head toward the counter, the floorboards creaking underfoot.

"Hey Jason." I return his smile.

"Looking for anything in particular or here to browse the newest Roxy or Rip Curl swimsuits?" He nods toward a new rack of tiny bikinis.

"Yeah, I'm not that confident in gravity." I eye the barely-there swimsuits with skepticism.

Destiny rubs her arms, dramatizing a chill. "Especially today."

"You're not surfing?" he asks, eyeing my lack of a wet suit. "Jada texted me in all caps: WAVES followed by sixteen exclamation marks this morning. I figured if Jada's there, then so is Cam, Ethan, and…"

"June." Destiny and Jason finish together.

The tones don't match though, and Jason must hear it too because he glances at her at the same time as I do, but she's already turned to study some turtle earrings on display.

"I dressed light today." I pull up the band of my O'Neil lycra leggings that match my rash guard under my joggers. "We're here for some wax, actually."

I head straight to the counter where there's a display of surfboard wax right where you need it. I drop a bar on the counter, reaching for my wallet.

Destiny holds up a bar of Sticky Bumps. "This is the one Ethan uses, right? I've seen it in his room."

"That's the warm-water formula," Jason says, grabbing a paper bag. He holds up the one I dropped on the counter. "Water's still too cold. It won't be warm enough for that one until spring."

Destiny glances between the bars before putting back the warm-water wax, her movements careful and controlled. "Right. Of course."

"Do I get the favorite Spanish tutor discount?" I ask, leaning against the counter.

"I don't know. Do I get a free cone at Sweet Rush?" Jason asks, scanning the items on the iPad.

"I could make that happen."

Jason beams, entering his employee number to get me thirty percent off. I drop another on the counter. He shakes his head. "You taking advantage of my generosity, Juniper Blake?"

I press a hand to my chest. "Never. When you come see me at Sweet Rush, I'll hook you up with two toppings."

He rolls his eyes. "Wow."

Jason slips the bars into a paper bag as the bell chimes and new customers enter—a group of tourist-looking guys who head for the surfboard display upstairs. Jason hands me the bag with our wax.

"Catch you later?" he asks. "Or should I say, *hasta luego?*"

I groan. "Your accent is still terrible."

"Some things never change," he calls as we leave.

The morning sun hits us like a wall of heat as we step outside. Destiny's quiet as we start back toward Jada's. We both check both ways again before we jog across the road.

"Jason's cute."

"Yeah," I agree absently and then catch her grin out of my peripheral. "Oh, no, you mean..."

"You were awfully flirty back there."

"I was not," I protest, hopping over a puddle from someone's sprinklers. "That's just how we talk."

"Sure," Destiny draws out the word. "You two seemed pretty comfortable."

"We spent a lot of time together during tutoring. And Jason is just friendly," I shrug, ducking through the gap in the seagrass. "It's not like that."

"What is it like, then?" She asks casually, grabbing a hibiscus flower off a passing bush. She twirls it under her nose. "Maybe you could ask him to take you to your mom's gala?"

I shake my head. "I don't think so."

"Come on, it could be fun." She bumps my arm.

I glance at her, surprised by the sudden interest in my love life. "I'm too busy with work and school."

She gives me a skeptical look. "You're not *that* busy."

"I'm not interested in anyone right now," I say, understanding now what she's really asking. What she's worried about.

We emerge back onto Jada's stretch of beach where everyone's as we left them. Through the morning haze, I can see Ethan waiting by our chairs.

"Oh." She studies my face like she's looking for something specific. "Well, maybe you should be. I mean, we could double date or something..."

The suggestion hangs between us as we make our way across the sand. There's a hopeful note in her voice that makes my chest tight. Like maybe if I was dating someone else, she wouldn't have to worry so much about my friendship with Ethan.

"Hey," Ethan calls out. "Did you get the right—"

"Cool temp formula," Destiny cuts in, tossing him the wax. "June made sure."

Something in her tone makes me wince, but Ethan grins. "Thanks, June-bug."

I catch Destiny's smile tightening at the nickname, the casual way he says it.

I kneel in the sand, my board propped up on my thigh to apply a fresh coat of wax as Jordan asks, "How's Jason?"

"Still terrible at Spanish."

"He seemed like he wanted to see you in that bikini," Destiny teases, her voice light but pointed.

"What?" Ethan asks with a laugh, glancing up from coating his own board beside mine.

Jordan perks up. "Oh? Are you modeling the new releases for the shop? Start with a private showing?"

"Ew, why are you such a pig?" I ask, but don't wait for an answer. "It wasn't like that." I shoot Destiny a glare. "He casually asked if we were here for the new suits, *very* benign, and perfectly normal for someone who works at a clothing store."

"She even got a special discount," Destiny adds as Ethan applies the wax in practiced circles. "*Very* flirty."

"Jason?" Tori snorts from behind her sunglasses. "Please. He's not June's type at all."

"Does June have a type?" Cam asks, rolling onto his stomach. "Other than fictional men?"

"Fictional men are less work," I protest.

"You need to write less about paper men and spend more time with real ones," Tori says, and I toss a piece of wax at her.

"You're one to talk," I say. Tori reads more paperback romances than I do.

"I volunteer as tribute," Jordan announces, flexing. The morning sun catches on the water droplets still clinging to his shoulders. "I'd make an excellent boy toy."

"Gross." Tori throws a handful of sand at him.

"What? I'm a catch." He dodges the sand. "Tell them, June. Remember that time when your car broke down—"

"And you made me wait two hours because you ran into Bianca at the gas station?" I finish. "Very chivalrous."

"See? She's already finishing my sentences. It's meant to be."

Ethan pauses in his waxing, his jaw tightening before it relaxes. "Don't you have waves to catch?"

"Aw, protective much?" Jordan teases, but he's already grabbing his board. "Fine, fine. But June, when you're ready to upgrade from your books..."

I throw my water bottle at him, but I'm laughing. "Go drown yourself."

Destiny's watching this exchange with that same probing look, like she's collecting evidence for something. Her fingers twist in the ends of her hair.

"Actually," she says, her voice carefully casual, "what about that guy from your work? The one who goes to Crystal Lake High?"

My face heats. "Chase? No way."

"He's cute," she persists. "And he's always chatting you up whenever I'm in there."

"They work together," Tori pipes up, wrinkling her nose. "You don't want to mix work and pleasure. Besides, June needs someone more..." she waves her hand vaguely, "intellectually stimulating."

"And someone who's bossier than she is," Cam mumbles.

"Good luck," I say firmly, hoping to end this line of conversation. "And I don't have time for—"

"That's what they all say," Julie sighs dramatically. "Right before they meet the one."

"The one what?" I ask flatly. "The one person who'll make me forget how much I hate dating?"

"You only hate it because you haven't given it a real chance," Destiny says, her voice edged with something almost desperate. I'm not the only one who hears it either. Ethan pauses mid-wax to look at her.

"Can I borrow the wax?" Jada jogs up from the water, her board tucked under her arm.

"Here." I toss her the stick. "Help yourself."

"Did I hear we're trying to set June up?"

"No," I say as Tori says, "Yes."

I shoot her a murderous look, *not you, too*.

"Must be something in the water—my mom was just telling me Sebastian Thorne's on the market."

Julie sits up straighter. "Sebastian? Really?"

"No way," Cam cuts in right away. "Absolutely not. You're too young and innocent for Thorne."

Julie rolls her eyes at her brother, but I catch the look she shares with Kai.

"June should throw her hat in the ring," Tori suggests, her tone too innocent. "You two already have history."

"Ancient history," I say firmly.

"Yeah, June hates Sebastian," Ethan says, not looking up from his board. "She needs someone more down-to-earth. Someone who gets her weird sense of humor, and who'll sit through all those awful horror movies on a Saturday night and not drag her around to fancy dinner parties, like she's just a trophy, and doesn't mind that she's stubborn as hell. Someone who won't try to change her, not some rich asshole who's never had to work for anything."

"Dude," Jordan laughs, "you just described yourself."

The silence that follows is deafening. I risk a glance at Destiny, whose fingers are frozen in her hair.

"Wow, you put a lot of thought into this," Destiny says, her voice dry.

"What? No," Ethan stumbles over his words, his ears turning red. "I meant like, you know, I'd say the same if we were talking about Lucy." He glances at Destiny. "June's family," Ethan finishes.

"Exactly." My voice is too bright. "Like how Cam's looking out for Julie."

"Don't bring me into this," Cam groans, but the tension doesn't quite ease though.

"Speaking of looking out for people," Tori cuts in, a beat too late, "those waves aren't going to catch themselves. And I was promised a show."

"Race you to the break," Jordan calls, already sprinting toward the water.

I grab my board, grateful for the escape. But as I paddle out, I can't help noticing how Destiny's stopped playing with her hair, her hands now twisted in her lap, or how Ethan's very focused on re-waxing a section of his board that's already done.

CHAPTER 4
The Deep End

TORI AND I leisurely tread water in one of the deeper lanes for our third period swim class. The swim team gets the best lanes, and the divers monopolize the diving board. Not that I want to swim laps or fill my ears with water after I blunder a dive. Tori could be over with them, but she's content to keep me company.

Coach Burton lounges in the lifeguard chair, attention flicking from his phone to the pool. His neon orange swim trunks clash spectacularly with the forest green Palm Vista Prep windbreaker he wears despite the heat, whistle dangling from a lanyard around his neck. He's never taken swim class too seriously. He saves that for the team. As long as you get in the pool and pass the written tests, he's content.

Tori pushes herself up out of the water and lies back on the side wall to tan. She wears the green and black practice suits the varsity team uses for non-competition days. A tie-dyed swim cap covers her red hair. I stay in the water. The sun will still tan me, but the water keeps me cool.

"Did something happen between you and Ethan?" Tori says after a stretch of companionable silence.

On the other side of the pool deck, you can see the soccer field through the eight-foot chain-link fence. Ethan has PE this period, and his class is on the field today. I've been tracking his location all morning, trying to figure out how to cancel our plans tonight after this weekend's awkwardness.

"What do you mean?"

"Things seemed weird at the beach yesterday." Tori drums her finger on her belly; her other hand makes lazy circles where it dangles in the water.

"It did, didn't it?" I sigh, knowing she won't let it drop. "There was just this little thing at Brandon's welcome home party where Brandon mistook me for Ethan's girlfriend." I catch Tori's grimace and I wave off the memory. "It was nothing," I say, but it sounds weak even to my own ears.

"Your tone says otherwise," she drones. "Did Destiny say something?"

"Well, no." I paint little shapes on the pool deck as I say, "But then right after, Brandon said something about knowing Ethan always had a thing for me..."

Tori half-sits up, her sunglasses sliding down her nose to gape at me. "Wait, what? That's what you call nothing?"

I wave my hand, brushing it off. "It's not a big deal," I insist. "I just don't want Destiny to think—I mean, Ethan is like a brother." I shake my head.

She hasn't said a word for at least thirty seconds, which is not like her. That she's holding back is more alarming than anything she could actually say. When I glance over, her face goes through different emotions in two seconds.

"What?"

Her face transforms into a partial cringe. "Well, I mean..."

"What?" My voice comes out an octave too high.

Tori shifts, sitting up and letting her legs dangle in the water. "I'm not saying I know *anything*, but maybe Destiny's mentioned *something*..." She shrugs again, but something about the tight lift to her shoulder tells me she's holding back.

Dread crashes over me in cold, unforgiving waves. I try to keep my voice level as I ask, "What did she say?"

"She said nothing *bad* about you," Tori says, picking up on my unease. "Only that sometimes... she feels like a third wheel."

"She said that?" I ask. Tori nods. "When?"

Tori shrugs, biting her lips, but says, "A couple of weeks ago?"

"Weeks, Tori? She's been feeling this way for weeks, and you're just now telling me?"

"You can't tell her I told you. You know how panicky she gets with confrontation."

I sink lower into the water, blowing bubbles out of my mouth. "We always hung out before they dated... the three of us..." It sounds like a weak excuse, now that I'm saying it out loud.

When Destiny confessed she liked Ethan, I wasn't surprised; she was always so shy around him, blushing and asking if he was coming along. I told her immediately that Ethan was only a friend, which I meant then, as I mean now, with my whole heart.

"I know you don't mean anything by it," Tori says quickly. "But, I mean, you and Ethan have all these inside jokes. His mom calls you Junie Bug. You're always together."

"I don't crash their dates on purpose," I say, a touch defensive. "Only when I'm invited."

Tori gives me a pitying look. "And who is always inviting you?"

I lift out of the water enough to say, "Ethan."

Tori lifts one delicate shoulder. The look she levels at me tells me I am missing something obvious.

"Ethan is always inviting me," I whisper.

Tori nods, biting her lip. I groan, sinking into the water.

When Ethan and Destiny started dating, nothing really changed between Ethan and me. And whose fault is that? When they started dating, I expected them to pull back, to prioritize their relationship. Instead, they....didn't. And I let them.

Now I'm seeing Destiny's tight smiles differently. Those small hesitations before she encouraged me to join them. Was that only polite obligation? She wanted to make Ethan happy and not appear to be the uptight girlfriend.

I should have been the one to change the dynamic, to insist on boundaries, but it was easier to pretend everything could stay the same.

I surface, water streaming from my hair. "I feel horrible."

"Yup." Tori doesn't pull her punches. "You really didn't see it, did you? Like you genuinely thought everything was fine." She sighs when I nod. "It's not like you were actively trying to hurt her, and Destiny's the one who kept saying yes when she meant no. And Ethan's not as clueless as he pretends to be. You all just... really suck at communication."

"Okay, so what do I do? Stop being friends with Ethan?" I ask, exasperation leaking into my tone. "She shouldn't have to feel like I'm a threat."

Ethan's been there for me through a lot these past four years at Palm Vista. The thought of giving up his friendship makes my heart ache in a way I wasn't expecting.

"No, not completely. Destiny wouldn't want that," Tori shakes her head, thoughtful. "But maybe... be more mindful? No more late-night phone calls or one-on-one hang-outs for a while."

I cringe into the water. We have plans to go skim boarding after school and to see the new horror movie on Friday. I need to cancel that immediately.

"He's going to get suspicious if I ghost him."

"Yeah, don't do that. Try a hobby, something that keeps you too busy to hang out?" Tori says gently, biting the side of her thumb. "Or you could start dating someone?"

"Not you too?" I splash water at her. "Now it makes sense why Destiny was pushing so hard on the idea of me dating Jason." *She was trying to solve her own dilemma without hurting my feelings.*

Tori laughs, kicking water back at me with little force. "Maybe Destiny was right. She just picked the wrong man." Her gaze drifts over my shoulder, and that hungry look crosses her face.

I turn to see Sebastian Thorne's sun-kissed back slicing through the water as he powers through another set. Each stroke identical to the last.

I choke on pool water. "Are you insane?"

"What? He's hot, smart, rich, athletic, and definitely single. Plus, you heard what Jada said. He's currently on the prowl—"

"No," I cut her off. "Absolutely not. Sebastian Thorne is the most entitled, antisocial snob at this school. He has impossibly high standards for everything, and that includes me."

"You used to be friends, didn't you?" Tori asks sweetly.

"When we were in elementary school. And only because our moms worked together," I lie.

Our moms' friendship brought us together, but there was a time when I thought Sebastian enjoyed having me around, before I learned what he really thought of me. Before I learned all those afternoons in his backyard, all those hours building sandcastles with battlements and corner turrets, and singing him songs while he painted meant something completely different to him than it did to me.

I wave dismissively toward his lane. "Look at him—he thinks he's too good for everyone here. I bet he's counting the minutes until he can go back to his climate-controlled mansion and sort his dinosaurs alphabetically and by time period."

Tori flicks water at me from her fingertips. "That's oddly specific hatred for someone you haven't talked to since elementary school."

I don't elaborate on how he'd once spent an entire afternoon teaching me his organizational systems, face scrunched in his trademark scowl, as he explained why the Stegosaurus couldn't possibly stand next to the T-Rex.

"It's not hatred. It's..."

Sebastian's no longer swimming. He's leaning over the sidewall two lanes over. Water glistens on his bare back, sliding down the contours of his muscles. You'd never have thought that dorky kid would grow up to be so—

Horror washes over me at how hushed the pool deck has become. The few students still talking near the diving boards voices carry easily over the water.

I mouth to Tori: *Did he hear me?* She answers with a shrug.

Sebastian's head turns, and the look he gives me freezes the blood in my veins. Those piercing green eyes, made brighter by the pool water, lock onto mine, making my heart skip a beat.

The moment stretches between us. Then someone calls, "Harsh, Blake," loud enough for half the class to hear.

A group of girls snicker. Sebastian's shoulders tense as more whispers ripple through our classmates. If there's one thing Sebastian Thorne hates more than socializing, it's people talking about him, period.

He pushes off the wall in one fluid motion, cutting through the water with sharp-edged strokes, but not before I saw the hard set of his jaw.

"Well," Tori breaks the silence, "that was..."

"I need to keep my big mouth shut," I mutter, already pushing myself up out of the pool. My skin hot despite the cool water.

"Don't run away," she says, looking up at me. "He was so far away." She tries, but at the incredulous look I give her, changes tactics. "It's not like you care what he thinks, anyway."

I don't. I really don't.

But as I grab my towel, I can't shake the image of his face in the moments before he turned away. A frosty glare that definitely didn't look hurt. There's this weird hollow feeling in my stomach that feels like guilt.

"I'm not running." I raise my chin. "I've finished my laps already."

Water slips down my arms and legs as I cross the concrete deck toward the changing rooms. Each plat plat plat of my footsteps thudding in sync with my heartbeat. I need to change into my uniform, cancel my plans with Ethan, and probably transfer schools. Not necessarily in that order.

THE LOCKER ROOM IS EMPTY when I push through the heavy door. The familiar smell of chlorine and artificial strawberry body spray fills the humid air, mixing with the metallic tang from the rusty corners of the old lockers. Water drips from my swimsuit, melding with the constant state of puddles on the cracked tile floor as I make my way to my locker in the back corner.

I pull out my phone, staring at the texts from yesterday where we made plans for this afternoon. That hollow ache in my stomach grows cold and heavy. How do you tell your best friend you can't hang out anymore because his girlfriend thinks you're trying to steal him? How do you explain that maybe everyone's been right about how weird your friendship looks from the outside?

The door creaks open, and I drop my phone into my bag, but it's only Tori. She gives me a look that's half sympathy, half exasperation. The fluorescent lights flicker overhead, casting weird shadows on the yellow walls that haven't been painted since our parents went to school here.

"You know," she says, sitting on the bench next to me, "for someone who doesn't care what Sebastian Thorne thinks, you're doing an awful lot of panicking."

"Ugh, I'm not panicking about *him*," I tell her, rubbing a towel into my hair. I stare at the locker door, wishing I could write myself out of this situation like I do with my characters. But real life doesn't have convenient plot devices or timely revelations. "How do I break up with my best friend?"

"Gently," she leans her head onto my shoulder. "Very gently."

I nod, but inside, everything already feels like it's falling apart.

CHAPTER 5

The Lunch Break-Up

THE CAFETERIA IS packed by the time I get there, the smell of today's mystery meat mixing with the lingering pool water in my hair. Through the wall of windows, weak October sunlight streams in, doing nothing to improve the institutional light blue walls or the scuffed linoleum tile floor. The usual chaos of conversation bounces off the high ceiling, punctuated by occasional bursts of laughter and the clatter of plastic trays.

Our usual table is already full. Ethan's arm drapes over the back of Destiny's chair as she picks at her pasta, Jordan and Cameron argue about something on their phones, and Tori picks apart a banana muffin while flicking through her European history notes. The empty spot next to the window might as well have my name on it. It's where I've sat every day since freshman year.

I take a deep breath and head over, my rehearsed speech already falling apart in my head.

"June!" Cameron calls out as I approach. "Tell Jordan that modding your game is absolutely cheating."

"It's a custom layout," Jordan protests. "How is that cheating?"

"Because you're getting an advantage—"

"Can we not do this again?" Tori groans, not looking up from her notes. "They've been at it for ten minutes."

"Hey," I say, sliding into my seat. Ethan angles his mom's homemade granola toward me, but I shake my head. "About after school—"

"Yeah, I was thinking about hitting DJ's after. I'm craving their famous Grouper Sammies."

He suggests as if us hanging out while Destiny is at work is not weird at all. So platonic that for a moment I consider backing down, but I don't miss the way Destiny picks at her food, the furrow in her brow, and I know I can't keep acting like everything's fine.

"I can't make it. I told Bree I'd take her shift tonight."

Ethan's brows pull down. "Okay, that's cool. We'll see you Friday at the movies."

"Yeah, um, about that." I focus on opening my water bottle, avoiding eye contact with Destiny or Ethan. "I need to skip the movie too."

"What? Why?" The disappointment in Ethan's voice is unmistakable.

"...stuff came up." The lie sits heavy on my tongue. "Family stuff."

"Since when?" His arm drops from Destiny's chair. "You were saying yesterday how excited you were about—"

"I know, I know..." I glance at Destiny, whose eyes drop to her fruit cup, her fork hunting around the shallow container. "Plans changed."

"But it's the new zombie movie you've been talking about for weeks," Ethan persists. "The one with—"

"She said she had a family thing," Destiny says while placing her hand on his arm and giving it a small squeeze. "If she can't make it, she can't make it."

"Oh, are we talking about *The Dead Rise*?" Cameron perks up. "Jordan, didn't you want to see that?"

"Yeah, actually." Jordan looks up from his phone, sensing an opportunity. "If June's not going, can I have her ticket?"

"No one's taking June's ticket," Ethan cuts in, his fork clattering against his tray.

Cameron whistles low. "Someone's territorial today."

Tori cuts him a sharp look.

Cam lifts his hands in surrender. "I'm just saying—"

"You should give it to Jordan," I interrupt, picking at my salad. "He will appreciate the movie more than me, anyway."

"Since when do you not like horror movies?" Ethan demands. "We watched the entire Walking Dead series last summer. You made us marathon all the web series."

"Yeah, well..." Destiny's fingers tighten on her tray. "That was different."

"June—" Ethan starts, but then his jaw clenches, and he stops himself.

"So anyway," Tori jumps in with forced brightness. "Did you guys hear about what happened in swim class today? When Sebastian overheard—"

"No, nothing happened, Victoria," I cut her off, gathering my uneaten lunch. "I need to talk to Mrs. Parker about that English assignment."

"You haven't even touched your apple," Ethan points out, a crease appearing between his eyebrows.

"Ethan—" Destiny starts, but he's already half-standing.

"June—"

"Ethan, your food's getting cold," Destiny says softly, tugging on his arm.

I catch the pleading in her voice, the way she's trying to keep him from following me. For once, I'm grateful for her intervention. Jordan and Cameron watch the exchange like it's a tennis match, and I sense heads from nearby tables turning our way.

"I'll see you guys in class," I mumble, hurrying to the door.

Behind me, I hear Cameron say, "Dude, what was that about?" followed by Jordan's "Seriously, what happened?" and the distinct sound of Tori kicking them both under the table.

I make it into the empty hallway when I hear Ethan's footsteps behind me, his stride echoing off the polished floors.

"June. Wait up."

When I turn around, he's frowning at me, a crease between his eyebrows that appears whenever he's trying to solve a tough math problem.

"What's really going on?" he asks, rubbing the back of his neck. "Is this about what Brandon said?"

My heart skips a beat. So it had rattled him too. The absurdity of it was eating at me all weekend, but I hadn't considered that Ethan might be as unsettled. After all, it *was* ridiculous—the idea that Ethan and I were anything more than friends.

"Kind of?" I step out of the main pathway, watching other students trickle past us.

"Because June—" he says as I launch in with, "Look, I've been thinking—"

"About?"

"That maybe I'm around too much." The words come rushing out. "You and Destiny should have time alone, without me always tagging along."

His frown deepens. "June, what are you talking about? You're my best friend. Of course I want you around." He glances back toward the cafeteria. Jordan's head turns when he does.

Ethan makes a frustrated sound, ushering me around the corner, away from prying eyes. "Is this about Destiny?" he asks. "She wants you there too. We're all friends."

"I know we're friends. I mean, Destiny and I and you and I—" I run a hand through my still-damp hair, growing frustrated with my own words. *Why is this so hard?*

"You and Destiny are serious, right?" I ask, fidgeting with my hands.

He shifts on his feet. "What are you asking exactly?"

"You like her a lot, right?"

"Yeah? Yes?" he says suspiciously. He rakes his teeth over his bottom lip. "I do but—"

I gesture vaguely between us, hoping he'll finally see what this looks like to everyone else. "I'm saying that maybe it's not fair to Destiny." I swallow at the way he shuts his eyes.

"Destiny," he says her name softly, with an absent nod.

I nod along with him. "It's weird, right? My always tagging along?" I try for a light tone, but he's still staring at the ground like a lost little boy. My heart constricts. It's not forever, I remind myself. I'm just giving them space.

"I have to run," I say, adjusting my backpack strap, needing something to do with my hands.

He nods, but it's as if he's not really hearing me. I walk backward when his eyes snap to mine. "I want to talk more about this," he says. "Later."

"Maybe."

He tilts his head, gaze narrowing. "You always do this June—disappear when things get uncomfortable. I let you get away with it, but not this time."

A flush of shame burns through me as memories flash behind my lids—all the times I've walked away instead of facing difficult situations. Am I that transparent? Or does Ethan know me too well?

I hold up my hands in surrender, trying to mask how deeply his words have cut. "I said maybe."

Then I turn and hurry down the hall, heart pounding. Desperately hoping I'm doing the right thing, even though it feels familiar in all the worst ways—like I'm about to lose someone important all over again.

And worse, I know Ethan's right. Running away when things get hard has become second nature to me. It's a pattern that started years ago, and I've never figured out how to break it.

CHAPTER 6

Doubts of Destiny

SMOKE LINGERS IN the air outside the second-floor bathroom. Someone's either inside smoking or just finished. Either way, I don't want the smell to cling to my clothes for the rest of the school day.

I take the stairs down the hall to the first-floor bathroom when the soft, feminine sounds of sobs stop me on the first descending steps. I hesitate, torn between checking on whoever is crying and giving them their privacy.

"So you think June is trying to break you up?" It's Emma Chambers, her voice sharp.

My heart stops at the mention of my name. My hand frozen on the railing.

"No, no," Destiny says with a sniff. "I don't think she's doing it on purpose. He's the one inviting her." *He*. She has to be talking about Ethan.

"Well, she should say no." Emma huffs.

Destiny draws a shaky breath. "I don't want to be the consolation prize."

"You're not," Emma's voice comes out soft and sympathetic. "She's pushing between the two of you. She's jealous. Ethan adores you."

One Mississippi. Two Mississippi. Three Mississippi. My heart cracks with every second it takes until Destiny says, "That doesn't sound like June."

Ethan *does* adore her. I've seen it firsthand. The way his whole face lights up when she walks into a room, how he'll pause mid-sentence to smile at her. She has this laugh—bright and infectious—that makes his eyes crinkle at the corners every single time. In the two years I've known him, I'd never seen Ethan so completely gone over someone.

"I just don't know anymore." Destiny's sobs continue. Suddenly muffled and I imagine Emma has wrapped her up in a hug because that's what I would do if I was down there.

I debate coming down the stairs, but Emma isn't exactly a friend, and it sounds like she thinks I have ulterior motives with my friendship with Ethan. And I might embarrass Destiny more knowing I overheard her confessions. No, I need to convince her I'm not trying to come between her and Ethan, Ethan wants her, and he and I are only friends.

I back away slowly, my heart pounding. Destiny's sobs echo in my ears as I slip out of the stairwell. The guilt churns in my stomach, twisting tighter with each step.

I take the hallway at a jog, quickly retreating down the opposite stairs and out into the afternoon sun. Palm Vista Academy sprawls around me, all tan brick and white columns, trying to look like a mini college campus.

I cut across the courtyard, past the pergola heavy with bougainvillea, and burst into the front office.

The office is cool and serene compared to the humid trek from the science building. There's a familiar smell of coffee from the teacher's lounge down the hall. The slight whirl of machines. Somewhere in the back, a printer is going.

Tori is at a small desk behind the main counter, where Mrs. Waller, the school secretary, sits with a book propped up covering most of her face. Neither of them seems affected by my sudden arrival. Mrs. Waller's current read, "His Unbridled Reign," features a shirtless cowboy on a horse—her usual fare. She keeps a stack of them in her desk drawer and trades them with Mrs. Parker from the English department.

Mrs. Waller shifts her novel, giving me a half-look, but when my focus moves to Tori, she resumes her reading. Tori pauses in her typing, waving me over. As office aide, she probably knows more about what goes on at Palm Vista than anyone—including most of the teachers.

"What's going on?" she hisses, leaning in.

"Destiny *does* think I like Ethan."

Tori raises a sculpted brow. "She told you that?"

"No. I accidentally overheard her telling Emma," I admit.

"Oh?" Her tone makes my spine straighten.

"Why'd you say it like that?"

Tori tilts her head. "Emma's not your biggest fan."

I wave off the obvious, shifting away from Emma. She's not the problem right now. "I wasn't spying. Just going to the bathroom." My heart races, voice rising as I say, "What more am I supposed to do? I'm canceling plans. Told Ethan I wanted space. Now, it feels like I'm making things worse."

Tori mirrors my exasperated panic. "I don't know, but you need to do it quickly."

"What else can I do?" My hands find my hair, twisting it up and letting it go. "I'm running out of options, and I don't want to lose both of them."

"You know what your real problem is?" Tori taps her black nails on the desk, already formulating. "Destiny can't picture you with anyone but Ethan because she's never seen you with anyone but Ethan. We need to change that." Her eyes get that dangerous gleam that means she's hatching a plan. "You need a boyfriend."

Not this again. I blink at her, then let out a groan. "*Tori.*"

"No, seriously. This is actually brilliant," she says, bouncing in her chair before she leans forward conspiratorially. "If Destiny sees you completely smitten with someone else, she'll stop seeing you as competition and start seeing you as... taken. Plus, she was already trying to set you up. It's perfect."

I tilt my head back and forth, not so keen on the idea of leading a guy along. But what other ideas do I have?

"I don't know." I shake my head. "Besides, where would I find a boyfriend, like today?"

Mrs. Waller's voice comes strong from the other side of her paperback. "Boys are like flies. Put a little honey out there. I'm sure you'll catch one."

Tori and I exchange a look. "I'm not sure if June has any honey," Tori says with a laugh. "She's all vinegar."

Mrs. Waller snorts, "Some flies like vinegar more than honey."

I wrinkle my nose at the interesting picture Mrs. Waller has painted. "I'm not sure I want to catch flies *or boys.*"

Tori slumps in her chair, putting her chin on her hands. "It won't work anyway, not unless you are sure the first one will say yes." At my confused look, Tori explains. "If you ask random boys out, it's going to get around school, and Ethan or Destiny will know something weird is going on."

"Fine, then, I'll invent a boyfriend."

"Nope, they'll know." She shakes her head again. "If not Destiny, then Ethan will. You are a terrible liar."

"Debatable, but *okay*," I grumble.

Tori drums her fingers on the desk, studying me with narrowed eyes. "You need someone who owes you a favor."

I suck in a breath. "I'm not sure I love the implication that my only shot at a boyfriend involves blackmail, bribery, or calling in a favor."

"What about Jason Wang?" she suggests, ignoring me. "Destiny already thinks you have a thing for him, and didn't you tutor him in French or something?"

"Spanish, but yeah."

"Perfect," she says, then, "wait! How good of a tutor were you? Did he get an A?" I give her a look, and she holds up her hands in surrender.

Jason is on the basketball team, and attractive enough to fake-date him for a couple of weeks. He always wears a big grin that makes him seem approachable despite his popularity. His Spanish sucked, but so did mine three years ago.

"I don't know..."

We turn at the sound of Mrs. Waller typing vigorously. "He's got geometry this period." She picks up the phone. "Want to call him in?"

"Yes," Tori says gleefully.

"No!"

Mrs. Waller types in his classroom number. Her clear secretary's voice comes a second later, requesting *Jason Wang to please come to the front office.*

Five minutes later, Jason walks through the open office doors with his backpack over his shoulder and a pencil tucked behind his ear. He does a quick look between the three of us, heading toward Mrs. Waller's desk.

THE NO-KISSING CONTRACT

"Hey there, Jason," I say, stumbling onto the front counter, as Tori pushes me forward.

Mrs. Waller takes his slip, stamps it, and hands it back.

"Uh, hey," he says, glancing behind me at the principal and vice principal's offices. "Am I in trouble?"

"Do you want to be?" Tori purrs, already in matchmaking mode.

I cut her a sharp look over my shoulder.

"June wanted to ask you a question," Mrs. Waller says, sitting back down in her desk chair, and picking up her novel.

"Oh-kay," he drawls, shifting his weight. Up close, I notice he's wearing what looks like a pastel-colored friendship bracelet—similar to the one that the volleyball team was selling last week for their fundraiser. He absentmindedly touches it, but when he notices me noticing, he pulls his dress shirt down.

"Jason, do you have a girlfriend?"

His gaze flicks behind me, quick as a cat. Probably assuming Victoria is documenting this for her extensive collection of school secrets. "Um, no?"

"Do you want one?" Tori purrs, a mischievous laugh in her tone.

"What Tori means is, I need a favor."

"A favor that requires knowing if I have a girlfriend or not?" he asks. "Is this about prom?"

"No," I shake my head.

Jason's face visibly relaxes, but it's short-lived.

"June needs a boyfriend."

"Actually, I need a *fake* boyfriend. Just for a little while."

Jason narrows his eyes at me, taking in my appearance. Warmth creeps over my scalp at his assessment. I shift as old insecurities creep in despite the years I've spent since middle school replacing the baby fat with lean muscle and curves I'm actually proud of.

I like how I look now, comfortable in my skin in a way eleven-year-old me never imagined, but I'm not so vain as to assume I'm everyone's type. But being sized up like this, especially when asking for such a weird favor, makes me feel exposed, vulnerable.

"I'm probably not your type—" I start, letting my insecurities take over.

Jason's dark brows go up. He holds out his hand. "Stop, it's not that. I…" he rubs a hand down his arm, his fingers brushing over that friendship bracelet again. "…like someone."

Tori puts her chin on top of her clasped hands. "Oh, who?"

Jason ignores her, but the slight pink tinge to his ears and the way his eyes dart toward the gym where the volleyball team practices tells me everything I need to know. "And a girlfriend, even a fake one, would ruin my chances."

"Ah, I see."

"I would," he rushes on, "I mean, maybe I still could…?" he rubs the back of his neck, voice trailing off. He looks like he wants to help, even if it ruins his chances with whoever made that bracelet.

Jason would have been a good choice. Safe. He'd keep the secret, and he's not the type to complicate things. Or me. Jason is the type of fake boyfriend that Ethan would never question, but I don't think anyone would believe that I would dump.

Besides, I can't ruin Jason's shot at true love, even if it only lasts in high school.

I wave a hand, dismissing the idea. "No, it's okay. It was a stupid plan, anyway."

Jason picks up the slip from the desk. I look up when he doesn't immediately leave. "What did you need a fake boyfriend for, anyway?"

Tori answers before I can come up with a vague reason. "She doesn't want Destiny to think she'd gunning for her man."

"Ethan?" he says. "Ah, I could see that." He furrows his brow, then his face lights up. "What about Sebastian?"

"Sebastian? As in Sebastian Thorne?" I scoff.

The one who overheard me trash-talking him in swim class like two hours ago? The same Sebastian with whom I haven't exchanged over ten words in the last four years. But I leave that embarrassing detail to myself.

"Not you too," I groan, scrunching my eyelids tightly before turning a sharp look over my shoulder at Tori. "Did you plan this?"

"See, I told you he was perfect." She shifts in her chair, with a satisfied pout on her lips.

I turn back to Jason, who's watching our exchange with raised eyebrows. "Why would you even suggest that?"

Jason, unfazed, says, "For one, Sebastian might be interested in a low-stakes relationship too." Jason raises a second finger before putting it down. "Actually, I only have one reason, but it's a good one."

"I don't think Sebastian wants—" Tori waves her hands near my face to shush me.

"Low stakes," she confirms and, at Jason's nod, turns to me. "That sounds right up your fake-relationship alley?"

I bite my lip. "Why does Sebastian need a fake girlfriend?"

Jason shifts, tapping his fingers on the counter. He glances at Tori, who's leaning forward, her big green eyes wide with curiosity, and Mrs. Waller, who's lowered her romance novel enough to peek over the top.

"Well, I don't know if he *needs* one," Jason says and leans in, lowering his voice, "but he might be open to it. It will get his parents off his back and solves your problem."

"And how did you come to this information, Jason?" Tori asks, voice full of suspicion.

She levels a stare at him, her eyes widening and then contracting like she's trying to use some version of mind control. And maybe she is. Tori thinks that if she looks people in the eye, they can't lie to her. That hasn't been true for me, but Tori swears by it.

Jason doesn't sweat under Victoria's laser-beam stare as he answers, "Sebastian and I are friends. We've been working out in the training room on Thursdays during lunch break, when it's mostly empty."

"And he just... confided in you about his dating problems?" I ask skeptically.

"Not exactly." Jason rubs the back of his neck. "His sister Sophie called one day while we were working out. And she was pretty worked up on the phone. I could hear bits and pieces." Jason's ears turn pink as he kneads his fingers into his palm. "I moved to the leg press to give him some privacy," he says, "after the call, I asked if everything was alright and he told me that his parents were pressuring his sister to—what did he call it?—'secure the Thorne legacy through advantageous social connections'. He said that he'd told his sister he'd take care of it. Get some of the pressure off her."

Mrs. Waller tsks behind her novel. "You should hear the things I do in my quilting guild. All those society mothers trading their children like poker chips. It's no wonder those kids grow up to be maladjusted adults, deciding for everyone else like their parents did for them. I say, let kids be wild. Mine were running around half naked on the beach, running in the rain, and now they're all happily adjusted. You'd think the salt air here would be cleansing, but it seems everyone's forgotten how to breathe."

THE NO-KISSING CONTRACT

The three of us blink at Mrs. Waller, who doesn't seem to notice our shock, except for Tori, who seems used to it. Mrs. Waller reaches over and plucks a picture off a corkboard, proudly displaying it to Jason and me.

In the photo there's about twenty people, all dressed in Christmas pajamas, for a photo shoot on the beach. People ranging from infants all the way to past Mrs. Waller's age.

She taps on a man, that could be younger than my dad but his beard makes it hard to gage and says, "That's my oldest Michael Jr, and his wife, Jen, and over here is my Gabe, and his wife Sarah, and my youngest Bethany, oh you know her, Mrs. Nesbit,"

"The algebra teacher!" I gasp, taking a better look at my ninth-grade math teacher.

"Her husband Patrick went to school here too," she laughs, lost in some memory. "He fell for my Bethany hard, but so did another boy. Oh! Mr. Harper, the automotive teacher—he used to race cars but—."

"Wow, Mrs. Waller," Tori interrupts. "That is quite a tale. You could write a romance novel yourself with the stories you've probably witnessed here."

"Oh, could I? Thirty-seven years here. I've seen more young love stories play out in these halls than I have time to write them all." She gets a faraway look before she pulls out a post-it note, hastily scribbling something down. "So much drama."

"Anyway," Jason continues, "Sebastian's been dodging his mom's setups for weeks, but it sounds like he's going to give in to help his sister. It might be perfect timing to help you with your, uh, *Ethan problem*."

Tori slings her arm around my shoulder. "Oh, this should be easy peasy, lemon squeezy," she says ironically, a big grin splitting her face.

My temple throbs. "I don't know..."

The idea makes me pause. Sebastian and me solving each other's problems through a mutual arrangement has a certain... elegance to it. And if he agrees, it should be pretty neat and clean, no strings, no feelings—just like Sebastian.

"Even if Thorne agrees—which he won't—how am I supposed to convince him after what happened—" *when we were kids,* but I don't feel like getting into all that in front of Jason, and Mrs. Waller "—um, what happened to rule number one of fake dating: pick someone who doesn't actively hate you?"

Jason furrows his brow. "Hate is such a strong word."

"Right." I mumble. I think hate accurately describes how Sebastian feels about me.

"Does Sebastian like honey or vinegar?" Mrs. Waller asks Jason, who shakes his head, obviously missing the subtext.

"The point is," Tori jumps in smoothly. "Sebastian needs a girlfriend to get his parents off his back, and relieve the pressure on his sister, and you need a boyfriend to get Ethan and Destiny off yours. It's perfect."

"Perfect," Jason claps. He pockets the return slip, giving Mrs. Waller a thank-you nod. "Tori, Juniper—good luck in your romantic endeavors."

"Not romantic," I correct. "Platonic. Sub-zero levels of platonic."

"Hey, Jason," Tori calls before he's out the door. He turns back, his brows raised expectantly. "You swear to secrecy, right? No blabbing?" She nods pointedly toward the bracelet we all know is hiding under his shirtsleeve.

Jason holds up his hands. "Why miss the fun?" He laughs, more to himself, heading out the door.

Once he's gone, I sink into one of the plastic office chairs. "Even if I *did* consider Sebastian, how could I approach him after what I said in swim class?"

"Yeah," she cringes. "I don't know how you're going to sweet-talk your way out of that one, but I know how you can start..." Tori's eyes glimmer. "You should totally come to practice today," she says casually. "See him in action."

"Absolutely not."

"Why not? You can sit in the bleachers, scope out the situation..." She waggles her eyebrows. "Maybe catch him when he's leaving the locker rooms."

"After I insulted him in front of everyone? No thanks."

"Actually, that's perfect," Tori insists, leaning forward. "You can apologize, clear the air. Then maybe suggest your... *little alliance*."

"Or he could drown me in the pool."

Mrs. Waller snorts behind her romance novel. "That boy's too proper to commit murder on school grounds."

"See?" Tori grins. "Even Mrs. Waller thinks it's a great idea."

I did already cancel plans with Ethan, and I'm technically free, which, judging by Tori's crazed nodding, she is coming to the same conclusion. "What am I supposed to tell people for why I'm there?"

"You're there to watch me, of course," Tori says, gesturing to herself. "Or if you don't want to approach him in view of those gossips on the swim team, you know, until you are official, you could head to his AP Euro class, room 204."

My gaze narrows. "How do you know his schedule?"

She waves a hand in the air. "As soon as Jason said Sebastian Thorne, Mrs. Waller looked up his schedule." She grins, waggling her eyebrows. "He could probably help *tutor* you for that chem test you're definitely going to fail since you've been in here all period."

"I'm not failing—" I start, but Mrs. Waller cuts me off.

"The boy has excellent grades," she says, turning a page in her book.

"Great, now you've switched to Team Sebastian too?" I ask Mrs. Waller with a groan.

"We're just trying to help with your... project," Tori says innocently.

"I hate you," I mutter, but we all know I don't mean it. "I'm going back to chemistry."

"Don't forget to text me!" Tori calls as I head for the door. "I want updates whether you pick swim practice or the private tutor!"

I let the door swing shut on her laughter, pausing in the empty hallway. The memory of Destiny's sobs echoes in my head, mixing with the sharp ache of Sebastian's name and the ghost of a friendship ruined long ago. I have options now—I could try to catch him after Euro, play it casual, maybe apologize for swim class... or I could go to practice, where at least Tori would be there for moral support.

As much as I hate to admit it, Sebastian might be the perfect solution. We have enough history to make it believable, and it sounds like he needs this as much as I do.

Either way, I'm apparently crazy enough to try.

CHAPTER 7
For Research Purposes

THE AFTERNOON SUN BEATS DOWN on the metal bleachers. I sit on the edge, tucking my skirt under my thighs to keep from burning my skin. Without the laziness of regular swim class, the pool area feels different—serious. The rhythmic splash of competitive strokes echoes off the chain-link fence surrounding the deck, mixing with distant sounds of football practice and the occasional screech of seagulls overhead.

I recognize Jase from history class warming up in lane two with Graham, and Jada's younger sister Riley stretching across the pool deck with the JV team. A few curious glances dart my way as I wave to Tori. Mallory from chemistry whispers something to her lane mate, both darting looks my way. After this morning's drama in swim class, I can only imagine what they're talking about.

Coach Burton paces along the central lanes where his varsity team practices, stopwatch in hand. Near the diving boards, the junior varsity coach works with newer recruits on their starts, their splashes less graceful than the synchronized movements of the varsity lanes.

Sebastian occupies lane four, his stroke powerful and precise. There's a fluid strength to his movements that draws the eye, making it hard to look away even when I want to. This is the most unguarded version of him—no pressed uniform, no composure to maintain, just him stripped down to the bare essentials.

"Enjoying the view?" Tori drops onto the bench beside me, still dripping from her warm-up laps. Water darkens the concrete where it falls from her practice suit. She runs her shammy over her face. "Though I guess the view would be better if they could still wear speedos? Like the college teams."

"This was a terrible idea." I pull my legs up onto the seat in front of me, wrapping my arms around my knees. "What if he sees me?"

"That's sort of the point." She wrings out her shammy, snapping it playfully in my direction. "Oh, speaking of *'the point'*, what about Dante? He's single, nice family, killer butterfly..."

Dante slices through lane five. He *is* nice—always holds doors open, helped me pick up my books last year when my bag split. But I've seen how he smiles when Destiny is around, the way her eyes follow him sometimes in the hallways. Not that it should matter—she's with Ethan. *Still.*

"I don't want a jock," I mutter, though my gaze drifts back to Sebastian's lane. He stops at the wall, pushing his goggles up to his forehead as he checks his time. Even from here, I catch the familiar crease between his brows.

Coach Burton's voice carries across the pool: "Pick it up, people! Santiago, watch that turn. Thorne, good form but I need more power on that finish."

Sebastian adjusts his black and silver cap before pushing off for another set.

"Um, hello?" Tori gestures toward Sebastian. "What do you call that?"

"That's different. Sebastian only does swim team because it looks good on college applications. And it's the most antisocial sport there is—him and his lane and his thoughts." I pause, watching him glide through the water on instinct. "He doesn't have to rely on anyone else. Doesn't have to talk to anyone else."

"You've put way too much thought into this," Tori says, something knowing in her tone that makes me squirm.

"I haven't—" But then Sebastian pulls himself out of the pool in one fluid motion, and something in my chest tightens. His dark green and black jammers fit snugly against him, outlining lean muscles and a physique that rivals most of the boys at school, even the best swimmers on the team. Like everything else about him, even his body is meticulous.

He's all long lines and stoic confidence now. But I catch glimpses of that serious little boy in the way he crosses his arms, jaw set as Coach gives him feedback.

"You're staring," Tori says with that smug smirk that makes me want to push her into the pool.

"I'm observing," I correct, very clinical. "For research purposes."

"You know," she says carefully, "it's okay if you actually like—"

"I don't." The denial comes quick. "He's... convenient. Perfect, actually. He hates social interaction, so it's not like I'll have to spend much time with him. He's got his own reasons for needing this arrangement, and he's just uptight enough that no one will question why we eventually break up."

"Uh huh." Tori's tone suggests she's not buying it.

"This is purely business. He needs a fake girlfriend to get his parents off his back. I need one to fix things with Destiny."

"Perfect," she repeats, but the excitement has deflated into concern.

I glance over at her. "Exactly. What's that look for?"

"June..." she starts, then stops as her expression grows troubled. "I was so caught up in solving your Destiny problem that I didn't really think about your shared history." She nods toward Sebastian. "Do you think you can handle it? Being around him again?"

My gaze drops to my lap, fingers twisting together. Tori's the only one who knows how much it hurt when Sebastian and I stopped being friends, but even she doesn't know everything.

The truth is more complicated than I care to admit.

There's something about Sebastian that's always gotten under my skin—not in a bad way, exactly, but in a way that makes me want to shake him out of his perfect composure.

Her question hits something raw I've been trying to ignore. The memory of the last day in the Thorne kitchen rises unbidden—hiding behind the counter, waiting to surprise him, only to overhear words that carved themselves into my eleven-year-old heart.

"We're not kids anymore," I say, but my voice comes out smaller than intended. "And it's not like we'll be really dating."

Tori doesn't look convinced. "Are you sure? We can find someone else." Her eyes glaze over like she's flipping through the entire school for potential replacements. "Maybe a freshman?" She shakes her head immediately. "Never mind."

Sebastian touches the wall and launches into another lap. Every stroke timed, every breath measured. Everything in its place, like always.

He hasn't looked up at the bleachers once—not even a flicker of recognition. I'm just another piece of scenery. Like I never mattered at all.

He's built this careful, untouchable world around himself—a fortress of straight A's, textbook technique, and ice-cold indifference. But perfection's just another type of armor. And even armor has weak spots.

"I can handle it," I say, more firmly this time.

Tori's expression softens. "You're sure?"

"Besides, I think Sebastian could use some shaking up."

Tori leans back on her elbows, eyes sparkling with mischief. "Would be a shame if someone... disrupted things."

"A real shame," I agree, already imagining Sebastian's face when I corner him after art class.

If I have to fake-date someone to save Ethan and Destiny's relationship, it might as well be the guy who's incapable of emotional attachments. And honestly? There's something weirdly satisfying about reminding Sebastian Thorne that no matter how hard he tries, he can't paint over me like another mistake on his canvas.

Coach Burton's voice cuts through our conversation: "Victoria! Social break's over—back in the water. We're working on relay transitions."

"Duty calls," Tori stands, giving my shoulder a squeeze. "Think about it, okay?"

I gather my things, not wanting to stay without Tori as a buffer. Awareness prickles under my skin like needles, and I glance toward the pool. Sebastian's gaze meets mine. Just for a second. The intensity there makes my stomach flip, but before I can read his expression, he's already pushing off for another lap, as controlled and unreachable as ever.

I hurry down the bleacher steps, the metal hot against my palm. Behind me, Coach's whistle pierces the air as he calls out splits, and I resist the urge to look back.

CHAPTER 8

Math Ain't Mathin'

THE NEXT AFTERNOON, I slip into study hall seconds before the bell, scanning the library for a safe spot away from Ethan's usual window table. The scent of old books and pencil shavings mingle with someone's vanilla body spray as I weave between the tables. Golden afternoon light streams through the tall windows, catching dust motes in its beams.

Jason's already claimed his spot in the back corner, dark head bent over calculus homework. Perfect. If I can look busy enough, maybe I can avoid the conversation that's been hanging between Ethan and me since yesterday's disastrous lunch.

"Avoiding someone?" Jason doesn't look up as I drop into the chair across from him. The cheap plastic squeaks beneath me.

"No, why would you ask that?" I pull out my chemistry notes, propping them up like a shield. The pages are wrinkled from being crammed in my bag, covered in my messy scrawl.

"Because you look suspicious and you're hiding behind your textbook." His dark gaze flicks toward the door as more students filter in. "Is it Sebastian?"

"Shhh!" I lean closer, frantically checking that no one's within earshot. My chair scrapes against the floor. "Could you be any louder?"

"Relax. He takes study hall in the art wing." Jason abandons his calculus, leaning in conspiratorially. His voice drops. "Heads up, though. I saw him talking to Avery Bennett this morning."

My stomach twists. "Oh?"

"Yeah. And she's not the first one I've seen circling." He taps his pencil against his textbook. "His parents must be cranking up the pressure because the vultures are definitely swooping in."

"That's..." Concerning? Expected? *None of my business.*

"Look," Jason whispers, glancing around before continuing, "all I'm saying is if you're really considering this dating thing, you might want to move fast. Before someone snags him for real."

I almost laugh. Sebastian Thorne wouldn't pick a random girl just because she batted her eyelashes. Even with parental pressure, he'd at least choose someone he could tolerate. Though that thought sends a sharp jolt through me. What if he's already found someone?

My gaze drifts around the library, taking in my options. Cam catches my attention as he walks through the doors, giving me a small wave. I return it, but quickly look away. Sweet as he is, Cam's like a brother. Plus, everyone knows he's had a crush on Mia since junior year.

"I'm still thinking about it," I mumble, picking at the corner of my notebook. "There's... history there. We were friends once... as kids."

Jason's eyebrows lift. "Sounds like you might have common ground, then?"

I make a noncommittal noise. "Let's say I learned exactly what Sebastian Thorne thought about being friends with someone like me."

Books drop onto our table with a thud. I jump, nearly knocking over my water bottle.

"You talking about Sebastian?" Jada slides into the chair next to Jason, wearing her gray Palm Vista Swim team shirt under her letterman jacket. "About his new groupies?"

Dante drops his gym bag before sinking into a chair beside hers. "You missed quite the show after you left practice yesterday."

"It's becoming a regular occurrence. I swear half the underclassmen show up to watch Sebastian in his skin-tight jammers." Jada's eyes dance with mischief. "Though they weren't the only unexpected spectators."

Heat creeps up my neck. "I was there for Tori."

"Those weren't just for Sebastian," Dante protests, pushing a hand through his brown hair. "They were supporting the entire team."

"Really?" Jada arches a brow. "'Sebastian, show us your BUTT-erfly' was team support?"

"I thought you had work?" Ethan drops into the seat across from Jada, his calculus book landing with a soft thud. His tone is casual, but there's something careful in how he glances at me.

"I did. Later." My voice comes out scratchy. "I was supporting Tori."

Dante grins. "Like how those freshmen were *supporting the team*' by taking yearbook photos?"

Jada turns to me. "Were you scoping out anyone in particular? Because Destiny mentioned needing a double date—"

"Hey." Ethan cuts her off, catching my eye. His familiar cologne washes over me. As he tilts his head toward the empty table near the reference section. "Got a minute?"

My chest tightens, but I nod. This conversation has been inevitable since yesterday. Might as well get it over with.

As I gather my things, I catch Jason's meaningful look. Maybe he's right. Maybe it's time to stop running from one awkward situation and face another head-on instead.

As I follow Ethan to the far table, I recognize the serious look he gets before deep conversations. The same one he wore when he told me his parents were divorcing in ninth grade. I can't let him start. Once Ethan gets going, steering the conversation becomes impossible.

"Before you get all intense," I say, sliding into the chair across from him, "I need help with something."

Wariness crosses his face. "June—"

"What's the rule about parabolas again?" I pull out my calculus homework, deliberately derailing his attempt at a serious talk. "The one with the vertex form?"

"That's not what I—" He stops, frowning at my notebook. "Wait. Did you seriously write—? June, *come on.*"

I hide my smile. If there's one thing guaranteed to distract Ethan, it's bad math.

"Really?" I tap my pencil against my chin innocently. "I thought h was the horizontal shift?"

"It is, but—" He's already reaching for my notebook, that familiar crease appearing between his brows. "If you write it like this—" He sketches a quick graph, totally immersed now.

When Ethan leans in to explain, I notice the faint freckles across his nose from surfing. Our shoulders brush as he corrects my graph, and suddenly I'm aware of the glances we're drawing. Emma whispers something to Julie that makes them both look our way.

I shift back, but Ethan moves closer, oblivious to how this looks—his head bent near mine, his arm resting along the back of my chair. Has it always been like this? This unconscious gravitation toward each other?

"June?" Ethan's voice breaks through my thoughts. "Are you even listening?"

"Totally." I point to his sketch. "Vertex form. Fascinating stuff."

He sets down his pencil with more force than necessary. "This isn't really about calculus, is it?"

"No, it's about me failing if I don't figure out these formulas." I pack up my books, movements quick but casual. "Actually, I should probably find a tutor. Someone who can explain it better than—"

"I can explain it fine." There's an edge to his voice. "You're not listening. Something else is going on."

"You're right." I stand, shouldering my bag. "I'm terrible at listening. That's why I need space to focus on school stuff. College applications. Work."

"Right," he scoffs, flicking the corner of the notebook. "Because you've always cared so much about your grades. At least be honest about whatever this is."

The dismissive tone gives me the perfect excuse to leave. "Thanks for the vote of confidence," I say coolly. "Really helping your case here."

I catch his flash of regret, but I'm already walking away. Behind me, I hear him call my name, but I don't turn back.

I can't.

CHAPTER 9
Proposition

I WAITED UNTIL AFTER school to find Sebastian, leaving Spanish IV early to hunt him down. Art is his last class, which is far enough from the student parking lot to give me time to catch him before he drives home.

I slip in as the bell rings, hanging back as students flee. No Sebastian. I edge into the classroom, breathing in turpentine and wet clay. Afternoon sunlight pours through the tall windows along the left wall, catching particles of dried paint and sanded clay in its golden beams. A few windows near the kiln sit cracked open to release the extra buildup of heat.

Most students have cleared out, leaving Miss Brooks and a couple of helpers to pack up table easels and discarded paper towels littering the desks and floors. At the back, a familiar sandy brown head is bent over a paint-streaked sink, methodically cleaning brushes like a practiced painter.

I move closer, studying his back. His white dress shirt sleeves are carefully rolled to his elbows, and a black apron streaked with dried paint is tied around his waist. His forest green sweater vest, the one he was wearing this morning, embroidered with the school's emblem, is probably folded neatly in his backpack.

A canvas on the nearest easel catches my eye. A study in blues and grays, a stormy sky brooding with uncast lightning before a waved churned sea. The longer I stare, the more the waves gently move, the clouds practically rolling in.

My eyes water, and I don't know why.

"Um, hi," I greet, stepping beside the sink, careful to stay out of the splash zone.

Sebastian continues the methodical movement of his thumb over the paintbrush, coaxing out the remaining pigment. For a second, I think he hasn't heard me. Then his whole body goes rigid, hands pausing as he glances at me sideways.

Okay, so I deserved that.

"Listen, I need a favor."

"Oh?" he says, adding pink soap to another brush and working it in. "From the elitist snob who only cares about himself?"

I rock back on my heels, shame burning my face. "I'm sorry; I shouldn't have said those things."

He huffs—more the movement of his shoulders than the sound—as the water drones on. "*You are unbelievable.*" He shakes out the brushes with three quick flicks before carrying them to a cubicle along the wall. He places a paper towel under what looks like a mini umbrella stand, hanging the brushes upside down to dry.

I frown at the contraption. None of the other cubicles have anything like it. I reach out to touch a brush, but he blocks my hand without looking.

"I think it might be mutually beneficial."

He cuts me a glaring side-eye, reminiscent of childhood when I'd dare suggest adding to his Lego sets. "I doubt it."

Before I can elaborate, he grabs his worn leather messenger bag and heads for the door, those long legs eating up the distance. I scramble after him, maneuvering around desks and Miss Brooks carrying a stack of dry-fired clay pots. I nearly clip my shoulder on the door trying to keep up.

By the time I catch up, he's pushing through the double doors into sunlight.

"Sebastian!" I call, annoyance leaking out after jogging to catch up.

"*Pip*," he says obnoxiously, using my old childhood nickname.

I clench my teeth but refuse to let him derail me.

A few lingering students turn to watch us pass. I'm practically chasing him like some groupie, while he glides ahead like a well-dressed wildcat. I'm pretty sure he notices me struggling to keep up, because he lengthens his stride. Sweat trickles down my back, and I'm certain my face is turning strawberry.

"Can you slow down?"

"Hmm," he hums, feigning ignorance.

He is such a brat!

Sebastian reaches the parking lot and heads straight for his Range Rover, dismissing me with a two-fingered wave that's both cool and condescending. Lights flash with a beep as it unlocks.

I sprint to the passenger door and fling myself into the seat before he can lock me out. The leather is warm against my bare legs where my uniform skirt has ridden up.

His eyebrows shoot up in surprise before letting out a long-suffering sigh, dropping his head back against the headrest. There's a paint smudge under his jaw and a hint of silver chain beneath his collar.

"What could you *possibly* want?"

"I want you," I blurt.

Fire blooms across my skin the second the words leave my mouth. It doesn't help the way his head slowly turns toward me, one perfect eyebrow arching, his elbow bumping mine on the center armrest as he shifts to face me.

I ignore the rising panic in my gut and push on. "What I mean is, I want a boyfriend."

He pinches the bridge of his nose, a gesture so familiar it yanks me back in time. "*Juniper.*" He says my name like it's the source of all that's wrong in his life.

"I need you to *pretend* to be my boyfriend." Then I remember Mrs. Waller's advice and add, "please."

He opens his eyes in a slow blink. I watch wariness shift into panic, before melting into something deeper. Vulnerable. He shifts in his seat, putting more distance between us even though we're already separated by the center console.

Silence stretches between us, broken only by the whisper of the engine and the soft hum of the air conditioner that struggles to cool the car. More sweat rolls down my back and temples. I reach over and turn the A/C to high. He tracks the movement back to my lap.

"No," he says, but his voice comes out rough, strained.

"You haven't even thought about it."

"I have." He gapes at me, looking less composed than I've seen him in a while... well, since the pool incident yesterday. "And nope, no way."

"Why? You don't even know the facts or terms! Or how it benefits you, too." I turn to face him more fully, my hand brushing his before he draws back.

He laughs, low and dark, the sound vibrating in the small space between us. "How could it possibly benefit me?"

"Okay, ouch," I say, shifting in his leather seats. Which are very comfortable. "That hurts a little."

Regret enters his face, but I'm not here for sympathy.

"It'll stop your mom from setting you up with ring-hungry debutantes and get you a no-strings-attached date to the gala our moms are throwing?"

I leave out Sophie's pressure to carry out the Thorne name as their eldest child. I don't need to remind him his parents want a marriage engagement, not a fake dating situation.

He narrows his eyes, ice-green and suspicious. "Did your mom tell you that?"

"Is it not true?"

He studies me before reaching up to loosen his tie, his movements quick and practiced. I glance out the window as he tosses the tie into the back seat, but my gaze drifts back to watch his artist's fingers move to the buttons of his crisp dress shirt.

"It's not *not* true," he mutters.

He shrugs out of his shirt, leaving him in his uniform slacks and white undershirt. The smell of his expensive cologne drifts toward me. The A/C finally kicks in, raising goosebumps along my arms.

"I have thirty—" he pushes a button to activate the dash clock. "—twenty minutes before I need to be somewhere."

I assume that's his Neanderthal way of telling me to continue, but quickly. "My friends Destiny and Ethan Cole—"

"I know who Ethan is." His hand tightens on the wheel.

"Well, I need them both to think I have a boyfriend."

"Why?"

"Because," I drag out the word. "It's a long story, but everyone thinks Ethan and I, well, that there's maybe—which is ridiculous, and Destiny is worried, and she's a good friend, and I want her and Ethan to be happy, and I don't want to be the reason they break up."

He tucks his bottom lip under his teeth. "Uh-huh."

"Does that make sense?"

"Sure." He flattens his mouth, which still conveys amusement. "You don't want Destiny thinking you have the hots for Ethan or vice versus, so you've concocted this *brilliant* plan to get a boyfriend."

"Uh-huh. Yeah. That about sums it up."

I'm wearing the short-sleeved polo version of the uniform, but inside the car—with Sebastian *right there*—it feels like a sweater. I pluck the fabric away from my skin, fanning it.

"Why don't you just get a boyfriend, Juniper?" He gestures at me with one elegant hand. "Like a real one."

"Because I don't want a boyfriend, *Sebastian*. And I don't want to fake *real-date* someone and crush their heart."

"But mine's okay?"

"You're not going to fall in love with me," I hiss.

He leans against the door, resting a paint-stained knuckle on his bottom lip, considering me with those intense eyes. "I still don't understand how this benefits me?"

I gesture as if it's obvious. "If your parents think you have a girlfriend, they'll stop setting you up with every eligible heiress in the state. Plus, your mom likes me."

He narrows his gaze. "My mom likes you *too* much."

I toss up my hands. "I guess I can be more unlovable, so it's easier when we break up," I say, exasperation pushing into my words.

"Juniper," he says, sighing.

"I don't know, Sebastian. You're the only one who can help me."

He glances out the window, and I can practically see the gears turning. I hope some are clicking in my favor. He reaches over, and for a second I think maybe he might... I flatten myself into the seat, heart jumping, but he only pulls the door handle, letting in a rush of hot air. It breaks whatever strange tension had built up in the car.

"I'll think about it," he says, leaning back. "Now get out. I now have only ten minutes. *Please.*"

"Okay. Great." I slide out with my backpack, about to say, *call me* when the door closes with a soft click.

I head to my car as his Range Rover disappears around the corner, sun glinting off its polished surface. Even his car manages to look condescending.

He didn't say no.

He didn't say yes either, but '*I'll think about it*' from Sebastian Thorne is practically enthusiasm. The boy I once spent two hours convincing to go swimming isn't exactly known for spontaneous decisions.

My phone buzzes in rapid succession. That could only be one person.

> **TORI:** Did you ask him???

> **TORI:** How'd it go???

> **TORI:** Did he say yes?

> **TORI:** Did he bring up you calling him a jerk???

> **TORI:** June???

> **TORI:** I can see you from the pool!!!!

I glance across the parking lot to the metal fence around the pool. A slender redhead waves at me through the gaps before Coach Burton's whistle blows a sharp warning.

I wave back and reply.

> **ME:** He didn't say no. I quote: "I'll think about it."

Three dots appear, then a flood of exclamation points and every emoji in Tori's arsenal. I pocket my phone without responding.

Whatever Sebastian decides, I still have to explain to Ethan what my *family business* is that's keeping me too busy for the movie tonight or how I'm going to keep dodging him without ruining our friendship. Or how I'll face Destiny, knowing she thinks I'm trying to steal her boyfriend.

And if Sebastian agrees... how long we can pretend to like each other if only ten minutes in his car has us both crawling out of our skin?

CHAPTER 10
The Thorne Ultimatum

I BARELY MAKE IT halfway to first period before someone grabs my arm and yanks me into the shadowy alcove between the auditorium and English building. My body reacts before my brain, already winding up for a solid knee to the groin when my vision adjusts in the dim light and I freeze.

Sebastian.

His tall frame fills the narrow space, jade eyes sharper than usual beneath furrowed brows, his face deadly serious as he studies mine. That expensive cologne hits me immediately—bergamot and something woodsy I've become too familiar with from his car. The alcove forces us closer than comfortable, and he releases my arm as abruptly as he grabbed it.

I retreat until the cool concrete wall hits my back, while he shifts to his side, but we're still close enough my skin prickles with his nearness. His face stays serious, his focus intense enough to steal my breath—until I remember it's Sebastian. Until I remember why that look makes my chest ache.

"What are the rules?" His voice comes out deeper than usual.

"You couldn't say my name? A little warning? I was this close to ruining your ability to reproduce."

"*Juniper.*" He says in the same exasperated tone from when I'd test his limits as kids.

"What are the stipulations?" He waves impatiently between us. "To this *relationship,* you're proposing."

I sigh, fingers finding my ponytail and twisting. I don't much care for the way his lip curls around *relationship*, but I answer truthfully.

"I haven't gotten that far. Just that we need to really sell it if anyone's going to believe we're a couple…"

He studies me longer than necessary. Then, "So what? Two lunches, some hand-holding, one hug a week?"

"What are you, a nun?" My voice bounces off the masonry walls. "Haven't you seen what a relationship looks like? We need to make it look real, like you actually like me and I actually like you?"

"Okay, well, I don't know how to fake that." His frustration echoes mine in the narrow space.

I clutch my chest. "Ouch again, Thorne."

"That's not what I meant." He pushes a hand through his hair, voice a harsh whisper. "You *do* know I've had, like, *one* girlfriend? And it was Mandy Carson in middle school. Right?"

"I don't know what you get up to in your personal life," I say cautiously, tapping my fingertips together.

I *do*, in fact, know that his only girlfriend was Mandy Carson, and it lasted six months, despite, or maybe *because,* they never saw each other outside school. *I also know* he turns down every invitation from anyone at school, and the few snippets my mom has slipped out over the years. *Not that I asked.* But I've never told her to stop, either.

He arches a brow like he knows I'm lying. I blink innocently, grateful I'm shorter and in shadow.

"No kissing." He crosses his arms, expecting an argument. The movement brings him half a step closer. I almost feel the warmth radiating from his skin.

"*Obviously.*" His eyebrow lifts at my tone. Hot embarrassment makes me look away. "You realize you're not that irresistible, right?"

"It's not about that," he says flatly, his eyes flicking to mine, fast and sharp, like I hit a nerve. "Kissing... complicates things."

For a second, I want to laugh; he says it as if I'm the one who might lose control. Like I'm the danger here.

"Sure," I say, eyes flashing. "No kissing. I'll try to keep my urges to myself." My eye roll could circle the moon.

He clears his throat. "Any other rules?"

"Social media."

He raises an eyebrow. "What about it?"

"We need to change our relationship statuses."

He frowns. "I don't have social media."

I stare. "What."

"I don't have it."

"None? That's insane."

"I don't see the point."

"You are such a robot," I mumble, then: "Well, now you need one."

Sebastian gives me a *you have got to be kidding me* look. "If I make a fake Instagram for my *fake* relationship, isn't that overkill?"

I wave a hand. "Maybe."

He exhales. "What else?"

"Pet name?"

"No."

I hold up my hands. The thought of Sebastian calling me baby or kitten—it's too weird. I smirk. "Okay, but you have to act jealous if someone flirts with me."

He hums as if the words are being pulled from him, "I could probably muster the energy."

He's silent, then: "You'll have to accompany me to my social *obligations*." His voice stays steady, but misery shadows his features.

"You make it sound like you're being forced." I snort.

He looks past me into the darkness between the buildings, at the small patch of light beyond. I follow his gaze, trying to picture what's there, and realize he's not really looking at anything.

Sebastian had everything I dreamed of growing up, but even with his wealth and privilege, something always seemed a little lonely about him. I remember his spark dimming whenever his parents mentioned another dinner party or business dinner he had to attend. He'd describe weekends filled with tutors for subjects no normal kid cared about, voice flat like reading from a script. Maybe it's not an exaggeration about being forced. Perhaps those "social obligations" weren't as optional as I'd assumed.

"I have work, so I'll need notice to arrange my schedule." I chew my lip, gathering courage. "And it only makes sense if you come to mine, too. Movie nights, or something."

His eyes widen slightly—Sebastian Thorne at casual friend gatherings clearly hadn't occurred to him. "I... okay. Fair enough." His gaze drifts like he's trying to picture himself at a movie night with my friends, and I can see an imperceptible shudder.

"No one is going to believe this." He gestures wildly between us.

I groan, rubbing my eyes. I pace three steps before I turn around. "No, it's fine. We just need to practice before we launch. Get to know each other." I flick a glance sideways. "Again."

"Practice?" he repeats. "In private?"

"Yes." I turn, rubbing my forehead. "I could come to your house?"

Butterflies bloom in my belly. I haven't been there in years. Whenever Mom invites me, I'm conveniently busy, or going somewhere with Ethan.

"No," he says too quickly, something flickering across his face.

Panic tightens my chest. I throw up my hands, nearly hitting him. "Look, this was stupid, but it's the only idea I have. Can you work with me here?"

He blinks. His focus shifts toward the alley mouth, where the sun beats down on the bleached sidewalk. His face clouds with worry, and I think he'll back out. A tight slithering dread crawls up my ribs. Who else would do this? Tori's right; my options are limited. At least I can count on Sebastian to be discreet.

The weight of this whole thing presses down, so I say the first dumb thing that comes to mind...

"What's your favorite color?" I blurt. "Is it still Egyptian blue?"

He eyes me as if I've officially lost it. Maybe I have. "Yes."

"Why'd you answer like that?"

"How do you remember my favorite color?"

"We *do* know each other... sort of," I say, bristling now that I sound like a stalker. "You'd go on about how it's made of calcium copper silicate and its iridescent hues, and we'd look at all those Egypt books. It was hard to forget."

"Yes, it's still my favorite color," he says, blowing out a tense breath, "and yours?"

"Purple, but not dark purple, like a creamy purple."

"Like manganese, or light violet?"

"I don't know what manganese looks like." I fight a smile. Trust the artist to get technical. "Maybe a mix of both?"

He nods, thoughtful, and for a moment we are little again, sitting in his playground tower with books piled around, and a string of Halloween bat lights twinkling around us, his brows furrowed like he's mapping me in some mental database.

"And we can't ever tell anyone it's fake, ever," I add, pointing my finger for emphasis. "Even when we break up. I don't want it getting back to Destiny or Ethan. That defeats the whole purpose."

He makes a zipping motion across his lips, then throws away an imaginary key. Reminiscent of the time I swore him to secrecy over pre-dinner brownies. I wonder if he remembers, or if he tries to forget everything about me.

"And if either of us wants to end it, we call it off." He adds, "amicably."

"Deal." I nod, twisting my bag strap. "No drama. No messy breakups. A clean exit."

"Of course," he agrees, his arms dropping and posture relaxing. "So when do we... publicize this relationship?"

I smirk. "I was thinking a full-page spread in the Times."

"You mock me, but this is your goofy plan."

"Goofy?" I glare, but it dissolves in a laugh. "This is insane."

"Oh, now you think that?" He finally cracks a smile. "So, Juniper Blake, are we really doing this?"

"Yes, I think we are." I smile back. "So, Sebastian Thorne, are you ready to be my fake-boyfriend?" I extend my hand.

He hesitates only a second before clasping it. His palm is warm, rougher than I'd expected for a pampered prince.

The warning bell shrieks. We both jolt like we're caught doing something wrong. His hand slides from mine to push through his hair.

Fake dating Sebastian Thorne. What could possibly go wrong?

"June?"

My stomach plummets at Ethan's voice. I spin too quickly, shoulder bumping Sebastian's chest. His hand steadies me automatically, fingers curling around my upper arm. The touch sends an unexpected jolt through me.

The sun blinds me as we emerge from the shadowed alcove. Ethan stands with Destiny beside him, his confident smile faltering as he takes in my flushed cheeks—*it's hot, okay*—and the hand on my arm as we emerge from the school's most notorious make-out spot.

His narrowed focus tracks up, recognition hitting as he realizes exactly who's behind me, all graceful menace in his perfectly pressed uniform.

"Thorne?" The name comes sharp with disbelief, darting between us. "What are you doing down there?"

The question aims for casual but misses, landing somewhere between confused and accusatory.

"Cole," Sebastian greets stiffly, letting go of my arm and sliding his hands into his pockets.

Sebastian's eyes drop to mine, brow raised as I try to telegraph a warning. I'm not sure what I'm trying to tell him, *exactly*, in three seconds, but I know I don't want to blow this fake dating scheme before it even starts.

Ethan's gaze darts behind us to the dark alley. I see him putting pieces together: the hook-up nook, Sebastian's mussed hair, the suspicious silence like we were caught.

It's Destiny who finally has the guts to ask. "June?" She offers a demure smile to Sebastian. "Were you two down there together?"

I can't logically explain what we *were* doing unless we let them think...

Sebastian's already watching when I glance up. Heat blazes up my neck. We haven't worked out our story yet, haven't had time to make this look like a believable couple instead of strangers closing a business deal.

I'm beaming my thoughts to Sebastian, but turns out I'm not psychic. The silence stretches, and it's obvious that something odd is going on between us.

Sebastian's jaw ticks, and I recognize the signs of him retreating behind his stiff and formal facade. He's going to deny it. Blow this whole thing before it even starts. I shake my head, but he's not looking anymore.

Then Ethan says, "Are you stalking her, Thorne?"

Whatever Sebastian was going to say dies as something dark crosses his features. Ethan's jab hangs in the air, then Sebastian grins. All teeth and no warmth.

"Stalking?" Sebastian's voice carries a soft menace. He chuckles to himself. His voice drops low, conspiratorial. "Well, Juniper, we'd better tell them."

My gaze goes razor thin. He really will blow this wide open, the jerk. Payback for all the hell I gave him as kids.

Sebastian's arm slides around my shoulder, pulling me closer like we've done this a hundred times. I feel the weight in more ways than one, especially when his thumb brushes my collarbone. "Right, babe?"

Sebastian raises one brow in challenge. *That jerk. Oh-kay.* I slide my arm around his waist, digging my fingers into his side. He lets out a small grunt, tensing.

The word "babe" hits Ethan and Destiny in different shades of shock.

"Yup, babe." I should get an award for saying that with a straight face. "Sebastian's my boyfriend."

"You guys are *together*?" Destiny asks. Blond brows still raised, but her small sigh sounds relieved.

"Boyfriend," Ethan repeats a second after, testing the word like maybe he didn't hear right.

"We, um, weren't going to make it official yet, but you caught us." I hold up my free hand. The other continues digging into Sebastian's ribs. Through his shirt, muscles tense at the pressure.

"Yup." He's smiling down at me, and I want to kick him.

His features are too perfect, too practiced—exactly what we need to convince them, and it's infuriating. Where has this Sebastian been?

"Okay," Ethan looks numb. He hooks his thumb behind him, toward where we usually meet before school. "We were looking for you."

Destiny's hand tightens on her backpack strap.

"You found us," Sebastian says, grinning as his deep voice vibrates between our pressed bodies.

"Us," Ethan echoes.

"Wow," Destiny laughs nervously, "I mean, wow, but, wow." She tucks her hair behind her ears as her laughter trails off. "Er, congratulations."

"Thank you." The words taste sour. I can't look at Ethan and see the hurt there. Best friends tell each other something like this. They don't spring new boyfriends on them.

"I would have told you sooner..."

"It's my fault," Sebastian picks up where I left off. "I asked Pip to wait."

"Pip?"

"It's an old nickname," I tell them as my elbow digs into his side. His thumb strokes my shoulder in retaliation.

"We've known each other since we were kids." Sebastian pulls me closer against him.

A new confusion twists Ethan's features, so I add, "You know my mom is business partners with Mrs. Thorne?"

Ethan blinks. "Yeah, I just didn't think—" Destiny tugs the hand she's holding when Ethan doesn't finish. "—that you too were that close."

I see the words forming on Sebastian's lips before he says them. Everything slows; my limbs turn to marble, and I can't stop him. "Like best friends."

The words hang in the air. Ethan's teeth clench behind closed lips. Sebastian tenses, the type of stillness of realizing he went too far.

Ethan's hand has dropped from Destiny's, and it clenches at his side. He's looking at me, but she is looking at him, her frown only deepening. This is exactly what I was trying to avoid. More wedges, more reasons to make me front and center in Ethan's world, pushing Destiny aside.

I need to defuse this quickly before it gets worse. I pull out of Sebastian's arm, sliding my hand into his. He can't hide his surprise as my fingers tangle with his. I wonder if he can tell how clammy mine are.

"We'd better get going," I say, then to Sebastian, "Walk me to class?"

"Yeah." He clears his throat, nodding.

"We'll see you two at lunch?" It's out before I can take it back. *Lunch.* Where we always sit together. Where everyone will see Sebastian and me together.

"Um, sure." I hear Destiny say as I guide Sebastian away.

I steer him toward the English building, casting a glance back, but Ethan and Destiny are already gone, swallowed by the crowd of students shuffling to class.

When we push through the doors of the English building, I pull Sebastian into the stairwell.

"I can't have lunch with your friends," he says before the doors even close, like he's been holding it in since I mentioned it.

"It just came out." I push my fingers through my hair, messing up my ponytail. "Wait, what else are you doing?"

He puts a hand on his hip. "I did have a life before this. I wasn't just waiting around on standby until Juniper Blake needed something." His face pinches in annoyance. "You haven't changed at all. You're still one-hundred percent entitled, and pushy, and—"

"*Me* entitled," I gasp, dropping my fingers from combing the tangles I created. "Says the guy with the custom playground."

"What?" he asks incredulously. "What are you talking about?"

"Never mind." I wave a hand dismissively.

"And yes, you're still a brat." He doesn't back down. His eyes flash in the dim stairwell lights.

The door swings open. Several students pour through the opening, stopping our argument. They cast curious glances at where Sebastian and I stand away from the stairs, and the main pathway heading to the second floor, in that shadowy place perfect for romantic rendezvous.

He gives me a final head shake before pushing off the wall and catching the door. I ignore the stares as I follow him. "Sebastian," I call.

He stops surprisingly, slowly turning so I can ask, "Are you still in?"

He hesitates, pushing both hands through his hair. "I hate crowds." He says finally. "And I thought we had a few days before we..." He gestures between us, hand wavering in the space that separates us. "Were a thing."

"You can call it off," I tell him in a small voice, my shoulders deflating.

The thought of forcing him into something he's clearly uncomfortable with sits uneasily in my ribcage. Sebastian's always been private. I remember how he'd tense up when too many people crowded around. If he really can't handle this...

I shrug. "I can find another way."

It's busier here than the stairwell, students slipping around us like water around a rock, but he doesn't move, studying me with those vibrant green eyes. His fingers tap against his leg—like when he's trying to make a decision.

Finally, he says, "I'll figure something out for lunch." Before I can respond, he adds, "But we need ground rules. Specific ones about how to act in public. And maybe..." he glances around at our audience, "...practice looking less like we want to kill each other."

CHAPTER 11
Public Displays of Confession

METAL LOCKERS CLANG and echo in the pool's changing rooms. Fabric rustling mingles with the gentle echo of conversation bouncing off the tiled room. Behind the bank of lockers, a toilet flushes.

"So he actually agreed?" Tori tugs her practice suit into place. "Just like that?"

I glance toward the sophomore girls changing at the far end, but they're too busy dissecting someone's breakup to care about us. "Lower your voice. And yes. For now."

I shuffle my one-piece swimsuit up under my uniform skirt.

"What does that mean?"

"It means..." I gather my thick hair and twist it into a tight bun. "It's complicated."

"Complicated, like getting caught at hook-up alley this morning?"

I drop my hands. "We weren't—who told you that?"

"Please." Tori pulls out her phone, scrolling through messages. "Emma Chambers saw you two sneaking down there. Madison

Davis swears she saw hand-holding, and according to the swim team group chat, you've been secretly dating for months."

"Months?" I grab her phone, scanning messages. A cold weight sinks in my belly at some theories about why we've been "hiding" our relationship.

She clicks her tongue. "And of course Destiny told me."

"What did she say?" I hand back her phone, the school gossip temporarily forgotten.

Tori shrugs, grabbing her towel. "That she thought you despised him."

I bite my thumbnail. "What did you tell her?"

"That your hatred was covering up your burning thirst for Sebastian Thorne," she coos.

"Oh, wow." I sink onto the bench. "This is..."

Tori smirks. "Exactly what you wanted? Everyone thinking you're off the market?"

"I didn't think it would be so..."

"Public? June, you're dating Sebastian Thorne. The guy turns down every girl at this school, and suddenly he's pulling you into dark corners..."

I groan, dropping my face into my hands. "I thought we'd have time to figure things out before everyone started talking."

"Speaking of figuring things out..." Tori's tone means trouble. "You realize you're about to spend forty-five minutes in a pool with your new boyfriend, right? In swimsuits?"

I peek through my fingers to find her grinning.

"Shut up."

"I'm only saying, if you're trying to sell this relationship..."

"We're new," I blurt. "Brand new. Too new for... whatever you're thinking."

"Mmhm." She stands, offering me a hand up. "Well, you better figure out how 'new' looks, because those girls haven't stopped staring since you walked in. I guarantee they'll report back every interaction—or lack thereof—to their friends."

We look over as three heads whip away, suddenly fascinated by their lockers.

"Fantastic." I grab my towel. "Just great."

"Hey." Tori catches my arm. "I think Sebastian might surprise you. Sounds like he was pretty committed this morning."

I groan, rubbing my temples. "That was..."

Shy, reserved Sebastian, suddenly comfortable touching me, playing it up for Ethan. We've barely spoken in years, and minutes before he said he didn't know how to act in a relationship. Well, he nailed the jealousy act perfectly. I'm still reeling from him calling me *'babe.'* Babe is not a word I thought was in his vocabulary.

"I don't know what that was."

Tori smiles. "Let's hurry; I want good seats for this show."

CHLORINE BURNS MY NOSE AS we push through the locker room doors, mixing with deodorant and sunscreen. Coach Burton sits in the lifeguard chair, whistle dangling on a black string around his neck, looking as interested in teaching as ever.

Mia and Rachael cluster by the diving board, their conversation cutting off as Tori and I walk past. Their stares follow us across the deck, and I try not to think about how many versions of our "hook-up alley" story they've already heard.

Tori nudges me, nodding toward Sebastian cutting through the water in his usual lane.

"So," she starts before he's even finished his lap, pitched low but gleaming with mischief. "What's the plan? Ignore each other? Make eyes across the lanes? Oh! You could pretend to drown and let him save you—"

"I hate you," I mutter, but I can't stop watching Sebastian move through the water.

"You love me. But seriously, people are watching. You should at least acknowledge each other." She nods toward Mia's group, who aren't even pretending not to stare.

I force myself to walk over to Sebastian's lane, conscious of every step on the slick concrete. The last time I was here, I was trash-talking him to Tori. Now I'm supposed to act like his girlfriend. It would be funny if my heart wasn't trying to escape through my throat.

Tori stops at the next lane, fitting her swim cap over her bun of red hair. "You're as red as Coach's whistle," she mutters.

"Shut up," I hiss, but then Sebastian reaches the wall and pulls himself up to adjust his goggles.

Water streams down his chest and shoulders, morning light catching on droplets that trace paths down his tan skin. He glances up, those impossibly green eyes meeting mine, and I forget to breathe.

"June," he greets flatly.

A group of students sits in the bleachers "studying," textbooks forgotten as they watch us like we're their favorite show. Totally within earshot.

I inhale and ease down onto the pool's edge, the rough concrete warm beneath my palms. Sebastian shifts back to make room for my legs, water sloshing between us. His arm grazes my knee by accident, but the contact sends goosebumps blooming across my bare legs. I smooth my hands down my thighs to chase them away.

Tori slides into her lane with the grace of a competitive swimmer, draping her arms over the green and white lane dividers. Her knowing smirk makes me want to splash her.

"So, Sebastian," she drawls, eyes dancing between us. "That was quite a performance this morning. Very convincing."

Sebastian studies his goggles, wiping away an imaginary speck. "Performance?"

He flicks a glance at me, and I send Tori a look that says *don't start*. "Tori knows. I told her."

He pushes a hand through his hair. Stray droplets land on my knee. "What happened to secrecy?"

"It was sort-of her idea?"

He inclines his head to Tori. "So I have you to thank for my new *girlfriend*?"

His smile is all teeth. A glimpse of his dry humor, but underneath is a playfulness that does dangerous things to my pulse.

"Yup, and you *are* welcome." Tori's grin turns devilish. "Our Junie is quite the little hellcat."

Sebastian snorts, but when he realizes we're both staring at him, his face goes red.

I splash water at her. "Don't you have laps?"

"Coach doesn't care." She nods toward where Coach Burton is deeply invested in a game of Block Blitz on his phone. "Besides, I'm here to keep things PG." She waggles her eyebrows suggestively.

Sebastian adjusts his goggles, amusement tugging at his mouth. "Well, I *do* have laps."

"Such an overachiever." Tori tips her head back in mock exasperation.

"Wait." I reach for his arm. My fingers glide down his wet skin, catching at his wrist. "What are we doing about lunch?"

He exhales a frustrated sound. "I hate the cafeteria. Can't we date without sitting together?"

"Yeah, if you want to ruin June's reputation," Tori chimes in. "It'll look suspicious if you only want to spend time with her in dark alleys and dim stairwells." She pauses meaningfully. "People might think you're ashamed of her."

His jaw clenches, a muscle jumping beneath the skin. "That's definitely not my intention."

I can't control what people think. The gossip will eventually move on. But Destiny and Ethan need to believe this is real, but not if it costs me the other—*necessary*—part of this plan.

"No, it's okay." I drop my hand from his wrist. "We'll figure it out. Not every couple spends lunch together."

Tori looks ready to argue, but a look from me has her clamping her mouth shut. We've already pushed him far enough out of his comfort zone. He looks like a caged animal eyeing an open door, ready to bolt.

Sebastian studies my face; while his is unreadable. He sighs, running a hand over his face. "Meet me at the library after fourth period."

"What?"

"If we're doing this," he says, low enough only Tori and I can hear, "we should at least try to do it right." He glances at the bleachers, where our audience still watches with poorly concealed interest. "Even if it means enduring the cafeteria."

"I mean it. You don't have to—"

"I know." Gaze softening before he says, "But Victoria's right. We need to convince your friends this is real."

"Did Sebastian Thorne just admit I was right about something?" Tori clutches her chest dramatically. "This is truly historic."

The corner of his mouth twitches. "I need to finish my laps." He slides his goggles over his eyes, all business again.

"Have fun, babe," I call after him, trying for love-struck girlfriend.

Sebastian freezes mid-motion, one hand still on the pool edge. His brows shoot up before he gives me a look of mild reproach.

I flutter my eyelashes innocently. "You started it."

He shakes his head, but I catch the way his mouth quirks before he turns away, vanishing under the water with barely a ripple.

"Well," Tori says beside me, loaded with implications, "that was…"

"Don't," I warn.

She lifts her hands. "I didn't say anything!"

"You're thinking it really loud."

"I was only saying—you two are really selling it." She shoots me a look. "Maybe even to yourself." She fans herself. "There's some real tension between you two."

I ignore her, but my heart hasn't stopped beating like a warning bell since Sebastian looked up at me.

"Well, at least you got Thorne to agree to eat in the cafeteria. That's progress, at least."

"He still might bail." I chew my cheek. He always hated crowds, but something warm flutters in my chest at the memory of his reluctant, *we should at least try to do it right*.

Tori watches me. "But he's trying. That's something, isn't it?"

"Let's hope it's enough to convince Destiny and Ethan." I slide fully into the lane. The water is sharp against my skin, shocking enough to clear my head.

CHAPTER 12
Soft Launch

"SO, JUNE, WHERE'S Sebastian?" Destiny asks, glancing meaningfully at the chair beside me.

I shrug, but everyone's staring, waiting for an answer. "Oh, um..." I scramble for an excuse that won't come back to bite me. "Some art emergency. We're meeting later."

I waited for him by the side doors of the library like he said, but the minutes kept passing as I stood there alone. It's what I deserve for the things I said about him.

Ethan drops his hamburger on his plate, slouching back in his chair. "So how long has this been going on?" He's pushed the accusation into the question, making a couple of our tablemates shift uncomfortably.

Cam and Jordan stare down at their plates. Emma and Cam's sister, Julie, have joined us too. I don't know if it's my sudden jump up the social ladder that's drawn Emma's curiosity, or if she's here to watch me crash and burn.

It doesn't help that the chair next to me is empty. A big sign proclaiming that I got stood up.

"Not long," I say, popping a grape into my mouth to buy time.

"How come you didn't tell me?" Ethan asks. Then, with a quick glance around the table, amends, "Us?"

"She told me," Tori says, trying to help—but then adds, "like weeks ago."

"*Weeks ago?*" Ethan blinks away his surprise. "How did this even happen?"

"Ethan," Destiny says softly, putting a hand on his arm. "June probably sees him when her mom meets with Mrs. Thorne. It's not that weird."

"Yeah, it's totally not weird at all," Tori adds.

I don't correct them; how I've avoided that very thing for years. But once upon a time...

"Is that when it happened, June?" Ethan says, sitting forward, his eyes flashing in challenge. "When you'd go with your mom to the Thornes?"

The question hangs in the air like a trap. Ethan is probably piecing together every negative comment I've made about Sebastian over the years, or the times I'd decline my mom's invitations to visit the Thorne's estate, even though she'd remind me how much I used to love it there. My aversion to Sebastian was never subtle—I barely acknowledged him at school unless absolutely necessary.

"We've recently reconnected," I say tersely, returning the challenge.

A shadow crosses the table before Sebastian drops into the seat next to me. My death grip on my napkin loosens.

I make room as he settles in, mumbling an apology as Tori and Jordan scoot their chairs and trays down. I always forget how physically imposing he is until he's right in front of me. My memory of him is always smaller, not this tall stranger who commands attention without trying.

But he's not supposed to be a stranger, so I look up at him and smile, trying to brush off the tension from Ethan's interrogation. "Hey."

"Hey, sorry I'm late." His hair is still wet from swim class, pushed back in sleek waves like he styled it that way. He carries the art room with him. Earthy clay, glue, and acrylic paint linger on his clothes as he pulls the wrapper off his straw with his lips.

"It's fine," I say, relieved that he showed. I know what this cost him. But the tone is all wrong—lower, gentler, and almost timid.

It must be strange because he does a double take, gaze moving all over my face before he leans in to say, "I lost track of time. I'm sorry."

"Where were you?"

"In the art room."

"I thought you had art sixth?"

"I do. Ms. Landry lets me come in at lunch, and I've got study hall after..."

"So... two extra hours to paint?"

One side of his mouth curves up. "Yeah."

Tori clears her throat. I blink and realize we've been staring at each other, talking in soft tones while most of the table watches. I slide back into my seat, my pulse buzzing in my ears.

The cafeteria, which hummed with noise moments ago, has quieted so every shuffle, cough or scrape of silverware echoes around us.

I can feel the weight of everyone's attention, measuring our every interaction. This isn't just lunch—it's the moment our fake relationship either becomes believable or falls apart spectacularly.

"So," Cameron says, volume cranked up to break the silence. "You're in art? You paint?"

Sebastian unwraps his cheeseburger, his movements precise. "Yes."

"He's really good," I say automatically.

Sebastian gives a modest shrug. "Your mom's really good too, Pip."

Emma and Julie exchange looks at his intimate use of my childhood nickname. Even Tori's brows climb up, but all I can think about is how easily it rolled off his tongue, like no time has passed at all.

Sebastian says, "My mom showed me the prototypes for the gala. It's going to be magical."

"I love your mom's crowns," Emma says, and logically you'd think she was talking to me, but the insult is clear when she turns to Julies and adds, "Sebastian's mom owns the Starlit Jewel downtown."

Julie touches her hair absentmindedly. "Oh, I've always wanted one of those clips with the little flowers on them. They look so lovely."

"Juniper's mom is the genius behind the Starlit Jewel. Even my mom will tell you that," Sebastian says. "She wouldn't have the shop if it wasn't for Mrs. Blake's creations."

I fidget with my napkin as I give him a grateful smile. Everyone always assumes the Thornes are the real power behind the business.

Mom always says meeting Bonnie Thorne changed both their lives. She'd been teaching local art classes when Bonnie walked in, already married to Sebastian's dad but desperate for a creative outlet from her societal obligations. Mom recognized a kindred spirit in Bonnie's appreciation for art, not only the technical skill, but the soul of it.

From there, a partnership bloomed. Mom's talent for crafting ethereal pieces that told stories in silver, gold and stone, combined with Bonnie's eye for beauty and business acumen. The Thornes had the capital that Mom, drowning in student loans from art school, could never have accessed on her own. But it was more than money—they shared a vision of creating wearable art that would be passed down through generations.

They built the Starlit Jewel together. Equal partners, even though the seed money came from Sebastian's father's fortune—the same fortune Sebastian will inherit someday. I wonder if that's why Sebastian and I clicked so naturally as kids because we both had mothers who saw art everywhere, who taught us to look for beauty in unexpected places.

Sebastian and I have spent years avoiding each other, when our mothers' friendship built the foundation of both our lives.

I glance at Emma, wondering if that's the new rumor she'll spread, that I'm after the Thorne fortune. The joke's on her. In a couple of weeks, we'll have broken up.

"I'm sure your mom's got something wonderful planned for you, June. For the gala?" Destiny asks.

I open my mouth to give my usual vague answer, but remember I all but told Mom I would attend, and now that I'm dating Sebastian, there's no reason not to. "Oh. Yeah."

The gala is definitely one of the social obligations Sebastian and I will have to navigate together. Where we'll have to convince his mother, his sister, and all of their society friends that we're actually dating. Where I'll have to pretend I haven't spent years avoiding their house, their parties... their son.

"Maybe Sebastian has something special picked out?" Tori smirks.

Sebastian shakes his head. "I don't think June wants me dressing her."

Cam whispers something to Jordan, and they both snicker. Tori kicks Jordan under the table. Whatever he said was too low for me to hear, but Ethan's hand clenches into a fist before he slides it under the table. He shoots a glare at Cam, causing them both to sober up.

Sebastian leans closer, his shoulder pressing against mine.

Across the table, Ethan reaches for his drink, but his hand hovers for a second too long before he grabs it, taking a drink with a frown.

"The gala's going to be beautiful," Destiny says quickly, salvaging the conversation. She picks at her salad, voice cheerful as she asks, "So you're escorting June?"

Sebastian nods with an agreeable noise in his throat. His knee started bouncing under the table sometime around talk of his painting, and his close-proximity makes my thigh vibrate. I place a hand on his knee under the table, giving it a squeeze. He stills.

"Yes, with June," he answers, more directly.

"That's months away," Ethan says, snapping my attention to him.

"Yes," Sebastian drawls. *Maybe too casually.* He's been composed all lunch, but something shifts with Ethan's incredulous tone.

Their gazes lock across the table, and then Sebastian leans back, draping his arm over my chair, settling into the seat like he belongs there. His fingers find my hair where it falls on my shoulder.

You have to act jealous if someone flirts with me. This isn't *exactly* what I had in mind.

"I've already wasted so much time without Juniper," he says, smooth as anything. "I don't plan on letting her slip through my fingers again."

Tori coughs, a grin splitting her face, one she tries to hide by downing the rest of her soda.

"I have to get something out of my car," Ethan says abruptly. He stands, glancing down at Destiny. "You coming?"

Her chair scrapes back as she hurries to follow him. "See you later," she calls to the table.

Emma gives me a bored look before her gaze moves with more interest to Sebastian. He still idly toys with my hair. His thumb makes lazy circles that remind me of how he cleans his paint brushes.

"So," Emma starts, leaning forward. "Will we see you at more social events now, Sebastian? You've always been so... selective about your appearances."

Sebastian's knee shifts under my hand. The warmth seeping through his pants floods into my bloodstream along with the realization that I never removed my hand. I slide it away to rub the back of my neck.

"I don't usually discuss my personal life," he says.

"Who does?" Tori adds helpfully, earning a look. "I certainly don't."

Over her shoulder, Bryce glances her way; blink and you'll miss it. It's not the first time. I shoot her a raised eyebrow, which she returns.

The bell rings, saving us from whatever Emma was about to say next. Sebastian's arm slides from my shoulders as he stands, but his hand finds mine, helping me up in a gesture that looks practiced despite being our first time.

"Walk you to class?" he asks, voice pitched loud enough for our lingering audience to hear.

"Sure," I manage, acutely aware of Emma watching us, of Tori's knowing smirk, and the empty chairs where Ethan and Destiny sat moments ago.

As we leave the cafeteria, Sebastian leans close, his voice low. "That was..."

"...yeah." I don't need him to finish the thought. It was intense, messy. Complicated in ways I didn't expect. I knew it'd be hard, but our first day as a couple was better and worse than expected.

His hand is still holding mine, even though no one who matters is watching anymore. I wonder if he's forgotten, or if, like me, he's too tired to figure out when we're supposed to stop pretending.

CHAPTER 13

Operation: Heir Unavailable

THE DOORBELL RINGS as I'm about to take a bite of my freshly made sandwich. A sharp sound in the still house. Mom is upstairs napping before dinner, exhausted from a long night packaging orders, and Dad is not yet home from work.

The silence has grown heavier lately, with Mom splitting her time between the tiny workshop and the commute to the store downtown. I avoid thinking about the realtor cards on the kitchen table, or her comments about needing a bigger workspace, better equipment. Seeing her less tired would be nice, but the thought of leaving this house makes my chest tight.

I set my plate beside my world history book and head for the door. Through the peephole, Sebastian stands on the front porch, hands tucked in his black uniform slacks. His white dress shirt hangs open over a plain t-shirt, giving him that prep school rebel look that probably makes half the girls at school swoon.

Taking a steadying breath, I pull the door open. It sticks against the thick carpet, forcing me to use my hip for leverage.

I slip outside quietly, not wanting to wake Mom, and yank it closed behind me.

"Um, what are you doing here?"

"I would have called, but I don't have your number."

"Oh. Right. Hand it over." I hold out my palm expectantly.

He pulls his phone from his pocket automatically, eyes locked on my face with enough intensity to make me fumble while typing in my number. "So what's so urgent it couldn't wait until tomorrow?"

He glances at his Range Rover parked in my driveway, then back at me. That familiar crease appears between his brows. "I need a favor."

"Oh?" My eyebrows arch as I plant a hand on my hip. "Oh, how the tables have turned." He presses his tongue into his cheek, but I'm just getting started. "For someone who couldn't handle both lunch and study hall, you sure are quick to call in a favor."

His mouth twists. "Lunch was torture enough."

"Wow, thanks." The sting comes viper quick, though I try not to take it personally. Sebastian avoids everyone.

He runs fingers through his hair while studying Mom's wind chimes. Made from copper pipes and the imperfect stones and gems that weren't quite perfect enough for her jewelry. The gentle clinking fills the silence as he visibly struggles with whatever he's trying to say.

"I need you to pretend to be my girlfriend."

I freeze mid-handoff of his phone. He gives a light tug, reminding me I'm still holding it captive. I let go. "Isn't that... what we're already doing?"

"My parents invited Avery and her parents to dinner."

"Avery?" The name clicks into place. The girl Jason mentioned. The twist in my gut is sharp and unexpected. "As in Avery Bennet—"

"Yes," he says curtly. "She's the one my mother keeps trying to set me up with."

"So you want to initiate Operation Heir Unavailable?"

"What?"

"It's a working title." I wave a hand airily.

He stares as if I've lost my mind but continues. "I thought I had more time to let her down gently, but her parents are leaving for Greece, so Mother invited them over before they left." The way he says it suggest he doubts the timing is a coincidence. "She's been... persistent."

I tilt my head. "Persistent how?"

"Well..." His fingers catch a copper disk carved with dragonflies hanging from the wind chime. Others bear leaves or swirls etched into their surfaces. "She doesn't seem as put off by my lack of interest as the others..." I raise my brow, pressing for more. "She's shown up at the house uninvited twice, and I keep conveniently running into her in the halls."

"Wow." I suppress a smile, and fail. "That's some dedication."

"It's not funny," he says, serious, and there's something sincere there, something that hits lower than it should. "She's actually very nice, which makes it worse. I don't want to hurt her feelings, but..."

I can't help my satisfied grin. Turns out Sebastian Thorne needs me as much as I need him. "But you need a girlfriend?"

Pink creeps up his ears. He takes a breath. "I... wouldn't put it that way."

"How would you put it?"

"I need..." He surveys the yard, the hibiscus bushes separating us from neighbors, as if someone might be lurking there. His hands disappear into his pockets. "Fine, I need you, June. You know my parents. You've never been intimidated by my family, or money, and we're familiar enough to make it look believable." He extends a pleading hand. "And I know you won't... expect anything from me."

His raw honesty pulls at me. "Yeah, I can help." The words come out easily. "That's what we agreed on, right?" I pause, realizing how quickly we're diving into this. Faster than my actual romantic relationships. "When is it? I might have to switch my shift."

"Thank you." His relief is almost touching. *Almost.* "Dinner's in an hour."

"Sebastian!" I shove his chest, making him rock backward. "That doesn't give me much time to—wait." A thought strikes. "What am I supposed to wear to dinner with the Bennets? I don't exactly stock ball gowns as everyday staples."

"It's not that formal—"

"Sebastian." I level him with a look. "Your family's 'not formal' is other people's black tie."

He waves dismissively. "Show me your closet."

Just like that, we're little again—Sebastian in my space, making demands. I go to argue that he can't barge in here making demands, but he's wearing those puppy dog eyes, and I remember the anguish he must've endured driving over here to admit needing my help as much as I need his.

He helps me push the door open. It yields easily under his strength, saving my hip for another day. He follows me down the hallway to my room. I half-expected him to hesitate at the threshold like he always did, no matter how many times he'd been in here, but this Sebastian walks right in, and heads straight for my closet, the bi-fold door perpetually open.

"You're going to hate it." To say Sebastian's a neat freak is an understatement. I close my bedroom door, then push it back open. *No reason.*

His lips twitch as he rifles through clothes like he does this regularly, before pulling out the sundress I wore to Brandon's welcome home party, and a black wrap dress I'd forgotten I owned. Tossing both on my bed. He selects a modest cream cardigan-black shirt combo, a silk emerald blouse and pencil skirt, offering them for me to grab.

Crimson fabric slides through his fingers as his gaze lingers on the red dress I bought for fun but never dared to wear out. Sometimes, when I'm feeling extra beautiful or especially sad, I'll put it on, do my makeup nice, and fold my laundry, or walk around and admire myself in the mirror before tucking it away again.

I maneuver past him to hang up Brandon's party dress. Its light linen keeps you stylish yet cool on sweltering summer days, but there's not enough fabric for a dinner party with his parents.

Sebastian lifts his hands, giving me room, but surprisingly doesn't flee from the small closet. I ignore how close he stands behind me, my back brushing his chest as I reach for a hanger.

"Your taste is... surprisingly good." I study the mix of daring and conservative pieces. Deciding to swap the hip-hugging pencil skirt for a flowy navy one that brushes my knees.

"What about this?" He reaches over me for a blue blouse.

I consider it, then nod. "That works."

He steps out of the closet. "All set?"

"Sure," I say, hanging up the rejected outfits. When I turn around, he's stationed by my dresser, arms crossed, surveying my belongings with the intense focus of an artist or mad scientist.

He catalogs the stack of abandoned sketches, crumpled receipts, protein bars, and a set of lime green hand weights like he's documenting how my room has evolved since childhood. He frowns at a battered notebook filled with story ideas and character sketches. Maybe he's confirming I'm still the messy, chaotic girl he used to know.

"Have you told your mom I'm coming?" I ask suddenly, "I don't want to crash a private family dinner."

"If you're my girlfriend, June, then you're included in the private family dinner." He picks up my notebook and thumbs through the pages, landing on one at random. A dangerous thing to do.

I dart over and snatch the book from his hands, tucking it into my dresser drawer and slamming it shut. "You have to tell your mom I'm coming *before* I show up."

"Fine," he grumbles. When he doesn't move, I flap my hand to his back pocket, where he put his phone. He yanks it out roughly, muttering, "You're so controlling."

I smile sweetly, and before I can stop myself, my voice goes smooth and teasing. "Isn't that what you like?"

Pink floods his ears as his thumbs work the screen. He's not typing long. Definitely not long enough to explain how he suddenly gained a girlfriend. I grab his arm to make him lower the phone, but he half-turns, blocking me.

"What are you telling her?" I grip the back of his shirt, rising on my toes to glimpse his screen while my other hand uses his shoulder for balance. "Are you really texting your mom? Or some random number?"

His laundry soap mingles with a day's worth of cologne as he goes completely still. Heat radiates through his shirt into my palms. I let go, tucking hair behind my ear and clearing my throat.

He arches a brow, lowering his arm so I can see the message. "You're so paranoid." His voice is gruff. "I'm really texting my mom. See."

I stay close but don't touch him again as I read his message.

> **ME:** I'm bringing Juniper Blake to dinner. We're dating now.

"Oh my gosh, Bash, that's how you tell your mom!" My voice rises enough to worry about the neighbors hearing.

Three dots appear, vanish, reappear, and then disappear again. I step back quickly, putting space between myself and his phone like it might burn me.

His phone pings.

He skims the message impassively before sliding it back into his pocket.

"What did she say?"

"She's excited to see you at dinner."

We stare at each other. My gaze narrows into disbelief while his remains half-lidded and dangerously aloof.

His phone rings and I groan. "Bash."

He slides his finger across the screen, ending the call. "It's fine. I'll drive. How long until you're ready?"

"I can drive myself."

"Pip." He draws out the nickname with a gentle reproach, the sound low in a way that makes my insides flutter. "A boyfriend picks up his girlfriend for dinner with his parents."

He has a valid point. This only works if we commit to the details. Though suddenly those details feel more intimate than they did at school. I'd imagined hanging on his arm at charity functions or sitting straight-backed at dinner parties, buffered by strangers. Now I have to sit at his family table and convince his parents we're a couple.

"Fine. Stay here." I step into the hall but turn back. "But if your mother shares any embarrassing childhood stories, I'm telling the one where you cried because I organized your books by color."

"I did not cry—" he starts, but I'm already heading to the bathroom, grinning at his indignant tone.

When I return to my room, he's perched on my bed with hands in his lap like he's afraid to touch anything. His gaze sweeps over me once. Efficient and impersonal. I don't know why I'm disappointed. Even if he's not interested, surely he can appreciate... I smooth my hands down my torso and hips, turning toward the mirror. I look great. Not a dog whistle, crawling on your knees *great,* but at least worth a raised brow, or a muttered *'Wow, Pip, you look nice'*.

"You ready?" he asks, already heading to the door.

"Sure," I say, not sure at all. I can do this. I can sit through dinner pretending to be his girlfriend, around his parents, and Avery... and... her parents. What does Tori say? Easy peasy?

I grab my purse and nearly collide with him at the threshold. Sebastian's hands braced against the doorjamb, blocking my exit. He's so close, it forces me to tip my head back to meet his gaze. He studies the light eyeshadow on my eyelids, two passes of mascara, and the red tint on my lips.

"I actually liked that arrangement," he says thoughtfully. "It was *aesthetically pleasing.* The minor meltdown happened when you decided my astronomy and physics books belonged with fantasy because 'they were basically magic'." His voice drops low, those summer green eyes flashing. "If you're going to embarrass me, at least get the story right."

I definitely don't smile. And a blazing hot fire definitely doesn't rush through my body, making my skin tingle. I push against his chest to pass; he yields easily, letting me brush past him as I escort him outside.

Completely straightforward. Low-stakes, no-kissing, zero-pressure contract with a mutual termination clause.

What could possibly go wrong?

CHAPTER 14
The Dinner Games

THE THORNE MANSION sits before us, grand and imposing in the fading light. Sebastian's grip tightens on the steering wheel as he pulls into their four-car garage. Beside us, a lineup of luxury cars gleam beneath the overhead lights: his mom's sleek black Audi, a metallic blue Range Rover that mirrors Sebastian's, and their dad's Mercedes-Benz G-Wagon—massive and military-grade. More suited for conquering terrain than suburban errands, but undeniably impressive.

"Ready?" Sebastian asks, but he makes no move to get out. His gaze is fixed straight ahead, with a familiar crease appearing between his brows.

"Are you?" I ask softly.

He exhales slowly, his shoulders dropping. "Yeah... It's just dinner, right?"

It isn't *just* dinner. Not in this house, with its weight of shared memories and quiet misunderstandings. It's stepping back into a life I convinced myself I didn't miss, and hoping I can pretend well enough that no one sees through the cracks.

I've spent so long avoiding this place, convincing myself I never needed to come back. Now here I am, playing girlfriend to the same boy whose words sent me running all those years ago.

We enter through the mudroom. The sage-colored walls are exactly as I remember, but the abstract painting that used to hang across the hall is gone, replaced by something new. This one captures the sunset over the bay in creamy pastels: orange, pink, and violet, the sun glittering on the still surface.

It's not the stormy one I saw in the art room, but I'd bet it's one of Sebastian's. I'm about to ask when Sophie Thorne appears in the doorway to the kitchen.

"There you are!" She's dressed in a black flowing blouse paired with cream-colored pants, her golden hair swept up in a sleek high ponytail. One of my mother's clips—ginseng leaves—sparkles in her hair.

"Mom has been freaking out since your text." She sounds elated, closing the space between him. Her attention lands on me, and her grin widens impossibly further. "You brought June. This is going to be so much fun." She squeezes Sebastian's arm with barely contained glee.

"Sophie," he chastises with a grimace.

Her dark green gaze sweeps over me with precision. "June, you look lovely. Did you tell your new *girlfriend* how pretty she looks?" Despite being four years older, she looks absolutely youthful in her delight over the situation.

But there's something extra in the teasing tone of her words. I arch a brow up at my new 'boyfriend'.

"She knows," he grumbles low, "I told her." I glance up in surprise when he adds, "Tori knows; call it even. Besides, we might need her." He shifts toward his sister. "Are the Bennets here?"

Sophie shakes her head, pressing her lips together. "Not yet, but you don't have much time to change." She looks her brother up and down critically. "You *are* going to change, right?"

Before Sebastian can answer, Bonnie Thorne comes down the hall, one hand clutched over her heart. "Bastian. You're not even dressed."

She turns a strained smile on me. "June," Her voice warms as she continues, "So nice to see you. We can discuss things more... intimately later, but for right now—" she grabs Sebastian's arm, tugging him toward the stairs "—I need you to get ready."

"Take good care of June," he calls to Sophie before they disappear.

As Mrs. Thorne leads Sebastian away, I take a steadying breath, trying to process the foreign feeling of being back in this house yet also exactly the same. As if only yesterday, Sophie and I were running through the halls while Sebastian trailed behind.

Every corner of this house holds a version of me I thought I'd buried. I just have to survive the evening without letting her resurface.

Sophie links her arm through mine, pulling me down the hallway and into a sitting room. The space is exactly as I remember—formal but cozy, with built-in bookshelves and soft lighting. A place designed for intimate conversations like this one.

"June," Sophie says, now serious. "Sebastian has told you about our predicament?" I nod, watching her carefully. She continues, "I didn't expect our parents to put the pressure on Bastian when I've so adamantly rejected securing a match. I thought they'd give him until after college, like they gave me, but... maybe they figured, with him, they needed to start earlier."

Sophie leans closer, her voice dropping to a whisper. "When Bastian told me he asked you to be his *girlfriend* to get mother off his back, I was so surprised. He's not usually so forward, especially not with this stuff."

She waves a hand in the air, and I can only speculate about what stuff Sophie means. Dating, romance, parents, people in general?

I let out a nervous laugh. Sebastian told Sophie it was his idea? That *he* asked me to be his fake girlfriend? Not that I came to him desperate to solve my Ethan-and-Destiny situation?

"Yeah," I manage, trying to sound casual. "He can be... persuasive when he wants to be."

She studies me for a moment, then lets out a little laugh. "I thought he was joking at first. Though it makes sense when I think about it. You two have so much history our parents wouldn't question it, and you're used to his mercurial moods."

I sink into the cushions beside her, mind still spinning. Why would Sebastian protect me like that? Why take the responsibility for this scheme onto himself?

I chew my lip, brow furrowing. "We haven't really spoken in years."

She waves a hand dismissively. "You were inseparable before that." She gives me a knowing look. "You know, he never told me what happened between the two of you."

"I don't really remember." I lie.

My eyes wander away from her, afraid that I might give too much away. That day. The words I wasn't supposed to hear. How easy it was to let our friendship fade rather than confront Sebastian and face rejection a second time. But that doesn't matter now.

"Ancient history," I say with what I hope is a casual shrug. "Besides, like you said, we were so close, it'll be like old times."

Sophie's smile turns less convinced. Maybe she's remembering something—she was there that day too, after all.

Voices from the foyer cut through my memories.

"—wonderful gallery opening," a man's voice carries down the hall. "The light installation was particularly—"

"Sophie?" Mr. Thorne's deep voice interrupts as he enters the sitting room. "I thought I heard—"

He stops when he sees me, his eyes—so like Sebastian's—widening in recognition. "June?"

"Hi, Mr. Thorne." I stand, smoothing my skirt. He looks exactly the same—tall, distinguished, with that air of casual authority that all Thornes seem to possess.

"What a surprise." He studies me for a moment. "Are your parents joining us?"

A couple appears in the doorway behind him. The Bennetts, I assume. Mr. Bennett is compact but clearly in good shape under his dinner jacket. Mrs. Bennet towers over him in her stilettos, and their daughter falls somewhere in between.

Avery is beautiful, with tawny skin and dark curls that catch the light when she moves. She carries herself gracefully, and there's intelligence in her eyes that suggest she's more than a polished extension of her parents. I can't see any reason Sebastian wouldn't want to at least consider her...

Mr. Thorne realizes he's blocking his guests and stands aside with an apologetic laugh. "Helen, Hampton, Avery, you remember Sophie and this is June—" he cuts off as if trying to think of how to describe me. "The daughter of Bonnie's business partner, Mariane, and the creative genius behind the Starlit Jewels."

Mrs. Bennett's eyes light up, her hands going to her plain pearl earrings. "Oh, my, I adore their pieces." Her cheeks flush.

"I was excited to be invited to the gala this year, to bid on the Wintergarden collection."

I nod politely. "Thank you. I'll pass along the compliment."

"I bought Avery one of those Goddess Crowns," Mr. Bennett says proudly.

"Siren," Mrs. Bennett corrects, "Siren crown, Ham."

"I wore it to homecoming," Avery says, one hand touching her dark curls as if the crown still sits there. Her movements are practiced, like she's used to being watched. "All the girls wanted to know where I got it."

When she mentions the crown, her whole face transforms, making her even prettier. I can see why Mrs. Thorne picked her for Sebastian—she has that perfect balance of poise and warmth that would fit seamlessly into their world.

"Is your mother here?" Mrs. Bennett asks me, her thin finger finding her ear again, "I'd love to tell her in person."

"Yes, June, is Mariane here? Paul?" Mr. Thorne glances toward the hall, as if expecting my parents to materialize.

Instead, Mrs. Thorne glides into the room in a silver slip dress, Sebastian right behind her in a black dinner jacket and brown slacks. She grabs her husband's arm as Sebastian cuts between Sophie and me.

"June is here as Bastian's guest," Mrs. Thorne says, smoothing an invisible hair back into place. Her smile is regal, practiced, from years of dealing with dramatic situations in high-profile settings.

"Your guest?" Mr. Thorne's eyebrows rise.

"My girlfriend, actually." Sebastian's voice is casual, but there's tension in his shoulders. "June and I are courting."

"*Girlfriend?*" Mr. Thorne lets out a nervous chuckle, eyeing Sophie like it's all part of some silly prank.

The Bennets' laughter comes a beat too late, not quite finding the joke humorous. Especially poor Avery. Her eyes widen as she glances at Sebastian. The flash of hurt that crosses her face makes him go rigid beside me.

"Yes, it's all very sweet." Mrs. Thorne's smile doesn't quite reach her eyes. "Childhood sweethearts. *Rekindled.* Shall we head into the dinner room?"

Childhood sweethearts. The words hang in the air like crystal wind chimes—delicate and breakable. Sophie makes a sound that might be a cough or a laugh.

Sebastian's hand finds my lower back as we follow the others into the hall, the touch so natural it takes me a second to realize it's part of our act. The Thorne's dining room is exactly as I remember it—the long mahogany table that seats close to twenty, the wall of windows overlooking the garden, the oil paintings of boats that Mr. Thorne collects.

Sebastian pulls out my chair, but before he can take his place beside me, Mr. Thorne gives a subtle tap on his nose that has Sebastian moving around the table to pull out Avery's chair.

Mrs. Thorne's voice cuts across the table. "Sebastian, you can sit with June anytime. Why don't you sit with our guests?" She points to the empty seat next to Avery.

"I'd like to sit next to June." His voice is firm but polite as he takes the seat beside me.

I try to catch his eye, silently warning him not to push too hard. It's one thing to pretend to be his girlfriend. It's another thing entirely to make his parents hate me.

Avery shakes out her napkin, placing it carefully in her lap. She traces the edge of her water glass, then catches herself and stops. I notice she's wearing one of my mother's rings, a delicate thing with silver flowers wrapped into the band and with a single bunny forever chasing the loop. I wonder if she wore it hoping Sebastian's mother would notice.

She's lost some of her confidence between the sitting room and the dining table. Still polished and poised, but smaller, like she's trying to take up less space at a table she thought would be hers to claim.

"Hampton," Mr. Thorne says as soup is served, "how's the merger with Soon-Up coming along?"

"Promising," Mr. Bennett replies, dabbing his napkin. "Though these tech startups can be... unpredictable."

"Avery's been helping with some of the social media aspects," Mrs. Bennett adds, patting her daughter's hand. "She has quite an eye for business."

Avery's face brightens at the praise, some of her earlier confidence returning. "I just help sometimes with content—"

"She's being modest," Mrs. Bennett interrupts. "Avery increased their online engagement by thirty percent last quarter. And she's already been offered internships at three different firms for next summer." Her gaze drifts meaningfully to Sebastian. "It's so important to have clear goals for the future, don't you think?"

Sebastian takes a sip of water, spine straight, but beneath the table, is the subtle vibration of his knee bouncing through the carpet. My hand finds his knee without thinking. He stills at my touch. I slide my hand back quickly, folding it in my lap.

"Sebastian's quite focused on his own future," Mrs. Thorne says with a tight smile. "His paintings were featured in last month's showcase at the Coastal Arts Museum."

"How wonderful," Mrs. Bennett says with practiced enthusiasm. "Though I imagine your parents hope you'll follow a more... traditional path?"

"Of course," Mr. Thorne cuts in. "Sebastian is a Renaissance student. Experienced in history, science, two languages, and has his pick at the top Ivy Leagues and private universities."

"I studied abroad at the Polytechnique in France before switching to Princeton, where I met my Hammy," Mrs. Bennett says affectionately. "Avery is entertaining the idea of attending abroad, but of course, she's flexible. Perhaps Dartmouth?"

"You're a Dartmouth man, right, Greg?" Hampton asks.

"I am," Mr. Thorne says with a slight puff to his chest.

"Sebastian, do you have plans to attend your father's alma mater?"

"Actually—" Sebastian starts, but his father cuts in.

"It's definitely on his list, but I'm not so proud as to insist he follow in my footsteps. He carves his own path. Harvard, Yale, Stanford—whatever he wants, it's ripe for his taking."

Sebastian sips his soup beside me, looking like choice has nothing to do with it. His gaze moves to me, and I flash him a sympathetic smile. The staff removes our soup bowls, replacing them with plates of rich red meat in a fragrant brown sauce, the bone still attached and pointing upward as if part of the presentation. It doesn't look like beef, but I'm not brave enough to ask. It's beef, I tell myself, as I cut into it.

"Though of course," Mr. Thorne continues, "we expect him to minor in business wherever he ends up. It's essential in today's market to understand both the creative and practical aspects of any industry."

"Art and business aren't mutually exclusive," Mrs. Thorne says. "Look at the Starlit brand. Mariane's designs have created quite the empire, haven't they, June?"

Suddenly, everyone's focus is on me. Even Avery looks up from her plate. I set my fork down.

"I'm sure my mom would be flattered to hear that." I dab at my mouth with my napkin. "Though you know she never takes compliments well."

"Oh, I do know." Mrs. Thorne's smile carries genuine warmth for the first time tonight. Having spent countless days and nights with my mom, pouring over their business plans, she knows exactly how my mother deflects praise.

"But success doesn't come naturally," Mr. Bennett interjects, motioning at Bonnie. "It wouldn't be a multi-million dollar brand if it wasn't for your business insight."

"I affectionately disagree," Bonnie shakes her head, placing a hand on her husbands where it rest next to his wineglass. "Even the sharpest mind can fail if the product is lacking."

I appreciate that about Mrs. Thorne. She never misses a chance to give my mom credit where credit's due.

"True enough," Mr. Bennett agrees, "Like Rogers' newest investment." He turns to Mr. Thorne, the two of them back to discussing business.

"Is that how you know each other?" Mrs. Bennett asks. Her voice carries a particular tone, as if she's onto something. Her eyes linger on Sebastian's hand, which has found its way to the back of my chair. "Sebastian, I don't remember you mentioning June when you and Avery had lunch together? That was last week, wasn't it, darling?"

Avery's cheeks color as she darts a look at me. She nods toward her mother as Mrs. Bennett waits for confirmation.

Sebastian pulls his hand away, placing it on the table, out of reach. My fingers twitch closer, wondering if I should take it. I turn my palm up, offering the chance to slip his fingers through mine.

Instead, he slides his hand off the table as he says, "No, I hadn't."

Bonnie, Mrs. Bennett, Avery, and I wait for him to elaborate. Avery's fork clinks against her plate.

When Sebastian doesn't explain, Mrs. Bennett observes, with careful precision, "These young relationships can be so... fluid at this age."

Sebastian's jaw tightens beside me. It isn't just about convincing his parents; it's about convincing the stud-hunting socialites that Sebastian Thorne is spoken for.

I reach for his knee under the table, hoping a small squeeze would give him the hint that he needs to explain that he wasn't leading anyone on, but he shifts away. Hot mortification pours over me as I turn to look at him. The physical rejection stings more than it should. He's shutting down when he needs to speak up. I see the doubt creeping into Mrs. Bennett's with every second of his silence.

Or maybe his hesitation isn't about nerves at all. Maybe sitting across from Avery has made him reconsider whether our fake relationship is worth it when he could have something real with her.

Our conversation has gotten the attention of Mr. Thorne and Mr. Bennet.

"Sebastian," Mr. Thorne says, but I'm not sure what he wants from his son. An explanation, to elaborate, to proclaim some affection and clear the air right now. Or to denounce me and pull a ring from his coat pocket and get down on one knee for Avery.

"It was bound to happen." Mrs. Thorne chimes in. "I remember when Sebastian was nine, and he decorated this little cave Greg made for him with light-up bats because June said they were her favorite animal."

Mrs. Bennett and Sophie exchange matching grimaces, but I don't take it personally. Bats were no longer my favorite animal once I found out that not all of them are vampire bats, but I don't add that little tidbit.

"Or when June would hold his hand everywhere they went." Mrs. Thorne continues, sharing a fond look at Mr. Thorne.

It was hard to convince Sebastian to do anything. I *had* to drag him everywhere.

"Sebastian would talk about her all the time," Sophie adds with a playful eye roll for her brother. "Pip this, and Pip that. Pip's favorite sound is a storm. Pip's favorite tree is a rainbow eucalyptus. Pip's not afraid of anything."

Sebastian has abandoned the rest of his meal, while most plates around the table are clean. He doesn't look amused by the trip down memory lane.

"Pip?" Mr. Bennett asks.

"It was my nickname for Juniper," Sebastian says tightly, like every childhood story is another weight on his shoulders.

It's probably reminding him of all the reasons he's spent years erasing me from memory. Why we were so different then, and still are now.

The staff arrive to remove our dinner plates, swapping them out with what looks like brownies with ganache frosting and a side of vanilla bean ice cream that everyone picks up a spoon to eat. I follow suit, taking small bites. The conversation moves on to other, safer topics that don't include me, but I can't help but see the sad slump to Avery's shoulders or the way Sebastian's eyes keep lifting to study her.

Sitting here, trying to read Sebastian's silences while vying with someone I didn't know was competition, isn't a version of me I want to be either.

CHAPTER 15
Borrowed Boyfriend

AFTER DESSERT, WE move to the formal living room for coffee. Mrs. Thorne glides to the French doors, opening them wide, letting evening air carry in night-blooming jasmine from the garden. The vents overhead continue pouring cold air into the room, waging an invisible battle with the warm air, causing a chill to prickle my skin.

"Cold?" Sebastian's voice is barely above a whisper.

Before I can answer, he's draping his dinner jacket over my shoulders. The fabric is still warm and carries his scent. Such a boyfriend thing to do, it *almost* makes up for dinner.

"Thank you." I pull the jacket closer, breathing him in despite myself.

Avery hovers near the bookshelf, fingers trailing over spines, but her attention stays fixed on Sebastian. Like she's waiting to corner him. Maybe to demand explanations about meaningless lunch dates and hidden girlfriends.

"You okay?" I whisper, catching Mrs. Bennett's sharp gaze tracking our every move.

"June," Mrs. Thorne calls, waving me toward the cream chairs where she sits with Sophie and Mrs. Bennett near the garden doors.

Sebastian's smile is polished, the one that never reaches his eyes. "Fine. Go ahead." He nods toward the mothers but his gaze drifts to Avery.

I hesitate, slipping off his jacket. What will he tell her? The truth? Apologize for leading her on? Actually, it's none of my business, but my chest tightens anyway.

His hand catches my arm. "Keep it. I'll get it when I take you home."

I settle beside Sophie on the loveseat while Mrs. Bennett immediately draws me into a conversation about her garden. I nod along as the mothers dissect camellia japonicas, tuberose, and whether plumerias complement hibiscus in tropical landscaping. Across the room, Avery's fingers skim Sebastian's sleeve before releasing him. He nods, following her into the hallway.

Mrs. Thorne points out garden specimens, her grip on my arm ensuring my attention stays with her. But my gaze drifts rebelliously to the two shadows in the hall, heads bent close in conversation.

Cold fire claws at my chest the longer they talk. Which is ridiculous. Sebastian isn't mine to control. I pull his jacket tighter around me, as if the physical reminder of our deal might silence the irrational pang of... whatever this feeling is.

"June." Mrs. Bennett's singsong voice snaps me back. All three women watch me with varying degrees of interest. "You and Sebastian? From childhood friends to... more. Rather sudden, don't you think?" Her smile turns razor-sharp. "Bonnie, you never mentioned Sebastian was seeing anyone."

Mrs. Thorne's smile barely wavers. "Oh, well, Sebastian doesn't discuss personal matters casually. Perhaps he waited to be certain of June's feelings before including the rest of us."

"How thoughtful." Mrs. Bennett's tone sharpens further. "He certainly never mentioned it during his many outings with Avery." She shifts primly, brushing an invisible speck from her lap. "Though young men can be so uncertain about their feelings."

The implication hangs heavy as her cloying perfume. I see exactly how this looks: Sebastian keeping his options open, stringing along two girls until he decides which serves his purposes better.

It's unclear whether Mrs. Bennett is annoyed or hopeful. I wonder how Avery would feel knowing her mother accepts her courting a player.

Mrs. Thorne's nostrils flare as her focus cuts toward the hallway where Sebastian and Avery remain visible. Is she more irritated at Sebastian for creating this mess, or at Mrs. Bennett for insinuating her son's a playboy?

Heat flares in my chest. Sebastian isn't cruel. Infuriatingly closed-off and impossible to read, yes. But not deliberately manipulative, and he'd never deliberately string someone along.

"Sebastian is oblivious, but never uncertain." I meet Mrs. Bennett's gaze directly. "Strange that Avery never mentioned seeing us at school. Though I suppose she could have missed us. Sebastian and I often spend our lunch hour in the art room."

Sebastian may not be a liar, but I have no such compunctions.

"Well, I—no, she didn't mention it," Mrs. Bennett admits.

"He told me ages ago," Sophie says, grinning into her glass. When Mrs. Thorne's head snaps toward her, Sophie shrugs, sheepish under her mother's startled stare. "Leave it to my brother to drop a bomb like this on everyone."

Mr. Thorne and Mr. Bennett emerge from the terrace, trailing cigar smoke, their eyes glassy from dinner wine.

"Where's Avery?" Mr. Bennett asks, scanning the room like he's misplaced his keys.

His wife's glare is sharp enough to make him swallow his next words on a hiccup.

"Catching up with Sebastian in the hall," I say with careful lightness, letting everyone know I'm aware my boyfriend is talking to another girl. "I told him to take his time."

I guess Sebastian was right. Years of observing from under the table with him at dinner parties and then later—when the Starlit Jewel took off—from the dance floor or trapped in conversations that hovered far above my station, taught me how to navigate his world.

Mom, Bonnie, and Sophie taught me to be confident but not aggressive, present but not demanding. Let them talk, smile graciously, and remember that their need to prove their worth usually reveals more insecurity than superiority. And never let them see they've gotten to you.

When I glance over, Sebastian watches me from the hallway. He murmurs something to Avery, who nods before they join us.

"Here's Bastian now," Mrs. Thorne announces.

I rise as Sebastian approaches, his hand finding my lower back with feather-light precision. "We should get going," he says, looking at only me. "It's getting late."

Avery rejoins her mother, her gaze lingering on mine before sliding away.

"Of course, I'll see you out." Mrs. Thorne's smile remains carefully neutral as she moves to follow us.

Mrs. Bennett's "lovely to meet you, June" sounds more like a final judgment than a farewell. Avery's quiet "goodbye" comes with another touch to Sebastian's arm that makes me wonder exactly what passed between them in that hallway.

"Don't be strangers," Sophie calls, raising her glass in mock salute.

Both Bonnie and Sebastian glance back with nearly identical *'behave yourself'* looks, which only widens Sophie's grin.

Mrs. Thorne stops her son with a pointed stare once we're out of earshot. Instead of the lecture I expect, she addresses me. "June, dear, you must come for dinner again soon. Perhaps next weekend?"

Sebastian answers before I can. "Actually, we have plans."

Mrs. Thorne's eyebrows arch. "Plans?"

"Yes." His voice turns firm. "Plans."

She leans in, voice dropping to a harsh whisper. "You spring this on me while I'm entertaining the *Bennett's*, and now you're denying me dinner with my son's *new girlfriend?* Who happens to be my *best friend's daughter?* Who you know I *absolutely adore? Bastian.*" His name becomes a reprimand.

"I'll think about it."

She straightens, unconvinced. "Maybe June can talk sense into you." Her expression softens as she looks at me. "I haven't seen you under this roof in so long, I'd like a real conversation without all the..." She tips her head toward the parlor, and I understand. *Without all the pomp and circumstance.*

"I'll see what I can do," I say with a conspiratorial smile, as if we're plotting together.

She squeezes my hand. "You've always known how to handle him." The teasing glint in her eyes takes any sting from the words, especially since we both know it's true.

"I'm not the little boy who cowered under Pip's glares, Mother. I can stand up for myself now."

She purses her lips, tilting her head to look at him directly. "I'm well aware you're not a little boy anymore, Bastian. If you were, you might still listen to me." Her hand smooths over her hair. "I never thought you cowered to June. If anything, I remember you driving her just as crazy as she drove you." She pauses, gaze narrowing. "Which makes this *reconnection*... interesting."

Sebastian's jaw ticks. "Right then." He inclines his head toward the garage door. "June, let's get you home."

We make it only a few steps when Bonnie calls my name. "Yes?"

Her fingers tap against her lips, then lower as she asks, "Does your mother know?" She waves delicate manicured fingers between us, almost hesitant. "About you two?"

"No," I swallow hard. "I haven't told her yet."

"I didn't think so." She spins, returning to the party, and ice settles in my stomach.

Of course. If Mom knew I was dating Sebastian, Bonnie would have been her first call.

I can't shake the feeling that Mrs. Thorne got exactly the answer she expected. I might have just confirmed her suspicions—and she'd be right. We need to be far more convincing, because right now we're not fooling anyone. Especially when my supposed *boyfriend* barely speaks to me at social events.

CHAPTER 16
Advanced Placement

SEBASTIAN LOOSENS HIS tie as we pull down the long drive, then yanks it off and tosses it into the backseat like he's shedding more than fabric. By the time we turn onto the main road, he's dropped his cuff-links into a cup holder and working the top buttons of his dress shirt free. His chest expands with what looks like his first full breath of the evening.

He hasn't spoken since we left his parents' driveway. I can't tell if he's upset about his mother's hurt feelings or preoccupied with whatever was said in his private conversation with Avery. The memory of dinner sits like lead in my chest—how he avoided my touch, how naturally Avery fit into their world of business talk and social connections. Even Sophie's stories about our childhood felt like evidence of everything that's shifted between us.

I fidget with the lapel of his jacket, annoyed by how good it smells. How good *he* smells—warm like a winter bonfire mixed with something crisp and expensive.

"Listen," I say, breaking the silence. "If you want to back out, I'll understand."

Sebastian glances over, startled. "What?"

"The dinner was..." I wave my hand vaguely, unable to find the right word for the disaster we just survived. "And Avery seems really nice. Your parents obviously approve—"

"Juniper." The way he says my name stops me cold. He pulls over suddenly, gravel crunching under the tires. When he turns to face me, there's an intensity there I wasn't expecting. "What are you talking about?"

"You barely spoke to me tonight, Sebastian." I slash a hand through the air, suddenly furious for... I don't know what exactly. "Your mother and Mrs. Bennett could smell the lies from across the table, and when it was up to you to defend our relationship, you *froze*."

"I don't know how to do this." His voice sounds like sandpaper.

"I know it's difficult, but if we can soldier on for a couple of weeks..."

He tosses me a moody look, pupils catching the headlights of passing cars. "Soldier on?"

I shrug. "It's just acting, right?"

He nods slowly. "Like when you'd make me play ponies? And you'd tell me to act like I was enjoying myself?"

He hated it at first, but there were moments when I thought maybe he actually was enjoying himself. He'd neigh and change his voice for different ponies and everything. I guess he was a better actor than I ever gave him credit for.

"What did Avery pull you aside for?" I ask, curiosity winning over pride.

He sits back, runs a hand over his mouth. "She told me she doesn't believe we're really together."

"Oh." The bottom drops out of my world. I remember how he shifted away when I tried to hold his hand at dinner. "Well, that makes sense. We weren't very convincing."

"No," he agrees, but there's something almost amused in his tone now. "She said we looked too awkward and stiff to be dating. That you didn't really like me, because if you did, you wouldn't be able to keep your hands off me."

I smack his arm. "You liar."

"I'm not lying." He laughs, warm and genuine, so unlike the stiff chuffs and scoffs I usually get.

"Wow. So I guess you can imagine what a relationship with Avery would be like. Congratulations?"

He rubs the center of his forehead roughly. "I'm trying to get *out* of a relationship, remember?" He exhales hard. "And I don't want to imagine."

"Right. So you want to call this off—"

"I don't." He runs a hand through his hair, messing up its perfect style. "If anything, I'm more committed now. Avery..." He pauses, that familiar crease appearing between his brows. "She made it clear she's still interested, even knowing about you. Said she'd *understand if things didn't work out between us.*"

"Wait." I turn to face him fully, arms crossed. "She hit on you? Even thinking you have a girlfriend?"

His mouth twists. "She doesn't think you're really my girlfriend, remember? And neither do my parents, probably. My mom wouldn't stop questioning me on the way to my room."

"Well, you didn't exactly help," I point out. "Every time I tried to act couple-y, you pulled away."

"Because my parents were there!" His voice rises. "And Avery..." He breaks off, frustrated. "I told you I didn't want to hurt her, and I thought feeling you up in front of her would be a dick move."

I scrunch up my face. "Feel me up, really? No wonder you don't bring dates around."

He stares at me blankly, not amused.

"This is what I mean, Bash." The nickname slips out easily as breathing despite years of avoiding it. "Tonight proved we can't fool anyone. We need more than holding hands."

Sebastian goes still, and I'm not sure if it's the nickname or the thought of having to touch me. "More?"

"Yeah, you know." I aim for casual, even as my pulse quickens. "The little things. Stuff couples do automatically. We won't break our no-kissing contract, I promise."

He's silent for so long, I regret suggesting it. Nerves dance in my chest, threatening to bring up the mystery meat from dinner onto his expensive car mats.

Then, his fingers drum against the steering wheel as he glances at the road. A car zooms by, red taillights vivid in the dark. Sebastian checks his mirrors, then executes a smooth U-turn.

"Where are you going?"

"To practice." He catches my look and adds, "The beach. It's usually empty at this hour."

"So no one sees us making fools of ourselves?"

Slowly, one corner of his mouth lifts into a lopsided smile. "Something like that."

SEBASTIAN PULLS INTO A MOSTLY deserted beach access parking lot. Two other cars sit with steamed windows, their owners clearly uninterested in the ocean view. I shiver as I step out. The temperature has dropped a few degrees as cool

January winds blow off the water. I leave Sebastian's expensive jacket in the car and miss it immediately.

He notices and reaches back in, but I stop him with a shake of my head. "That jacket's too nice; leave it."

"June?" His tone carries gentle reproach.

"I'll be fine."

He gives me one last look before ducking into the backseat for a forest green hoodie from his gym bag. He holds it open, gesturing for me to slip my arms through, then tugs it over my head like he doesn't trust me to manage alone.

"Better?"

I burrow into the soft material. It smells like him. I'm surprised how familiar his scent has become, but it's impossible to avoid. It clings to his uniforms, his car, his clothes. I've been suddenly immersed in all things Sebastian, and it's imprinted on my senses. I should give it back immediately. And I will. *Later.*

"This will do," I say.

He rolls his eyes dramatically, but there's a small smile playing at the corners of his mouth. I ignore his sassy attitude and hold out my hand, feeling strangely vulnerable. He stares at it for half a second before taking it. His skin is warm, his grip firm and solid.

"Do you still come out here?" I ask as we hit the boardwalk. He glances at me questioningly. "When we were kids, you and your dad would bring your telescope to look at planets, or meteor showers..."

He raises a quizzical brow and says slowly, "Yes."

"We came with you once. Do you remember?"

"I do," he says, then carefully, "But it's just me these days."

"Oh." I say, "Yeah, my mom's pretty busy with the shop now, too. If she's not in the workshop, she's in the store."

"Sorry, June."

"It's fine. And sorry about your dad too."

He looks at the night sky, the stars barely visible through the coastal haze. "I'm comfortable being alone."

Our feet crunch on the sand as we reach the end of the boardwalk. I pull off my low heels, transferring them to one hand before we walk toward the water, stopping where dry sand meets wet. The ocean moves like a living black thing, undulating softly, lit only by the moon and distant fishing boat lights on the horizon.

I glance back toward the parking lot, where light poles illuminate the car tops and palm trees. The strips of condos and hotels lining this stretch of beach, and the occasional grand-looking beach house dwarfed by massive hotels.

It's easy to hold his hand right now. With the cool wind brushing my knuckles and cheeks. The night blanketing us in privacy. There's something about darkness that's both scary and seductive. Both to be feared.

I tug him down the beach, listening to the waves arrive and retreat in a constant rhythm like breathing. Now that we're actually here, alone, my confidence falters. It's one thing to suggest practicing, another entirely to figure out what that means when we're standing on a dark beach.

Sebastian seems content to walk, and maybe that's enough for now. Maybe we both need to work up to whatever comes next.

I pull my phone from his hoodie pocket and open my notes app, typing a line that's been echoing in my head since dinner.

"Am I boring you, Juniper?" Sebastian's voice carries over the waves.

I glance up, the light from my phone illuminating his face. He's smiling. "Not yet." This makes his shoulder shake with silent laughter. I slip my phone back into the pocket.

"So, is this it?" he asks, swinging our hands gently. "We walk around the beach until we're experts at hand-holding?"

"I think you have negative third-base covered."

He raises his eyebrows. "Are we working up the bases? That might breach our contract."

"You're so far in the negative, Mr. Thorne, we won't even come near first base." I nudge him with my elbow, smothering a smile. "Your no-kissing contract is firmly intact. *Trust me.*"

That earns me a soft chuckle, and his shoulders relax. "Okay, point taken. So what now?"

I take a steadying breath and release his hand to wrap my arms around his waist. He stiffens immediately, tension rippling through his back.

"I felt you tense up," I say gently, stepping back to give him space.

"I wasn't expecting it," he says, defensive.

"That's the problem, though." I keep my tone light, understanding rather than wounded. "You can touch me just fine, but when I touch you..." I motion between us. "People will notice if you go rigid every time your girlfriend touches you."

"Fake girlfriend," he corrects firmly.

"Right. But people don't know that, and if you're tensing up every time I touch you, it's going to look weird or like I'm holding you hostage in this relationship. I don't want anyone to think this is a pity date. You were fine when I touched you in front of Ethan. You didn't pull away when we were younger, unless... unless..." My voice gets smaller as the implications hit me. "Unless something happened, or I did something wrong, or—"

"Hey, hey, June." He steps closer, hands hovering as if he might touch my face before dropping them. "It's not about anything that happened," he says quietly. "It's my problem, okay? That's why we're here, right? Because I need to work on this?"

"*We* need work, but yeah."

He takes my hands and slides them around his waist again. "See? I'm working on it."

His muscles are tight under my palms, not quite trembling, but like a wire pulled tight. He's not flinching or pulling away, though. Progress. I move carefully, letting him set the pace, my fingertips barely pressing into the starched fabric of his dress shirt. "Tell me if it's too much."

I tease the edge of his shirt, where he's pulled it free from his slacks. The air between fabric and skin is warm, almost humid. When he nods, I slip my hands gently underneath. His skin is fever-hot compared to the cool night air. The contrast raises goosebumps on my arms.

The planes of his back are smooth, interrupted only by the ridge of his spine and the flex of muscle when he inhales. I can feel his heartbeat against my left palm, a rapid thud-thud-thud that seems too fast for someone trying to appear calm.

"Okay, now, you?"

"You want me to put my hands under your shirt?" His voice cracks at the end, and he clears his throat.

"I'm not asking you to—never mind—here." I guide his hands to my hips, tugging them up under the hoodie's thick cotton. Yes, tugging, because he's gone so rigid I'd swear he'd fossilized. His palms rest against my waist with the careful pressure of someone defusing a bomb—there, but barely.

The borrowed hoodie traps heat between us, his body warmth mingling with mine in the space beneath the fabric. I can feel the exact shape of his fingertips on my skin, each one a point of contact that seems to burn brighter than it should.

"See? It looks like more than it is."

His eyebrows rise, and the look he gives me—like I do this often—makes my cheeks flame. "Is this what you've picked up in your books, Pip?" he murmurs, amused again.

I'm thankful for the darkness hiding how my face has turned as red as Tori's hair. The night air does nothing to cool my burning skin.

When I don't answer, he says, "And this is what's expected of us at school?"

"Not always, only when someone's watching," I admit. "But couples touch, Sebastian. They lean into each other, they sit close, they...exist in each other's space." I pause, remembering our conversation in the car, and add meaningfully. "Besides, if we want to convince Avery..."

His mouth quirks up. "Right. Can't have her thinking you don't really like me."

"Exactly," I say, looking away. "We need to look comfortable touching or they'll see right through us."

He nods, thoughtful. "Anything else we should work on?" His voice is quieter now, rougher at the edges.

I search his face for signs of discomfort. "I don't want to push—"

"I'm not made of glass, June." His smile shows real amusement. "I understand the role I'm supposed to play now."

His fingers tighten against my sides, bunching into the fabric of my shirt. We're close enough that I can count each freckle the Florida sun has left across the bridge of his nose.

Face to face. Staring into each other's eyes. The distant lights from shore catch in his pupils, making them look wide and dark, the green irises reduced to thin rings.

His hoodie suddenly feels overwhelmingly hot. A bead of sweat forms at my hairline despite the chilly air.

"That's... that's probably enough for tonight. We can figure out the rest as we go." I slip from the circle of his arms, and the night air rushes in where his warmth had been.

I walk toward where the soft white sand meets the dark saturated edge. During the daylight, it's a darker off-white, creamy tan, but under moonlight it looks like a trap, like quicksand. I dig my bare feet into it, feeling grittiness between my toes.

"And you think this will be enough? Without crossing any other lines?" he says. I glance down to where his bare feet sink into wet sand.

"No kissing," I affirm. "Besides, if we keep getting caught down dark alleys, rumors will take care of themselves."

He hums low in his throat, hands in pockets. A soft beep sounds from his phone, and he checks the screen. "My mother," he says, eyes flicking to mine when he sees me watching. "She's wondering where I am."

"You should tell her we're at Gator's Landing." I rock back on my heels, waiting for the tease to land.

He nods, distracted, then jerks back. "Isn't that where people go to hook up?" But then understanding dawns, and his face pinches into disappointment. "June, are you trying to give my mother a heart attack?"

"I'm just kidding." I turn my evil grin back to the water.

"You did always love to tease me," he says dryly, but I've given him plenty of reasons to smile these past few days, so I don't take it personally.

"It would solve any doubt that you're my girlfriend," he murmurs, fingers moving over the screen.

"You are *not*—" I reach for his phone, but he holds it up out of reach. Which isn't hard. "Sebastian!"

He lowers it so I can see he was only randomly typing letters in his notes app. I shove his phone back at him, relieved, but my pulse still races. "Wow, you've grown a sense of humor."

He exhales a laugh, shoulders moving. But then something shifts as he pockets his phone. His half-smile fades, replaced by something serious. "A lot has changed since we were kids, June."

His gaze connects with mine meaningfully. The sharp reminder of our past brings me back to the present, to my body still humming from his touch, to all the reasons I've spent years avoiding exactly this. Him.

The rules were clear from the beginning—but this fake relationship is cracking open things I thought I'd buried years ago.

I pull my hand from his arm and slip it into the hoodie pocket.

The night air has grown colder. "It's getting late," I say, already heading back to the boardwalk.

Sebastian nods, falling into step beside me. Our feet leave parallel tracks in the sand, mine smaller and less defined than his. Wind picks up as we walk, carrying the scent of salt and seaweed, plus a faint smell from the fast-food chain a couple blocks over.

"There's a meteor shower next month. Could be a *couple-y* thing?"

"Oh?" I say, failing to hide my surprise. "Yeah. Sure. I'll invite Destiny and Ethan." I clear my throat. "We can show off our new techniques."

"Right," he says tightly.

I brush the sand from my feet before slipping my shoes back on. Sebastian waits, hands in pockets, his gaze fixed on the horizon like he's searching for something in the darkness.

"Worried about school tomorrow?" I ask.

He blinks, snapping back to the present. He nods. "Among other things." He gestures toward the parking lot. "Ready?"

THE NO-KISSING CONTRACT

Sebastian turns on the radio as soon as we're buckled. Some indie pop station I'd bet money he never listens to, but he doesn't change it. The music fills the space where conversation should be.

We keep taking one step forward, and two-steps back, like some complicated dance where neither of us knows the steps.

The warmth from our practice session is already fading, replaced by the careful distance that's kept us safe for years. And tomorrow we'll have to pretend the comfortable intimacy actually exists.

"Thanks for the ride," I say when his car stops in my driveway. "And for... dinner."

"I should thank you, Juniper, for dinner."

Juniper. Not June. Not Pip. Back to formalities. I slip my purse over my shoulder. "Well, see you tomorrow at lunch?"

He nods once. Something crosses his face before he goes carefully blank. "Tomorrow," he agrees.

I slide out of the car; the door clicking softly shut behind me. His engine idles behind me as I walk to the door, pull my keys out, and turn the lock. I wish more than anything right now that Dad would fix the stubborn door as it hinders my smooth retreat. Finally—finally—his car reverses from the driveway. Headlights sweep over the window as he leaves.

CHAPTER 17
No Kissing. No Boyfriend. No Problem

I DROP MY TRAY onto the table, claiming our usual lunch spot. The cafeteria builds around me—trays clattering, conversations overlapping, bursts of laughter from the cheerleaders' table, sneakers squeaking on linoleum. After last night's dinner disaster, I'm not sure if I'm more nervous to see Sebastian or Ethan.

Tori slides into the seat next to me, red curls bouncing. I'd texted her about the unexpected dinner at Sebastian's house, including how his sister had joined our little conspiracy. Her nose wrinkled—miffed about losing status as sole secret-keeper. I'd conveniently left out our moonlit "practice session" afterward. Something about those moments on the beach felt too private to share, even with Tori.

Jordan and Cam appear next, their conversation about basketball continuing to the table. They settle into their usual seats, leaving Ethan and Destiny's spots conspicuously empty.

Since Ethan and Jordan share fourth period, I try for casual as I ask, "Where's Ethan?"

Jordan's shoulders stiffen as he suddenly focuses on arranging his fries into neat rows.

"Jordan, where is he? Seriously?" I lean forward, elbows sliding across the polished surface.

He glances around the cafeteria as if he's looking for an escape route. "I don't know. He and Destiny slipped off right after class. Maybe he forgot something in his car?"

The words tumble out too fast. I know Jordan well enough to recognize a lie.

"Did Ethan tell you not to tell me?"

His shrug is overly casual as he turns to Cam, cutting off any further probing. Cam gives me an apologetic look before they both retreat to their conversation, my drama already forgotten.

Tori's eyes collide with mine, her brows raised in silent communication. I stare at my lunch tray, picking at the chicken sandwich as my appetite vanishes. I figured there'd be fallout from this whole 'dating Sebastian' thing. I just didn't think it'd sting this much.

"Where's Thorne?" Tori's cuts through my brooding. My head snaps up to find her fixing me with an exasperated look that clearly says, *shouldn't you know where your boyfriend is*?

"He's, um..."

Tori leans across the table, her silver necklace dangling over her salad as she whispers, "Yeah, you two aren't convincing anyone." She spears a cherry tomato with unnecessary force, brandishing it like evidence. "Except maybe Ethan, since he'd rather hide in his car than see you together."

"Victoria!" I hiss, darting a glance down the table. Jordan and Cam are hunched over Cam's phone, probably checking Adrian's Insta-feed again, but my pulse still races.

She tilts her head, exaggerated and dramatic in typical Tori fashion. "I haven't even heard anyone talking about you two today." She gestures with her fork, Italian dressing droplets hitting her tray.

"That's a good thing. It means our relationship is completely believable." I take a defiant bite of my sandwich, though the bread feels like cardboard.

She snorts, nearly choking on lettuce. "The only believable part is how unbelievable it is."

"That makes no sense," I mumble around my mouthful.

"What makes no sense is that you avoid each other." Tori's mouth develops a mischievous glimmer that makes me nervous. "If he was my boyfriend, I'd have my hands all over him."

I shift in my seat, the plastic chair creaking. *Avery said practically the same thing.* Unbidden images flash through my mind—my fingers sneaking under his shirt at the beach, water beading on his collarbone... I set my sandwich down with more force than necessary.

"*Please.*" She stuffs a huge bite in her mouth, talking while chewing in the way she knows drives me crazy. "You cannot tell me you don't think he's attractive. I have swim class with you. I know you check him out."

My cheeks burn as I fidget with my napkin. "I can admit—"

"—that you think he's hot." Her grin turns absolutely wicked.

"There are things about him that are pleasant." I try for neutral, professional, like I'm discussing artwork rather than my fake boyfriend's... hotness.

"Very pleasant." She waggles her eyebrows.

"And hypothetically, if I was interested..." *Which I'm not. Definitely not.* The flutter in my stomach is totally irrelevant.

"You'd be all over it." She practically sings the words.

"Let's stop talking about this." I gather my trash, needing something to do with my hands.

Tori brandishes her fork like a conductor's baton. "June, if you want to sell this, you need to sell it." She shakes her fist for emphasis, nearly launching a cucumber slice across the cafeteria.

I lean in close, hair falling forward to shield our conversation. "We're working on it," I whisper, hating how defensive I sound. "We've been practicing."

"Practicing? What does that *even mean?*" Her eyebrows shoot up so high they nearly disappear into her hairline.

I wave a hand impatiently, wishing I hadn't brought it up. "Just getting comfortable after last night's disastrous dinner."

"And how'd that go?" There's a teasing lilt that makes me want to throw my sandwich at her.

I shrug, aiming for nonchalance and probably missing by miles. "Fine. It's just acting, Tori."

"Okay," she says slowly, "June, you have to *pretend* to be attracted to Sebastian Thorne?" Her look says she's not buying it.

"It's not me," I whisper, face burning. "We have a no-kissing clause."

Her lips curl into a knowing smirk. "So you're saying you would have been?"

"No. Just no." *Don't think about his lips. Do not think about his lips.*

She stabs at her salad, speaking between bites. "There's more than kissing." At my warning look, she smirks. "Like holding hands, *of course.*" She points to the empty seat beside me with her fork. "He could be here?"

Yes, I *am* hyperaware of the empty chair. Where the hell is my fake boyfriend? After the progress we made last night, you'd think he'd be here?

A laugh from the next table draws my attention. Two girls glance over their shoulders, whispering but not quietly enough. "Guess Thorne's over it already?"

"Or she's his stalker," the other says, flicking her wrist in a lazy, dismissive arc.

Tori waves her hand in front of my face. "You're getting that wrinkle between your brows again. The one that shows up when you overthink."

I smooth my forehead self-consciously. "He seemed fine in class." Though '*fine*' might be generous. It's hard to talk when your face is underwater.

"You mean, where you two ignored each other?" Tori's fork spears another tomato with unnecessary force.

We didn't talk in the car on the ride home from dinner. Last night I'd convinced myself it was because he was tired from socializing, or because our beach practice had made things too real for him too. Now I'm not so sure. Maybe he regrets asking me to dinner. Or worse, maybe he's off with Avery.

I scan the cafeteria despite myself, looking for Avery's shiny dark curls. I don't see her, but that doesn't mean anything.

"There's not much talking when you're swimming laps." I fidget with my water bottle, watching condensation drip.

"No one takes swim class seriously," she says, calling my bluff. "Except the dive team. Everyone else is getting a tan or flirting."

"Sebastian does," I say, and she doesn't argue. She can't.

I push my tray away, groaning at the table. Last night, it had felt almost easy standing close to Sebastian in the darkness, his hands warm against my sides, waves crashing softly in the background. But then something shifted, and now he's nowhere to be found. We'd practiced being a couple, but had it helped at all?

The bell rings, saving me from having to respond. As I gather my things, my mind races. Maybe this was a mistake. I mean, what are we even doing? Playing house with his family one minute, acting like strangers the next. And for what? So

Ethan can hide in his car with Destiny while Sebastian... does whatever he's doing?

I shoulder my backpack; the weight matching the heaviness in my chest. I should call this off. Make up some excuse about focusing on school or whatever. Before things get messier than they already are.

But as I head to class, another thought sneaks in, unwanted: Why does the idea of ending it make me feel worse?

Tori and I head toward our next class. I stare at my phone screen, wondering if I should text Sebastian and ask why he ditched me. But no—I'd rather see his face when I confront him. I scan the hallway for his tall frame and golden brown hair. I want him to tell me what his problem is instead of ghosting me. Unless this is part of his whole 'breaking up amicably' thing? A spontaneous affair that fizzles out before it can really burn?

It doesn't give me much to convince Destiny that she has nothing to worry about. But we agreed he could quit anytime. Was dinner last night really that bad? I analyze our interactions and can't find any obvious reasons he'd be disappointed in my performance. Unless...

He saw Avery last night—polished, poised, ambitious—and decided he'd like to give her another chance. She fits better into his world than I do. The daughter of a rich entrepreneur with ambitions toward the senate.

Tori elbows me, snapping me out of my thoughts. Destiny stands at her locker, switching textbooks.

"Hey," I call out, closing the distance between us.

Destiny turns, her smile delayed, and not quite as believable. "Hey." She ducks behind her locker for a moment, adjusting her books around a heavy sweatshirt.

Tori cringes beside me.

Destiny closes the door, pushing her blonde hair back. A silver bracelet dangles from her wrist. The sight gives me pause. It's Ethan's. My mom made it for him for Christmas last year.

It was his gift to do with whatever he wanted, but seeing on her wrist makes me strangely hollow. Destiny pulls her sleeve down over her hand. Our eyes meet briefly before Tori nudges me, brows drawn in concern. *Right.*

"You weren't at lunch." It comes out more accusatory than I intended. I clear my throat as ice spreads, making my hands numb.

"Oh. Yeah." She moves down the hallway, creating distance between us. Tori and I follow. "Ethan and I, he, we," she corrects, "wanted to be alone."

"Oh?"

Destiny's cheeks turn pink in the silence as we continue down the hall. Tori pivots to look at me.

Destiny flips it back to me. "Did something happen at dinner?" Her tone is a gentle probing, like when someone's behaving unhinged. I try to rein everything I'm feeling, but I honestly don't know what's wrong with me.

Oh. Right. I'd sent both Tori *and Destiny* a picture of my outfit in the bathroom mirror before I left for the Thornes.

"Um, no."

"I'm only curious because I saw Sebastian heading toward the art room right before lunch," she continues, each word careful. "Did he not sit with you again?"

Again.

"Oh. That." I glance at Tori, hoping she can help provide an excuse. The knowing look she gives me says *I told you so.* "Sebastian really likes to paint." I hear myself say, the excuse falling flat.

Destiny nods, but I know what she's thinking—that if things were serious, if we were as into each other as new couples are,

THE NO-KISSING CONTRACT

then we'd be spending all our time together. Like when Tori dated Sota. There were several lunchtimes when we didn't see them. The key factor being *them* together, sneaking off to be alone.

The three of us continue down the hallway until we reach the science building, and Tori veers off with a light touch on Destiny's arm before tossing me a good luck shrug over her shoulder. Destiny blows out a sigh like she's holding in steam, clearly itching to leave, but we both have math this period, so we continue on in tense silence.

She's the first to break.

"June, you and Sebastian," she says slowly. "It's just... weird. Ethan said you hated him, and I don't remember you ever mentioning you two were friends..."

"I don't think I said *I hated him*." My eyes drift upward in mock contemplation. I have definitely muttered the words, *I hate Sebastian Thorne* under my breath in the last four years.

Like when he saw me crying in the hall after a terrible day and tossed me a pack of tissues and waltzed off. Or the time when Ethan and I got paired in creative writing and he mumbled loud enough for me to hear that I could do better.

"Besides, enemies to lovers is so hot right now." I shift my backpack. Instead of fumbling through an excuse, I say, "The heart wants what the heart wants."

She eyes me like she doesn't buy it. Tori might be right. I am a terrible liar. "Sure, it's just kind of convenient?"

"Convenient?" I repeat, voice climbing higher than I intended.

"I mean..." Her cheeks flush and she looks away, biting her lip. When she looks back, there's something close to panic there. "I didn't mean convenient like that. I meant—" She's backtracking rapidly, words tumbling over each other. "I'm not saying you're lying or anything. It's great that you and Sebastian—"

"Destiny, it's okay—"

"It's..." She takes a shaky breath. "Ethan and you have always been close, and I respect your friendship, but Ethan's my boyfriend now."

I turn, giving her my full attention. "Whoa, you're not messing with anything. Destiny, I support your relationship. I'm the one who pushed Ethan to ask you out."

The real question—the one she's been holding back—finally breaks through her people-pleasing facade. "Are you doing this to make him jealous?" She recoils, as surprised by her outburst as I am.

"No," I say quickly, then again, firmer. "Destiny, no." I touch her arm gently, afraid she might recoil away. "I promise you I'm not doing this to make Ethan jealous."

I'm doing it to prove I don't want him at all.

And I know—I know—I'm making everything worse, but if I back down now, everything crashes and burns. I will lose Destiny and Ethan and all of this will be for nothing, but maybe if I confess now, it won't be so bad?

The truth sits ready on my tongue when she says, "Good. Because it was looking like you were using Sebastian to get at Ethan, which would be so messed up, for both of them. And I couldn't handle being played like that."

I press my lips together. "Right. That would be sick."

She laughs, nervously, and I'm not sure if it's from her vulnerable outburst or the lack of conviction in my tone.

"Ethan is still hurt," she says, "He doesn't like Sebastian, but I told him that if he cares about you—as a friend," she amends, and I don't miss the nervous flick of her gaze to mine, "then he needs to be supportive of who you choose to love."

Love?

I shoot her a look, and her face shifts, suddenly unsure. "Like how you're supportive of him." She twirls a strand of hair around her fingers.

"Of course," I hear myself say.

Destiny sighs, relieved. "I think we just need to clear the air. How about a double date?"

"A double date," I say automatically.

"Yes." She beams, dropping her hair. "Exactly. Something to get the boys bonding."

"Yeah." I shake myself. "Sure, text me the details. I'll make sure Sebastian's free."

If I can even find him. If he agrees. If this whole fake relationship hasn't already imploded, and he didn't bother to tell me. Even thinking about asking Sebastian to spend an evening with Ethan is bad enough. But not asking, and having to admit I can't even get my fake boyfriend to go on a double date with us? That's worse.

CHAPTER 18

Touch Me Like the Swim Team is Watching

I CATCH SEBASTIAN AS he's about to enter the locker room for swim practice. His gym bag's slung over his shoulder, attention locked on his phone, completely oblivious to my approach. The moment I step into his path, his shoulders drop in resignation.

"Juniper," he says, already noting the hard press on my mouth, my gaze narrowed on him.

"Where were you at lunch?" I don't wait for an answer. "You said you'd be there. I came to your dinner last night. You owed me a lunch."

He sets his bag down and leans against the wall beside the locker room door, letting his head fall back with a sigh. "I know. I'm sorry."

"Why did you bail on me?" The words come out sharper, exposing the hurt underneath.

His head lifts, searching my face. "I should have texted you. I'll come tomorrow."

"That's not the point." I drop my voice as students pass by. "You're supposed to be my boyfriend, and it's humiliating. I sat there with Tori while people whispered that I'm some stalker, pretending you're my boyfriend. You said you wouldn't ruin my reputation, Sebastian. And it's Friday. There's no school tomorrow."

He steps forward, hands settling on my upper arms. The seriousness in his eyes stops my rambling. "I'll fix it, June."

I stare up at him. "Do you want to call it off? You can."

"I know I can." His hands move up and down my arms, like he's trying to ease my nerves. It's working. "And no, I don't want to call it off." His brow furrows as he studies me. "Did something happen?"

I shake my head, then shrug. "It's... Destiny thinks I'm making this entire relationship up." He gives me a look that says *you are*, but I ignore him. "To make Ethan jealous."

Sebastian's eyebrows shoot into his hair. I wave dismissively. "I know. *Weird*." My phone weighs heavily in my pocket, Destiny's text burning a hole through my skirt fabric. "So now it's my turn to call in a favor."

"What do you need?" Suspicion creeps into his voice.

I bite my lip, bracing for the fallout. "I may have told her we'd do a double date with her and Ethan."

He groans. "A double date? With Cole?" He rubs his forehead. "Please tell me you don't want me to attend one of those drunken debaucheries Bryce calls a party?"

"No, not this time." I twist my fingers together. "Just the four of us. Destiny thought it would help 'clear the air'." I make air quotes.

"Clear the air," he repeats, voice flat. "Between me and Cole."

"Well, yeah. You two clearly have an issue."

His head tips back, as if he's physically trying to distance himself from the conversation. His next words come out clipped. "You could say that."

"Okay," I say, "we can unpack that later."

"There's nothing to unpack." His gaze drifts beyond me, as if he's seeing something I can't.

But there is.

It would explain his weird behavior when we ran into Ethan and Destiny coming out of the alley. How he could suddenly summon the affection toward me to needle Ethan.

I've rarely seen Sebastian and Ethan interact, but that's not unusual since Sebastian barely talks to anyone. I never questioned Ethan's dismissive comments about him because I made them too. I was too focused on my own grievances to wonder what Sebastian had actually done to earn Ethan's hostility.

There's definitely a story, but now's not the time to push.

Whatever their history is, we'll all have to set it aside long enough to salvage this situation so Sebastian and I can end things without raising suspicions.

Down the hallway, a group of swimmers heads toward the locker room, gym bags bouncing against their hips, swim caps already in hand. Dante gives Sebastian a questioning look as he passes, his eyes darting between us before he pushes through the locker room door. Two more boys trail behind, nudging each other and whispering as they spot us.

"Coming, Thorne?" one calls.

Sebastian gives a casual nod, making no move to hurry. The boys exchange glances before disappearing into the locker room.

After what feels like an eternity, Sebastian's demeanor shifts. "Actually, this might work."

"Really?"

He nods, a thoughtful look crossing his face. "There's a charity event at the aquarium tomorrow night. A fundraiser for the marine conservation program."

"The aquarium?" I blink.

"I volunteer there during summers and school breaks," he says, almost shyly. "I wasn't planning on attending this year... I have a few tickets... it's semi-formal. Wear the blue dress in your closet." He ignores my arched brow, focusing on something over my head. "Good cause, low pressure. And public enough that Destiny can't question the legitimacy of... *us*."

I can't hide my amusement at the thought of serious, reserved Sebastian spending his free time among tropical fish and school groups. "You volunteer at the aquarium?"

"Since I was fifteen." He shifts, looking uncomfortable. "I like the seahorses."

The image of Sebastian watching over delicate seahorses makes something warm unfurl in my chest. "That's... unexpected."

"I'm full of surprises, Pip." His mouth quirks up at the corner. "So, what do you think? Aquarium event instead of awkward bowling for four?"

"How did you know they suggested bowling?"

He levels a look at me. "It's always bowling or mini-golf."

"I *like* mini-golf." I leave out how that was Destiny's other suggestion.

"The aquarium could work," I nod slowly. A public event means less intimate conversation, which means less interaction between Sebastian and Ethan. "And I'm terrible at bowling, and you know how much I hate that."

"Exactly." His shoulders relax. "It benefits a great cause, and even if the evening's a disaster, something positive still comes from it."

"Always the pragmatist."

"One of us has to be." His eyes find mine, that familiar intensity returning. "So, tomorrow night? Pick you up at seven?"

"I'll tell Destiny." I pull out my phone, already composing the text in my head.

His voice drops, meant just for me despite the thrum of voices echoing from the pool deck. "And... I'm truly sorry about today."

My body betrays me, goosebumps racing along my arms at the intimate rumble of his voice.

I step back, out of his singular focus, brushing my hands over my arms. "You can make it up to me by naming a lionfish or maybe a sea turtle after me."

My phone buzzes with a text from Tori. *Kiss.* I quickly lower my screen, shoving it in my pocket. "I should probably go. I have work..."

"Yeah," his voice is rough.

My phone erupts in rapid succession. Sebastian raises his brows. "Do you need to check that?"

"No, it's just.. Tori." I squeeze my eyelids shut for a second. "We should probably, um, hug or something. Apparently, they can see us from the pool."

He pushes off the wall in one fluid motion, closing the distance between us. My arms come up automatically as he reaches for me, one hand settling on the small of my back while the other finds my waist. I rise on my tiptoes, hands settling around his neck as he draws me closer.

His hand slides under the fabric of my shirt where it's ridden up, warm and steady against the sensitive skin above my waistband. I smile into his shoulder at how he's already using the skills we practiced after dinner with his parents. I press my cheek into his shirt. Beneath it, he's all solid muscle, shifting slightly as his arm tightens around me.

My scalp tingles as his breath brushes my temple—it carries the faint mint of whatever gum he'd been chewing. His heartbeat thrums through his shirt, faster than normal, a rapid flutter that mirrors my own.

The hand on my back spreads wider, fingers spanning from spine to ribs, and I become aware of how completely I'm pressed against him. Chest to chest, hip to hip. My own hands explore the base of his neck, fingertips just barely touching the edge of his hairline where his skin is impossibly soft, like sun-warmed velvet.

I have to remind myself to inhale.

For our audience, I remind myself. Part of the show.

"Seven o'clock tomorrow," he says, his deep voice reverberating through me. Then quieter, his lips so close to my ear that I feel the movement of them forming words: "Try not to get me into any more social situations after this?"

"No promises," I manage, too aware of how natural this feels. I force myself to step back, my fingertips trailing down his shoulder, sliding over the curve of muscle. Too slow, I realize as his gaze catches mine, deeper than the ocean.

I hear a shout in the distance. I swear it sounds like Victoria.

"See you tomorrow." I spin, heading straight toward the parking lot.

I collapse into the driver's seat, trapped heat hitting me like a furnace. I start the engine and roll down my windows, desperate to release both the stifling air and the heat still coursing through my body.

My phone buzzes. Probably Tori again. Shouldn't she be busy training? I glance at the screen. Most texts *are, in fact,* from Tori, but one's from Destiny, confirming they're in for the aquarium, and one emoji from Ethan responding to the parody video I sent him earlier. At least he's still talking to me, even if he *is* avoiding me.

I drop my phone into the cup holder without responding, suddenly wanting to scream. The parking lot is emptying now, with only a few cars remaining, most because of sports practice.

I press on the gas, realizing as the engine revs that I never put it in gear. "Get yourself together," I mutter.

When I look up, Sebastian is still standing under the colonnade by the boys' locker room, watching with concern. I flash him a two-finger wave to show I'm fine. *No need to walk over here.*

Maybe I *do* need help? It felt nice wrapped in his muscular arms... No. I need to get to work. At least that'll distract me from obsessing over tomorrow and having to perform in front of Destiny and Ethan with them scrutinizing our every move, look, and touch.

The aquarium. Seahorses. Another piece of the Sebastian Thorne puzzle I never expected to find.

CHAPTER 19

Breakfast for Dinner, Lies for Dessert

I PAD INTO THE kitchen Saturday morning, still in my oversized sleep shirt and shorts, hair braided from the night before. Bacon sizzles on the griddle while maple syrup perfumes the air, mixing with the sweet scent of pancake batter.

Mom's at the griddle flipping pancakes while Dad beats eggs in a yellow bowl. Weekends are the only time I catch them in the same space anymore.

"Morning, sleepyhead," Dad says without looking up. "Late night at Sweet Rush?"

"Yeah, we didn't close until eleven." I snag bacon from the plate on the counter, still warm and crispy, on my way to grab a glass. "Fridays are always crazy."

Mom glances over her shoulder, spatula in hand. "You're up early for a Saturday. Plans before work?"

"Actually, I switched shifts with Chase." I pour orange juice into my glass. "I'm going out tonight."

"Oh?" Mom turns back to her pancakes. "Plans with Ethan and Destiny?"

"Yup." I slide onto a breakfast bar stool, wrapping my hands around the glass. "We're going to a charity event at the aquarium. With Sebastian Thorne."

Mom's spatula freezes halfway to the next pancake. "Sebastian? Bonnie and Gregory's Sebastian?"

"Yeah." I sip my juice, trying to appear casual.

The coffee maker releases a soft gurgle as it finishes its cycle. Batter continues to bubble and hiss on the griddle, as Dad's fork scrapes against the mixing bowl.

"That's..." Mom finally flips the pancake, though it's slightly darker than the others. "Unexpected."

Dad's beating becomes more deliberate. "I didn't realize you two were talking again."

"We have swim class together. And he's been sitting with us at lunch." I scroll through my phone to avoid their searching looks. My thumb moves across the screen without really seeing anything. "We've been... catching up."

"Catching up," Mom repeats, wariness threading her tone. She pours more batter to the griddle. "And this won't interfere with your friendship with Ethan?"

I resist telling her that's exactly the point—that my "relationship" with Sebastian is meant to convince Destiny I'm not interested in Ethan. Instead, I say, "Of course not. Why would it?"

But my voice sounds defensive, and I immediately regret my words.

"June-bug," Dad says gently, "this is the first time you've willingly spent time with Sebastian in... what, six years?"

I set my glass down too hard. "People change. We're not kids anymore."

"Of course," Mom says, returning to her pancakes. "It's just surprising."

Dad pours eggs into a waiting pan in the silence that follows. The weight of their concern presses down on me. I tear bacon into smaller pieces rather than eating it.

"So, is this a double date?" Mom asks, flipping pancakes with more precision than they require.

The word 'date' hangs in the air. My throat constricts as guilt settles in my chest. I knew we'd have to tell my parents to convince the Thornes, but lying to their faces feels wrong in a way I wasn't prepared for. But this was my idea, and I can't bail on Sebastian after giving him such grief about following through.

"Um... Yes, that's exactly what it is." The words tumble out.

A fork hits tile with a metallic clang. Dad's shoulders tense as he retrieves it, then turns to face me fully.

"Dating," Dad says slowly, testing the word.

"Does Bonnie know?" Mom asks, something careful in her tone. "I saw her yesterday, and she didn't mention it."

My hands turn slick around the glass. I rotate it slowly, watching pulp swirl. "Uh, yeah, I'm pretty sure she knows. I had dinner there a couple of nights ago."

Another loaded look passes between my parents. Dad moves to stand beside Mom, a united front of parental concern.

"You're dating Sebastian?" Dad crosses his arms.

A flush creeps down my neck. "Yes," I say, though even I can hear how unconvincing it sounds.

"June," Mom says softly, "are you sure about this?"

The gentle concern almost undoes me. Because standing here in our kitchen while they look at me with such protective worry, I'm not sure about anything.

"Why wouldn't I be?"

Mom turns off the burner and wipes her hands on her apron. When she looks up, her expression has softened.

"Remember when I would set up those little easels for you two while Bonnie and I were brainstorming?"

The sudden shift catches me off guard. My fingers find a loose thread on my shirt. "I remember him getting mad because I didn't care about the color wheel."

"All your paintings would eventually turn brown," Dad chimes in with a grin. "Big brown blobs covering the refrigerator. We called them mud pies."

"But then you two made that little mountain scene with the rainbow," Mom says, pressing a hand over her heart. "I wonder what happened to that one."

"It probably got tossed when I redid my room." Definitely not stuffed in the bottom dresser drawer with the other ridiculously sentimental things I couldn't throw away.

Mom and Dad exchange one more look—softer this time, more resigned.

"You're not that little girl anymore," Mom says quietly, untying her apron. "I trust you know what you're getting into."

The words settle over me like a heavy blanket. Because even as she says she trusts me, I'm not sure I trust myself. I'm remembering eleven-year-old me crying in my room after Sebastian shattered my heart. The memory still ambushes me sometimes when I see him in the hallways.

"He's... really changed," I say, the words emerging softer than intended. "But also the same. He still notices when I'm cold, and still bounces his knee when he's nervous."

Mom's expression grows knowing as Dad turns back to the eggs, but not before I catch his smirk.

I clear my throat.

"Anyway." I stand, eager to escape. "I should call Tori back—she wants to video chat about picking a dress for tonight."

I head toward the hallway before they can ask more questions. "Sebastian's picking me up at seven."

"June?" Dad calls after me. I pause in the doorway. "Have fun tonight."

The kindness in his voice constricts my chest. "Thanks, Dad."

As I head down the hall, their hushed conversation resumes in the kitchen. They remember everything—the years Sebastian and I were inseparable, and how abruptly it ended. But they don't understand this is different. I'm not that naive little girl anymore.

Once, Sebastian was my best friend, and his opinion meant everything, but that shattered long ago. I know exactly where the lines are drawn between us, and I won't cross them again. This setup is simple—we help each other, then return to our separate lives. No risk of getting hurt when you're both playing parts.

At least that's what I keep telling myself as I stare into my closet, trying to figure out what to wear to convince everyone this is real—while keeping the truth locked safely away where it can't hurt either of us.

CHAPTER 20

He's Just Not That Into You Unless You're a Leafy Seadragon

SEBASTIAN'S RANGE ROVER pulls up at seven sharp. I check the mirror one last time and slip out before my parents decide to turn this into an interrogation.

He waits on the porch in navy slacks and a sage green button-down that brightens his eye color, and a dark blazer that fits perfectly. For someone who spends most of his time scowling, he cleans up criminally well.

"Hi," I say, suddenly shy. Which is ridiculous. It's just Sebastian.

His gaze travels from the straps at my shoulders down to where the fabric brushes my knees. Something distinctly un-Sebastian-like flashes across his face, making my pulse flutter.

"You look..." He stops, swallows. "Beautiful, Juniper."

The raw sincerity in his voice trips something in my chest. No practiced charm, no calculated compliment. "Thanks. You're not bad yourself."

His smile softens the sharp lines of his face, almost boyish. "Ready?"

"As I'll ever be." I grab my purse and call over my shoulder, "Bye! I'm heading out!"

"Hold up, Junie."

Dad materializes in the archway, dish towel slung over his arm. His casual stance doesn't match the scrutiny in his gaze.

Sebastian nods respectfully. "Mr. Blake."

"Sebastian." Dad extends his hand, and Sebastian shakes it firmly. "It's been a while."

"Yes, sir."

Mom emerges from the kitchen, not bothering to hide her curiosity. "Sebastian! Right on time." She wipes her hands hastily on her apron before offering him one. "You've grown quite a lot since we last saw you."

"Mrs. Blake." Sebastian's voice hits that perfect note between polite and warm. He gestures to her left cheek. "I think you have a little..."

Mom swipes flour from her face with a flustered laugh. "Oh! Thank you. I'm making cobbler. You're welcome to join us after your—"

She stops before finishing the word *date.*

"Your home always felt like a second one to me." His attention drifts to the corner where we used to build pillow forts while our moms discussed business. His expression turns wistful.

"Well, you're always welcome," Mom says.

She nudges Dad, who clears his throat. "Not too late tonight."

The dad-voice is out in full force now—the one reserved for anyone taking me out.

"Yes, sir. I'll have her home at a reasonable hour."

"And you're meeting Ethan and Destiny there?" Mom's tone suggests confirmation rather than a question.

"Yes, Mom," I say, edging toward the door. "They're waiting for us."

My parents share a look that makes me want to disappear—concern, curiosity, and definitely something they'll dissect once we're gone.

"Have fun," Mom says, but her tone promises a longer conversation in my future. "It's nice seeing you back in our house, Sebastian."

"Thank you, Mrs. Blake." Sebastian smiles, though I catch a flash of nostalgia before he turns to me. "Ready?"

"Definitely," I say, perhaps too eagerly.

The door clicks shut behind us, and I exhale. "Well. That wasn't awkward at all."

Hiss mouth quirks as he opens my door, holding it while I slide in, making sure my dress clears before closing it with care.

"Smoother than my house," he says, settling into the driver's seat.

I hum an agreement as the engine purrs to life. "Only because we left. Just wait—my mom will be waiting up with 'just some tea' while she interrogates me about our relationship."

"That reminds me." He pulls from the curb, his look pointed. "My mother's still demanding I bring you over."

"Poor Sebastian." I layer the tease thick. "Think you'll survive another Thorne family dinner?"

His lips twitch. "Maybe if you promise to behave. No jokes that might scandalize my mother."

"Me? I'm always perfectly behaved."

He shakes his head, but I catch the smile he's trying to suppress.

His thumbs tap a nervous rhythm on the steering wheel as familiar streets give way to the coastal highway. The air between us feels different tonight—heavier, charged with expectation beyond our usual performances at school.

"So this charity event..." he begins, and I'm grateful for the subject change.

He launches into an explanation about sea turtle rescue programs, the rehab center renovations as we drive.

More animated than I ever see at school—hands alive with motion, dimples flashing. I'd forgotten how passionate he gets about things that matter.

"They're creating artificial reefs to help restore the ecosystem," he says, bright with enthusiasm. "And the new filtration system will house more species during rehabilitation—"

He stops mid-explanation, shoulders drawing in. "Sorry. You probably don't care about the details."

"No, it's nice," I say truthfully, watching as self-consciousness colors his cheeks. "I didn't know you were so into this stuff."

He shrugs, fingers adjusting on the wheel, that familiar distance creeping back into his posture. "I like the ocean."

"Like your paintings. The stormy ones," I say. "Is that why you paint them?"

He glances over, gaze lingering before returning to the road. "Something like that."

A slight smile plays at his mouth, and I look away before my thoughts wander somewhere stupid. I keep trying to figure out this newer, more complicated Sebastian, but he keeps shifting just out of reach.

"Are you still writing?" The question comes out hesitantly, focus never leaving the road. "I saw the notebooks in your room. Like... before. You were always creating stories, jotting down words you liked from my books."

He noticed. More than that—he remembers.

"You remember that?"

His face twists as if pained. He glances over. Holding my gaze for one, two, three seconds, before he's forced back to the road. "Why wouldn't I remember, Juniper?"

The question lands with Sebastian's particular brand of stillness—more dangerous than shouting.

It wraps around my heart and squeezes. For years, I convinced myself he'd moved on. That our friendship was a phase he outgrew along with Legos and Saturday morning cartoons.

"I... yeah, I guess I never really stopped," I admit, my voice softer than I intended.

He nods once. "You were always good at it."

The warmth in his tone does something funny to my breathing, so I turn toward the window before I do something catastrophically stupid. "Thank you."

The engine hums, tires whispering on asphalt as downtown swallows us. High-rises crowd in on all sides while neon lights from restaurants, tattoo parlors, bars paint us in shifting colors as they slide over the car interior as we pass.

Sebastian's fingers drum lightly on the bottom of the wheel as we stop at a red light. "So. Will your parents be there tonight?"

"No, thank God." A faint smile ghosts across his face. "Just the usual donors, board members, and a few head scientists. Should be relatively painless."

"Good. So we only have to worry about Ethan and Destiny."

He makes a sound caught between a groan and a growl. "Right." The light turns green. "Though we'll be stuck with them all evening."

I smile down at my lap. "Maybe there's a room you can flee too?"

I meant it as a joke, but I hear how it sounds the second it's out. "I didn't mean—I know why you avoid the lunchroom."

Misery floods his face. "I really am sorry, June. I won't do it again."

"Maybe we can trade off days? I'll come to the art room?" I fidget with my dress as the car seems to shrink.

His response comes quickly, softer that I expect. "I'd like that."

His hand rests on the gearshift, close enough to touch if I wanted to. *If I dared.*

He bites his lower lip, and I watch him weigh whatever comes next. "And it's not too much. Spending time with you. The... touching."

The business lights fade. Only occasional streetlamps move through the dark car now. The way he says *'touching'* sends heat racing through me, memories of the beach flooding back; his hands on my skin. My hands ball into fists on my lap. I need to stop this train of thought. It's easy to get caught up in the whispered confessions, the intimate declarations, but it's all in my head.

I can't let myself think otherwise. Not when it's so catastrophically stupid.

"Good." I shift in my seat. When he looks over, my gaze drops to his mouth. I ball my hands into fists on my thighs. He follows the movement to my lap. "Then you won't mind touching me all night."

The car jerks, tires catching the lane markers with a rough *bump-bump-bump* for several tense seconds before he corrects course.

"I meant for show," I say quickly, checking the road. My cheeks are burning now that I've said those words out loud. "Like we practiced."

"Yes," he says suddenly, cool and detached. "I figured that was expected tonight as part of this *double-date* charade."

The word *'charade'* stings more than it should.

I turn to the passenger window, watching the city blur past. Downtown's lights give way to something more industrial as we approach the waterfront district. Through the buildings, I catch glimpses of the bay. The dark water reflecting the scattered lights from boats and piers. Salt and seaweed drift through the vents.

Sebastian slows as we turn into an upscale area where renovated warehouses have been converted into galleries and event spaces. Streetlights line the road at perfect intervals, casting warm pools of light on the sidewalks.

The aquarium glows against the dark sky, its curved front resembling a giant wave frozen in time. Spotlights shine on the modern glass structure as banners announcing the charity event flutter in the evening breeze. Twinkling lights line the stone walkway leading to the entrance, where well-dressed couples make their way inside.

"Wow," I breathe, tension momentarily forgotten. "It's fancier than I expected."

"Yeah, these events attract serious donors." Sebastian pulls into the valet area, handing his keys to an attendant in a green vest. "The Thornes have been involved for years."

"Of course they have," I mutter. This is Sebastian's world—charity galas and valets and donors with deep pockets.

He touches the back of my hand lightly as we walk toward the entrance. "You okay?"

"Fine." The lie comes automatically. "Just hoping I don't embarrass you in front of all your fancy fish friends."

He laughs, the sound warm and real. "First, fish can't judge your table manners. Second..." He leans closer, voice dropping. "None of these people matter, Pip. You couldn't embarrass me."

His breath ghosts over my bare skin, raising goosebumps. "Right."

We step into the grand entrance, where a massive cylindrical tank rises through the center like a liquid pillar, filled with colorful fish that move in hypnotic patterns around the column. The usual fluorescents are dimmed, replaced by soft blue and green illumination from the tanks that casts everyone in an ethereal glow. A string quartet plays near the gift shop while servers in all black circulate the room with silver trays of champagne and hors d'oeuvres.

Sebastian takes two glasses from a passing server, offering one to me.

I hold up a hand. "I don't drink."

"It's sparkling cider. Non-alcoholic."

"Oh." I take it from him, tasting something fizzy and citrusy. "Thanks."

His expression shifts. I follow his gaze to where Ethan and Destiny stand near a stand of tropical fish by the gift shop. Destiny looks stunning in a pale green dress that complements her blonde hair and fair skin. Ethan's in dark slacks and a white button-down with a green tie matching her dress. His arm's around her waist as he points at something in the tank.

They look perfect—comfortable, happy, like they belong in this elegant world.

I wonder what Sebastian and I look like. Are we really convincing anyone, or can they see right through us?

"June?" Sebastian's voice pulls me back. "You all right?"

I glance up at him, surprised he noticed, but Sebastian always noticed everything, didn't he? "Everything's fine." I reach for his hand. "Let's go say hi."

His fingers lace with mine, his thumb running across my knuckle, strangely intimate despite all our practice at school. The warmth of his palm is oddly reassuring.

Destiny spots us first, her face lighting up. "June! Sebastian!"

"Hey." I accept Destiny's quick hug. "This place is incredible."

Ethan's eyes drop to our linked hands. "Yeah, quite a step up from bowling."

The edge in his voice earns him a look from Destiny.

"The aquarium does important work," Sebastian says smoothly, slipping into the polite, distant tone he uses for people he doesn't trust. "Plus, the tickets support the marine conservation program."

"Always happy to support the Dolphins," Ethan says, glancing away.

An awkward silence threatens to settle over us until Destiny jumps in. "Should we look around first before we find our table?"

"Yes, I've heard the seahorses are particularly adorable." I squeeze Sebastian's hand, smirking up at him.

The corner of his mouth lifts in a private smile.

As we head toward the seahorses, Destiny falls in beside me, our dresses swishing. Sebastian and Ethan trail behind, carefully apart, hands shoved in pockets. Whatever history lies between them, it clearly won't be resolved tonight.

"This *is* better than bowling," Destiny whispers after glancing behind us. "He's just grumpy he had to wear a tie."

Ethan hates dressing up. He even chafes under the Palm Vista uniform, keeping a gym bag full of T-shirts to change into the second he's in his car. I smile, remembering the pack of clip-on ties I got him the Christmas ago.

"Though I wouldn't have minded mini-golf." I bump her lightly with my hip.

She wrinkles her nose. "Sweating under sunscreen while you and Ethan trash-talk about hitting a tiny ball into a clown's mouth? Over air-conditioning, cold drinks and free food?" She laughs, shaking her head. "You're nuts. Though I guess you'll have your fill of these events as Sebastian's girlfriend, huh?"

"I guess." I look away. "Though he fits in way better than I do."

She gives me a quizzical look. "June, do you not see yourself?" She doesn't wait for me to answer. "You belong here as much as he does. Honestly, you've been moving through this world your whole life. Maybe you never left it. Maybe you just convinced yourself you did."

Her words stun me into silence. I've spent so long viewing the Thornes' world as something separate—something I once accessed as a child but lost. But maybe the lines have been blurring all along without me noticing.

I glance back at Sebastian, who's enduring some stilted conversation with Ethan. Even here, surrounded by wealth and people who clearly know him, he maintains that careful reserve. Always watching, never quite joining in. Excelling at what's expected while maintaining crucial distance.

I know that feeling. Different reasons, maybe, but the same discomfort of not quite fitting the role you're supposed to play.

Maybe we're more alike than I thought.

"I never thought about it that way," I admit, watching a couple examine the exhibit while the woman's earrings catch the blue light. "I've spent so long avoiding everything."

"You know, avoiding something doesn't make it go away. Just makes it harder to deal with when you finally face it." She pauses, eyes following mine to where Sebastian and Ethan are talking. "Trust me, I know."

Destiny straightens her shoulders. Whatever somber thought gets washed away, her bright smile returns.

"Anyway," she says with a lighter tone, "where are those seahorses I was promised?"

THE SEAHORSE EXHIBIT IS BATHED in soft orange light, making everything dreamlike. Delicate creatures sway in their tanks, tails curled around strands of seagrass, their movements almost hypnotic.

"They mate for life," Sebastian explains to Destiny, who seems genuinely fascinated. "And it's the males who carry the babies."

"Really?" Destiny gasps, leaning closer. Her face glows in the warm light. "How long do they stay pregnant?"

"About two to four weeks, depending on the species." Sebastian points to a larger seahorse with a distended pouch. "That one's probably close to giving birth."

I catch Ethan's eye over Destiny's shoulder. He looks as surprised as I feel seeing Sebastian passionate, knowledgeable, almost... charming. When Ethan notices me watching, he quickly looks away, suddenly fascinated by a small crab scuttling across the sand.

I move toward the next tank when Sebastian's hand finds the small of my back, sliding around my waist as he leans down. "Want to see my favorite exhibit?"

I nod, trying to ignore the warmth spreading from where his fingers rest against my spine.

As soon as we're out of earshot, I turn to him. "Destiny was certainly impressed with your seahorse lecture, Professor Thorne."

"Was she?" His brows lift innocently, but something knowing glints in his eyes.

"You know she was." I knock my hip into his, surprised when his fingers tighten on my waist. "All those questions, the way she was looking at you..." The words come out sharper than intended.

His mouth quirks up. "And this bothers you because...?"

"It doesn't," I blurt out. "I thought you were cleaning tanks or something. Not becoming the seahorse whisperer."

This earns me a laugh, the sound echoing in the cavernous room. He rubs the back of his neck. "I help with the educational programs sometimes. Kids are usually fascinated by seahorses."

"They're not the only ones," I mumble, crossing my arms. When I glance up, he's smirking. "What?"

"Jealous Blake?"

"You wish," I shake my head, taking a step away to hide the flush creeping up my neck. "I just didn't realize you had a whole secret life here."

"Not a secret," he corrects quietly, falling into step beside me. "Just separate."

We stop at an easily overlooked tank beside the seahorse exhibit. Inside, among rocks and coral, is what appears to be seaweed... until it moves.

"Leafy seadragon," Sebastian says softly with appreciation. "Most people walk right past them."

I lean closer, marveling at its perfect camouflage—delicate, leaf-like appendages flowing from its body, nearly indistinguishable from the plants. "It's beautiful."

"They're incredibly rare in captivity. This one was rescued after a storm. Couldn't survive in the wild."

The compassion in his voice makes me turn to study his face. Blue light from the tank plays across his features, softening the usually sharp angles.

"You really love this place, don't you?"

His eyes meet mine, startlingly green in the aquatic light. "It's peaceful here. Everything has its place, its purpose." He turns back to the tank. "No expectations or reputations to live up to. Just life."

I bite my lip. We've shifted into dangerous territory—real conversations, and real feelings.

"Well, you clearly know your stuff. But you always did, didn't you?"

"It's only memorization," he says with a dismissive shrug, shutters descending over that brief moment of openness. "Like anything else."

"Don't do that."

"Do what?" His brow furrows, creating a crease in his forehead.

"Act like it's nothing." I step closer. The narrow alcove makes our proximity feel more intimate than I intended. My hand grips his arm like he might bolt. "You're good at this, Sebastian. Probably good at a lot of things you don't give yourself credit for."

Surprise and confusion flicker across his features, then something altogether different that makes his pupils dilate.

For a moment, we just stare, the soft bubbling of the tank the only sound between us.

We're standing so close it would be easy to do something stupid like hook my fingers in his belt loops and pull him closer or run my hands up his chest. The thought makes my pulse trip.

Sebastian glances at my hand on his arm. I wonder if my fingers betrayed my thoughts. I deliberately step back. "We should probably catch up with Ethan and Destiny. Our reason for being here?"

His fingers dig into the hair at the back of his neck. "Right."

As we navigate back through orange-lit corridors toward the jellyfish exhibit, my heart refuses to slow. My brain really needs to inform my body that the charming, attentive boyfriend and lingering looks are only part of the act.

We find Ethan and Destiny in the jellyfish room. Translucent creatures pulse rhythmically in tall cylindrical or square tanks, long tentacles floating behind them like ghostly ribbons. The lighting shifts from blue to purple to pink, casting everything in an ethereal glow.

"These are moon jellies," Destiny reads from a plaque. "They don't have brains or hearts."

"Sounds like my ex," a voice says behind us.

We turn to a tall woman in an elegant black dress. She's somewhere in her thirties, with sharp features and a perceptive gaze. She extends a hand. "Sebastian Thorne. I thought you were skipping out on us this year."

"Dr. Zhao." Sebastian shakes her hand with familiarity. "My girlfriend, Juniper, deserves the credit. She takes conservation almost as seriously as I do." He glances at me, eyes teasing. "And I couldn't miss the opportunity to show her my second favorite girl."

"Ah yes, Penny," Dr. Zhao's face lights up. "She's much better. And I think she misses you." She gives me a friendly once-over, offering her hand. "I'm glad someone can drag you out of the water long enough to wear shoes."

Color rises in Sebastian's cheeks at the inside joke. There's clearly a history, which makes me curious. When I raise my brow, he gives a nod that promises to explain later.

"Well, enjoy your night." Dr. Zhao's sharp eyes move between us, then to Ethan and Destiny, still examining the jellyfish. "Lovely to meet you, Juniper."

When Dr. Zhao walks away, I lean into Sebastian. "Friend of yours?"

"She runs the rehabilitation program. We've worked together on several projects."

"And who's Penny?" I place a hand on my hip.

He looks down with a half-smile, a dimple appearing in his left cheek. His hand slides down my arm, leaving a trail of heat before settling on my hip, fingers tapping. "Jealous, Blake?" His grin widens. "Twice in one night?"

I scoff as Ethan clears his throat. He and Destiny are standing right there, watching our exchange.

"Yeah, who's Penny, Thorne?" Ethan asks, tone challenging.

Sebastian pivots, his smile sharpening. "She's a sea turtle." He leans down, voice pitched low but loud enough for them to hear, "and maybe if you're *nice to me,* you'll get to meet her."

His breath grazes my ear, and I swear I feel it in my spine. I catch Ethan tense beside us, but Destiny quickly links her arm through mine, pulling us ahead.

"Don't worry, they'll get used to each other soon enough," she whispers with a laugh, squeezing my arm. Her tone turns conspiratorial. "But you two are so adorable. I've never seen Sebastian like this with anyone."

"Like how?" I ask, suddenly self-conscious.

"You know, all attentive. The way he looks at you—" She sighs dreamily. "He's obsessed."

Heat rises in my cheeks. I steal a glance behind me to find Sebastian watching us, eyes finding mine immediately. He gives me a small, private smile before turning back to a particularly large jellyfish.

"I don't know about that..."

"Babe, didn't you want to see the touch tanks?" Ethan calls back to us. "They're right up here."

"Perfect!" Destiny tugs me forward. "I've always wanted to touch a stingray."

The touch tanks brim with vibrant sea stars, knobby chocolate chip starfish, and soft, motionless sea cucumbers nestled among the pebbles. In the center of the room, a circular pool lets guests lean over the edge to feel the velvety texture of the stingrays swimming around the tank.

Despite the formal event, several guests have rolled up their sleeves, reaching cautiously into the water to brush their fingers against the passing rays.

Sebastian hangs back. I follow his gaze to see Avery standing with her parents near the coral reef display. She wears a pale pink dress that makes her look like a tropical flower. Her eyes light when she sees him, giving a small wave.

Sebastian's posture shifts almost imperceptibly. Shoulders tense, jaw tight. He returns her wave before checking the time on his phone.

"Go say hi." I nod toward Avery.

He turns back to be, searching my face. "That's unnecessary."

"She clearly wants to talk to you," I press. "And it would look weird if you completely ignored her after the dinner at your house."

He hesitates, glancing back at Avery, who's whispering to her mother. "I don't know if that's appropriate."

I flash him a reassuring smile. "I'll be fine with Destiny at the touch tank. Just don't be too long."

He nods, holding my gaze as he brushes my hair back, fingers trailing along my jaw. My breath catches. There's a self-conscious urge to glance at my friends. *Sebastian Thorne is touching my face*, but of course, the display is for Avery. I relax a little, though there's still a hurricane in my stomach.

He gives my arm a squeeze before heading toward the Bennett's. I watch him go, noting how his movements become more formal with each step. Avery's face brightens as he approaches, her hand touching his arm briefly during their greeting.

"What's that about?" Ethan asks, appearing beside me.

I shrug, trying to be casual. "Friends of his parents."

Ethan watches Sebastian shake Mr. Bennett's hand, suspicion pulling his mouth down. "Isn't that Avery? I've seen him talking to her at school."

"She has a crush on him." I wave a dismissive hand. "It's not a big deal."

Ethan gives me a strange look. "Right." His tone suggests he's not entirely convinced.

Before I can respond, Destiny looks up, waving for me to join her. "June, come feel this! It's so cool!"

I slide closer, careful of my dress as I reach into the water.

"Fingers out like this." Destiny demonstrates a two-finger touch as a small stingray glides beneath her hand. "It feels like wet silk."

I gently brush against a ray as it swims by—smooth and cool, alive in a way that makes me grin.

One of the aquarium educators approaches with small pieces of shrimp. "Would you like to feed them?" She asks with a friendly smile. "Hold the shrimp between your fingers and keep your hand flat below the surface. They'll swim right over and take it."

I do as instructed, gasping as a ray brushes my fingers and takes the shrimp.

"Tickles," I laugh, watching the graceful creatures circle the shallow pool.

"I know, right?" Destiny's face is lit with childlike wonder. "I can't believe I've never done this."

I glance over to find Ethan watching Sebastian and Avery, arms crossed.

I grab his hand with my dry one. "Come on, grumpy." I pull him toward the water. "Try it."

I repeat the educator instructions. Lay our hands flat, letting the shrimp stick up between our fingers. Ethan copies me, but then his hand traps mine under his. I glance up, but he's watching the water.

"Look." He nods as a ray glides over our hands, vacuuming the shrimp in what feels like forever, but I know it only lasts seconds. "Cool," he murmurs, face close to mine.

Ethan and I have touched countless times. When he'd grab my hand to lead me, or smack it away when I'd steal his popcorn. The times he'd pick me up and toss me in the pool. So why is my heart racing now?

I try to pull away, but his hand remain firmly over mine. I narrow my eyes. "What are you doing?"

"What are *you* doing?" he hisses back. "Thorne, seriously?"

Destiny glances over, brows pulled down to match her deep frown. "*Be nice.*"

"I am being nice," he insists, though his moody expression suggests otherwise.

He finally lets go. I pull my hand free to flick droplets at him, hitting his dress shirt.

He smooths a hand down his chest. "I just think it's messed up that your boyfriend is talking to another girl. I'd never do that to—" He pauses. "Look, guys like Thorne have different rules. Different expectations."

"What does that even mean?"

We move down to let other guests have a turn and huddle near the paper towel dispenser, but only Destiny takes one to dry her hands.

"I'm only saying what everyone's thinking. He's got college friends, other connections. A whole other life you know nothing about." Ethan gestures toward where Sebastian still stands with Avery, her hand on his arm as she laughs at something he's said.

The sight makes my chest clench uncomfortably. Ethan gives me a knowing look. "You think pretty boy doesn't use their boy's club discrepancy?"

"Sebastian's not like that."

"Really?" He asks like I'm purposely being dense. "You think he—I mean, come on. Look at Mitchem, Simon, hell, even Bryce and Fiona? They don't date classmates, but they sure aren't celibate."

I stare at him, shocked by the ugliness in his voice. I step back, eyes snagging on Destiny, who's also looking at him in surprise.

Ethan runs his hand through his hair, frustrated. "Forget it. You're right. I'm being weird." But he can't let it go: "I just don't want you to get hurt when he gets bored and moves on to someone more..." He trails off, realizing how that sounds.

"Enjoying the touch tank?" Sebastian's voice cuts low behind me.

CHAPTER 21
Penny for Your thoughts

I TURN SLOWLY, MEETING Sebastian's narrowed jade eyes. Not angry; they're cold, calculating. He holds out a paper towel.

I carefully take it, wiping my hands.

Ethan grins, sliding his hands into his pockets. "Yes, Thorne, immensely."

"Great," Sebastian says, all teeth.

If I had any doubt he overheard our conversation, that shark-like grin confirms it.

"Sebastian," I breathe his name, guilt making me hot and cold all at once.

His jaw jumps, and he won't look at me. "I appreciate your concern, Cole, but I promise you, June knows exactly where she stands with me."

The temperature drops several degrees. Destiny and I share a look.

"I'm just looking out for her," Ethan says, though some of his bravado fades.

"Of course you are." The flat delivery makes the hair on my neck stand on end. "But if you two will excuse us. I need to steal June for a moment."

His hand finds my elbow, and I turn to follow.

"Hold on." Ethan steps forward, his arm barring our path. "This isn't June's fault."

"I know," Sebastian says, glancing up from Ethan's arm. "I know it's not June's fault."

"Ethan, I'm fine," I cut in, trying to deescalate the situation. "I'll see you at the table."

Destiny puts her hand on Ethan's chest while asking with her eyes if I'm okay. I give a small nod. She returns it before saying with a forced smile, "We'll see you there."

I slip my hand through Sebastian's waiting elbow, tossing one last placid smile at Ethan and Destiny as Sebastian gently steers me away from the main corridor.

Once we're out of earshot, I brace for the fallout. "Sebastian, I'm sorry—"

"Not here." He sounds tired. He pushes a hand through his hair as he smiles at one of the aquarium employees. "Please."

The quartet fades as we cut through the shark tunnel. Curved glass walls arch overhead, blue-green lights wash over the other guests, who gaze up at massive sharks swimming above as we move briskly through.

Ethan's words echo in my head, and I cringe all over again.

"Where are we going?" I ask when he stops at a door marked 'staff only' and swipes a key card.

"You'll see." His expression gives nothing away as he holds the door.

We enter a dim back hallway. The air is cooler here and carries a stronger scent of saltwater. He takes my hand as we move through, his pace slowing as we approach another locked door requiring his key card.

"Sebastian, about what Ethan said—"

"Juniper." He turns to face me, his eyes gentling for the first time since the touch tank. "I didn't bring you back here to talk about Ethan."

He uses his back to push open the door. We enter a large room with several round fiberglass tanks. Unlike the exhibition tanks, these are clearly medical in nature—plain light blue interiors with gentle ramps and platforms.

"Welcome to the rehab pools." He leads me to a tank where a sea turtle about the size of a dinner plate floats near the surface, one flipper noticeably damaged. "This is Penny."

He grins, a teasing glint in his eyes. "I don't think you've completely earned it yet." He backs away, grin still in place, "but I couldn't come all this way and not sneak her one of these."

He crosses to a refrigerator on the far wall, and returns with two skinny, smelly fish.

We approach the edge of the pool, watching the turtle's graceful movements despite the obvious injury. Her shell bears a deep gash, carefully treated and sealed.

"What happened to her?"

"Caught in fishing gear. She was barely alive when they found her." His voice softens. "But she's a fighter."

The turtle surfaces, seeming to recognize Sebastian, or maybe she smells the fish in his hand. She swims to the edge where his arm rests on the tank, poking her head up in greeting.

"Hey, Penny," he says, gently stroking the side of her head. "Feeling better today?"

I smile watching him. He catches me, color rising in his cheeks. "I helped with her treatment when they brought her in." He shrugs, but there's unmistakable pride in his voice.

"That's pretty cool."

Another shrug. "They think she'll be ready for release in a few months."

"You like saving things, Thorne."

He looks at me, lips incredulous. "I didn't save her; the trained staff did. I only... helped. A little."

I shoot him a face. He's doing it again. "Don't sell yourself short. Dr. Zhao is definitely impressed with you."

Sebastian looks away, focusing on feeding Penny another fish. "I just volunteer when I can."

"All those times I thought you were off at fancy country club events?"

His mouth quirks up at one corner. "Some of those too. Can't escape everything." He holds out the last fish. "Want to try?"

I wrinkle my nose at the smell, but take it. "What do I do?"

"Hold it above the water. Let her come to you." His voice is gentle as he guides my hand, fingers warm against my wrist. "And watch your fingers."

I move in closer, carefully dangling the fish above the surface. Penny paddles over, dark eyes watchful. She stretches up her beak, and tugs the fish from my fingers.

"Oh!" I laugh, startled by her speed.

Sebastian smiles. "She likes you."

I level him a look. "She likes the food in my hand."

"Yeah, maybe." He laughs, fingers trailing her shell as she glides past.

We watch Penny circle back, hoping to find another fish waiting in our hands. Her injured flipper makes her slower than she should be. Something in my chest squeezes.

"What's next for your writing?"

"What do you mean?"

"Ever thought about trying to get published?"

I stifle a nervous laugh. The idea is both thrilling and terrifying. "I don't know if I'm good enough yet. I still have a lot to learn."

"You were always good at it." He smiles at the tank. "Even those dinosaur love stories."

I groan, covering part of my face with one hand. "I had hoped you'd forgotten."

"I especially liked the one where the T-Rex fell in love with the Brachiosaurus, despite their differences."

My cheeks flush beet red as my fingers trail through the water. "Yeah, well, I've expanded to people now."

His brows dance. "It's still one of my favorites." The teasing smirk fades into something more serious. "Is that what you want to do? After high school?"

"Maybe. I'm also... exploring animal psychology." I brace for his suggestions or critiques. But he doesn't rush to respond, doesn't offer careers that might be more lucrative. Just listens and waits. "Everyone else has a plan. Even Ethan and Destiny have it figured out. And I'm..." I flap my hand, searching. "Unmoored."

He nods. "Everyone thinks I'll do something with painting, but it's only a hobby." He tips his chin to encompass the room, the aquarium, maybe even the entire ocean. "My passion's here."

"You'd be great at it, Sebastian." I say wistfully, letting my knuckle drag over Penny's leg when she gets close.

"You'd make a great writer, June." His voice is equally soft. When I look up, his eyes are on mine, catching the blue light from the tank, and appearing teal.

"Sorry about Ethan." I clear my throat. "What he said wasn't fair."

A shadow crosses his face before he exhales. "I hate what they say—" He shakes his head. "It doesn't matter."

"He doesn't know you like—" I catch myself, aware of how presumptuous that sounds. I *knew* Sebastian once. But it feels like I'm discovering him again. "He doesn't know the real you."

"Like you do?" He asks, barely audible, his gaze burning into mine.

"Yes," the words slip out. "Or I'm starting to. Again."

It feels like a confession.

He holds my gaze. His fingers brush mine on the edge of the tank—not accidental—sending electricity up my arm. My fingers twitch, and then his larger knuckles part mine.

Why is he still acting like a boyfriend when we're alone with no one here to see?

My gaze drops to his mouth before I catch myself.

Sebastian's breath goes shallow. Our faces are closer than they should be. He leans forward a fraction, gaze fixed on my lips.

For one wild moment I think even if it's pretend, it couldn't hurt to see what it would be like...

He pulls back, sighing at the tank. His hand slides away from mine. "We should head to the table." He clears the roughness from his voice. "Ethan and Destiny will be waiting."

Of course. *The rules.* The ones put in place so this wouldn't happen because even though we remind ourselves this is not real, it's so easy to... forget.

I grip the side of the tank. "Right."

He was right to pull away. This would complicate everything. And I'm not sure I've even forgiven him for... everything that happened before.

THE NO-KISSING CONTRACT

SEBASTIAN LEADS THE WAY TO the dining area, hands in pockets, nodding to staff members and guests who recognize him. The corridor feels endless, filled with the soft murmur of other guests and distant laughter. We pass a small group of well-dressed donors admiring a lionfish display.

I keep pace beside him, trailing my fingers along the textured wall, when really I'm using it as an excuse. I smooth my arms. Adjust my necklace. Anything to avoid the temptation to reach for him.

I've become too comfortable, forgetting that contact is only necessary when we have an audience.

"Cold?" Sebastian asks, noticing my fidgeting.

"No," I say, polite, professional even.

I spot Ethan and Destiny at our table as soon as we enter the dining room. I grab Sebastian's hand, ignoring the thrilling jolt it sends through my body. His fingers close immediately around mine, but then he glances down, brow lifted in question.

"They need to see we're fine," I say quietly, reassuring both him and myself that this is for them. "That you didn't drag me off to lecture me."

"Right," he says blandly, almost bored. "All part of the act."

"Exactly," I say, ignoring his jaw tightening.

His gaze tears from mine to the table. "Let's just get through this."

I'm not sure whether he means dinner or something bigger.

And just like that, we're back to the deal. I should be relieved he's keeping things professional. Instead, it's like I'm losing something I never really had.

"Everything okay?" Destiny asks as we sit, her gaze bouncing between Sebastian and me.

"Perfect," I say. "Sebastian wanted to introduce me to his turtle."

Ethan's eyebrows shoot up. "His... turtle."

"Penny," Sebastian clarifies coolly. "She's in rehab after a fishing accident."

"Oh, that's so sad," Destiny says, immediately softening. "Is that part of the program we're supporting tonight?"

As Sebastian explains where the charity money will go, his voice transforms into the calm, confident tone I've known for years. The same one that usually hides the anxiety underneath.

His knee bounces lightly under the table. My hand moves instinctively toward his leg out of habit, but I catch myself mid-motion, fingers curling back into my lap.

That's what a real girlfriend would do.

But I'm not his girlfriend. I'm a stand-in who keeps forgetting where the performance ends and reality begins.

We agreed to maintain boundaries: only what's necessary to be convincing, and nothing more.

CHAPTER 22
A Study in Repression

*P*EACE OFFERINGS SHOULDN'T look this good in a school uniform.

Sebastian stands at the south gate when I arrive Monday morning, his green and gold tie knotted precisely under his sweater vest. Our school uniform becomes something editorial on him—an effortless polish that can't be taught. That's not unusual. What is unusual: he's waiting for me, holding what appears to be a bribe.

I spent Saturday convincing myself this could work without anymore... complications. When Ethan invited me to watch movies with everyone, I texted Sebastian to coordinate alibis. No need to subject myself to lingering touches or meaningful glances. Just business.

So why is he here now?

His black sunglasses hide any emotion as I approach, but then the dimple appears. "Juniper."

"Sebastian."

In one hand, he holds a coffee cup from the nice place downtown. In the other, a brown paper bag that smells like bacon and fresh bread.

He extends the cup. "Vanilla latte, extra shot, oat milk."

That's my exact order. Down to the milk alternative.

I take it, letting warmth seep through the cardboard sleeve. This means nothing. He's observant. And he's always been meticulous, and what's more thorough than learning your fake girlfriend's coffee order?

"Thanks."

"And a breakfast sandwich, if you're hungry."

Now I'm really suspicious. I peek inside the bag—eggs, bacon, sourdough. My stomach betrays me with a small rumble.

I sip the latte. "Are you trying to bribe me?"

Pink floods his cheekbones, but he doesn't look away. "Maybe."

I wait. Students flow past us through the gates, their chatter a buffer against whatever's coming. The morning air is crisp with the promise of rain. I take another sip of my drink, determined to maintain the emotional distance I'd worked so hard to establish yesterday.

Sebastian pulls off his sunglasses and pushes a hand through his sandy-brown hair, messing up his morning style. I raise an eyebrow.

He sighs, resigned. "Saturday night didn't end the way I expected. It seems like we got off track."

There it is. Delivered in typical Sebastian fashion—understated, revealing nothing about what actually went wrong.

"Off track," I repeat, rocking back on my heels. "Is that what we're calling it?"

He tilts his head. "What would you call it?"

The challenge underneath is subtle. We're standing close enough that I can see the faint shadows under his eyes. Like maybe he spent all night replaying moments from the charity event too.

"I don't know." Which is both true and completely false. I *would* call it: the moment I made a complete fool of myself.

Yes, there were moments Saturday night where I could've sworn he wanted me too. But wanting something in the moment and actually wanting it are two very different things. I learned that lesson at eleven. I'm not making that mistake again.

"You tell me. You're the one with the peace offering."

His exhale is caught between frustration and relief. "June." The way he says my name makes something twist in my chest that I immediately try to suppress. "You're obviously keeping your distance, and your texts were—"

"Were what?"

"Brief."

"I'm not mad at you, Sebastian." I shake my head. "And my texts weren't brief."

He doesn't call me out on the lie, but his look says he knows.

He glances over his shoulder at the main building and crosses his arms. "Is this because of what Ethan said?"

"No, he's confused," I say, and when Sebastian tilts his head, I ramble on, "about us. I knew it would weird everyone out."

His brows lift. "Because it's sudden."

He's nodding slowly, but the look he's giving me is making my insides squirm. "Right."

The word hangs between us, loaded with everything we're not saying. My resolve wavers, the distance I'd maintained all weekend threatening to crumble under the weight of his attention.

I need to stick to the plan. Keep it simple. Keep my heart out of it.

Sebastian motions toward the stone tables under the overhang. I follow, dropping my backpack between us on the bench—a deliberate barrier.

I unwrap the sandwich. It's almost to my mouth when I notice him staring.

"You're going to watch me eat?"

He looks away, but not quickly enough.

I say with a coy smile, "You're always so serious."

"You like it." His gaze snaps back to mine. "Because you enjoy it when I break."

His tone says he knows exactly what I'm doing.

He's not wrong.

His weighted stare acknowledges the game, the push and pull, the way I chip at his self-control to see what's underneath.

I take a bite, closing my eyes as pesto mayo and sourdough melt together. "Oh my gosh."

When I open them, he's staring again.

"What?"

"Nothing." But his voice has dropped half an octave. "You're... enjoying that."

He looks like he's going to break right now. Heat crawls up my neck. I force myself to look away first.

He shifts. "It's working, you know. Our arrangement. My mother's stopped hounding me. She even ordered you a dress for the gala."

"Oh." I pick at the bun. "That's... generous. She really shouldn't have."

I'd planned on wearing the champagne dress with the other girls walking the floor.

"I'm almost certain she was already planning it. You know my mother; she always loved dressing you up. And now that I'm escorting you, she's figured you can't say no."

Mrs. Thorne would dress me in Sophie's old party dresses. I'd spin around in circles or run through the house feeling the air around my legs. Making Sebastian be the knight who saved me, or the dragon Sophie and I slayed, depending on the day.

I never felt left out then. Not until my last day at the Thornes'.

"Your mom's clever," I murmur, and he sounds an agreement.

"You don't have to wear it," he says. "You can wear whatever you want."

I squeeze his hand. "No, it's an important night. I'd love to. I'm sure it will be lovely."

He grabs my coffee, testing its weight before taking a sip. "So what did we do Sunday?"

Right. Our fake date. "You took me to Romano's. You had salmon, and I had steak, of course."

"Romano's?" His eyebrows lift.

"Yeah, you can afford it." I wave a hand breezily. "Plus, I heard their lemon cheesecake is divine."

A smile tugs at his mouth as he traces the cup's edge with his long fingers. "And after? Driving around until curfew? Or did you invite me in to watch crime dramas with your parents?"

I tap my chin. "We parked by the pier, obviously."

"Obviously." He sounds almost amused. "Is that what you told Cole?"

I rotate the coffee cup, careful not to let our fingers touch where his rest on the table. "I kept our after-dinner activities private."

"Shame."

"Jealous Thorne?"

"That was part of the deal," he says, watching me.

I angle my gaze at him—sharp, deliberate. "What's your deal with Ethan anyway? And don't tell me it's nothing."

He runs his free hand through his hair, making it even more disheveled. "Isn't the bell about to ring?"

"Better make it quick, then."

His fingers drum once against his thigh. "You heard his opinion of me on Saturday. That's not new."

"There's more than that."

"I don't have a singular issue. We just clash." His gaze meets mine and holds. "Cole's trash talking doesn't affect our agreement."

I cringe. "I'm not worried about that."

His brows pull low. "Isn't that why you need this? So he backs off?"

"For Destiny," I say carefully, "so she doesn't see me as a threat."

"Right. Same thing."

His tone suggests otherwise, but the bell rings before I can push.

Sebastian straightens, glancing toward the main building where students move faster now into the school. "I'll walk you to class."

He reaches for my backpack before I can protest. I fall into step beside him, acutely aware of whispered conversations that pause as we pass. When a group of girls openly stare, I grab his hand.

"So, are we good?" Sebastian asks as we approach the English building. "With the deal, I mean."

"Yeah." Though something unresolved still hangs between us, I'm not naming it first. "We're good."

He studies my face as we walk, and I wonder if he can tell I'm lying. If there's one thing that hasn't changed about us, it's that I'm good at running, and Sebastian doesn't chase.

"I listened to the song you sent."

"Oh, what did you think?"

"It was nice."

I shoot him a flat look. "You can be honest if you hated it."

"I would, if I did." He pulls out his phone, not bothering to hide his passcode, or disguise the suspicious amount of strategy games filling his home screen, and shows me my songs added to his favorites.

"Strategy games?" I lean closer. "Let me guess—you're the type that builds elaborate civilizations for perfect efficiency? I bet your armies are undefeated."

"Is there another way to play?" His mouth quirks into an equally teasing smirk. "Not as sophisticated as blowing zombies' brains out for in-game currency."

"Hey, you might like it. Release some of your frustrations." I bump my hip into him. "You're kind of uptight."

He rubs a hand down his face. "The only thing frustrating right now is you."

"Oh?" I grin devilishly up at him. "Sounds like you need to shoot some zombies."

"Are you inviting me over?"

I swallow. "I'm not sure you can handle my room. You might start cleaning."

"I contained myself last time." He makes an indistinct sound in his throat. "Besides, I think that's the real reason you invited me over as kids."

We stop outside my classroom. For a moment, we stand there, looking at each other.

He shifts his weight from one foot to the other. "How about we spend Mondays, Wednesdays, and Fridays in the cafeteria, and Tuesdays and Thursdays in the art room?"

I smile up at him. "You're always so reasonable."

His mouth quirks up at the corner. "One of us has to be."

I shake my head, smiling as I take my backpack from his shoulder. "See you at lunch, Bash."

"See you later, Pip."

I watch him merge into the hallway crowd. Even in uniform, Sebastian draws attention—something about the way he moves, unhurried and self-contained.

Destiny waves from her seat when I enter the classroom, her brows wiggling suggestively. Behind her, Ethan leans close to whisper something that makes her face change.

"Fun weekend?"

I pull out my notebook to hide whatever's showing on my face. "Very."

CHAPTER 23
The Red Dress is a Threat, Actually

SEBASTIAN'S ALREADY AT his easel when I slip into the art room Tuesday during lunch, arranging brushes with a precision that probably extends to his entire life.

After the uncertainty of the weekend, Sebastian and I have found our rhythm. What started as an awkward partnership has settled into a comfortable new routine.

"Won't I disturb your peace or whatever?" I wave at the mostly empty room.

He doesn't look up. "You thrive on disturbing my peace, Pip, but no—I'm not the only artist at school, despite what people seem to think." He mumbles this last part.

"Then where is everyone?"

"I didn't realize being alone with me made you nervous."

"It doesn't," I say too quickly.

Though the last time we were truly alone was at the beach, and I'm not counting the rehab room since technically Penny the turtle chaperoned.

He hums low in his throat while setting up a second easel. "This is Ms. Landry's lunch break. She'll be back before the next period."

I snort. "Of course you'd work on two paintings at once."

"While I do sometimes do that—this is yours."

"Mine!" I squeak out. He nods, already squeezing paint onto his palette. "I haven't improved since we were kids. I almost failed art."

"You did not," he says matter-of-fact. "I saw your sketches at the art fair."

"They put everyone in the art fair. Even Kenny's weird black blobs."

He pats the stool next to him with a smile that's very un-Sebastian-like. Wolfish, you could say.

"Don't you have better things to do than teach me to paint?"

"Not currently." He places a paintbrush in my hand, fingers curling around mine like he knows I want to toss it. "But you don't have to paint. You can go back to your web novel—is that what you were reading yesterday?"

"Yes." I eye him, noting the earnest way he glances at me, carefully arranging his workspace beside mine. In the way his knee bounces, just barely, until he notices and stills it with a clearing of his throat. "Okay, what are we painting today?"

He works with efficiency and skill, roughly sketching out an overall design before coating the canvas in a burnt orange underpainting that quickly transforms into something masterful. A fall landscape of reds, oranges, and yellows—leaves dusting a country road—while teaching me to paint something similar.

I focus on mixing the colors he shows me. Muscle memory takes over: the familiar rhythm of painting beside Sebastian, the quiet concentration, his patient corrections when I get heavy-handed with the yellow ochre. We were friends once. I think we could be again. I've missed this, missed him, more than I wanted to admit.

Avoided him was easier than letting myself feel the ache of his absence.

I steal a glance as he works. The tension melts from his shoulders when he's painting. This is Sebastian in his element—not the intimidating figure stalking our school hallways, but the boy who used to show me how to see light differently, how colors tell stories.

I sit back to study my canvas. "You're a great teacher."

"You take directions better now." His brows furrow as he adds details to the trunks, the leaves, the little blue bird perched on a branch.

I laugh. "You've learned how to use your words."

He grunts, but the corner of his mouth twitches upward. I dip my brush in our shared palette, catching the light yellow he's using for highlights. His sleeves are rolled to his elbows, revealing the lean muscle of his forearms, and when he leans forward to add detail, sandy hair falls across his forehead. He pushes it back with his wrist.

He's beautiful when he's like this, unguarded and in his element.

"I charge extra for art lessons that include staring."

"I wasn't staring at you." I quickly return to my painting. "I was watching you blend."

"Right." He finally glances up, one brow arched. "My mistake."

He turns his brush like he's going to mark me with it, a familiar mischievous glint in his eyes. I flinch back with a squeal.

"Relax, I wasn't—" He dips his finger in cadmium red and paints my nose.

"Sebastian!" I move to do the same, but he's dropped his brush, letting it clatter to the floor to grab my hands.

The art room is no longer empty. Ms. Landry has returned to set up for her next class, and a few students trickle in as the bell approaches. Sebastian and I have study hall next, but he often takes his here. Ms. Landry is letting me stay by association, though the side-eye she's giving us now suggests she's regretting it.

"You're causing a scene," I whisper-hiss, snatching one of his paper towels to wipe off the paint.

When he comes up from retrieving his brush, he's still laughing.

"I'm so going to get you back."

"Oh, I know." He says it as if he's looking forward to it.

I'M FOLDING A BLUE SHEET of paper at our lunch table on Friday when Tori drops her tray dramatically as she sits. I'm surprised her water bottle doesn't fall. "Well, look who's graced us with her presence. Juniper Ann Blake, I thought we'd lost you to the art geeks forever."

"She was on loan," Sebastian says beside me.

"You're no art geek, Thorne. Don't even. You're more like an art god."

A V forms between his brows at her compliment. He takes a bite of his burger and fries while I smooth my fingers over the paper creases, folding it back on itself, bending and curving until I have a tiny paper seahorse. I set it on Sebastian's tray.

He picks it up carefully, examining it. The corner of his mouth lifts, his knee pressing into mine along with his shoulder. "Aw, you made this for me?"

My smile goes crooked as I press more into him. "No, I made it for the turtle. Tell her I said hi."

He twirls it between his fingers before tucking it carefully into his blazer pocket. "I will. I'm seeing her this weekend." His smile turns smug.

Jordan scoffs as he approaches, shaking his head. "You rescue baby turtles, you paint, and you just smashed the 100-meter freestyle record at regionals," he says, dropping into the seat across from us. "Is there anything you're not obnoxiously good at, Thorne?"

"Yeah, June, is there anything he's not good at?" Tori has her straw between her teeth, tone laced with double meaning.

My face burns as I raise my hand to block as I mouth *'shut up'* to Victoria, who bats her eyelashes in response.

"Yeah, who knew Thorne had a soft spot for prickly sea creatures?" Ethan says, stealing one of my fries. I smack his hand away, but he lifts his brows in challenge.

"Room for one more?"

Bryce Matthews stands at our table, one hand on Cam's empty chair. His letterman jacket hangs open over his untucked uniform shirt—a deliberate flouting of dress code that somehow never gets him in trouble. His dark hair falls perfectly across his forehead, and his lazy smile suggests he knows exactly how good he looks.

"Thorne," he nods, "nice to see you slumming it with the rest of us."

"Bryce," Sebastian acknowledges. "Charming as always."

I glance between them, sensing underlying tension until Bryce laughs, extending his hand. Sebastian shakes it briefly. The type of handshake born on golf greens or in private yacht clubs. A ritual of mutual recognition rather than friendship.

"So." Bryce takes a seat, leaning back with the confidence of someone at the top of the social hierarchy. "I'm having a thing at my place tomorrow night. The parents are in Greece for *business*." He makes air quotes around "business". "The bungalow's all mine for the weekend."

"Bungalow," Tori snorts. "Your beach house has an elevator."

"Details," Bryce waves dismissively. "You guys in? I know Jordan is."

"Absolutely," Jordan nods with a wink.

"Count us in," Ethan says automatically, then glances at Destiny when she doesn't automatically agree.

"Actually, I can't. My grandma's birthday dinner is tomorrow, remember? We talked about this last week."

Ethan's face falls. "Right. I forgot." He turns to Bryce. "Maybe next time."

"Dude, you don't need a plus-one to party," Jordan protests.

Destiny shoots Jordan a look. His shoulder lifts in what could be an apology.

"Nah, I promised I'd be there. I should be there." Ethan glances down at the table, giving her hand a tender squeeze.

Bryce tips his chin toward me. "What about you, June? You haven't been to one of my get-togethers since... sophomore year, was it?"

The shift in Bryce's attention has me fidgeting with my napkin. "I don't know... I'm not really a partier."

"Neither am I." He lies smoothly through his movie star grin. He leans forward. "You should come. You'd make it significantly less boring."

Sebastian stiffens beside me. His knee, which had been casually touching mine under the table, pulls away. Bryce notices the shift, tracking the space opening between us. His smile widens.

"Thorne's invited too, of course." He gives Sebastian a knowing look. "You still remember how to have fun, right, *old man*?"

Sebastian's exhale is almost a laugh—dry, followed by a bored glance with Bryce, like this is a common tease.

"I prefer quieter settings," Sebastian says evenly, though his hand curls into a loose fist on the table.

"Ah, yes, I remember," Bryce nods. "But maybe June wants to spend her senior year living it up and not sequestered in the art studio watching you brood over oil paints, or whatever it is you two do." He grins at us with obvious implications.

"I like watching him paint," I reply, with a defensive edge.

"Of course, I'm sure it's riveting, but a change of scenery is good for the plot, don't you think?"

"Certainly." Tori nudges me. "It'll be fun, plus it's the last big bash before semester finals. Everyone's going."

I flick a glance at Sebastian, searching for how he's handling Bryce's invitation, but his face gives nothing away. I know how he feels about these things, but it's tempting to enjoy one last party...

I bite my lip. "I'll think about it."

"Don't think too hard. Just show up." Bryce stands, his gaze lingers on me a moment longer than necessary. "Seven o'clock. Bring swimsuits... or don't." He winks at Tori and saunters away.

I send Tori a look at whatever the hell that was, and the small smile she flashed him.

Sebastian takes a long deliberate drink as his gaze follows Bryce across the cafeteria.

"Wow, was Bryce flirting with you?" Destiny asks me, voice dropping to a conspiratorial whisper.

"He flirts with everyone," Tori says, shaking her head in his direction. "But yeah, he totally was."

"In front of your boyfriend," Jordan adds, eyes darting between me and Sebastian. "That was... bold."

"He wasn't actually interested. He's just being Bryce." I wave a hand in the air.

Sebastian sets his water bottle down with controlled precision, but his fingers drum against his thigh.

"I have no doubts Bryce thinks you're beautiful, but he's aware of the boundaries. That display was for me."

I glance at him, surprised by the casual way he called me beautiful. Does Sebastian really believe that or is this another clinical observation, as simple as admiring a flower or the sunset? We both had our reasons for this arrangement, but I never considered he might actually find me attractive. I duck my head before he can see my face.

"Well, looks like it worked," Tori mumbles.

"So, are you guys coming or what?" Jordan leans forward eagerly. "It'll be fun, and don't worry, Thorne, I can take care of June for you."

"I can look after myself, thanks," I shoot back.

Sebastian leans down, his whisper grazing the side of my neck as he asks, "Are you actually considering this?" He tilts his head, silently asking if this is one of those obligatory fake dating things he's forced to attend.

"June, you should totally go, and you don't have work tonight," Ethan adds, too enthusiastically. His smile sharpens as he catches Sebastian's eye. "Come on, Thorne, you can let her out for one night. Or are you afraid to let your *girlfriend* have some fun without your supervision?"

Sebastian's knee stops bouncing under the table. "June makes her own decisions," he says, deceptively calm, "as you know."

Ethan's smile falters.

"Ethan," Destiny says under her breath, nudging him with her elbow.

"What? Sebastian knows I'm kidding." Ethan holds up his hands in mock innocence.

"So that's a yes?" Jordan asks, looking around the table, either oblivious to the tension or not caring.

Tori shares a worried glance between Ethan and Sebastian. "What do you say, June-bug, one last hurrah for the year? You know you'll have fun, and I can drive."

I'm shaking my head, my knee bouncing when Sebastian says suddenly, "I'll drive." His tone leaves no room for debate. "June will ride with me."

"Always the gentleman," Ethan says lightly, but his attention stays on Sebastian a moment too long. He turns to Destiny with a forced smile, his face shifting to confusion at the annoyed look she gives him.

I dip my head toward Sebastian, keeping my voice low. "You don't have to go if you don't want to."

He doesn't answer right away, watching Ethan whispering something to Destiny, their heads bent close together.

"It's fine." His serious mouth transforms into a slow, feral grin—the kind that appears when he's figured out exactly how to win. "Besides, I've been wanting to see you in that red dress."

I roll my eyes at the blatant performance, even as heat unfurls under my skin. If Sebastian wants to make a show of this, then I can match his energy. He's not the only one with a competitive streak.

I shift closer, letting my hand slide up his knee. "Be careful what you wish for, Thorne."

The challenge settles between us. He stills under my touch, surprise giving way to something darker. Something that says, *try me.*

His hand covers mine. I stop breathing for a second as his thumb traces my knuckles.

"Sebastian," I whisper, not sure what I'm asking.

"June," he murmurs right back.

Tori's laughter rings out at something Jordan says. Ethan and Destiny gather their things. The table has moved on; no one's even watching us anymore.

The bell is the cold water I needed.

We both straighten quickly at the sound of the bell and join the others as we scrap leftovers into the bins, and stack our trays on the way out. As we head down the hall, Sebastian falls into step beside me as we trail behind the others to study hall. There's a deliberate space between us. Our hands sway at our sides, close enough to brush knuckles, but never quite connecting.

His shoulders are set, and when I glance at him, his features have shuttered closed. It's classic Sebastian. One minute he's flirting about red dresses, the next he's retreating into himself when things get too public for his comfort level. I've seen this all before, and understand now when he needs space.

Tori has her arm looped through Destiny's in front of us, heads bent as they whisper. Further ahead, Jordan's voice carries back in cheerful bursts, but he's too far away for me to make out the words. Ethan walks beside him, only half-listening—his attention keeps drifting behind him.

Tori and Destiny eventually break away as they head to the science building.

When we near the library entrance, Sebastian stops me with a hand at my elbow. I half turn, waiting for the usual excuse—*you should go to study hall without me* or *I have a project I need to finish*. We both know he's lying, but we're only fake dating. It's not like it should hurt my feelings.

"June." His voice is low, uncertain. He looks ahead to where Ethan and Jordan have paused outside the library doorway, clearly waiting for us. "I need a minute."

"Oh." The word comes out smaller than I intended. "Sure."

He watches Ethan deliberately linger, now openly staring in our direction. Sebastian exhales sharply, rubbing his forehead. "Will you come with me?"

My chest does this stupid little flutter. *He wants me to come?* "Okay."

He takes my hand, leading me away from the main flow of students around the corner of the library into a small courtyard tucked between the library and administration buildings. A memorial garden donated by the class of 1999 in memory of a student who drowned during their junior year. Most students rush past the bronze plaque without stopping, but this hidden space has become a refuge for those who need solace.

A wooden pergola draped in jasmine vines offers shade over the concrete benches. Glossy leaves twist around the beams, thick with clusters of star-shaped blossoms. Their perfume drifts in the warm air, sweet enough to compete with the scent of mulch and sun-baked concrete. Birds flutter in and out of the green tangle, nests hidden deep inside, where no one can see.

"Is this about Bryce's party?" I ask once he stops. "We don't have to go. I can say we're doing something else—"

"No." The word comes out resigned, almost defeated. "It would look weird if we didn't show now. I'd be the controlling boyfriend, right? Trying to isolate you from having fun with your friends?"

His words sting. "I was trying to help."

"I know." Sebastian sits, dropping his head into his hands. The sun filters through the plants overhead, casting shifting patterns across his shoulders. When he looks up, his guard drops. "It's fine. Besides, we need to look like a convincing couple, and Bryce's party is the perfect stage."

"You don't sound fine."

"I'm not miserable to hang out with *you*, June," he exhales slowly. "It's just... if I can't stand sitting in the cafeteria while everyone either preens for my attention, my father's money, or gossips about me, why would I want to subject myself to a concentrated dose?"

Sebastian isn't like Bryce or Jordan, who thrive on attention. Even as a kid, he'd rather spend hours in his room with his watercolors than at his own birthday parties.

I move to stand directly in front of him. His knees part to allow me to step between them. He tips his head up to meet my eyes, exhaustion lingering as he watches me, shoulders curling inward like he's trying to make himself smaller.

"It's not my usual scene either." I study his face. "Look, it's not fair to you. You've been holding your end, and here I am barely pulling my weight. Is there a family dinner I can attend? Maybe crash a ball? Show everyone that Sebastian Thorne is taken?"

"Everyone is well aware that I'm taken." He rests his hands on my hips, studying me for a long moment. "No, I said I'll go. I know Bryce's type. The way he was looking at you..." He looks away, shaking his head. "I don't trust him. Or Jordan's idea of 'looking after you.'"

"I can handle myself." I fight my smirk.

"I know you can, Pip." He smiles fondly at the nickname. "It shouldn't mean you have to. Besides—" his eyes flick to the path to the library, then back. "I'd rather not give Cole the satisfaction of thinking he chased me off."

I raise an eyebrow. "Since when do you care what Ethan thinks?"

A flash of vulnerability that's gone so quickly I might have imagined it—and for once he doesn't pull away, or shut down. Sebastian's fingers curl in the fabric at my hip. "Since he started acting like he has a claim on you."

My thumb and forefinger find the soft cotton of his collar as I say, "Ethan doesn't have a claim on me. We're just friends."

Sebastian tips his head back, a sound rumbling in his throat. His thumbs trace my hip bones through my clothes, and heat crests through me in waves.

"Eight o'clock tomorrow?" My voice comes out huskier than intended.

"I'll be there." His voice is quieter now, meant only for me.

A group of girls passing nearby slow their steps, obviously trying to catch snippets of whatever is unfolding between Sebastian and his maybe-girlfriend. The pose is quite intimate—me standing between his knees, close enough that I could wrap my arms around his neck or climb into his lap. Part of me wants them to see, to know that Sebastian is mine. *I shouldn't think like that.*

"People are watching," he murmurs, not looking away.

"They're always watching."

Like they'll be watching at Bryce's party. The red dress hanging in my closet will definitely turn some heads, but I want to wear it for Sebastian, not a bunch of our drunken peers.

"I thought your favorite color was Egyptian blue?" I tease, and when he frowns, I clarify, "The red dress?"

His brows lift in sharp understanding, his sun-tanned cheeks flushing. "Ah, yes. The red dress..." The way he says it makes my stomach flip. "You can—of course—wear whatever you want."

I hide my smile, humming under my breath. "Maybe if you're *nice to me*, you'll get to see me in it one day."

His hands tighten on my waist as he exhales. Slow and careful. And I can't help but smile at how, for once, he struggles to maintain his control. I very much like watching him crack.

He gently nudges me back a step as he stands, hands sliding away. The loss is immediate.

"Come on." He says it lightly, but he doesn't look at me right away. "Let's go before Cole arrives on his white horse to drag you back to the library."

He reaches for my hand, and when I don't immediately follow, glances back, a question already etched in his furrowed brows.

"The art room is a lot quieter," I offer.

"It is," he drawls cautiously, like he thinks it's a trap.

"And I've got an unfinished mountain landscape that needs attention." I shrug.

His mouth curves up. "Well, we can't leave a perfectly good mountain unfinished, can we?"

"It's practically a capital offense."

We hover there a minute longer, both waiting for the other to move. The afternoon sun catches his hair, turning it golden at the edges. He's still serious—Sebastian has always had that intensity about him—but there's something softer there now too, something I haven't seen since everything fell apart between us.

Maybe it's time I forgave him. A lot of time has passed. A lot has changed.

Sebastian takes a tentative step toward the art wing, like he's giving me time to change my mind. Instead, I fall into step beside him.

CHAPTER 24

My Fake Boyfriend's Got Game. Pool Game

SEBASTIAN'S CAR GLIDES through the gates of Carrion Island, a macabre name for something so lush and exotic. Native and imported palms line the winding drive like sentries, their fronds lit by hidden landscape lights. The trees continue to frame Bryce's circular driveway, where luxury cars are already parked three deep. A Maserati gleams on the front lawn like someone couldn't be bothered to find a proper parking spot.

Bryce's "bungalow" is also criminally misnamed—the three-story glass-and-concrete masterpiece is five times the size of my house. Every window blazes with light, and music pulses from somewhere inside. People spill onto the multi-level decks that wrap around the house, their laughter carrying across the manicured lawn. Partygoers are already splashing in the pool despite dark clouds gathering offshore.

Sebastian parks and heads around to open my door. He looks effortlessly put-together in a gray slim-fit Gucci shirt, dark Fear of God jeans, white Alexander McQueen sneakers, and a Cartier watch flashing on his wrist. I'm wearing black jean shorts with frayed edges, a jeweled blue wrap halter and my Nike Air Max 1s.

Tori offered to loan me one of her form-fitting designer dresses, but I'm not trying to catch anyone's attention tonight. Just Sebastian's. Strictly for appearances, of course.

"Everyone's watching already." His voice is low, eyes cutting to the second-story balcony.

At Bryce's parties, what you wear matters less than who you arrive with. Walking in on Sebastian's arm makes me feel less like the outsider—even with Bryce's invitation.

"That's the point, right?" I square my shoulders, channeling Tori's confidence. "One big happy couple."

Madison and her friends lean over the balcony railing. She gives Sebastian an appreciative once-over before her gaze lands on me with bland recognition.

"Hey, Sebastian," she says, sugary. "June."

We nod as we continue to the front door, which is ajar. Sebastian's hand settles on the small of my back, steering me forward.

"You might owe me for this one," he murmurs near my ear. "We've been here thirty seconds and I'm ready to flee."

"An hour should be long enough to show everyone—we totally heart each other." I bat my lashes at him.

"June!" Jordan's voice booms through the foyer before I've cleared the threshold. A couple of guys I don't know echo his greeting, their calls bouncing off the walls, competing with the bass coming from the living room.

"Hi," I smile, eyeing his enthusiasm. He sweeps me into a hug before I can dodge him; sweet tobacco clings to his clothes.

"Okay." I push gently at his chest.

Jordan throws his hands up, grinning at Sebastian. "Sorry, man. Not trying to steal your girl."

"June, should I be worried?" Sebastian asks smoothly.

I shake my head. "Sorry, Jordan."

The guys behind Jordon howl and shove his shoulders. He bows theatrically. "Worth a shot, yeah?"

Sebastian's arm slides around my shoulders, steering us toward the living room. "The lady has spoken."

Floor-to-ceiling windows frame the ocean beyond. Palm trees and ornamental fountain grass create a natural border between the house and the shoreline, while the sky clings to deep cobalt blue, reluctant to surrender to night. Dark clouds mass over the water, promising rain.

I can't help comparing them to Sebastian's paintings—how he captures storms with such intensity it feels more authentic than the real thing unfolding in front of me.

The glass wall slides open completely, merging the living space with a multi-tiered deck that wraps around the house. Salt air sweeps through, cool against my skin. We navigate through clusters of people, the music loud enough to feel but not deafening.

Sebastian weaves through the crowd, my hand in his as he heads to the game room, where according to him, everyone congregates.

Sand crunches under my shoes near the back doors, dusting across the limestone. The music is quieter back here, and I'm grateful for it.

I freeze in the doorway, Sebastian bumping into me.

At the pool table, cue in hand and lining up a shot, is Ethan.

Sebastian mutters a curse over my head.

Ethan glances up. Something unreadable crosses his face before he arranges it into a friendly smile, nodding.

Bryce and Cam turn to follow his gaze.

"June! Sebastian!" Bryce straightens from his shot. "Didn't think you'd actually show, Thorne."

"Wouldn't miss it," Sebastian says, voice dry.

Bryce grins, finishing his shot. "Drinks are in the kitchen. Make yourselves at home." His attention linger on me before he adds, "Glad you could make it, June."

"Thanks." I avoid looking at either of them as heat crawls up my neck.

"I wasn't sure if you were coming." Ethan passes his cue to Cam, tone casual, one hand in his pocket. "You seemed unsure when I texted earlier."

The six inches between Sebastian and me feels astronomical.

"Where's Destiny?" My gaze travels around the room.

Ethan's hand goes to his neck. "Yeah. Change of plans. Turns out it was immediate family only."

"Oh." The word comes out flat.

I glance at Sebastian, willing him to look down and read my pleading. *Put your arm around me. Hold my hand. Something, Thorne!*

But an older guy with dark red hair bumps his elbow, pulling his attention.

"Bastian? Thought that was you." Sebastian takes the offered hand, covering it with his own like they're old friends. "Haven't seen you around in years."

"Yeah," Sebastian says, offering no further explanation. "Nate, this is my girlfriend, Juniper. June, this is Nate, Bryce's older brother."

My brows lift and I instinctively glance at Bryce, who's lining up his next shot. They have the same dark red hair and stocky build, but Nate is obviously older, with a light beard dusting his face.

"Girlfriend?" Nate's eyebrows climb as he looks between us. "I heard your mom was trying to set you up. Looks like she finally succeeded."

"Something like that," Sebastian says tightly.

"How's Sophie?" Nate's tone shifts, more careful.

"Good," he says, sizing Nate up. "Home from college. She's applying for placements in New York, maybe even Washington."

Nate rubs his scruff. "That's great. I always knew she'd do amazing things."

"Yes."

"Heard Brandon's back." Nate laughs. "It's surreal seeing everyone here. Even you, Bastian. I thought you'd stopped coming to things like this."

"I came for Juniper."

Someone calls Nate's name from across the room, and he nods before patting Sebastian's shoulder. "It was nice seeing you, Bastian. Tell Sophie I said hi."

After he leaves, Cam drifts closer, red cup in hand. "You know Nate?"

"He dated my sister briefly."

"And never got over her," Bryce adds, rejoining our circle. "Sebastian also used to hang out with us back in the day, before he became a hermit."

"Looks like June got you out of your shell, Thorne." Cam's look is pointed.

Ethan watches this exchange, his smile turning curious. "Well, I was about to win fifty bucks off Cam." He gestures toward the table. "You guys want to play winner?"

"I don't think—" Sebastian starts.

"Come on, Thorne," Ethan's voice sharpens. "Or are you afraid of losing in front of June?"

Sebastian's eyebrows lift. As Ethan returns to the table, Sebastian leans close. "You realize I'll have to spend the next hour pretending I don't want to strangle him?"

I turn, our noses nearly touching. "Think of it as practice for your acting skills," I whisper back.

His gaze is heavy on mine as a slow smile spreads across his face. "Fair enough. But you're buying me ice cream after."

"Deal."

Cam whoops as Ethan sinks his shot. "That's twenty," he says, pulling bills from his pocket.

"Thought you said fifty." Ethan grins.

"Twenty was the bet. Don't try upping it now."

"Fine, fine," Ethan laughs, pocketing the money. He turns to us. "You up, Thorne? I'll even give you a handicap."

"I don't need one." Sebastian's smile shows teeth.

"You sure? When's the last time you played with actual people instead of just yourself?"

Sebastian stills, but his voice comes out amused. "I think I can manage."

"Twenty says you can't," Ethan challenges, holding up Cam's money.

Before Sebastian can respond, I spin my finger. He arches a brow but obeys. I grab his wallet from his back pocket and pull out two twenties. "He'll take that bet," I say, plucking the bill from Ethan's hand. "And we'll double it."

"June," Sebastian says, voice dropping.

"What? I have complete faith in you." I smile up at him, hoping I appear as an adoring girlfriend rather than someone who just made a reckless bet.

I don't even know whether Sebastian can still play pool.

Ethan grins. "Confident, aren't you?"

"Always," I reply, even as my stomach flips.

Sebastian removes his jacket, draping it over a chair. The motion emphasizes his shoulders, the lean muscle beneath his shirt. The way his clothes tease what's underneath is as distracting as when he walks around shirtless at the pool. I force my attention back to the game.

"Ladies first," Ethan says.

"Actually," Sebastian cuts in, "I'll go first." His eyes are sharp, mouth ready for war. "If that's alright with you, June?"

"All yours." I step back to give him room.

Sebastian circles the table with deliberate grace, selecting a cue and testing its weight. He spins it once on the table before lining up his shot.

The crack of the break echoes through the room, followed by the satisfying clack of balls falling into pockets. Sebastian straightens, a smile playing at the corners of his mouth as he surveys the table.

"Lucky break," Ethan says, surprise edging his voice.

"Luck has nothing to do with it," Sebastian replies, lining up his next shot. "Physics. Geometry. Precision." Sebastian sinks another ball with each word, moving around the table with methodical efficiency.

A grin spreads across my face as Ethan's confidence falters. Sebastian's always been detail-oriented to a fault, but watching him apply it to something as ordinary as a game of pool is undeniably attractive.

"Didn't know you were a pool shark, Thorne," Cam says, watching as Sebastian circles the table like a predator.

"I'm full of surprises." Sebastian looks at me as another ball drops.

The heat in his gaze makes my cheeks warm. I don't remember him ever looking at me like that. I dig my nails into my palms, grounding myself before I get too caught up in the game.

By the time Sebastian misses—and I'm not convinced it wasn't intentional—Ethan's face shifts from surprised to wary.

"Your turn," Sebastian says, stepping back.

"Nice to see you're still good at this," I murmur loud enough for everyone to hear.

Ethan lines up his shot but misses, cursing under his breath.

"Looks like we're sixty dollars richer," I say as Sebastian moves past me.

"We?" His shoulder brushes mine. "Are we a 'we' now?"

"Aren't we?"

"Fair enough."

The game continues, drawing a small crowd. Word spreads that Sebastian Thorne is destroying Ethan Cole at pool. Ethan's shoulders tense with each shot Sebastian makes. This isn't about pool anymore—it's about territory, about proving something.

When Sebastian sinks the eight ball, scattered applause breaks out. He straightens, face deliberately neutral as he extends his hand.

"Good game."

Ethan hesitates a fraction before taking it. "Yeah. Good game."

His carefree smile returns as he pulls out another twenty. He holds it out but yanks it back before I can grab it. "Scammed by my own best friend."

"Maybe don't goad my boyfriend next time." I snatch it, pocketing the cash.

"Does anyone else want to challenge the champion?" Cam calls.

"I'll take that bet," a senior from the soccer team steps forward, already selecting a cue.

I move aside, still buzzing from our victory. Sebastian lines up the break, his fingers as skilled with the cue as with a paintbrush.

"He's good." Ethan's voice beside my ear makes me jump.

"Yeah." I can't keep the pride out of my voice. "He is."

Ethan studies me, his face unreadable. "You really like him, don't you?"

The quiet way he asks gives me pause. "Of course. Why else would I be with him?"

"I don't know, June." His voice drops, ensuring only I hear. "Maybe because it keeps people from asking questions about... other things."

My stomach clenches. "What's that supposed to mean?"

Before Ethan can respond, Bryce appears with two cups. "You need drinks," he announces, offering them to us.

Ethan leans forward, mouth turned down. "What is it?"

"Just water," Bryce says, sipping his own. "Despite my famous blowouts, I try to stay sober."

"Try," Ethan mutters skeptically.

Bryce's jaw tightens, but he hands Ethan a cup anyway. "I should've warned you about Sebastian's surgical pool skills, but that was too much fun to watch."

"Yeah, thanks." Ethan takes a long drink, shrugging. "June didn't warn me either."

"Sebastian's good at anything requiring finesse," Bryce says, watching Sebastian sink another shot. "Except women." He smirks at me, ignoring my look. "Tell us, June, has he improved in that department?"

Maybe letting Bryce think he's getting a glimpse into our private life wouldn't hurt. I watch Sebastian destroy his opponent, and it's easy to imagine those large hands on my body, mine exploring the muscles I've glimpsed in the pool.

"Wow." Bryce grins, tapping his cup against mine. "I'll take that look as a yes."

My cheeks catch fire. I glance at Ethan, and his face is almost as red.

Sebastian glances up as if sensing we're discussing him. He misses his next shot, to the clear relief of his opponent, who has yet to take a single turn, and hands his cue to Cam.

Bryce smirks over his cup rim as Sebastian joins us.

"I saw your exhibit at my mom's gallery," Bryce says. "The whole collection is incredible. Love the paintings of marble statues in the dark forest, but those stormy oceans..." Bryce's gaze goes distant. "It does something to me."

"Thanks. Pip helped inspire a few."

Is that how Sebastian sees me? Even now, I'm storming through his carefully ordered life with this fake dating scheme, stirring waters that had been still for years.

"Oh?" I keep my tone light. Despite the tight ache in my chest. "Because that's how I made you feel? Overtaken by chaos or a destructive force of nature?"

"Not exactly." Sebastian tilts his head. "More like... you remind me of the ocean. Always moving, never controlled. Filled with life. Just like you."

The party fades. His eyes lock with mine. "Besides," his voice drops to a rumble, "what's wrong with being completely overtaken?"

"But you painted those months ago..." The realization lands harder than it should.

Or is this all a performance for everyone watching?

Sebastian only nods, but Bryce tips his drink toward me with a grin. "Guess Thorne's been crushing on you for a while, June."

Emma, hovering nearby, perks up. "Really? Funny. I thought you two barely spoke before dating. Especially since June was always so... busy with Ethan."

Before I can respond, Julie—Cam's sister, and until tonight someone I considered a friend—joins in. "Yeah, but I guess not anymore."

I shoot her a sharp glare before I catch something raw in her expression before she turns away. I hadn't realized her crush on Sebastian ran this deep.

"Yeah, June," Emma presses with false innocence. "Is that your secret? Keep bouncing back and forth so you don't have to choose?"

Before I can stammer a response, Jada materializes beside me, arms crossed, glaring at Emma like she might throw her out of Bryce's house.

"Or maybe some people can maintain friendships without turning everything into drama?" She raises an eyebrow.

"There's nothing to pick," Ethan cuts in. His grin empty of warmth. "My friendship with June didn't change when she dated that guy sophomore year. Why would this be different?" He waves a hand dismissively.

Sebastian's arm comes around my waist. I place my hand on his chest in a gesture I hope conveys I don't need him to play jealous boyfriend. This isn't his fight. Emma's defending Destiny the only way she knows how—by stirring up trouble.

Sebastian's hand covers mine, but he doesn't back down. "Right, Ethan's in love with Destiny. But you're wrong about one thing, Cole." His voice is smooth, but there's no mistaking the protective edge. "I'm not some random guy she's dating."

His words—*not some random guy*—send heat racing through me. His thumb slips under my shirt, brushing the bare skin at my waist, searing a path with each stroke and making my knees weak.

"Alright, alright, enough with the romance novel," Bryce laughs, breaking the tension. "Cole, take your shot. Unless you're too distracted?" He waggles his eyebrows.

"I'm not distracted," Ethan says too forcefully.

Sebastian clears his throat, looking at me with an intensity that makes everyone else disappear. I wonder how serious he was about our no-kissing rule.

What am I thinking?

"I need a drink," I announce, louder than necessary.

Sebastian dips his head until his lips nearly touch my ear. "Want me to come with?"

Goosebumps race along my skin. My heart pounds so hard he must feel it. "No, I—" I step back, needing space to breathe. "I'll just be a minute."

CHAPTER 25

Mocktail Confessionals

I NAVIGATE THROUGH THE busy living room into the kitchen. Music still thumps from other rooms, but the kitchen feels less chaotic. A few people mill around the massive center island, where bottles and mixers spread out, but mostly it's grab-your-drink-and-go. Victor plays bartender, theatrical with his pouring as he shows off for Bree and Stacia.

"June!" Victor calls when he spots me. "Want to try my signature drink? It's a no-mocktail cocktail."

"A what?" I laugh. "No alcohol cocktail?"

"No, a no-mocktail cocktail." He grins.

Bree adds, "It's sweet with pineapple and peach soda."

"Perfect for tonight." Victor beams, already pouring me a cup.

I catch the scent of Ethan's cologne and the laundry detergent his mom uses, and I know Ethan's behind me before he speaks.

"Don't drink that." He catches my wrist mid-reach, waving Victor off with his other hand. "We need to talk, June."

How would Destiny feel about Ethan and me talking alone at a party she's absent from? Bass pulses through the walls, mixing with clinking glasses and laughter bursts from the island where Victor still plays bartender.

"Please, June." His hazel eyes plead.

I let Ethan lead me out to the back deck, down to patchy grass sprouting between the flagstone pavers. Storm clouds have thickened, turning the sky into one of Sebastian's paintings. Music and voices drift from open doors behind us, muffled enough to create privacy.

A few people linger by the shore, their voices indistinguishable over the salt-heavy breeze. I wrap my arms around myself, though the chill has nothing to do with the night air, and everything to do with Ethan.

"June, what are you doing?"

"You said you wanted to talk?" I lean against the stair railing, not wanting to get too far from the house, in case onlookers want rumor fuel.

"What are you really doing with Thorne?" His jaw works as he says it.

"We're dating," I clarify cautiously.

He scoffs, the sound incredulous. "You're too careful around each other. I know you, June. You've never been careful about anything. You don't act like you're dating him."

"What do you want? For us to make out on the couch in front of everyone?" I say, irritation pushing through.

Ethan flinches. He shoves both hands through his hair—already a mess—before dropping them heavily. "Is this because of your mom?"

"What?"

"Some publicity thing? The kids of Starlit Jewel in love to promote her new jewelry line?"

Now I'm the one who looks slapped. "You think our moms arranged this? That they forced Sebastian to date me?"

He grimaces. "No, that's not what I meant—but come on, June. Thorne? That guy's a dick. And he's not your type." He steps closer, voice dropping.

"I know you'd rather be in sweats watching bad horror movies than at some fancy party cuddled with that ratty stuffed bat you still sleep with from third grade."

"Sebastian is my type, obviously." Wind pushes hair into my face. I swipe it away. "He does get me."

"You two really connect, huh?" His voice turns sharp. "You hate this stuff." He gestures at Bryce's house, his status. "What are you even doing here?"

I glance at the house, warm light spilling from the windows, our friends visible inside. Ethan comes to these parties, yet judges me for it.

"*You're here.*"

His brows lift, annoyance draining from his face. "That's why you're here? For me?" He stares with a desperate intensity that makes my breath catch.

My eyes dart to the open doors, voices suddenly too close and too far away.

"I didn't mean it like that." I gesture sharply toward the party, carrying on without us. "I meant you also choose to be at these parties."

Ethan's face falls, taking on the same wounded look from when his parents announced their divorce. Despite how increasingly uncomfortable I am with this conversation, it makes my chest ache.

"Yeah, but I have to care, don't I? Play along? But Sebastian doesn't. He gets to decline social obligations and still everyone thinks he's a god."

"You know that's not true. You've seen how people treat him at school. They watch him in the cafeteria, picking apart everything from his clothes to his solitary lunches in the art room." Sure, they envy him—but they also tear him apart.

"But they still want his attention, don't they?" Bitterness edges his voice. "Still crane their necks when he walks by. Everyone here would throw themselves at his feet. I mean, look at you."

My jaw drops, and he blanches. "June, I didn't mean—I'm screwing this up." He drags a hand through his hair, leaving it in dark spikes. "The other week, when you said you needed space, I thought..." He swallows hard. "I thought you were trying to tell me something."

My heart stutters. "Ethan—"

"We've been friends forever. Best friends." His voice cracks. "And lately, I've been thinking maybe..." Something raw and vulnerable breaks through. "And then suddenly you're with him?"

"You *are* my best friend," I whisper. "But don't do this." I push my hands through my hair, stifling a growl. It's all falling apart. "This was supposed to make things easier. You and Destiny were supposed to be happy, and I was supposed to stay out of the way."

"What are you talking about?"

"Nothing. Forget it."

"No, don't do that. Don't shut me out." He puts his hand on the railing behind me, leaning in close enough that I can't look away. "Did Destiny say something? Did she ask you to stay out of the way?"

I shake my head. "No, nothing like that."

"Then what? You think dating Sebastian makes it easier for me?" Something broken threads through his words. "I've been trying to figure out what's been going on with you for weeks, and now you're telling me you orchestrated something to keep Destiny and me a happy couple." He dips his head, chuckling darkly, before lifting it. "June, we haven't been happy in months."

"I can't do this right now." I slide away from the railing. "This isn't what I wanted."

"What did you want?"

I look at the house, at our friends visible through the windows. "I'm with Sebastian."

"Yeah, and I'm with Destiny. Funny how that works out."

The words hang heavy with everything we're not saying. I feel sick. "I need to go."

Resolution enters his posture—the same look he gets when he's not giving up.

"Don't. Whatever you're about to say, don't. Go fix things with Destiny and stay out of my relationship with Sebastian."

He flinches, staring for a moment before his hand clenches into a fist. "Fine, June."

We climb the stairs quickly. Ethan takes a sharp left toward the game room, but I'm not ready to face everyone, or answer questions about why we're returning together. Even though a couple of weeks ago it wouldn't have been a big deal, now everything carries a double meaning.

I head into the living room, letting the makeshift dance club swallow me up. I push through the crowd, which has doubled since we first arrived, and into the kitchen.

Victor's still there, a short brunette perched on the counter beside him.

"Hey, June. Changed your mind about my signature drink?" He grins, poised to pour. "Don't listen to Cole—he just hates pineapple." He nods to the girl. "Tell her, Jen."

She downs the rest of her cup, throat bobbing through several swallows. "Mm," she says, wiping her mouth with the back of her hand. Her eyes are bright, almost glassy. "You should try it."

"Sure." I take the cup from the counter.

The sweet tropical scent hits my nose first, along with the carbonation. It tastes like the pineapple peach kombucha Mom buys. I wouldn't be surprised if Victor is trying to pass it off like he's some superb mixologist.

"Its good. Thanks." I take another deep gulp, handing my cup back for a refill. The sweetness lingers as the fermented drink warms my chest.

"I knew you'd like it, June." Victor grins.

"There you are!" Tori materializes from the other doorway. "I've been looking everywhere."

Something on my face must show because she quickly assesses the group refilling drinks, Victor and his friend, and immediately recognizes we need privacy.

Her timing couldn't be more perfect. I'm still not ready to deal with whatever's gotten into Ethan or the scorching heat racing through my blood every time I look at Sebastian.

"Come on." She drags me into the mostly empty hallway.

A couple sits on the stairs, body language suggesting they're stuck in an argument. They probably won't care about our conversation.

"You look amazing." I tell her. Tori's dressed in an Isabel Marant cotton mini wrap, silver halter and black boots.

She flutters both hands as if that's irrelevant right now. "So how's it really going?" Her eyebrows bounce. "Any more scandalous hugs?"

"No, because I don't want you whooping like I just scored the winning goal."

"It's true, though. Sebastian Thorne is quite a score. I've already heard all about it, and I've only been here twenty minutes." I shake my head. "You look fabulous too, by the way. Very *Juniper.*" Her smile says it's a good thing.

"Thanks, but I don't feel fabulous."

"Thorne?" Her brows furrow with concern.

"No, Ethan." I give her the highlights of our backyard conversation.

"I'm sorry, June-bug. This is getting complicated, isn't it?" I nod, and she chews her lip. "I can't believe him. That's so unfair to her and to you."

Two girls burst from the bathroom down the hall, laughing, before disappearing back into the living room.

"I don't know what to do," I admit. The hallway tilts slightly when I shake my head. "I just wanted everyone to be happy."

She squeezes my shoulder. "I know you did. But you're not responsible for Ethan or Destiny's happiness. They need to figure this out themselves."

"Should I tell Destiny?"

"No," she says quickly. "She'll hate you."

"I feel like I should."

Tori looks skeptical. "Maybe wait until after the fallout from whatever happens between her and Ethan when she finds out he came here without her." She makes a face. "What a dick."

"I know." I rub my temple instead of shaking my head again, since the hallway finally stopped spinning. "Ethan doesn't even believe I'm really dating Sebastian."

Tori gives me a look, and I wave away the obvious.

"You might need to lay it on thicker with Sebastian, especially if he thinks this whole thing is a PR stunt."

I take a long pull of my drink, watching her over the rim of my cup. The drink has gone room temperature because it's much warmer going down. "How am I supposed to do that? You know the rules."

"Fine, you don't have to kiss, but find a private corner to be so obsessed with each other the world fades away."

"Have you been reading Mrs. Waller's novels?"

"Maybe." She grins, unashamed. "But am I wrong?"

My mind drifts back to Sebastian's thumb tracing circles on my skin earlier. Maybe Tori has a point. We promised to make this look real. And I've wondered what it would be like to be closer to him, to have those artist's hands cup my face, to feel those muscles with my bare hands.

The no-kissing rule suddenly seems both crucial and cruel. I blame the heat in my cheeks on the stuffy hallway and Bryce's dad's rigid stance on keeping the A/C at a humid seventy-eight degrees.

"Come on." Tori tugs my arm, breaking through my wandering thoughts. "Let's find your boyfriend before anyone wonders if you're avoiding him."

CHAPTER 26

The Kombucha Made Me Do It

TORI AND I weave back through the crowd, cutting through the kitchen so I can top off my drink with more of Victor's sweet concoction—which has lost its bite now that I'm used to it—and Tori can grab a soda.

"Don't drink too much of that stuff," Tori cautions meaningfully to my cup. "Victor's 'special recipes' are usually stronger than they taste."

"It's nonalcoholic." I take another sip. "A no-mocktail cocktail, whatever that means."

We push back through the crowded living room, and right before we cross into the game room, her steps falter. She grabs my elbow, leaning close.

"Uh-oh," Tori nods toward the far corner. "Look who's here."

I follow her gaze. Destiny walks across the room with Ethan, obviously locked in a tense conversation. She's dressed in a pale green dress that makes her look like a woodland fairy, but there's nothing ethereal about her expression.

"You think Ethan lied about Destiny's family dinner tonight?"

"*Something's* not right," Tori murmurs.

"When do you think she got here?"

Something in my voice stops her mid-shrug. "Oh." Her eyes widen. "You think she saw you and Ethan talking outside?"

The timing would be about right, and from the rigid set of her shoulders as she pulls him through the patio doors, something is definitely wrong.

"Should we check on her?" I ask, guilt churns my stomach.

Tori bites her lip. "Let's… give them a minute before we dive into that mess."

I nod absently, still watching the door they disappeared through. My throat is suddenly too dry, and the room suffocating.

"Come on." She links her arm with mine, leading us to the pool table.

Sebastian has his back to me, engaged in a game with Dante. He lines up the shot, fingers holding the cue so delicately. When he leans over the table, his shirt pulls taut across his shoulders.

The room is even hotter than the hallway. I press my cool cup to my forehead as Tori whispers something about finding Bryce before heading toward a set of caramel-colored couches across the room.

Sebastian's shirt rides up enough to expose a strip of skin on his lower back, and the edge of his black underwear. I run my hand along that patch of skin as I drift by.

He jerks, the cue slipping in his grip and missing the shot. His head snaps around. "June?"

"You're up, Hoffman," someone calls.

Sebastian passes the cue off to a girl with flaming red hair.

"Sorry," I mumble, realizing I cost him the shot.

"It's okay." His voice comes out rough. He searches my face like he's checking for something. "You were gone for a while. Everything all right?"

I wave my hand in the air, the gesture feeling looser than usual. "Everything's fine."

Sebastian's eyes narrow. "Cole followed you out." A statement, not a question.

I swallow the urge to glance where Ethan and Destiny walked out, and instead smirk. "Jealous, Thorne?"

He steps closer, forcing me to tilt my head back to hold his stare. "Maybe I should be." His gaze drops to where my hand now rests on his chest. "Are you sure you're okay?"

"I'm with you, aren't I?" His heartbeat thrums steady and strong under my palm.

Across the room, I catch sight of Destiny and Ethan by the couches. Their body language is tense and restrained, Destiny's laugh forced, Ethan wearing an overly bright smile.

Tori's brows lift at their performance, and when she catches me looking, she gives me a subtle head tilt that says: *Can you believe them?* She subtly waves us over, and when I hesitate, she becomes more obvious about it. Practically jarring Bryce beside her as she bounces, her hand in the air, calling my name.

"I think she wants us to join them," I murmur to Sebastian. He follows my gaze, nodding.

As we make our way over, Jordan and Cam have joined, along with Mia, who Cam's been trying to date for weeks.

There's only a wide armchair left, so I move to squeeze in next to Tori on the couch, but she blocks me, shaking her head with a grin. "I'm sure Sebastian won't mind?"

I offer Sebastian an apologetic look, inclining my head that we should play along. He shifts over the fraction he can to let me slide in next to him. It's a little cramped, and after some adjusting, I'm practically on his lap, his arm warm around my waist.

He smells so good I lean into him to get more of his scent. "What cologne is that?" I ask, surprised at the low, seductive quality of my voice. I press my fingertips to my lips, wondering where that came from.

"Gypsy water," he mumbles automatically.

"So, Thorne," Bryce leans forward, a beer dangling from his fingers, "You going to business school, or did you convince your dad to send you to art school?"

"I don't want to go to art school." Sebastian's deep voice rumbles through his chest where I'm pressed against him.

"Oh?" Cam furrows his brow. "But all your paintings…"

"Are a hobby."

"Well, I wish I had half the talent you have," Bryce says.

Sebastian snorts, the sound surprisingly inelegant for him. "You *do* have half my talent, and I get to hear about it from my father. He's very impressed." The dry way he says it could sound insulting, but Sebastian delivers it with such familiarity that it's clear it's an ongoing joke between them.

The group erupts in laughter, and Sebastian relaxes beneath me. It's easy to forget that he grew up with these people. This easy camaraderie is just as much him as the aloof persona he wears for school.

"Well, I get to hear all about the Renaissance man, Sebastian Thorne, so I guess we're even," Bryce grins. "Though I'm not ready to follow in your footsteps and settle down yet, despite my mother's protests." He nods toward me. "No offense, June, I can completely see what turned our boy around."

I wave a hand airily, no offense taken. When I put it back down, it instinctively rests on Sebastian's chest, against the hard planes of his muscles beneath the soft cotton of his designer shirt.

"Where are you headed after graduation?" Mia asks, flashing a smile at Bryce.

"Harvard, of course. *Papa*, wants nothing less." Bryce grimaces before taking a sip. It seems he, too, is feeling the parental pressure.

"You're heading to H as well, right, Cole?" Bryce asks, directing the conversation to Ethan.

"That's the plan," Ethan responds.

Since when? I frown, turning sharply at Ethan, making the room spin. Ethan wants to go to Duke and play soccer. He even had a scout talk to him about a full scholarship. The Ethan I know would never give that up. Harvard doesn't even give scholarships. Has his plan changed while I've been caught up in this charade with Sebastian?

"We're thinking of going together," Destiny chimes in, her voice a touch too enthusiastic. "I can study psychology while Ethan does pre-law."

"Pre-law?" The words slip out before I can stop them. "But what about marketing and your soccer scholarship?"

Ethan's shoulders tense as surprise, regret, and something almost defensive wash over his features, before finally settling on the last one. "I can play soccer there, June."

Destiny's smile tightens. "We're making plans for our future together." There's an emphasis on *together* that feels pointed.

"That's great," I say, but it's hollow.

The conversation drifts around me, voices blending together as I take another sip of my drink. My attention drifts across the room, landing on a girl walking past wearing what looks like—

Sebastian follows my line of sight. He inclines his head with a questioning look.

"She's wearing one of Mom's pieces," I explain, my hand still resting on his chest. "The silver leaf circlet. It's from last year's collection."

His features soften. "Last year's gala, you were working backstage."

"You saw," I say, not really a question.

He nods slowly. "You were wearing a navy dress with thin straps, and your hair was braided."

I nod slowly, my fingers tracing the edge of his shirt, wandering to the warm skin beneath. "You were escorting Kiki Anderson that year."

"You saw," he echoes, his voice rough.

The party fades around us, the conversation now background noise. His free hand comes up to brush a strand of hair from my face, and I wonder if he even realizes he's done it.

My fingers find the edge of his shirt, wandering to his bare skin. "Did you really hang bats in your little play cave because of me?" I ask, unbidden.

He shifts beneath me, the muscles in his thighs tightening. I wrap my arm around him tighter, my body molding to his. His cologne fills my senses—that mix of citrus and spice that's uniquely him.

"Yes," he admits. "You loved bats."

"I still have the stuffed bat you gave me," I tell him. "Do you remember that?"

He nods. "I remember a lot of things," he murmurs, his gaze sliding away from mine briefly.

My hand slides up his neck, plays with his soft hair. My finger traces the shape of his mouth, fascinated by how soft his lips are. Sebastian catches my wandering hand in his, his grip gentle but firm.

"Pip," his voice is a low warning. It reminds me of how he was always trying to protect me and keep me from getting hurt.

My attention drops to his mouth, the soft curve of his bottom lip. "You know there are plenty of things we can do besides kissing," I hear myself say.

Sebastian tenses beneath my touch. He studies my face, before he leans in so close I think he might break his own rule. His breath hitches, and I close my eyes…

"Juniper, have you been drinking?" He asks in a low, disapproving rumble.

"No, of course not," I frown. My features feel like putty.

He gives me a disbelieving tilt of his head, his mouth tightening. He shifts, leaning over to grab my drink, taking a sip.

His face goes hard. "This is spiked."

"No, it's not. It's a mock-fail… no-tail." I try again. "No-alcohol tail-mot-something?" I wave a hand airily. "I don't know what Victor calls it."

He groans, "Victor's signature drink is hard kombucha." *Well, at least I got that right.* "Meaning it has liquor in it."

His words finally connect in my very slow to connect brain. I gasp, putting a hand over my mouth. "Sebastian, I don't drink."

"I know you don't."

"My mom," I gasp again. I try to get up when his hand comes firmly around my hips to hold me in place. "Sebastian, what about my dad? What are they going to say when I come home intoxibrated?"

"Intoxicated."

"Mmhm," I nod. "That's what I said."

"I'm going to kill Victor," he growls through his teeth.

I pull his face to mine. "Don't Bash. I don't want anyone to know."

He flicks a glance at our little group, his brows pulled down. I push my finger against the V on his forehead. "Grumpy-kins, just like when you were a kid. Except now you're so tall, and you have so many muscles." I grab his bicep, feeling the bulk. "You must work out *a lot*."

"June, I need you to drink some water." He grabs his bottle next to my discarded cup, unscrewing the lid and handing it to me. He doesn't let go until I've set it on my lips. "Slowly," he instructs.

"You two are getting awfully cozy over there," Tori calls out playfully, but then I catch her double take. I see the moment she realizes something's wrong. "Um, actually, maybe it's time to call it a night."

"Seriously, like, get a room," Jordan coughs out a laugh, but when he glances at Ethan, he sobers up.

"They make a cute couple, don't they?" Destiny says, her voice carrying across the group with brittle cheerfulness. She looks between Sebastian and me before focusing pointedly on Ethan.

Ethan takes a long drink before answering. "Adorable," he mutters, head turned away from me.

"Who knew Thorne could be so sweet?" Mia says, nudging Cam.

"I'm still not convinced," Ethan says under his breath, wincing when he realizes he's spoken loud enough for everyone to hear.

Sebastian's jaw tightens, the muscle there jumping visibly. He stares Ethan down across the circle.

"Shh," I tell Sebastian, my voice a conspiratorial whisper. "Don't be mad at him, Bashy. He's just in love with me."

I squish Sebastian's mouth with my fingers, as it's turned into another frown.

The room goes silent. Someone coughs awkwardly. I glance around, confused by the sudden tension, until my fuzzy gaze lands on Destiny. Her face has gone pale, her blue eyes wide as she stares.

Then she studies me more carefully. "June, are you drunk?"

"No," I protest, but it comes out whiny.

But then Sebastian rats me out. "Victor's Hard Kombucha," he says dryly.

"I told her not to drink that," Ethan says with a flat smile. "Good job looking out for your girl, Thorne."

Sebastian goes rigid beneath me, turning to stone. The tension builds in his muscles right before he stands, bringing me with him, with a firm grip under my thighs. He sets me down smoothly, keeping his arm around my waist to steady me.

Ethan rises to his feet quickly, shifting from smugness to alarm at the look on Sebastian's face. "Whoa, I tried to warn her—" he holds up his hands defensively. "I figured she'd picked something else. June's a big girl."

"Boys," Tori interrupts sharply, stepping between them. "Maybe focus on June instead of your pissing contest?"

"June's mom is going to flip," Destiny says.

"Guest rooms upstairs if you need it," Bryce offers. "Keep the puke in the bathroom."

"You smell like Christmas trees and pineapple cake," I whisper-tell Sebastian, my hand wandering up to touch his soft hair.

"I need to get her home." Sebastian's voice is clipped. His arm tightens around my waist as I sway.

The word "home" cuts through the haze coating my brain like ice water. I grip Sebastian's shirt, panic flaring in my chest.

"No, no, no. My mom will know I've been... drunking." I frown, frustrated with my tongue. I try again. "Drinking?"

"You can't take her home like this," Destiny says, her voice surprisingly gentle. "Mrs. Blake will ground her until she leaves for college."

"Take me to your house," I tell Sebastian, still gripping his shirt. "You can build me a blanket fort, and we can talk about dinosaurs."

Sebastian's eyebrows lift, and something close to affection crosses his face before he wipes it away. "That's not a good idea, Pip."

"My house," Tori suggests, already gathering her things. "My parents are in Miami for the weekend. She can sleep it off there."

"Perfect." Sebastian swoops me up into his arms, carrying me across the room out the door, but I'm focused on the way the lights catch in his hair, making it look like spun gold.

"Your hair is pretty," I tell him seriously, reaching up to touch it. "Like wheat fields in the sun. Did you know I used to watch you paint during your art class? I had biology across the courtyard. You get this little wrinkle right here." I poke between his eyebrows again.

"Juniper." He catches my wandering hand, but his voice is a gentle rumble. "I'm going to need you to keep your hands to yourself for a few minutes, okay?"

"Okay," I agree easily.

He carries me through the house, past mostly amused faces, like girls being carried from Bryce's house is normal. Maybe it is. A girl waves at me as I pass, and I wave back.

The night air is cool against my clammy skin as we exit the front door. It's lightly drizzling. Drops of fine mist kiss my skin, and collect in my hair as we continue to his car.

Sebastian carefully sets me down by the car, making sure I'm leaning against it before he digs his keys out. The ground is soft under my sneakers; the grass slippery from the rain. I take a deep inhale of salty air and tip my face up to the soft rain to cool my warm cheeks.

Thunder rumbles in the distance as Sebastian opens the passenger door and helps me inside. I'm fumbling with the seat belt before he gently nudges my hands away to buckle it.

"I texted you my address," Tori says, voice nearby.

"Tori," I call, and when she appears beside the door I say, "Victoria, I'm sorry you have to leave so soon."

"It's okay, June-bug. It's been a very entertaining night. I can't wait to tell you about it tomorrow." She squeezes my hand through the open door, a mix of amusement and concern. "Get some water in her," she adds quietly to Sebastian before carefully closing the door.

Sebastian and Tori exchange a quick conversation, and then he is sliding behind the wheel. I rest my head back against the headrest, as the wealthy homes of Carrion Island blur past, letting the cool, salty air blow over my face, hoping it will cool the burning sensation and clear the nausea that has suddenly bubbled up from Victor's special drinks.

THE CAR IDLES OUTSIDE TORI'S two-story ranch-style house, its recently landscaped yard barely visible in the dim porch light. But you can still smell the fresh mulch through the open windows.

Sebastian takes my phone when I fumble with it, tapping the screen until Tori's voice message plays—she's making a hangover supply run.

"I can't believe this happened." I press my forehead against the seat."How was I supposed to know the drink's name was a joke?"

"I know." His voice is gentle, not like when he was talking to Ethan.

"Are you mad at me?"

"No, Juniper." He glances over. "I have no reason to be mad at you."

"This time," I mumble. I study his profile lit by the streetlights. "What about when I rebuilt your Lego castle?"

"No."

"What about when I took your tiger's eye stone?" I ask, "Oh, by the way, I borrowed it."

"Stole." His mouth curves. "You *stole* my tiger's eye. And no. I knew you wanted it but wouldn't ask, so I left it under some papers, so you'd think I wouldn't notice."

"You set me up." I smile, lost in the memory.

Sebastian goes quiet. I've said too much, maybe revealed how much I remember of the past.

"How's your stomach?" he asks.

"Floaty. Like the roller-coasters at Busch Gardens."

He reaches behind his seat and produces a water bottle. "You should drink more water."

I take it, cradling it between both hands. "This isn't what I expected at all."

"No?"

"No." My head drops back against the seat. "I thought pretending to date you would be harder."

He turns to face me fully taking on a calm intensity. The dashboard light carves shadows across his cheekbones, and suddenly I'm eight years old again, confessing all my secrets, while he wordlessly organized the chaos wrought, never once complaining.

"And sometimes, like tonight…" I pick at the bottle label. "It's almost…"

"Like what?" He shifts closer.

I open my mouth. The truth hovers there, dangerous and honest and absolutely ready to destroy everything.

Headlights sweep across us as Tori's car pulls into the driveway, the harsh glare saving me from regrets when I'm sober.

"We don't have to talk about it tonight," he whispers.

Tori opens my door carefully, plastic bag swinging from her arm. "Any vomit?"

"No." I fumble with my seatbelt, actually get it unlocked this time.

"Good. Maybe we can skip that rite of passage." She shoots Sebastian a grateful look. "Thanks for taking care of her."

"I'll walk you in." He's already out, coming around to my side. Rain begins to fall in earnest. First, as light splattering as we follow Tori to her front door, then heavy drops hammering the roof and ground.

Sebastian keeps his hand at my waist, steady, as if he's prepared to catch me.

Tori pushes the door open and grabs my hand. "Thanks for all your help, Thorne."

He nods, sliding his hands into his pockets. "Text me when you wake up." His eyes haven't left my face. "I want to know you're okay."

"I will."

Tori clears her throat. "I've got her from here."

Sebastian steps back. Rain darkens his gray shirt in patches. "Goodnight, June." Then, almost as an afterthought: "Tori."

I watch him jog to his car, rain soaking his clothes. I can't stop looking until Tori gently tugs me inside.

"Come on, drunk girl." She closes the door. "Let's get you to bed, so you can have sweet dreams about your boyfriend."

The warm house hits me, and I realize how cold I'd gotten. I wrap my arms around myself as Tori leads me to her bedroom. The evening spins in my head. Ethan's strange behavior, Sebastian's hushed confessions, and how much I really enjoyed playing the part of his girlfriend.

CHAPTER 27

Today's Forecast: Regret, With a 90% Chance of Ethan

I WAKE TO TORI humming along to music. My head feels stuffed with cotton, muscles tense like I've run a marathon. Sunlight streams through her gauzy curtains, way too bright for whatever time it is.

"Morning, lightweight," Tori's voice comes from above. When I crack open one eye, she's perched on the bed, way too amused, and holding a bottle of water and ibuprofen. She gives it a shake.

My brain rattles with the sound.

"Remind me to kill Victor." I groan, pushing myself up against her headboard. The room takes a moment to settle, and I wince.

"It looked like Sebastian was going to last night."

"What did he say?"

"He didn't have to *say* anything. You could see it in his face. That boy knows how to give a death glare."

I press my fingers to my temples, not wanting to think too hard about why that information makes my chest feel warm.

"I should have known something was off when you started feeling up Sebastian's biceps and calling him 'Grumpy-kins.'" She grins. "Which, by the way, was absolutely adorable."

Fragments of memories float back. Sebastian's cologne. My fingers in his hair. *Oh no.* "Please tell me I didn't—"

"Ask him to break the no-kissing rule? While practically in his lap?" Tori's green eyes sparkle. "You sure did. And let me tell you, the look on Ethan's face..."

"Ethan?" More memories surface—our disastrous conversation in the backyard.

"Yeah, that was... interesting." Tori's voice turns thoughtful. "For someone who claims to be *just friends*, he looked ready to murder Sebastian every time you touched him. Which was often." She pauses. "Very often."

I pull the covers over my head with a groan. "I was following your advice about making it look real!"

"Oh, it looked real alright. For both of you. I've never seen Sebastian Thorne look at anyone the way he was looking at you."

The memory hits me with startling clarity—his gentle touch as he brushed hair from my face, the way his voice softened when he called me Pip. "He was playing along," I mumble into the blanket.

"Was he though?" Tori pulls the cover down so I'll look at her. "Because the way he took care of you after... Ethan couldn't even be bothered to warn you properly about the drink, but Sebastian wouldn't let you out of his sight once he realized."

I close my eyes, not wanting to examine why that comparison stings. "He was being nice."

"Nice?" Tori snorts. "Sebastian Thorne doesn't do *nice*."

Before I can argue, my phone buzzes on the nightstand. The small vibration grates on my overly sensitive nerves. I reach for it with deliberate care.

THE NO-KISSING CONTRACT

> **SEBASTIAN:** How are you feeling?

My pulse quickens. Even through text, he manages to affect me. I stare at the message until Tori leans over my shoulder.

"Ooh, the boyfriend's checking on you."

I unlock my phone, trying to think of a response that doesn't scream *'mortified about everything I did last night.'*

> **ME:** Alive. Barely.

His response comes quickly.

> **SEBASTIAN:** That bad?

> **ME:** Mostly embarrassed. Sorry about... everything.

> **SEBASTIAN:** Don't be.

Clipped, short. Classic Sebastian. He's probably checking the fake-boyfriend obligation box. *Don't be.* I'm about to toss my phone when another message comes through.

> **SEBASTIAN:** But we should probably talk. You still at Tori's?

> **ME:** Yes

> **SEBASTIAN:** Perfect. I'm bringing lunch. 20 minutes ok?

Through the screen, I can't tell what he's feeling. Angry? Amused or something worse—disappointed. What does he want to talk about? The way I climbed him like a jungle gym? Or maybe he's finally realized this whole relationship is more trouble than it's worth.

"You look like you're about to throw up," Tori observes.

"He wants to come over." I shove my phone at her. "To talk."

She reads the exchange, a slow grin spreading across her face. "Tell him yes."

"But—"

"June." She gives me a look, sliding my phone in front of me. "The boy is bringing you food. Let him."

I make an undignified whimper.

"Besides, do you really want to spend all weekend overthinking? And what if your moms see pictures from last night? You two need to coordinate."

I groan, dropping my head against the headboard. Bryce's parties usually end up plastered all over social media—either for the absolute shenanigans or for the bragging rights. Sometimes both. Mrs. Thorne might not be checking up on Sebastian, but Sophie would definitely know. Would she tell her mom?

Or if anyone tagged the boutique in a post. Mom might trace it back. Emma is one of Starlit's biggest customers, and she might do it out of spite.

I scowl, knowing Tori's right.

> **ME:** Ok.

> **SEBASTIAN:** See you soon.

"There." Tori looks satisfied.

"What am I supposed to say? Sorry I made you come to a party with people you've been avoiding for years. Sorry I dragged you into my drama with Ethan, who might secretly be in love with me. Oh, and sorry I groped you all night?"

Tori grimaces, but says, "I'm pretty sure one of those he's okay with." At my look, she laughs, "Now you have eighteen minutes to fix your makeup—I don't think you want Sebastian to see your adorable raccoon eyes."

TWENTY MINUTES LATER, I'M SITTING cross-legged on Tori's couch in her Taylor Swift concert tee, and a gold belt cinched around my waist, my hair wrangled into a messy braid.

"Stop fidgeting," Tori says. "You're making *me* nervous."

"I'm not fidgeting."

I am absolutely fidgeting.

I can't stop picking at my nails while memories from last night flit through my thoughts. Each remembered moment makes me cringe harder.

The doorbell rings.

"Showtime," Tori says, pulling open the door.

Sebastian stands in the doorway holding a takeout bag from Charlie's Cafe that smells amazing and a drink carrier from Healthy Sprouts with what looks like green smoothies. He's in dark jeans and a plain black t-shirt, his hair damp.

"Late lunch for the party girl," he says, holding up the bag, ignoring my glare. "I figured you'd need to sleep in after last night."

"Hilarious," I tell him, snatching the bags, and setting them on the coffee table.

"...and detox smoothies for the hangover," he adds with a grin, sitting them down.

"My hero," Tori declares, taking one of the paper-wrapped sandwiches from the bag. She grabs her purse and keys. "And that's my cue. I need to run some errands. You two crazy kids behave."

"Tori—" I protest, but she's already heading for the door.

She takes a long sip of the smoothie as she walks. "Mmm, so good," she calls over her shoulder. Then the door clicks shut behind her, leaving us alone.

Sebastian sits on the couch, pulling out a sandwich and fries, ignoring how Tori conveniently made herself scarce. I sit down carefully, leaving an appropriate amount of space between us.

"About last night," I start, picking at the wrapper of my sandwich.

"You don't need to apologize." He passes me my smoothie.

I take a sip—it's good, sweet like watermelon candy, and not overwhelmingly tart. "Thank you for coming last night. I know you hate those things."

Sebastian's silent for a moment while he chews. "I don't hate them *exactly*." He grabs his drink, taking a quick sip. "I went to plenty back in the day."

Even though Bryce had hinted as much, it still surprises me. I've kept a peripheral awareness of Sebastian Thorne all these years, but I must have missed that side of him.

"Why did you stop?" I ask softly.

He considers this, swirling his drink. "I was tired of the expectations," he finally says. "The constant performance. The way everyone watches you, waiting for you to slip up or show weakness." His voice takes on an edge I've never heard before. "It's exhausting, having to be what everyone wants you to be."

I study my smoothie intently. "And now I'm making you do exactly that."

"No, you're not." He shifts on the couch to face me. "Last night wasn't... It didn't feel like performing with you."

My heart stutters. "What did it feel like then?"

He runs his thumb along the edge of his cup, disturbing the condensation. When he speaks, his voice is low, almost vulnerable. "Like back when we'd spend hours in my backyard and I didn't have to think about..." He waves a hand through the air. That one airy gesture encompassing not only Tori's parents' beach house, but everything that separates us. "...all of this."

I remember too—how simple it was then, before I learned some gaps can't be bridged by childhood friendship alone.

I take a breath and force myself to address what happened at the party. I've never had to apologize for coming on to someone before.

"I should apologize for coming on to you." He has stopped chewing. My fingers pull at the hem of my shirt, my burger and fries forgotten. "For trying to break your no-kissing rule—"

"Stop." He sets his sandwich down. "You don't need to apologize."

"But—"

"I liked it." The words come out rushed, almost angry. "I more than liked it, and I'm disgusted with myself." He breaks off, looking miserable.

"Oh." My stomach drops. Of course he's disgusted.

The words twist in my chest, stirring up memories of my last day as Sebastian Thorn's friend. I'm back in their kitchen hiding behind the counter, waiting to pop out and yell "boo", but what I overheard made me leave and never come back.

"I'd never like someone like her," he'd told Sophie, and those words had carved themselves into my heart, defining how I saw myself for years. Messy. Loud. Unrefined. Not enough.

I set the burger down and wrap my arms around myself. All these years later, and I'm still that insecure girl, waiting to be rejected. "Right."

He sweeps over my face, and then he groans, "Not like that, June." He forcefully pushes a hand through his hair. "I'm disgusted with *myself*," he repeats, and it doesn't feel good the second time either, "because you were drunk, and I should have stopped it sooner."

"Because sober-me would never..." I wave my hand between us, mimicking his earlier gesture. *Kiss you?* The unspoken words taste bitter.

He opens his mouth, then closes it. "Right." The familiar crease forms between his brows, but I don't need him to explain anymore.

"Well," I say, forcing brightness into my voice as I reach for my sandwich. "Glad we cleared that up."

He watches me as I chew, but I don't look over.

"Good news. I think my drunken groping was enough to convince everyone we're a couple. And you sweeping in like a white knight sold it nicely too. We can ride that high until the gala."

He sets his sandwich down. "I wasn't performing."

"I know. You would have done the same for me, Avery, or any other girl who needed help. That's just who you are."

Underneath all the scowling and long-suffering sighs is a heart of gold.

Though I don't know why it's making me so angry.

The look he gives is complicated. But whatever he's about to say is cut off by my phone buzzing.

Ethan's name flashes on the screen. Both Sebastian and I stare at it. The buzz seems louder in the awkward silence. Part of me wants to let it go to voicemail—I'm not ready to deal with Ethan after last night—but the alternative is sitting here with Sebastian with this horrible hole in my chest.

A knot forms in my stomach. I'm caught between them again—Ethan, who thinks he has feelings for me as soon as I'm taken, and Sebastian, who clearly sees his reactions as nothing more than biology.

The phone continues to buzz as I stare at it.

"I should get that," I say, reaching for it.

Sebastian's jaw tightens, but he doesn't move from the couch.

"Hey," I answer, trying to sound normal.

"June." Ethan's voice comes through tinny and hesitant. "I'm glad you answered. I was worried you'd never want to talk to me again." The pain in his voice makes my chest tight—this is Ethan, my best friend, sounding lost and broken.

The weight of Sebastian's attention makes me fidgety, so I push to my feet, needing distance. I wander over to the breakfast bar with a clear view of the ocean.

"What is it you wanted?"

"Right," he laughs nervously. "Can we meet? Please?"

I shut my eyes. Of course, he wants to meet. Because apparently today is designated Most Uncomfortable Conversations with Juniper Day.

"Um, nows not a great time..."

"Please, June. I can be at your house in twenty minutes?"

I glance behind me at Sebastian on the couch, who's carefully studying the contents of his drink. "I'm still at Tori's," I say, watching the muscle in his jaw jump.

"Okay. I can head over..."

"No," I say quickly, and then I hear myself say, "How about you meet me at my house in an hour?"

Why not? What's one more mortifying conversation to add to my day?

"Great, I'll see you—" I end the call before Ethan can finish.

Sebastian gathers up the wrappers and uneaten food. "So, you're meeting Ethan," he says, his voice carefully neutral as he stands.

When I nod, he says, "I'll drive you home."

I fidget with my phone, not quite meeting his eyes. "You don't have to. I can get Tori to—"

"June." He says my name with a stubborn finality that means arguing is pointless. "Let me drive you."

The car ride threatens to be excruciating—fifteen minutes trapped with the weight of our unfinished conversation and Ethan's impending visit hanging between us. But as soon as were buckled he turns on the radio.

For some reason it's worse.

We're almost at my house when Sebastian finally breaks the silence. "About what I said before—"

"It's fine," I cut him off. Another rejection right now would shatter me, especially with whatever Ethan has to say waiting. "Really. We're good."

He frowns at the road ahead, his hands flexing on the steering wheel. "I think I should explain—"

He stops when he sees Ethan's car parked in front of my house.

He's early. I mumble a curse as Sebastian pulls up to the curb.

"Thanks for lunch," I say, reaching for the door handle. "And for... everything." Before I open it, the question spills out. "We're still going to the gala together, right?"

His grip on the steering wheel loosens. "Of course. Unless you've changed your mind."

"No, I want to." The words rush out, too eager. I clear my throat. "I mean, the deal still stands, right?"

"Right." His voice is flat. "The deal."

I'm closing the door when his hand shoots out, stopping it. "Call me later?"

I blink, surprised, until he says, "So we can figure out our schedules for the week."

Right. Our compromise on how much time is acceptable to convince everyone we're a couple. I nod, not trusting myself to speak.

As I walk toward my house, I hear Sebastian's car idle for a moment before pulling away.

I don't look back to watch him go.

CHAPTER 28

How to Lose Your Best Friend in One Confession

ETHAN SITS IN one of Mom's thrifted wicker chairs when I step onto the porch, chin resting on his hands, wearing the Duke sweatshirt I got him last Christmas. In a couple of weeks, it'll be too warm for sweaters.

He's waited on these steps hundreds of times and spent many summer afternoons sprawled across my front yard, planning adventures or complaining about homework. Now, the sight of him here feels unfamiliar.

"Hey." He stands, stuffing his hands into his pockets. He nods toward the road. "I thought you were at Tori's?"

I turn as if expecting to see Sebastian's car still idling there. "Oh, I was. Bash brought us lunch."

"Bash." He repeats the nickname softly, incredulous, furrowing his brows.

"Do you want to come in?" I'm already fishing out my keys and setting them to the lock.

"Yeah."

The door opens on the second try, and I mutter an apology.

"You don't have to apologize for the door. I know it sticks." A sad smile pulls at his lips.

Dishes clinking and running water drift from the kitchen, along with my parents' murmured voices.

A cabinet door closes, and my mom calls out, "June? Is that you?"

"Yeah, Ethan's here too," I answer, already angling toward my room.

Usually, he'd call out a greeting, maybe wander into the kitchen to charm my mom. Today, he follows silently. It feels like I'm sneaking him in, like there's something between us I need to hide.

"Oh, Ethan!" Mom appears in the kitchen doorway, drying her hands on a dish towel. "We just finished lunch if you're hungry. There's still some—"

"We're good, Mom." I take a step toward the hallway and wave at Ethan to follow. "We'll be in my room."

"Ethan!" Dad brightens, appearing beside Mom with a stack of dishes. "We haven't seen you in weeks. How's Brandon settling back in?"

"Good, good." Ethan shifts automatically, moving to help Dad like he's done a thousand times. "He's looking at job opportunities downtown."

I sigh, following them into the kitchen. I should have known we couldn't sneak past.

"And how's Tori?" Mom asks, looking between us. "Did Ethan pick you up at her house?"

"Uh, no, Sebastian did. He brought us lunch and then drove me here."

"Oh." Mom exchanges a look with Dad that I pretend not to see.

"He didn't want to come in?" Mom's watching me with that look she gets when she's trying to figure something out.

My mind scrambles for a believable explanation that won't make this more awkward. My temples throb just thinking about how to explain this weird quadrangle we got ourselves into.

"It's my fault, Mrs. B," Ethan cuts in smoothly. "I texted June about helping me with my college application essay. The deadline's coming up and, well…" He shrugs sheepishly. "You know how I am with words."

Relief floods through me. Trust Ethan to come up with the perfect excuse. When they turn around, I give him a grateful squeeze on his arm.

"Uh-huh," Mom murmurs, turning to add another cup to the cupboard.

"We should probably get started." I'm already edging toward the hallway, grabbing Ethan's sweatshirt and pulling him with me. "These essays won't write themselves."

"Leave the door open," Dad calls after us.

I freeze mid-step. Beside me, Ethan stops too.

Dad's said those exact words a thousand times before. I'd always roll my eyes, make some quip about how Ethan was basically my brother. Ethan would laugh it off, promising to behave himself with exaggerated seriousness.

"Got it, Mr. B," Ethan says, but his voice comes out higher than normal, and his face has gone blotchy.

I spin away toward the hallway before anyone can see my burning face. Ethan follows behind me a heartbeat later, leaving a space between us that's never been there before.

MY ROOM IS EXACTLY AS I left it yesterday. Discarded outfits tossed onto the bed, the closet door hanging open, fairy lights creating pools of soft light in the growing dusk. Everything feels different. The Juniper who was here yesterday isn't the same one walking in now.

Ethan gravitates to my papasan chair like always, then stops halfway, like he's not sure of his place anymore. He ends up perching on the edge of my desk instead. That small change makes everything feel worse.

His gaze wanders to the collage of our shared memories on the wall—Ethan and me skim boarding, us at homecoming with Tori and Jordan, the stupid faces we made in the mall photo booth last summer. They tell a different story now.

The sound of Mom loading the dishwasher drifts from down the hall. I wrap my arms around myself, fighting the urge to close the door, to shut out the real world until we can fix whatever this is. Maybe sometimes growing up means growing apart, even when you don't want to.

"June—" he starts, as I say, "Ethan—"

We both stop. There's something there that I recognize—the same look he gets before every difficult truth he's ever had to tell me. And I know exactly why he's here, and I'm not ready for it.

"Before you say anything..." I start, but he's already shaking his head.

"June, I'm sorry." His voice is rougher than usual. He runs both hands through his hair, leaving it disheveled. "About last night. I shouldn't have—" He breaks off, looking anywhere but at me. "I was out of line."

"It's okay," I whisper, sinking onto the edge of my bed. My hands twist in my lap. "Last night was... Everyone was a little..."

"I wasn't that drunk when we talked." He meets my stare directly, his mouth caught between a smirk and a grimace. "But you were, when you were all over Thorne."

We've waded into alligator-filled waters now.

"Please—let's not go there."

"Just... let me say this." He leans forward, elbows on his knees. "Last night, seeing you with him—" His eyes close briefly like it physically hurts. "The way he touched you, the way you looked at him..."

Jealousy threads through his words, sharp and painful.

"Ethan, you shouldn't even be thinking—whatever you're thinking," I snap. "That's not fair to Destiny."

His face crumples. "I know. Don't you think I know that?" He stands, pacing to the window. He breathes out a long exhale coming from somewhere deep in his soul. "We broke up."

My stomach drops. "You broke up."

He nods miserably. "She said she deserved someone who wasn't thinking about another girl. Said she didn't want to be anyone's consolation prize." His voice cracks. "She was right."

"Ethan..." I start, but he's already talking, words spilling out like he's been holding them back for too long.

"She asked me point-blank if I had feelings for you, and I couldn't... I couldn't lie to her anymore. I can't keep pretending. It's not fair to anyone." His voice is rough. "I can't be around you and act like I don't feel this way anymore."

"You told me you loved her," I say, barely above a whisper.

"I did. I do." He holds my gaze. "But not... not like this. Not like what I feel for you."

"Why are you telling me this now? Why date Destiny? Why put her through—"

"Because—" He scrubs a hand down his face. "You've never looked at me the way you look at Thorne." He's quiet for a long moment, staring at his hands. "And I didn't want to lose your friendship. I thought… I thought I could get over it."

He sinks back into the chair. The fairy lights cast soft shadows across his face, making him look younger somehow. Like the boy who held my hand at my grandpa's funeral. Who taught me to surf even though I was a terrible pupil.

My chest aches for them both—Destiny, who did nothing wrong but loved a boy whose heart was elsewhere, and Ethan, who's been lying to himself as much as everyone else.

"I really did care about Destiny. I *do* care about her. But she was right—I've been lying to myself, thinking these feelings would go away if I just tried harder with her, but—"

"Stop." The word comes out strangled, as I stand. "You don't get to do this. You don't get to come here and—"

The words catch in my throat because seeing him like this, vulnerable and broken, is almost too much. But underneath is the realization that—

"This is my fault." My voice cracks. "I'm the reason you broke up. I'm the reason she—"

"No." He moves like he's going to comfort me, then stops when he sees my face. His hand drops. "This is on me. All of it."

I sink onto the edge of my bed, my hands twisting in my lap. "Gosh, Ethan, this is so messed up."

"I know it is," he says quietly.

"Then why are you here?" I ask, sharper than intended. "What am I supposed to do with this?"

"It's killing me, June. Watching you with *him*—"

"This isn't about Sebastian."

"Isn't it?" His face twists between hurt and frustration. "A month ago you couldn't stand him. And now you're what—in love?"

"It's complicated."

"Complicated how?" He leans forward. "Explain that to me, Juniper."

Ethan using my full name cracks something inside me. He deserves honesty, but I can't—not with his breakup like an open wound between us.

"I'm with Sebastian," I say. "I want to be *with* Sebastian."

The lie tears out of me, bleeding so absolutely with the truth.

He studies my face, searching. Whatever he finds makes him look away first.

I wipe my cheeks. "Destiny deserves better than this. Better than both of us." My vision blurs. "I can't... I won't be the reason you two broke up."

"Is that really what you want? Go back to Destiny and keep lying?" There's a challenge in his voice now. He takes a shaky breath. "I love you, June. I have for a while."

The words hang there, and I can't breathe. He's telling me he loves me, and all I can think about is how this ruins everything.

His face crumples at what he sees on mine. "I'm sorry I messed this up. I never wanted to hurt anyone."

"I know." And I mean it.

"Destiny deserves someone who's all in. Not someone thinking about his best friend when he should be focused on her."

The parallel hits hard. I've been doing the same thing—loving someone who doesn't love me back. Except Sebastian isn't in love with someone else. He's just... not in love with me. Period.

Mom's footsteps in the hall make us both freeze. Ethan steps back immediately, and suddenly we're as far apart as my small room allows.

I turn away, wiping my eyes as Mom appears. She looks between us but doesn't mention my red-rimmed eyes.

"Everything okay up here?" she asks carefully.

"Fine," Ethan says quickly. "I should go. The essay's more complicated than I thought." His attempt at casualness fools no one.

He backs toward the door, not looking at me. "Thanks for letting me come over, Mrs. B."

"Of course." Mom watches him go.

I don't move as he leaves. Don't watch him go. Each sound of his footsteps retreating down the hall, the front door closing, his car starting—feels like another crack in our friendship.

But through the sadness cuts something sharper: the terrifying realization that I've been lying to myself as much as Ethan has. Because somewhere in the middle of this fake relationship, I fell for Sebastian Thorne all over again. And just like when we were kids, he probably doesn't feel the same way. After today, I'm pretty sure he can't.

Mom lingers in the doorway. "Want to talk about it?"

I shake my head, sinking onto my bed. "I'm fine." The words come out hollow. "Tired."

"Honey, four years of friendship doesn't hit a rough patch for no reason."

"It's complicated," I mutter.

"Because of Sebastian?" She asks gently, "Or something else?"

I pause. "Both, I guess."

She nods, not pushing further. "Just remember, friendships change as we grow up. Sometimes those changes are painful but necessary."

"It still hurts, though." I slide off the bed to hug her.

She squeezes tight before leaving me alone with the wreckage of what used to be the simplest relationship in my life.

I sink onto my bed, hugging a pillow as I stare at my photos on the wall. Frozen moments of our friendship stare back, tainted now by this new reality where Ethan loves me, I broke

Destiny's heart, and I'm falling for someone who might not want me back.

My phone buzzes. Tori's name lights up the screen:

> **TORI:** 911. D called me. WTF happened with E??

The message blurs until the screen goes dark. The fake relationship was supposed to fix things, not implode everything around me.

And then there's Sebastian. I close my eyes, remembering his hands on my waist, how he took care of me last night, brought us lunch today just because.

'I liked it; I more than liked it,' he'd said, followed immediately by, *'I'm disgusted with myself.'*

The message felt clear enough—he cares, but not like I'm starting to.

> **TORI:** June? Answer me!

> **ME:** It's all falling apart

I type another message, thumb hovering over the send button. *And I think I've fallen for Sebastian.*

Sebastian and I still have to attend the gala. Still have to pretend everything's fine at school. Play our parts even as everything crumbles.

And now we definitely can't break up. It would look like I dumped Sebastian for Ethan, giving Ethan false hope.

I delete the unsent message and let the phone drop.

I've spent seven years avoiding Sebastian Thorne because of something I overheard. The worst part is I'm terrified that when this partnership ends, I'll lose him all over again. Only this time, it will hurt so much more because I know exactly what I'm missing.

I have to figure out how to untangle this mess—how to save my friendship with Ethan, help Destiny heal, and face the truth about Sebastian.

Tomorrow, I tell myself. I'll figure this out tomorrow.

Tonight, I want to disappear under my covers and pretend none of this ever happened.

CHAPTER 29
Morning Reckoning

ON MONDAY MORNING, I consider faking sick. But hiding under my covers won't un-break Ethan and Destiny's relationship. It won't erase my feelings for Sebastian. And it definitely won't stop the gossip spreading through Palm Vista's halls.

So I get up. Get dressed. Try to look like someone who didn't spend all weekend staring at her ceiling avoiding the world until I had no choice but to face it.

My hands tremble as I zip my jeans. The exhaustion sits heavy in my bones, making even simple movements feel like I'm wading through water. I barely slept—every time I tried, I replayed Ethan's confession. Pictured how devastated Destiny must have been.

I splash cold water on my face, but it doesn't help the dark circles under my eyes. At least concealer exists for a reason.

The student parking lot is full when I pull in. My stomach drops when I spot Ethan's blue Charger three spots down, Jordan's truck beside it. They're leaning against the hood, talking. The familiar sight makes my chest constrict—how many times have we stood like that, the three of us, laughing about something stupid before first period?

Before I can decide whether to hide in my car until the last bell or make a break for the side entrance, a shadow falls across my window.

Sebastian stands there, two coffee cups in hand, uniform pressed and pristine, sunglasses perched on his nose like he's modeling instead of heading to first period. My heart does that stupid flutter thing I really need to get under control. The one that makes my pulse pick up and my skin feel too warm.

I roll down my window. "What are you doing here?"

"Bringing my girlfriend coffee." He says it loud enough for heads to turn. Including Ethan's.

Right. *Girlfriend.* After Friday's party and Ethan and Destiny's breakup, we can't suddenly act distant. We still have to play the game, even though everything else has gone sideways.

I grab my bag and climb out, accepting the coffee. The cup is warm against my palms—solid, real, grounding. "Thanks."

His head tilts, sunglasses blocking whatever stirs behind those intense eyes. His hand settles on my shoulder, and the weight of it steadies something inside me. His voice drops as he asks, "What's wrong?"

I take a sip to buy time, letting the bitter warmth slide down my throat. I'm going to have to tell him about Ethan and Destiny. How our fake relationship might have caused exactly what I was trying to prevent.

My gaze flicks toward Jordan and Ethan. It's a quick look, but Sebastian glances behind him, like he already knows who he'll find.

"We should probably talk," I say quietly. My voice sounds thin, even to my own ears. I catch sight of Emma and Julie getting out of Emma's car. Emma locks eyes with us and whispers to Julie. Both watch with poorly concealed interest.

Destiny's parking spot sits empty. She hasn't returned any of my texts. The sight makes my stomach twist harder. I'll have to have a conversation with her eventually, if she'll let me.

Sebastian's thumb brushes my collarbone, pulling my attention back. The touch sends a shiver down my spine that has nothing to do with the morning chill. "Is this connected to your conversation with Ethan yesterday? Why you didn't call me? And why Cole is glaring at my back right now?"

I nod, not trusting my voice.

He takes a deep breath, steeling himself for what's to come.

"Come on," he says, sliding his hand around my waist and guiding me away from my car. Away from Ethan.

His Range Rover is parked on the far side of the lot. Past Ethan's car. Past Emma. Past what feels like the entire student body waiting for the first bell in the parking lot of all days. Sebastian's fingers lace through mine easily, like we've done this a hundred times. Like my heart doesn't skip every time he touches me now. Like my skin doesn't tingle where his palm presses against mine.

Ethan's stare burns into my back as we pass. The weight of it makes me want to disappear. Jordan's silence weighs heavy too—he's been Ethan's best friend longer than I have. Emma's not even trying to hide her interest anymore, phone forgotten as she and Julie track our movement across the lot. Her smirk suggests she knows exactly why Destiny isn't here.

The walk feels endless. Every step echoes in my head, mixing with the pounding of my pulse in my ears.

"Here." Sebastian stops at his car, turning me to face him. He takes my coffee and sets both cups on the roof. I sag against the door, exhaling. The cool metal presses through my shirt.

"Better?" he asks softly, pulling off his sunglasses and hooking them on his blazer pocket.

Behind him, Ethan pushes off his car and heads toward the entrance, shoulders rigid. Jordan follows, shooting us one last look I can't decipher. The tension in my chest loosens, but doesn't disappear.

I nod.

"Okay, Juniper. What's going on?" His hand brushes my hair back, fingers lingering along my jaw. The touch is gentle, careful—so different from the casual way Ethan used to ruffle my hair or bump my shoulder. This feels intentional. Important.

Just a performance, I remind myself, even as warmth spreads from where his fingertips rest against my skin. *It doesn't mean anything.*

"Destiny and Ethan broke up." The words rush out on an exhale, like releasing pressure from a valve.

He freezes. His hand stills against my face, his profile sharp in the morning light.

"When?" The question is too controlled, like he's bracing himself.

"After the party." I swallow hard. "Everything's messed up now. Destiny won't talk to me... I thought I was helping, but I broke it instead."

His hand drops. The loss of contact makes me feel suddenly colder. "Is this why Cole was so desperate to see you?" Each word comes out precise, clipped. A muscle works in his jaw. "He couldn't wait to tell you?"

"He's my best friend, Sebastian." The words feel hollow even as I say them. "*Was* my best friend."

"What did he say, exactly?" There's an edge to his voice now.

I look away, focusing on a discarded soda can rolling across the pavement. Anywhere but his face. "It doesn't matter."

He shifts back, already pulling away. The space between us suddenly feels vast. I grab his sleeve, pulling him back before I can think better of it.

He stares at where my fingers grip his uniform—white-knuckled and desperate. I watch him realize the tight space between us, watch his gaze slowly lift to mine. "Juniper." His expression guarded. "If this is getting too complicated, we can call this off."

"No," I cut him off too quickly. My voice comes out sharp, panicked. His brows lift like I've said something crazy, and I modulate my tone to sound less desperate. "We can't break up now. Not right after they did. Everyone would think..." I let him fill in the blanks, imagine what people would say if we broke up the same weekend as Destiny and Ethan.

His eyes drop to where my fingers twist in his uniform. I let go, smoothing the wrinkled fabric. Something shifts across his face as he watches me. "Okay. Whatever you need."

The tension drains out of me in a soft exhale. My hands fall away.

The first bell rings, cutting through the parking lot chatter. He reaches past me for our forgotten coffees, his arm brushing mine. When he hands me my cup, his fingers brush mine deliberately—not an accident. "I'll walk you to class." His voice is low, almost rough. "Ready?"

I nod, even though I'm not sure what I'm agreeing to anymore. His fingers lace through mine as we head toward the building, and I let myself enjoy it—the way my heart flutters at something so simple, the way his palm fits against mine, warm and solid. The way it makes me feel less alone, even if it's all pretend.

Even if it doesn't mean to him what it means to me.

CHAPTER 30
Fallout Island

FIRST PERIOD AP Literature feels hollow with Destiny's empty seat next to me. I've already texted her three times since Saturday, each message showing delivered but unread. My attention keeps drifting to her vacant chair while Mrs. Parker discusses *Persuasion*—how Wentworth and Anne orbit each other for years, pretending indifference while carrying the weight of an old hurt.

I meet Tori outside French, and we walk toward the pool together. "Have you heard from her?"

"She's home sick." Tori's sympathetic, but careful. "At least that's what she's claiming..."

"Yeah." I shift my bag higher on my shoulder. "So you've talked to her?"

"June..." Tori barely hides her wince. "Give her some time, okay?"

By lunchtime, the division becomes clear. Ethan and Jordan have claimed a corner table near the vending machines, heads bent together in conversation. It's strange seeing them separated from our usual group—Ethan has sat with me every day since the first week of freshman year. Jordan glances up as Sebastian and I enter, but quickly returns to his lunch tray. Ethan gives me a tight smile as we pass.

Emma always divided her time between us and Bryce's table, mostly for Destiny, and today she sits with them, capturing the attention of another girl at their table. Their voices carry enough that I know they're talking about me without being able to make out the words. Every few minutes, Emma's attention cuts to our table, probably collecting more material for whatever story she's spinning.

Cam hovers uncertainly with his tray before settling at a table with some guys from the baseball team. He gives me an apologetic shrug, which I return with a small smile. I get it. Torn between worlds. It still stings, though.

I stare at the empty table, except for Sebastian and me. I'm about to suggest ditching the cafeteria for the art room when a tray hits the surface. We both look up as Jason Wang drops his bag before settling next to Sebastian. A girl I recognize from the volleyball team—Mina Baker—takes the seat beside him.

"Mind if we join?" Jason asks, though he's already sitting. "Mina, you know June and Sebastian, right?" There's something soft in the way she looks at Jason, and I catch Sebastian hiding a smile behind his water bottle.

"I know Thorne," she greets, her short hair swaying as she nods, "but June, I don't think we've officially met."

I take her offered hand. "Hey."

Tori arrives last, dropping dramatically into the chair across from me. "Well, this is new," she says, surveying our makeshift group. "I like it. Very *Island of Misfit Toys* meets *Breakfast Club*."

THE NO-KISSING CONTRACT

She steals one of Sebastian's chips, ignoring his raised eyebrow. "Though I refuse to be Molly Ringwald."

Julie slides in next to Tori, offering me a small smile. At Bryce's party, she was openly hostile, but now she's choosing our table over Emma's, even if she keeps glancing over her shoulder. Whatever animosity she felt then has softened enough for her to join us.

"Hey," she says, and when our eyes meet briefly, I see regret, or maybe just awkwardness. I give her a cautious nod.

"So," Jason says, unwrapping his sandwich, "anyone else completely lost in calc this morning?"

"You mean anytime Mr. Reynolds talks?" Mina groans. "I thought my brain was going to explode."

Sebastian leans forward. "I could help, if you want. I took AP Calc last year."

"Speaking of things Sebastian's good at," Jason says, "Mina was telling me about your art exhibit at the gallery."

"They're incredible," Mina says, tucking her hair behind one ear. "June, have you seen it?"

Before I can answer, Sebastian says with a smirk, "I haven't subjected her to that torment yet. June's seen enough of my art to last a million lifetimes."

I tug on his hand so he'll look at me. "I love your paintings. Especially the stormy oceans, the lightning off the water."

His fingers tighten around mine, and I wonder if I've said too much, revealed that I've spent more time studying his paintings than I should admit.

He leans back, his arm sliding around the back of my chair. To anyone watching, it probably looks like a casual boyfriend gesture. But I feel the weight of it, the warmth of his fingers brushing my shoulder.

"I'll have to take you then, maybe after the gala is done and over with."

Maybe after. The casual way he mentions a future beyond the deadline of our agreement. Like we're still going to be… something. That's dangerous to hope. The kind that leads to real heartbreak when this all ends.

Emma's laugh cuts across the cafeteria. "I give it a month, tops," her voice carries just enough to reach us. "I mean, once the novelty wears off, and he realizes she's using him for social climbing." She leans closer to the girls beside her, keeping her voice deliberately loud. "Though I guess she traded up—from Cole to the Thorne heir. Wonder who she'll set her sights on next?"

The implication hits like a slap—that I'm using Sebastian to elevate my status. *As if I'm that calculating.* The cruel irony is that our fake relationship had nothing to do with popularity or business connections and everything to do with protecting the people we care about.

Sebastian's fingers tighten on my shoulder. When I glance over, he's watching me, not Emma. He pushes halfway out of his chair. I catch his hand, giving him a small shake of my head.

"Ignore her," Tori says firmly.

I huff. "She's always looking for something. This is just her latest excuse." I say, pushing my food around.

But suddenly Ethan is there, his hands planted on Emma's table. "That's enough, Emma."

The cafeteria hushes around us. Several people stop mid-sentence to stare.

"What?" Emma blinks up at him with fake innocence. "I'm only saying what everyone's thinking."

"No, you're not." Ethan's voice is calm, but there's an edge to it I've never heard before. "You're being cruel because you can, and you need to quit."

"Cruel?" Emma's eyes narrow. "I'm not the one who—"

"Yes, you are," Ethan cuts her off. "And June doesn't deserve it. None of this is her fault." His gaze finds mine across the cafeteria before he turns back to Emma. "So back off."

No one speaks until Jordan appears at Ethan's side, tugging him away. As they pass our table, Ethan doesn't look at me again, but his words hang in the air. *None of this is her fault.*

Sebastian's thumb brushes across my knuckles, making me aware I'm still gripping his hand. When I try to let go, he holds on tighter. He watches Ethan leave with something like grudging respect before giving me a small smile.

"Well," Tori says into the silence. "That was dramatic."

The cafeteria slowly returns to its normal volume, but now there's a new undercurrent to the whispers. I catch fragments—*did you see* and *Cole just*—before Sebastian tugs gently on my hand.

"Want to get out of here?" he asks quietly.

My gaze drifts to Bryce's table, where Emma's already bent close with a friend, probably spinning this into something worse. Then at Ethan's empty seat by the vending machines. Running away won't make any of this better.

It didn't before.

"No." I squeeze Sebastian's hand before letting go. "I'm good here."

Something like pride glimmers in his eyes. He leans back, arm returning to its place on the back of my chair. I lean into him, not caring if it's real or pretend. Right now, I'm just grateful he's here, helping me face whatever comes next.

"So," Mina says, clearly trying to cut through the tension, "anyone planning to come to our game on Friday?"

"Of course," Jason answers quickly. Pink creeps up his neck as we all look at him.

"Smooth," Tori mouths at me across the table, and for the first time all day, I actually laugh.

CHAPTER 31
Exit Wounds

WHEN I WALK into first period, Destiny is already in her usual seat. She's wearing the forest green Palm Vista cardigan, her blond hair pulled back in a neat ponytail. She looks exactly the same as Friday morning before everything imploded. We lock gazes across the filling classroom. She gives me a small smile that pumps hope into my stuttering heart.

I take my seat next to her, hyperaware of every movement, every whisper. The second I sit down, conversation drops to hushed murmurs. Madison and Bree steal glances our way, looking between Destiny and me before quickly turning away. News of the breakup has clearly made the rounds. Now everyone's waiting to see what happens next.

Destiny turns to face me, guarded but gentle. "Hey."

"Hey." The knot in my chest releases with my breath. "I'm glad you're back."

She nods, playing with her cardigan sleeve. "Yeah, I needed a day before I faced... well, you know."

"Yeah, I know." I stifle a grimace. "Destiny. I—"

She holds up a hand. "I'm not ready to talk." Her voice is steady, but hurt lingers underneath. "I don't blame you. Not really. I did. At first, but—" She shakes her head, more for herself than me. "I think I need space from Ethan... and you right now."

Even though I should have expected them, the words still land like a punch. "I understand," I say, though I really don't.

"I need time to... process." Her eyes turn glassy, and she dabs at unshed tears with her sleeve. "I hope you can respect that."

"Yeah." The whisper barely makes it past my throat. "I'm so sorry."

"I know," she whispers back.

Mrs. Parker launches into her lecture about Anne Elliot and Captain Wentworth. Her passionate analysis of how time and distance can both heal and deepen old wounds suddenly feels painfully relevant. I stare at the back of Jase Donovan's head in front of me, hearing words without processing them.

This is exactly what I tried to prevent with this whole charade. The irony is that my plan to protect their relationship might have actually contributed to its end. I was so focused on proving to Destiny that she didn't need to worry about me and Ethan that I never considered how my solution might create an entirely different problem.

When the bell rings, Destiny gathers her things quickly. Unlike our previous years of walking to second period together, she gives me one last look—polite but distant—before disappearing into the hallway alone. I watch her go, the space between us feeling wider than a few feet of classroom tile.

Sebastian's waiting outside my classroom—something he started doing last week. He follows Destiny's retreating form before settling on me. "You okay?"

"Not really." The weight of everything presses down on me. "She said she needs space."

Sebastian nods, understanding immediately. His hand finds mine, squeezing gently. "I'm sorry, Juniper."

My chest aches with something complicated—grief for the friendship I've damaged, mixed with unexpected comfort from the boy who was recently just someone that I used to know.

"You up for the art room today?" His voice is gentle as he guides me through the crowded hallway. A group of sophomores watches us pass, their whispers following in our wake. "You can paint out your feelings?" He grins at the look I give him. "Or I can drive us somewhere if you want to get away completely."

The thought of staying on campus, feeling the weight of whispers and stares everywhere we go, makes my stomach twist. Part of me wants to take him up on his offer to leave until all this blows over, but Destiny came back today. She's facing this, facing everyone's judgment and curiosity. If I disappear now, she'll have to face all the gossip alone. At least if I'm here, some of the attention will be on me instead.

"The art room sounds nice." I say, looking up at him.

He nods, a smile spreading across his face. "Art room it is."

As we walk toward my calculus class, I notice how naturally he's shifted from reluctant fake boyfriend to actual... friend. When did Sebastian Thorne become the person I turn to when everything falls apart?

CHAPTER 32
Sweet Rush

THE SATURDAY AFTERNOON surge at Sweet Rush hits like clockwork—families fresh off the beach, kids smelling like sunscreen, and locals hunting their sugar fix. The bell above the door chimes constantly as I scoop cookies and cream into waffle cones and ring up bags of saltwater taffy. String lights glow against mint green and pink striped walls as I move between the register and ice cream counter.

"Two scoops of strawberry cheesecake, sprinkles on top!" I slide the cone across the counter to a little girl with braids. Her mom hands over a ten as the vintage-style register makes its satisfying ka-ching.

A busy shift is exactly what I need to keep my mind occupied. It's been four days since Destiny asked for space, and seven since Ethan confessed he loved me.

All week has been a minefield. Every interaction with them is strained, polite in ways that ache. Destiny's talking to me again. She came back to our table on Friday, but I catch her watching Ethan and me with something between sadness and anger. I'm never sure which one's meant for me.

Ethan avoids me, and honestly, I don't blame him. Guilt turns my stomach to lead every time I see him in the hallway. How do you look at your former best friend after breaking his heart?

"June!" Macy, the fifteen-year-old new hire, calls from the candy wall where she's restocking the glass jars of jellybeans. "Can you grab more rock candy from the back? The blue raspberry's almost out."

I'm halfway through nodding when the bell chimes. I glance up automatically and nearly drop my scoop.

Sebastian walks through the doorway, afternoon sunlight streaming behind him. He's wearing pressed chinos and a heathered blue henley, with the sleeves pushed up to his elbows. A leather sketchbook tucked under one arm, sunglasses perched on his head. He takes in the explosion of pastels—the chrome accents gleaming in the light, the unicorn mural that sparkles with actual glitter paint—before finding me behind the counter.

My bubblegum pink polo, mint green shorts, and the glitter purple suspenders that seemed cute when I was hired now feel ridiculous. The visor with "Sweet Rush" in bubble letters doesn't help.

He joins the line, ignoring whispers from a group of sophomore girls who definitely recognize him. When he reaches the counter, his mouth twitches with amusement.

"This is..." he says as he takes in my uniform.

"Don't." I point my scoop at him in warning, though my lips betray me with a smile. "Not one word about the suspenders."

"I wouldn't dare." The way his eyes crinkle at the corners says otherwise. "Though the visor really brings out your eyes."

Macy snorts beside me, abandoning all pretense of restocking the sprinkles.

"What can I get you?" I ask using my best customer service voice.

"What would you recommend?" He leans on the counter, close enough that his cologne mingles with the freshly made waffle cones.

"Well," I tap my scoop against my chin, "The Unicorn Parade is popular." I point to the swirled cotton candy ice cream dotted with rainbow sprinkles. "Especially with the under-ten crowd." I lean in, assessing him with exaggerated seriousness. "Though you strike me as more of a vanilla bean guy."

"You think you have me figured out, Pip?" His voice drops lower, just for me.

"Classic. Traditional." I hold his gaze. "Safe?"

He hums low, knuckles rapping the counter. "What's your flavor, Juniper?" His gaze hold mine in challenge.

The room turns hot, despite the cooler of ice cream beside me. "Strawberry cheesecake."

"Perfect. Two scoops." He glances at the candy wall. "And some of those orange chocolate alligators."

I scoop his order, aware of his attention as I do, and Macy's poorly concealed grin. "Anything else?"

"Just one thing." He accepts the cup, fingers brushing mine. "What time do you get off today?"

"Four," Macy answers for me, biting her lip as I move to the register.

I shoot her a look, but she beams back, completely unrepentant.

"Perfect timing, then. I'll wait." Sebastian's smile has Macy sighing. He makes his way to a sparkly vinyl booth, settling in with far more grace than anyone should manage on seats that squeak. He opens his sketchbook, seemingly content to wait.

"Oh my gosh," Macy whispers, elbowing me. "Your boyfriend is like, stupid hot."

"Shouldn't you be restocking something?"

"Already done." She grins.

I serve customers, but my attention drifts to Sebastian's corner. His head bent over his drawing, that familiar crease between his brows, teeth digging into his bottom lip as the world disappears around him.

Every few moments he glances up, taking in details of the shop before returning to the page. His hand moves in quick, confident strokes, so different from the hesitant movements of the boy who made me sit still for *"just five more minutes"* while he got the shadows right.

Once, I catch him watching me. The warmth in his gaze makes me fumble the sprinkle shaker.

"June," Macy whispers. "You're a disaster. Go ahead and take a break. I've got this."

I glance at the clock—it's almost my fifteen-minute break, anyway. "You sure?"

"Totally." She's already moving to ring up the last customer. "Besides, I want to hear all about it when you get back."

I slide into the booth across from Sebastian. The vinyl is warm from the afternoon sun streaming through the windows. He doesn't look up immediately, adding one last detail to his sketch. Graphite stains his thumb where he used it for shading. His left hand absently traces the edge of his empty ice cream cup.

"So," I say, and his eyes lift, making my heart stutter. "This is unexpected."

"I was in the neighborhood."

"The neighborhood," I echo with a raised brow. Sweet Rush is twenty minutes from his house, in the opposite direction of two other ice cream parlors.

"Is that why you asked if I was working today? You planned a surprise visit?"

"You seemed like you could use some cheering up after this week."

I lean back against the vinyl. "And you're the cheer squad?"

His lips quirk as he takes the last bite of strawberry cheesecake ice cream. "I actually want to ask you something."

My brows lift. "Was it to model for you?"

His cheeks flush pink. I incline my head at his drawing.

"Oh, that." He coughs.

He turns the sketchbook toward me. He's captured the light through the window, the varied shapes and textures of the candy jars on the counter. But what is most startling is how he's drawn me—not only the ridiculous uniform, but how I'm caught mid-motion, a soft smile as I hand over a cone to an unseen customer. There's a gentleness to the lines, an attention to detail that feels intimate.

"You're a good subject." His focus stays on the drawing, thumb brushing over a corner in an absent gesture. His tell when he's nervous about showing his work. But this isn't like when we were kids and he'd proudly display his latest masterpiece, demanding my opinion. This feels vulnerable, like he's revealing more than just his artistic skill.

"But I came to ask if you're free this afternoon? After your shift?"

I narrow my eyes. "Why? What are you planning?"

"Some friends from the aquarium are monitoring the manatees at Warm Springs Preserve this afternoon. Would you like to come?"

I sit up straighter. "The manatees? Really?" I can't hide my excitement. I've always loved manatees—their gentle movements, curiousness. They're like water puppies.

He nods with a grin. "There might be other interesting people there too." His gaze glimmers with something secret, and I'm nervous and excited for different reasons.

"In this?" I gesture at my uniform, suddenly self-conscious again. "No way."

He shrugs, a smirk playing across his mouth. "I kind of like it."

"I'm serious," I tell him, though his teasing smirk makes it hard to keep a straight face.

"I have a shirt in my car you can wear," he says. "It'll be fine. The manatees will love it."

I let out a soft helpless laugh, already mentally sorting through what I have in my car to change into. "What time are they meeting?"

"Four-thirty."

"And it'll be just us?" This isn't part of our deal. This is Sebastian choosing to spend his Saturday trying to cheer me up.

"Is that okay?" His fingers trace the edge of his sketchbook.

"Yes." The word slips out before my brain catches up. "I'll meet you in the parking lot at four?"

His smile—not the teasing one, but something tender, almost shy—does things to my body I've been trying to ignore since the Aquarium.

"Perfect," Sebastian says, gathering up his things.

I slide out of the booth with him. His fingers on my wrist stop me from immediately bolting. I tilt my head as he whispers, "See you then."

Goosebumps race down my arms as I push through the swinging door into the kitchen. Macy pounces when I return.

"Details," she demands. "All of them."

"He's taking me to see the manatees after my shift." I try for casual even as my pulse quickens.

"Manatees?" Macy sighs dramatically. "That's so cute."

I shake my head but I can't stop smiling. "I need to finish these orders."

The rest of my shift crawls. Finally, four o'clock arrives. I change quickly in the back room, ditching the suspenders, and swapping my pink polo for a white tank top from my gym bag.

Sebastian waits by his Range Rover when I emerge, late afternoon sun casting him in golden light. He straightens when he sees me, something unreadable flickering across his face.

"Sorry to keep you waiting."

"I wasn't waiting long." His eyes drift over my tank top and mint shorts, lingering before he reaches into his backseat. "Here." He pulls out a cream-colored hoodie. "Did you still want this?"

"Yes, thanks."

He passes me the cashmere bundle, impossibly soft against my fingers. It smells like him. A memory flashes quick as a viper, from Bryce's party—*"you smell like Christmas trees and pineapple cake."*

I pull his sweatshirt over my head using the motion to hide my burning cheeks. My ponytail gets caught in the fabric, so I tug the elastic free and finger-comb through hair that still carries the sticky-sweet scent of sugar and vanilla from my shift. I'm all too aware of his gaze on me like he's committing this to memory.

Sebastian's hand lifts, hesitates, then his fingers catch a strand of my hair. The touch is gentle, reverent. He follows the movement as he lets it slip from his fingers.

"It's just fifteen minutes down the coast." His voice is rougher than usual. "Ride with me, or you can follow?"

Everything about this feels different. The empty parking lot. No classmates watching, no parents to convince. Just us, and whatever this is growing between us that feels less and less like pretend with each passing day.

THE NO-KISSING CONTRACT

I wonder if I'm the only one feeling the shift.

"I'll follow you," I say, because I need those few minutes alone to calm my racing heart.

CHAPTER 33
Manatee Meet-Cute

THE PRESERVE OPENS before us as we drive in—a sheltered lagoon where freshwater springs meet brackish water, creating a perfect manatee habitat.

I pull into the small lot beside Sebastian's car, already crowded with aquarium vans and research equipment.

The rich smell of saltwater and mangroves hit me as I climb out, mixed with the earthy scent of the springs. It feels wild, untouched—like Florida before development claimed the coastline.

"This is beautiful."

"Wait until you see what we really came for." He leads me toward the group scattered around the shore.

Dr. Zhao looks up from her waterproof tablet near the shoreline. Two grad students wade knee-deep in the shallow bay, holding equipment, while a marine biologist documents the massive gray shapes gliding below the surface.

"Sebastian! Right on time," Dr. Zhao calls, waving us over.

"Dr. Zhao," Sebastian's hand finds the small of my back. "You remember June?"

"Of course, nice to see you again." She extends her hand. "Welcome. We've got quite an operation going today."

"Thank you for allowing me to tag along," I reply, shaking her hand.

"You're in for a treat," Dr. Zhao gestures toward the water. "We've got three regulars in the lagoon—Marty, Fleur, and Pickle, plus two we haven't identified yet."

"Pickle?" I can't help smiling.

"She has a thing for cucumbers." Dr. Zhao laughs. "Sebastian, why don't you show Juniper the observation deck? Then you two can help with tagging the new arrivals."

Sebastian guides me down the boardwalk to a wider platform extending over the clearest part of the lagoon. The boards creak under our feet, as small fish dart between the mangrove roots visible in the crystal-clear water below.

"Look." He points to ripples several yards out.

I lean against the railing as a large gray shape glides beneath the surface. The manatee rises, its whiskered snout breaking the water as it takes a breath. Two more surface nearby.

"They're beautiful," I whisper.

Sebastian points out the pattern of scars on Marty from a boat propeller, the pinkish tint to Fleur's skin.

Smart looks devastating on him—attractive in a way that has nothing to do with his perfect face. Though that doesn't hurt either.

From the platform, I can see the full scope of the operation. One researcher has moved to the sandy shore, preparing what looks like tagging equipment, while two aquarium volunteers carry crates of donated produce.

"Hey." He nods toward the group below. "There's someone I want you to meet."

I follow his gaze to a woman with highlighted brown hair talking with Dr. Zhao. She's vaguely familiar, but I can't figure out why.

Sebastian leans closer, shoulder pressing into mine. "That's Lucia Navarro."

I stare blankly before it hits me—Sebastian in my room, perusing the paperbacks on my bookshelf. The well-worn copies of *Beneath the Siren's Song* and *Midnight Tide Prince* with their cracked spines and well-loved pages. All penned by local writer Lucia Navarro.

"The author?" I gasp. "You mean that's really...?"

His face breaks into a grin. "She's a regular volunteer with the rehabilitation program. Would you like to meet her?"

"I could kiss you right now."

The words escape before I can stop them. When I finally dare look, his ears are pink and he's blinking like a baby fawn.

"I won't, obviously." I try to laugh it off. "That'd be a breach of contract."

Sebastian's mouth curves dangerously. "Good thing you're such a stickler for the rules."

Heat blazes down my spine. His words sound like a dare to break the rules.

"Do you want to go say hello?" His voice sounds higher now.

"Do we just—I mean, I can't just go up to her." My hand grips his arm. "Is that stalkerish?"

He grins. "Not when she asked to meet you."

"She asked..." I jump up and down, taking part of his arm with me. "You told her about me? Wait, what did you tell her about me?"

"Come on."

"Thank you," I whisper, my voice thick.

"We haven't even talked to her yet."

"I know." The words catch. "It's... you arranged this. For me." I blink hard against the tears threatening to spill. "That's incredibly thoughtful."

This isn't part of our contract. This is him paying attention—noticing what I love—and caring enough to share it with me. It goes beyond our fake-dating parameters, into something that feels dangerously like he still knows me.

Are we friends again, Sebastian? I want to ask him, but I don't want to break this moment by reminding either of us of the reasons we stopped.

He looks away, kneading his palm. When his gaze find mine again, I have to remind myself of the boundaries.

He opens his mouth, then closes it. Whatever he was going to say gets replaced by a simple, "Of course."

Sebastian guides me toward the monitor station, where Lucia Navarro stands chatting animatedly with a young man in a teal polo bearing the aquarium logo. Up close, she looks a few years older than her author photo, on the back of *His Ocean Bride*, but she still has that knowing smirk.

"Lucia," Sebastian greets as we approach. "I'd like you to meet June."

"Hello!" Lucia smiles warmly, extending her hand. "Sebastian's told me so much about you. He says you're a writer too?"

I shake her hand, grateful Sebastian is still beside me because my knees feel weak. "Oh, I mean, I hope to be a writer someday. I'm just an amateur."

"Oh, you're a writer all right." She grins, fist on her hip. "You've already got the self-deprecating impostor syndrome going for you."

I let out a nervous laugh. "Does it get easier?"

She makes a show of thinking it over. "I'll let you know. But meeting fans helps kill the self-hating goblin for a little while."

"Your books are incredible," I say, fangirling despite telling myself to play it cool. "The way you write yearning, and the humor woven through everything. I've read *Midnight Tide* so many times the spine is falling apart. I'm still thinking about that ending."

"Oh, I thought my editor was going to kill me over that ending. I really had to fight for it." Her smile is warm. "Sebastian says you've been writing since you were little. That you're very talented."

I glance at Sebastian, eyes wide. "Well, I forced him to listen back then. My short stories were... interesting."

Lucia laughs. "The best kind are. Listen, there's a lot of writing advice out there, and here's my pitch: listen to it all, but only take what gives back." She squeezes my arm. "I'd love to help you; see if this old gal can offer any wisdom. Even if it's just to grab coffee and talking shop."

Sebastian glances toward the shoreline where marine staff are still unloading equipment, then back at me. His hand brushes my arm in parting. "I should see if they need help," he murmurs before heading down the dock.

For the next ten minutes, I live in a dream as Lucia asks me thoughtful questions about my writing process, shares stories about her own rejections before getting published, and even offers to read a few pages if I want to email them over. She's sharp, encouraging, and so much more generous than I ever imagined.

One of the researchers signals they're ready for the volunteers. Lucia gives me an apologetic smile to cut our chat short, but before we join the others, she presses a card into my hand with her contact information. "Email me. I mean it," she says with mock sternness.

I clutch the card as if it's solid gold. "Thank you. I will."

We work alongside the research team. Sebastian with the grad students on technical tasks, me helping Dr. Zhao's daughter feed the manatees while staff take measurements.

I can't stop watching him work—sleeves rolled up, hands steady as he calibrates equipment with the grad students. This is Sebastian when he's passionate about something. Not performing for parents or playing a role at school, just... himself.

My eyes find him without conscious thought, drawn like a compass needle. And more often than not, when I look, he's already looking back.

Our gazes catch and hold for a beat too long before one of us remembers we're supposed to be working. It's the strangest form of foreplay, in the way it's not at all. We're surrounded by people and not even near each other, yet it's as intense as if his hands are on my skin, his mouth whispering my name. The space between us feels charged, electric, even with thirty feet of brackish water and a team of marine biologists separating us.

When he catches me staring for the third time in ten minutes, his mouth quirks in that barely-there smile that's only for me. I nearly drop the bucket of fish.

This is dangerous territory. Fake relationships aren't supposed to include thoughtful surprises that make your heart want to burst. They're not supposed to make you forget there's an expiration date, or dread the end.

My heart pounds against my ribs as the truth hits: I'm falling for him. For real.

CHAPTER 34
Sugar Crash and Burn

THE SUN HANGS low when the research team begins packing equipment. Lucia left twenty minutes ago, and most of the grad students are loading gear into aquarium vans.

"Thank you," I say as we rinse our hands in a bucket of clean water. The words feel inadequate. "For all of this. Meeting Lucia, the manatees... it's been perfect."

"You don't have to thank me again." He grins down at me while we dry our hands. "I like making you happy."

His attention drifts to the sun painting the trees in hues of gold. "I missed this," he admits, absently turning a ring on his finger. "I missed... you."

The setting sun makes his irises glow like jade, accentuating every individual eyelash. When his gaze drops to my mouth, the yearning ache becomes almost unbearable.

Before I can overthink, I rise on my tiptoes, hands finding his shoulders. His skin is warm beneath the fabric, still damp from the water. His eyes widen as I lean in.

His breath catches—a sharp intake—and he tilts toward me. His hands slide up—then his entire body goes rigid.

"June—" The word comes out strangled. His hands drop but hover uncertainly, like he doesn't trust himself to touch me. He takes a step back, then another. "I can't—"

He glances toward the volunteers, then back at me, something desperate before shutting it down.

Rejection stabs me in the heart, followed by ice-cold reality. Our fake-dating rulebook with a spotlight on the obvious: *no kissing*.

"Oh! That was—I shouldn't have—I thought—" I stumble backward, nearly tripping.

What had I thought? That Sebastian arranged all this because he wanted me? It's the kitchen incident all over again—me wanting Sebastian to feel something that doesn't exist.

Why do I keep doing this?

"I am so sorry." I wrap my arms around myself trying to hold everything in.

"You don't have to apologize," he says, but his voice comes out rough, strained. He reaches for my hand, but I jerk away, moving toward the walkway. "June, wait—we should talk about this."

"No, it's okay." I hold up a hand. "I'd rather not."

Sebastian falls into step beside me. We pass an aquarium worker carrying a black case. Once they're gone, Sebastian says, "No, June, I don't think you understand."

Heat crawls under my skin, hot and prickly, making me want to dive into the ocean and disappear like the mermaids in Lucia's novel *Tide of Passions*.

My embarrassment flares into anger, burning away threatening tears. "Really. Let's forget this ever happened."

Sebastian stuffs his hands into his pockets. The space between us speaks volumes. The perfect evening lies in ruins, shattered by my stupid impulse and his crystal clear rejection.

When Dr. Zhao stops to ask Sebastian about volunteering this weekend, I seize my chance. "I should get going," I say, voice overly bright. "Thank you for allowing me to help today, Dr. Zhao. It was incredible."

Before anyone can protest, I'm heading for my car, steps quick and purposeful. I hear Sebastian calling after me, but I don't turn around. I can't face whatever gentle letdown he has prepared.

I dig into my bag for my keys and unlock the car with the fob as my hand closes around the handle. A palm slams against the frame above me.

I jolt, a strangled gasp escaping as my head whips up. Sebastian looms over me, chest heaving like he sprinted the entire distance. When I shoot him a glare, his face is a mask of anguish.

"Juniper—"

"It's fine. We don't need to talk about it." I cut him off. "I made a mistake. It won't happen again. We got carried away—that's why we made the rules, right?"

"That's not—" He runs both hands through his hair, exhaling hard. "Don't run away. Not like before."

We hold each other's stare. Is that what he's worried about—losing my friendship again?

"I'm not," I say, voice catching. *I am.* I break eye contact to pull my keys from my bag. When I look up, he's still watching me like I'm a wounded animal. "I tried to kiss you; you didn't want it. I feel stupid, but I'll see you Monday."

His face crumples like I've physically wounded him. "Please let me explain—"

But I can't bear to hear him explain how he was just being kind, how he doesn't want to hurt my feelings.

"Please," I beg, shutting my eyes. "Let me go."

My desperation must get through because when I open them, he's stepping back, allowing me to slip into my car.

As I drive away, I catch him in my rearview mirror, still standing there, one hand pressed against his mouth like he's trying to keep words from escaping. A statue in golden light, watching me go.

At least I've finally learned my lesson.

CHAPTER 35
Love Triangles Are Not My Shape

I AM STARING AT the pages of *Tides of Temptation*, Lucia Navarro's bestselling romance about a pirate captain and a governor's daughter who turns out to be a powerful water sprite. I've been trying to read it for the past hour, but every lingering look and touch between Cordelia and Captain Beaumont reminds me of how I made a fool of myself last night. How the very idea of kissing me sent Sebastian cringing away.

Late Sunday afternoon light warms my skin where my pajama shorts end and my knee socks begin. I haven't moved much since I woke up, only taking the occasional snack trip to the kitchen.

At least I don't have to work today. I couldn't have managed my shift staring at the booth Sebastian sat in, which led to our disastrous encounter at the spring.

Though there are plenty of reminders around here, like Captain Beau's sea glass green eyes and storm-forged jawline. I toss the book with more force than necessary to the floor, then throw my arm over my burning eyes. The smell of his cologne is shoved into my senses, clinging to his hoodie I pulled on this morning because apparently, I like pain. I let out an irritated growl. I refused to cry another tear over Sebastian Thorne.

"Wow, what did that book do to you?"

I jerk upright as Ethan steps into the room. He looks different—still the same messy-headed boy who ate dinner at my house on weeknights when he was avoiding his stepdad, but something has shifted. Maybe it's him. Maybe it's us.

I slide up from the bed, pushing the sleeves of Sebastian's hoodie up. "What are you doing here?"

He closes the door before stuffing his hands in his pockets. "Your mom said I could let myself in."

"No, I mean here, at my house?"

"You're still mad at me, huh?"

"I'm not mad at you, *exactly*," I say cautiously. The carpet is soft under my socked feet as I shift my weight. "But things are different now. Destiny broke up with you because of me."

"Not because of you, but because of me," he says firmly. "I failed her. I failed you both. The way I acted at Bryce's party, how I've been acting since you started dating Sebastian… I made things weird between us."

He grabs the ends of his hair and releases them with a frustrated sigh. "And I hate it. I hate that I messed everything up. I miss you, June."

"Miss me like a friend?"

He glares at me. "I will not apologize for having feelings for you. I *am* sorry for how it went down, though. How selfish I acted toward Destiny and you. How I hurt her." His voice catches. "How I'm hurting you now."

He holds his hands out, palms up. "I cared for Destiny. That part wasn't a lie, but it was different with us. Can't you see that? It was easy with you. I looked forward to our game nights, playing Zombie Killerz. Cuddled up on your couch watching those stupid romantic movies you pretend to hate." He glances down at the discarded book, picks it up, smiling at the cover before setting it on the nightstand.

"I want you to forgive me. Can you do that?"

I think about it. The memories we've shared over the years. The ticket stubs to summer fairs still pinned to my bulletin board, the friendship bracelet his younger sister Lucy made me. I nod. "Yes."

He kneels by the bed in front of me, his hands, partly calloused and warm, gingerly take mine. The daylight catches the copper in his hair from all his days at the beach.

"Good," he says, but he's still apprehensive. "I have one more favor? It's a big one, but hear me out."

"What is it?"

"I want you to kiss me."

I pull my hands from his and stand. The air in my bedroom is too thick to breathe. "Ethan, why would you ask me something like that?"

He smirks. "Because I know you'd punch me if I went for it."

He stands, and I back up until the edge of my desk presses into my thighs. Ethan doesn't follow me and instead stuffs his hands in his jean pockets.

"I think you have feelings for me, too, and I want you to really think about it before you push me away. Don't think about Thorne, or Destiny. Think about us. All the time we've spent together, how much fun we've had."

At my hesitation, he nods. "I need to know, June. If you kiss me and feel nothing, then I'll drop it, and we'll never talk about it again. But if there is something..."

"And if there's nothing?" I ask, already knowing the answer but needing to hear him say it. My mind races ahead to all the ways this could go wrong, how I could lose him completely if this ruins things between us, but also how I might lose him if I don't allow him the closure he needs.

He swallows, the sound almost audible. "Then I guess we go back to being friends."

"Friends? You can go back to being friends? After you told me you loved me?"

He looks miserable as he considers this. "I don't know. Maybe not," he admits. "Not if you stay with Sebastian."

"That's not fair."

"I know. But it makes me sick seeing you with him."

"Ethan, he's my..." I start, but the words catch. *My boyfriend.* Sebastian is still technically my boyfriend, and Ethan doesn't know the difference.

I wrap my arms around myself as I sit on the bed, anger cutting through my confusion. "You understand this is messed up, right? You ask to kiss me when I have a boyfriend. Whether you like Sebastian or not, I'm with him."

His face flushes, shame replacing the desperate hope. "I know it's shitty. Trust me, I know."

The truth about our fake relationship sits heavy on my tongue. How, after the gala, he doesn't have to worry about Sebastian and me dating. Our relationship will dissolve like paint in the rain.

Maybe I owe him the truth about my feelings, even if it's not the answer he's hoping for. Maybe we both deserve to know where we really stand, instead of wondering "what if" for the rest of our lives.

I stare at this boy who's been beside me through most of high school. Who's never been afraid to reach for me, even now.

"One kiss, June."

I touch my fingers to my lips. I wanted to kiss Sebastian yesterday, and he pulled away. He had every right to set boundaries, but the heat of rejection still burns.

Maybe Sebastian feels something, maybe he doesn't. But here's Ethan, willing to risk it all for one kiss. What would it be like to be wanted that openly? To not have to wonder and guess and read into every careful gesture and touch? It feels good to be wanted, even if it's not by the someone I want.

A paper seahorse I made for Sebastian sits undelivered and judgmental on my desk. But maybe I need closure, too.

"Okay."

Neither of us moves. But my heartbeat picks up in anticipation, knowing that things will never be the same after this.

Ethan takes a step toward me, his hand finding mine. He waits until I step toward him. My arm slides around his waist, and I rest my head on his shoulder, catching his familiar scent of fresh laundry and citrus body wash he's used since sophomore year. His hand rubs along my back. The gesture is so familiar it should be comforting. Instead, it reminds me how different this feels from Sebastian, how my skin doesn't tingle where Ethan's hand meets my back.

His chest moves with a deep inhale. He lets it out slowly.

"You don't have to, June," he says, low, his other arm coming up to hug me tighter. "I'll figure something out, okay? I'll get over it."

But I'm already tilting my head up to meet his gaze. His blue eyes dance between mine. Little stars catch in them from the string lights fighting with the harsh sunlight outside. The freckles across his nose from too many days surfing, the small scar at his temple from when he crashed his bike in tenth grade.

Ethan is attractive. I've always seen that, but there was never any zing, any flutter whenever I looked at him, or when we touched. I try to find it now. My hands cup his face. Was there always that bit of fire when he looked at me and I chose not to see it?

"I know I don't have to," I whisper.

And then I kiss him.

His lips are soft and warm, and for a second that stretches like eternity, I let myself fall into it. Let myself pretend this is what I want, that this familiar boy with his gentle hands and honest heart could be enough. That maybe Sebastian's rejection was the universe telling me to choose what's safe, what's easy, what won't shatter me into a million pieces.

But even as Ethan's arms tighten around me, even as he kisses me back with years of pent-up longing, all I can think about is how wrong this feels. How his lips don't make my knees weak, how his touch doesn't set my skin on fire, how this sweet, careful kiss is nothing like the storm I crave.

I pull back, and I see the moment Ethan realizes. His arms flex tighter around me, his head dropping to my shoulder. We both exhale. "I don't know if I'll ever get over you, Juniper."

Tears spring to my eyes, and I hug him tighter, resting my head against him. After a moment, I hear him sniff before he says, "You really love him?"

I wipe my cheeks. "I do."

He pulls back to look at me, understanding in his glassy gaze. He loosens his hold as I slide out of his arms.

"Does he know?"

I shake my head. He releases a breath that puffs his cheeks, like he's deflating, before he moves to sit on my bed. The old bedframe groans under his weight. When his gaze returns to mine, there's acceptance there. "It was unfair of me to ask that of you."

"It's okay." I take a seat next to him; the mattress dipping further under our combined weight, nudging us closer. For a moment, we sit in the silence of all we've confessed.

"So what now?"

I don't have an answer. How do you go back to normal after this? After he's told me he loves me and will never get over me, and I've told him I love someone else?

"I don't know."

"I really made a mess of everything," he says after a while.

"We both did," I confess, but Ethan give me an incredulous look.

Someday I might tell him about the catalyst, about my part in it at least, but not today. Not when all it will give him is a hope he doesn't have. Maybe some paintings are meant to stay behind gallery glass, untouchable and perfect. Some storms are better weathered alone. And some secrets need to stay unspoken. Destiny, though she deserves the truth, I just need to work up the courage to tell her.

"What about Destiny? Are there still feelings there?"

He shakes his head. "She made the right call ending things." He rubs his brow. "I hope one day she'll forgive me for how things went down, but we're better as friends."

I lean back on my hands and stare up at the ceiling. "So much has changed this year."

"Yup." He flops back on the bed, folding his hands on his belly. The mattress bounces with the movement. "Like you and Thorne."

"Don't start," I warn.

He lifts his hands up in surrender before lacing them again. "It'll take some time for me to get used to that."

I snort. "I think he feels the same about you."

"Yeah," he laughs.

I rub the spot where my heart rests, wondering if this ache will ever go away.

"What is it with you two, anyway? You've had this secret rivalry for years, and neither of you wants to tell me what it's about."

Ethan gives me a look, like I should have figured it out by now. "Wasn't it obvious?" He shrugs, but there's no humor in it. "We were both in love with you."

"Oh."

"Yeah, 'oh'." He stands up, surveying my room as if it'll be the last time he sees it. "I better go. Brandon and I are going fishing." He heads toward the door, his hand resting on the knob. He chews his cheek. "You want to come?"

I want to. I want to pretend this afternoon never happened, that we can go back to being the kids who spent summer days fishing off the jetty without all this weight between us. But I kissed him knowing I loved someone else, and that changed everything.

"Next time?" I say, but we both know things will be different. Maybe not bad different, just... different.

Ethan gives a last nod before he slips out into the hallway. I listen to his footsteps fade, wondering if this is how growing up feels–losing pieces of what you were to become whatever you're supposed to be next.

I touch my lips, thinking about the two kisses in twenty-four hours. One with the boy who laid his heart bare without fear, but stirred nothing inside me, and the almost-kiss with the boy who let me run away but makes my heart race with only a look. One kiss that gave me the answers I needed, and one almost-kiss that left me with nothing but questions.

Ethan's wrong, though. Sebastian was never in love with me. Whatever we had as kids died a long time ago, and this arrangement was just convenient for both of us. But knowing that doesn't make it hurt any less.

I wanted clarity, revenge even—to forget all about Sebastian Thorne and go back to hating him again, but all I did was confirm what my heart already knew: some feelings can't be undone, no matter how much better it would be if they could.

CHAPTER 36
Shallow End, Deep Hurt

THE POOL'S HEATER battles with the cold front that blew in Monday night. It keeps it at seventy degrees, which wouldn't be too bad if the breeze didn't feel like it was coming off Antarctica.

Most of the class huddles on the bleachers, bundled in either layers fit for a Milwaukee snowstorm, or underdressed, in thin Palm Vista sweaters and sandals. Coach Burton perches in his lifeguard chair dressed in a windbreaker of the school's colors, apparently content to let us choose between freezing in the water or out of it.

A few students seem immune to the weather. Sebastian is one of them. I dangle my feet in the lane beside his, watching him cut through the water, one powerful stroke at a time, like the cold doesn't touch him.

We've been cordial since the *incident*. He walked me to class, ate lunch with us yesterday, but there's some unspoken tension that sparks every time our gazes accidentally meet. Neither of us wants to address the almost-kiss, so maybe we never will.

I keep replaying that moment in my head since Saturday. How he almost leaned in before jerking back. The pained look when I tried to leave. I keep going in circles: does he want me or not? Everything felt real until I actually tried to kiss him. His rejection has curdled into something darker inside me.

Tori shivers beside me in her fleece-lined sweater. "This is inhumane. It's like, sixty degrees."

"Seventy-two," I correct, though I'm shivering too.

She nudges my shoulder, voice dropping. "So? Are you going to tell me why Ethan's suddenly acting normal again?"

"What do you mean?" I slowly scissor-kick my feet in the water.

Tori gives me a face. "He ate lunch with us yesterday, when last week he couldn't stand seeing you with Sebastian." Her eyes narrow. "And you're doing that thing where you won't look at me. Did something happen?"

"He came over this weekend."

"And?" She leans closer.

"We talked." I kick my feet, watching ripples spread.

Tori's voice drips with skepticism. "About what?"

I check that our classmates are still huddled at the far end, their chatter creating a buffer of noise. "About us. He thought I had feelings for him too."

"And what did you tell him?" She asks slowly, biting her nail.

"I told him no, Tori, of course."

"Yeah, sorry," she mumbles, looking chagrined.

"But he didn't believe me." I grimace. "He wanted to see if anything was there."

"See how?" she asks, her brows pulled low. At the look I level at her, she gasps, loud enough that I shush her. "Juniper!"

I lift a shoulder. "He wanted to see if there were, I don't know... sparks?" I try to sound casual, like I haven't spent all weekend feeling guilty about it.

Ethan's request for closure made sense. Since my relationship with Sebastian is a facade, I didn't see how it could hurt anyone. If anything, it felt like the mature thing to do—instead of leaving Ethan wondering.

Especially since I know how that feels.

Sebastian pulling back was all the closure I needed. He wasn't interested in anything beyond a platonic friendship. I can either accept his boundaries, or go back to being acquaintances who occasionally orbit each other.

Tori grabs my arm. "Please tell me you didn't."

"He asked me to," I say defensively, though my voice wavers. "He said if I felt nothing, he'd drop it and we could go back to being friends."

"And?" Tori's eyes are wide, searching my face.

"Nothing." The word comes out flat. Final. "I felt absolutely nothing when we kissed. It confirmed what I already knew."

"Ethan kissed you?" Sebastian's voice cuts through the air like ice.

We both jump. Sebastian floats in the next lane, arms draped over the dividing floats. Water streams down his face as he stares straight through me.

"Sebastian." I breathe his name, my heartbeat switching gears. "Yes, but it's not what you think—"

"You kissed him?" His voice is dangerously low. I nod. "Does he know about us? Did you tell him it was fake?"

"No."

Something dark flashes across his face. Without another word, he hauls himself out of the pool in one fluid motion, water cascading off his shoulders.

He stands there, water pooling at his feet, his face completely blank. Then his eyes meet mine, and something shatters before he turns away.

Guilt punches my stomach, but anger quickly follows. How dare Sebastian be mad when he's made it clear how fake this all is?

"June!" Tori warns, with a groan. "You should have told him."

I wave dismissively, though my heart races. "It's not real, Tori. Why would he care? This whole thing ends after the gala, anyway."

"Uh, June, I think he's really pissed." She nods toward Sebastian striding across the pool deck, leaving a trail of wet footprints.

"I didn't think he'd care."

Tori stares like I've grown a second head. "Are you serious right now?" she asks but doesn't wait for me to answer. "Of course, Sebastian would care that you kissed another guy. Sometimes you're really smart, June, and sometimes..." She gestures helplessly.

"I'm an idiot?"

"I was going to say oblivious, but yeah."

The weight of my mistake settles like a rock in my stomach.

"Um, June," Tori's voice turns urgent. "I don't think he's handling this well."

Sebastian pushes open the side gate hard enough to make the chain-link fence shudder. He cuts across the cement pathway toward the athletic field.

"Where is he—"

Tori and I track him to where Ethan's PE class runs drills. Dread drops like ice in my belly. "Oh, no."

I'm already moving. Pulling my legs out of the pool, I run after him.

The guilt evaporates with each step, replaced by a growing fear of what Sebastian plans to do next. I've never seen him this angry. Even from here, you can see the rigid line of his shoulders, his hands balled into fists.

Coach Burton's whistle screams behind us. "Where do you think you're going? Blake! Victoria!"

I push through the gate, Tori right behind me.

"Sebastian, wait!"

My bare feet slip on damp grass as we reach the field. Sebastian's already halfway across, water still streaming from his practice jammers. A couple of students stop and stare as he cuts straight through their drills.

The fence rattles behind us, followed by hoots and cheers. I can imagine our classmates gathering to watch the show. Coach's whistle keeps screaming, mixing with my heartbeat and feet pounding on wet grass.

Ethan helps Coach Mackey arrange cones, his back to Sebastian. He turns at the sound of whispers, confusion crossing his face when he spots Sebastian approaching—shirtless, barefoot, in green and black swim jammers. If anything, it's more unnerving, like some avenging god risen from the water.

Ethan's gaze flicks to me, running barefoot across the field with Tori, then back to Sebastian. Understanding hits.

"Thorne, wait a minute." Ethan holds up a hand.

But Ethan's trying to tame a dog, and Sebastian is a feral wolf. Fury vibrates through him, controlled violence in every step. This isn't my careful, reserved Sebastian anymore. This is the storm he's always painted, finally breaking.

"Hey, what's going on here?" Coach Mackey calls, but his voice seems distant, drowned by the rushing in my ears.

Someone in the growing crowd gasps. And I swear Ethan nods, resolved, like he's been expecting this—maybe even deserves it—right before Sebastian's fist connects with his jaw.

CHAPTER 37
Experiment Gone Wrong

SEBASTIAN SITS MOTIONLESS beside me, shirtless and dripping pool water onto Principal Wagner's carpet. Tori's uniform is damp from when I yanked my legs from the pool to chase after Sebastian. Ethan is beside her, holding an ice pack to his jaw. All four of us face Principal Wagner's desk like defendants awaiting a verdict. Sebastian won't look at me.

Coach Mackey leans against the filing cabinet, arms crossed, glaring at the boys like he expects trouble. Principal Wagner studies us over wire-rimmed glasses, fingers steepled.

I bite my nails as my foot drums against the floor. The wall clock's mechanical ticking fills the room like a countdown to our doom.

"Would someone care to explain what happened?" His voice is deceptively calm. When none of us speak up, he sighs. "Miss Hastings, since you and Miss Blake felt the need to abandon class and follow Mr. Thorne, perhaps you'd like to enlighten me?"

Tori shifts, gaze meeting mine. I see her calculating how much to reveal without exposing everything.

"We were worried," she says carefully. "When Sebastian left suddenly, we thought he might need help."

"Enough to abandon class but not alert your teacher?" Principal Wagner's eyebrows climb. "And Mr. Thorne, what prompted this sudden departure during class?"

A muscle in Sebastian's jaw feathers as he stays silent. Water drops from his hair, tracking down his shoulder.

"Mr. Cole?" Principal Wagner pivots. "Any insights?"

Ethan lowers the ice pack, revealing a bruise already blooming along his jaw, dark against his skin. "It was a misunderstanding, sir."

"A misunderstanding that required physical violence?"

"I might have deserved it, sir," Ethan says quietly, gaze flicking to me before dropping to his hands.

A half scoff, half growl, comes from Sebastian, drawing Principal Wagner's attention.

"Mr. Thorne, do you have something to add?"

I hold my breath, wondering if Sebastian will reveal the web of lies that brought us here. But he just shakes his head once, droplets of water scattering from his hair.

"And Miss Blake? What's your role in all this?"

The words stick in my throat. How do I explain that I'm the reason we're all here? Before I can answer, Mrs. Waller pokes her head in.

"Mrs. Thorne is here."

Something flashes across Sebastian's face—the first real reaction since his fist connected with Ethan's jaw.

Mrs. Waller's gaze moves between us, lingering on Sebastian's bare chest and Ethan's bruised jaw. "And Mr. Cole and Mrs. Nelson are on their way."

Ethan's shoulders slump. He hasn't seen his father much since his mom remarried, and I know it always brings up complex feelings, especially seeing his dad this way after months of barely talking.

Principal Wagner nods. "Send Mrs. Thorne in, please."

I sink lower in my chair, wondering if permanent exile might be preferable.

Bonnie Thorne sweeps in wearing a cream-colored suit, eyes widening at the sight of her half-dressed son.

"Sebastian?" The question holds volumes.

"Mrs. Thorne," Principal Wagner stands. "Thank you for coming so quickly. We've had an... incident."

"So I gathered." Her gaze sweeps efficiently over Sebastian, then Ethan's bruised face, to Tori and me between them. Understanding dawns too clearly as she asks, "June? What's going on?"

I open my mouth, but nothing comes out.

"Your son assaulted another student," Principal Wagner says bluntly. "Normally, this would result in immediate suspension, possibly expulsion—"

"I'll accept whatever punishment you deem appropriate," Sebastian speaks for the first time, voice rough.

"Sebastian," Bonnie's tone holds a sharp warning. "Let me handle this."

She turns a diplomatic smile to our principal. "Walter, I think we all recognize that while this behavior is unacceptable, it doesn't require the severity of explosion," Mrs. Thorne says, her voice carrying that perfect blend of concern and authority—the same tone she uses to convince reluctant donors to increase their contributions. "I'm sure once Ethan's parents arrive, they'll see this for what it is—a simple testosterone-fueled misunderstanding. You know teenage boys; they're always getting worked up about something. Sports, *girls*."

Another knock brings Ethan's mom and Mr. Cole into the room. Sarah rushes to her son in hospital scrubs. Mr. Cole follows in athletic pants and a polo shirt with "Cole's Fitness" embroidered on the chest.

"Oh my gosh, Ethan!" Sarah turns his face, examining the bruise. "What happened?"

Mr. Cole's face darkens as he takes in Sebastian's perfectly bruise-free face. "I'd like to know that myself." His voice carries the same edge he uses when breaking up fights between hotheaded gym members. "Why exactly did this boy attack our son?"

"Now, let's not jump to conclusions," Bonnie says smoothly, sliding into damage control. "I'm sure once we understand the full situation—"

"The full situation?" Mr. Cole cuts her off. "My son has been assaulted on school property. We could be looking at legal action."

The word 'legal' hovers in the air like smoke. Principal Wagner clears his throat. "Perhaps if we could hear from the boys themselves—"

"Ethan, how old are you? Eighteen?" Mrs. Thorne asks.

"What does that matter?" Sarah hisses.

"He's technically an adult." Mrs. Thorne raises a brow. "He would be the one to decide whether to press charges against his classmate."

"Your son assaulted ours for no reason—"

"I think we all assume the reason." Mrs. Thorne waves succinctly at Tori and me. "The reason most schoolyard fights start." She turns to Principal Wagner. "Perhaps we could discuss this privately? After my son has had a chance to... make himself presentable?"

Tori shifts beside me, and I know we're thinking the same thing. How quickly the Thornes make problems disappear—but this isn't something money and influence can smooth over. The damage is already done.

Principal Wagner flushes, caught between offense and consideration. Before he can respond, Ethan's mom steps forward.

"Absolutely not," Sarah says, voice tight. "You're not discussing anything without us present."

The parents argue back and forth while Principal Wagner fails to calm them. Coach Mackey blows his whistle, making us all flinch. Tori yelps at the high-pitched assault on our eardrums.

"I kissed June," Ethan blurts.

The air leaves the room. Sebastian turns to marble beside me.

"June-bug?" Sarah says, hand dropping to her side.

Mr. Cole's righteous anger deflates. "What does that have to do with this boy?"

"June's my girlfriend," Sebastian says, gaze cold on Ethan.

Principal Wagner holds up his hand in a stay-calm gesture, darting between Ethan and Sebastian.

"That's why Sebastian hit me," Ethan continues, looking at Principal Wagner. "I knew they were dating... I deserved it."

"Oh," Sarah says softly, understanding clicking into place as she looks between me and Sebastian.

"I see." Bonnie's voice loses its political smoothness, replaced by the look of a mother who is seeing past the surface.

Mr. Cole runs a hand down his face, indignation transforming into paternal exhaustion. "Ethan..."

"While this... clarifies things," Principal Wagner says carefully, recalculating the situation. "It doesn't excuse physical violence on school grounds."

"Of course not," Mrs. Thorne agrees quickly. No longer trying to sweep things away, but seeking a favorable resolution. "Sebastian will accept whatever punishment you deem appropriate for this *obvious* provocation."

Mrs. Thorne's translation: *Ethan started it.*

I watch the adults navigate this new understanding, how everything shifted once they had a simple explanation they could grasp—boy likes girl, boy kisses girl who has a boyfriend, fists fly. Such a clean narrative. So much neater than what's actually happening here.

Sebastian still won't look at me. I study his profile, trying to make sense of him.

His jaw is set like stone, even sitting perfectly still, he radiates the same energy that sent him storming across that field. Part of me wants to reach for him, to touch his arm, to say something—anything—but the rigid line of his shoulders warns me away.

The boy who pulled away when I tried to kiss him just risked expulsion, and called me his girlfriend like he meant every word. Either he's the world's best actor, or I've been completely wrong about everything.

I keep replaying those seconds when something inside him just... broke. I've never seen him lose control like that. The careful, controlled Sebastian I know doesn't exist in violence—doesn't throw punches or risk his future over anything.

But he did. For me. Or *because* of me.

When Sebastian finally turns to look at me, the movement is slow, deliberate. The moment our gazes meet, something inside him collapses.

The anger drains from his face like color bleeding from a photograph. What's left behind is so much worse. He looks at me as if he's watching something break in his hands. Like

I've taken everything he offered and thrown it back at him in pieces.

And suddenly, I see it all. The pattern I've been repeating my entire life. All those mixed signals I thought I was reading, all the confusion about his feelings—what if I was the one creating the mess? What if every time things got real, I ran?

I'm such an idiot. This is exactly what Ethan meant when he said I always disappear when things get uncomfortable. It's what I did when Sebastian and I were kids—I ran instead of asking him to explain. I've been running from hard conversations my entire life, and look where it's gotten me.

And I did it again. I kissed my best friend—betrayed Sebastian's trust—all because I was angry and hurt and too scared to have one honest conversation.

Because I do love him. Whether this started as fake or not, what I feel for Sebastian is real. More real than anything I've ever felt.

And I might have just destroyed it all.

I'm tired of guessing, tired of assuming the worst, tired of being the girl who runs away instead of fighting for what matters. I want to know if this is about saving face or rivalry with Ethan or something else entirely.

We need to have the conversation he wanted to have at the preserve and I wouldn't let him. The conversation we should have had five years ago.

For once in my life, I want to stop running toward the exit and start running toward the truth. Whatever that might be.

The question burning in my chest isn't whether he'll forgive me—it's whether I'll finally be brave enough to tell him the truth. About how I feel. About why I ran. About how sorry I am for always assuming the worst instead of giving him the chance to explain.

THE NO-KISSING CONTRACT

I'm done running.
I owe Sebastian—I owe myself—that much.

CHAPTER 38
Splendidly

WE'RE DISMISSED IN stages: first Tori, who got detention for leaving class, same as me, then Ethan, who got three days' in-school suspension for instigating. Finally, Sebastian's allowed to retrieve his clothes from swim class before he's sent home to serve his three-day suspension. When he comes back, he'll serve a week of school-wide community service emptying cafeteria trashcans or building sets for the drama club. He's going to be miserable, which is what Ethan's parents and Principal Wagner want.

Tori and I walk to swim class to retrieve our bags. Mrs. Thorne and Sebastian talk quietly behind us until the parking lot comes into view, and she kisses his cheek and heads to her Audi convertible.

I slow my steps. Tori squeezes my arm before continuing without me, disappearing into the girls' locker room.

"Sebastian, I—" The words stick in my throat. What can I even say? Everything feels insignificant.

"Not now, Juniper." His voice is distant. Like we're strangers again.

"Please let me explain." His palm lands on the boys' locker room door. I grab his arm, but it was the wrong move. His stare cuts to mine, stealing my breath. I've seen him mad before, but never this cold fury.

He drops his hand and steps closer. I release him, afraid that touch is what's igniting his fuse.

"I should have known you'd run again. You always run when things get messy. You should have told me you had feelings for him."

"I don't." The truth.

"Then why the hell did you kiss him?"

The question hangs between us. I could offer a half truth—say we never meant to hurt anyone; I knew I didn't have romantic feelings for Ethan; it was for closure. I could admit I violated his trust and screwed everything up.

But the honest reason, the one sitting in my personal hell, the one I'm most ashamed of—

"I did it to hurt you." Tears swell in my eyes, unbidden. "I wanted you to feel something, Sebastian. Anything."

His chin dips in confirmation, like he'd known all along. "Well, it worked. Are you happy? You got me back for whatever I did to piss you off when we were kids." His mouth presses into a bitter line before he says, "You know you never told me. I still don't know what I did, but it must have been bad," he grabs his chest, fingers twisting the fabric in agony, "because this is horrible. You wanted to hurt me. It worked. *Splendidly.*"

"I didn't think you'd care," I say, frustration raising my voice. "When Ethan asked me to kiss him... I didn't think you'd care."

He swallows hard. "How could you think that?"

"You kept pulling away. Every time I tried to get close, you'd retreat. I thought I was imagining everything between us." Tears burn my throat, and my next words come out small and pathetic. "You didn't kiss me."

"When we were kids? June, I was eleven when you left—"

"No. At Warm Springs, at Bryce's party, at Tori's house. You had plenty of opportunities."

He stares at me for a long time. "You were drunk at Bryce's."

"That's what stopped you?"

"June—" He brushes a hand over his mouth. "What does it matter now? You kissed Ethan."

"I know." I press my palms into my closed eyelids. "It matters that I hurt you, and I'm truly sorry for that. But you hurt me too."

He runs a hand through his hair, gaze lifting over my head before returning. "Let's not do this now, okay?"

"When, then?"

His stare goes unfocused. "I don't know. Maybe never." When he looks at me, exhaustion weighs his features. "Isn't that what we do? Avoid the hard conversations and pretend it doesn't hurt?"

The truth stings. "I'm not running this time. Sebastian—"

"No. I can't do this right now." He shakes his head. "I'm suspended. Wagner's probably dying to have security escort me off campus. I can only handle one humiliation today." He turns, then stops. "Punching Ethan was my choice, June, just—let me go." When I nod, he adds, "I'll see you at the gala. We made a deal, after all."

The word 'deal' hits like he wanted. Because that's all this ever was to him, right? A business arrangement. One last favor between old friends.

He pushes through the locker room doors, bare feet on the tiles. The space between us feels impossible to cross. But this time, I put it there. A metallic bang echoes behind the door. It sounds like a fist hitting the metal lockers. I cringe.

I really screwed things up, didn't I?

Tori appears with my things. "Well," she says with forced brightness, "at least no one got expelled."

I lean against her shoulder. "Yeah. At least there's that."

The words taste hollow. Expulsion might have been easier than facing Sebastian at the gala. Pretending everything's fine while trying to figure out if the boy who called our relationship a "deal" is the same one who couldn't bear another boy's lips on mine.

One certainty remains: Sebastian Thorne keeps his word. The question is whether he's keeping it from obligation, or because there's something left worth saying.

CHAPTER 39
Spilling the Tea

I PULL INTO THE driveway beside Mom's champagne Toyota—she's home earlier than usual. I wonder if it has anything to do with today's incident. The school definitely called.

I ease the front door closed, but it still announces me with a betraying thump. Maybe our next house will have a door that doesn't require dislocating a shoulder.

"June." Mom appears in the living room doorway, still wearing her flowy skirt and tan tank, sunglasses perched on her head like she just walked in herself.

"Hey." I take my time with my backpack. No sudden movements.

She watches me, hands on her hips. "You're home early?"

I pause. "Short day."

"Principal Wagner called."

The words hang between us like a guillotine blade. She crosses her arms. "Ah, yeah, about that."

Her face shifts from stern to concerned. "Come on. I'll make tea."

THE NO-KISSING CONTRACT

Minutes later, I'm clutching a cup of chamomile tea, letting the heat seep through my palms. The familiar honey-floral scent should be comforting, but my stomach still churns as Mom settles across from me, her own mug cradled like a shield."

"So." Mom cradles her mug. "Want to tell me why you, Sebastian, and Ethan were all sent home today?"

I trace the rim of my cup. "There was a fight."

"I gathered that much from the phone call." She takes a measured sip, watching me. "What I want to know is how my daughter ended up in the middle of it."

"It's... complicated."

Her voice stays gentle, patient. "Start from the beginning."

I stare at the fruit basket on the table—overripe bananas browning beside one stubborn unripe avocado. Where do I even begin explaining how everything I've done has backfired spectacularly?

"Sebastian and I weren't really dating." The words tumble out, like a dam breaking.

Mom's eyebrows lift, but she stays silent.

"We made a deal. I'd pretend to be his girlfriend so his parents would stop trying to set him up, and he'd pretend to be mine so everyone would stop thinking I was after Ethan."

"I see." Mom sets down her mug. "And how did that work out?"

I wince. "Not great. Ethan got jealous anyway. Destiny got hurt. They broke up." I avert my gaze. "And then there was the kiss... with Ethan."

She makes a surprised sound, and I rush on.

"Ethan wanted to know if there was something between us. I thought if I proved there wasn't, he'd drop it and we could go back to being friends."

"And was there?" Mom leans forward.

"No. Nothing. Very platonic." I dart my gaze away from her knowing look. "Then Sebastian heard me telling Tori." I spin the mug in my hands. "He wasn't happy."

She covers her mouth, already guessing. "So he punched Ethan."

"Yup. And it gets worse." I sigh. "I knew he might overhear. I just didn't think he'd care."

She hums low in her throat, that disapproving mom sound.

"I also didn't think he'd march across the field and deck him."

She tries to hide her smile behind her mug. "And that's why the three of you were sent home?"

I nod, heat crawling up my neck. "I never meant for anyone to get hurt. The fake-dating thing was supposed to fix everything. Instead, I made it worse."

Mom studies me. "And what about your feelings? In all this protecting everyone else, what did you want?"

The question catches me off guard. I've been so busy being the emotional lifeguard for everyone else that I forgot I was treading water too. "I wanted everything to go back to before the weirdness started."

"But that's what you wanted before." Mom's voice is gentle but persistent. "What do you want now, June?"

The truth sits heavy in my chest, demanding to be acknowledged. "I missed him, Mom." My voice drops to a whisper, fragile like soap bubbles. "I love him."

Mom reaches across the table, squeezing my hand. "And does he want that too?"

I don't know what Sebastian wants. Maybe he doesn't either. I've seen the flash of yearning in him, watched him pull back every single time. Walls up; shutters dropping like storm protection. What keeps him from following through? Is he such a stickler for rules that he can't even break the invisible ones he's created?

"Yes, and no. I don't know." I rake my fingers through my hair, tugging at the tangles like I can unsnarl my thoughts too. "We have too many years of dodging the truth. Neither of us can be honest about our feelings. What if we completely ruin it this time?"

Mom's eyes sparkle with something that looks like satisfaction. "He's been half in love with you since you were kids, June. The question isn't whether he has feelings—it's whether he's brave enough to act on them."

"He really hurt me last time."

She reaches across the table, grabbing my hand. "I know Junie." Her squeeze is gentle. "But you never asked him why he said those things, or if he even meant them. There's obviously more to it. You were so young. He obviously doesn't feel that way anymore."

I stare at my tea, watching the surface still and turn glassy. When did I become someone who kisses one boy while thinking about another? When did I become someone who lies to her best friends? The girl reflecting back in the amber liquid looks like me, but I barely recognize her.

"How do I fix this?" I look up, desperate. "How do I make things right with Destiny? How do I talk to Sebastian? Or face school tomorrow when everyone's talking about us?"

I groan, burying my face in my hands. "It's too late. I've ruined everything."

"Honey," Mom says firmly, "you haven't ruined anything. Yes, you made questionable choices, but your heart was in the right place. Take it one conversation at a time. Start with Destiny.

Be honest about your feelings and mistakes. As for Sebastian..." She smiles. "I think you already know what you need to do."

"Tell him how I feel?" The words come out like I'm six again asking Mom if monsters are real.

"Yes. But first, maybe apologize for kissing another boy."

I cringe but nod, feeling slightly steadier. "So you're not mad?"

"No." Mom sighs, reaching over to tuck hair behind my ear. "I wish you'd felt you could come to me when this started. We used to talk about everything, remember?" Her look turns pointed. "Even Sebastian."

"Trust me, I've learned my lesson." I wrap both hands around my mug, drawing comfort from its warmth. "Do you think Destiny will forgive me?"

"Destiny cares about you," Mom says carefully. "But she's hurting, and that takes time to heal. Be patient and honest with her."

She stands, circling the table to drop a kiss on the crown of my head. Her lips linger a moment longer than usual. "I'd better call your father before he paces holes in his office floor. The school called him too."

I groan, rubbing my forehead. "Can you leave out the part where I kissed Ethan?"

"Maybe." Mom's smile turns mischievous.

I watch her go, feeling lighter than I have in weeks. But I can't float here in this moment of relief. I still need to talk to Destiny before the school gossip machine starts churning. News of Sebastian hitting Ethan will spread through our hallways like spilled paint, staining everything it touches. And for once, the whispered rumors will be uncomfortably close to the truth. Destiny deserves to hear what happened from me.

And after that, figure out if Sebastian can forgive me.

CHAPTER 40
Chat with Destiny

THE SUN MELTS toward the horizon, bleeding brilliant oranges and roses across the sky like watercolor on wet paper. Destiny and I sit side by side on a worn beach blanket, watching waves chase each other to shore in their endless, hypnotic rhythm. Each crash sends a fine mist that flavors the air. A few distant silhouettes drift along the water's edge, but this section of beach belongs to us—perfect for the conversation that's been eating me alive since I sent that text.

When I asked her to meet, saying I really needed to talk, I wasn't sure she'd agree. Rumors have been flying faster than seagulls fighting over dropped fries, and I know she's heard them.

But she came. She's here, hugging her knees to her chest, blonde hair lifting and falling with each salt-tinged breeze. After everything that's happened, she probably has a dozen theories about why I wanted to talk.

"Thanks for meeting me."

Her fingers worry at loose threads on the blanket's edge instead of looking at me. "I heard what happened." Her voice carries a careful neutrality people use when they're holding back.

I trace aimless patterns in the sand beside our blanket. "What did you hear?"

"Sebastian punched Ethan, and you and Tori were involved somehow, and everyone got sent home." She risks a sideways glance. "People think it's about the four of you. You know. Together."

I wince. Of course some complicated love quadrangle would make for excellent gossip. "That's not what happened."

"I figured." The tiniest note of dry amusement colors her voice before it vanishes. "We both know what really happened, right? Why Sebastian would want to punch Ethan."

My heart hammers against my ribs as I stare out at the darkening horizon. This is it. The conversation I've been dreading but should have had weeks ago.

"Destiny, there's something I need to tell you." The words barely carry over the waves.

"I already know Ethan's in love with you. You don't have to explain it." Her mouth sets in a bitter line that transforms her entire face.

"I overheard you a couple of weeks ago. In the bathroom with Emma. You were worried Ethan had feelings for me." I ramble on in a rush.

She goes rigid beside me, fingers clawing into the sand to her left. "And I was right."

"Yes, but I didn't know that then." Her eyes narrow dangerously as I continue. "I thought if I dated someone, you'd see I wasn't trying to take him from you."

Her face drains of color. "What do you mean?"

"Sebastian and I..." The words stick in my throat. I force them out. "When we first started dating, it was fake."

Destiny goes completely still. The only sound is waves hitting the shore and a seagull crying somewhere behind us.

"What?" Her voice is barely audible.

"It was fake. From the beginning."

She blinks once, twice, like she's trying to process a foreign language. Then her eyes widen, confusion melting into something much harder. "So you lied. To me. To everyone."

"Yes." The admission sits between us like a stone dropped in still water, sending ripples I can't take back.

She stands abruptly, pacing toward the water's edge before spinning back toward the parking lot, like she can't decide whether she wants to scream, run, or swim until she hits the horizon.

When she finally faces me, her arms are wrapped around herself so tight it looks painful. There's fury in her gaze, but beneath it lurks a broken heart.

"I can't believe this. You and Sebastian were faking the whole time? Did Ethan know?"

"No, it wasn't like that," I protest, scrambling to my feet. "I was trying to give you space. To show you that you didn't have to worry about me and Ethan."

"By lying to my face every day?" She shakes her head, the light catching the glassy sheen in her eyes. "Do you have any idea how humiliating this is for me? Everyone at school thinks I'm the pathetic girlfriend who couldn't see what was right in front of her, and now this?"

"I thought I was helping," I say desperately. "I never wanted you to get hurt."

"So what's the reason your fake-boyfriend punch my ex-boyfriend then?" The bitterness in her voice cuts deep.

I swallow hard. "Ethan needed to know if there was something between us." My voice cracks on the admission. "We kissed."

"And was there?" The question emerges as barely a whisper. "Do you love him back?"

"No." I don't look away, letting her see the truth there.

She sinks back onto the blanket, head dropping into her hands. "This is so messed up."

"I know. I'm so sorry." The words feel pathetically small against the magnitude of what I've done. "I never wanted this to happen."

We sit in silence, listening to the steady percussion of waves meeting the shore. When she finally looks up, her eyes are red-rimmed, but the fire has gone out of them. Now she looks...tired.

"Maybe you didn't make it worse. Maybe you... sped up the inevitable. I kept telling myself I was being paranoid, but..." She laughs, but it sounds broken. "We were never quite right together. I was always trying too hard to be what he wanted. And Ethan..." She exhales, then turns to me. "Ethan was always looking at you."

A tear slips down my cheek, and I wipe it away. "Destiny—"

"Not always romantically," she clarifies quickly, like she needs me to understand the distinction. "But you were his standard. The one he always turned to first." She grabs a handful of sand, watches it slip through her fingers. "Part of me is almost relieved. At least now I know it wasn't in my head."

My chest aches at the pain threading through her voice. "I never wanted to come between you two."

"I think I know that now," she says, nodding slowly.

We fall quiet again, watching a pelican dive into the waves in the distance. A cool breeze lifts off the water, raising goosebumps on my arms.

"I should hate you for this."

"I know."

"But I don't." She turns to look at me, and there's a sad clarity there. "It's better this way, really. Before we wasted any more time pretending we were in love."

I shouldn't feel relief when she's still hurting, but I do. *She doesn't hate me.*

"You're way more understanding than I deserve."

"Don't give me too much credit." A weak smile crosses her face. "I'm still pretty mad. And hurt. It's going to take me a while to trust you again."

"I understand." And I do. Trust can be shattered as easily as glass, but I'm determined to mend it, even if it's piece by piece.

She studies my face for a moment. "Can I ask you something?"

I nod.

"This thing with Sebastian though..." she hesitates, like she's not sure she wants to know. "Why'd he punch Ethan if you two were faking it?"

"Because..." My throat tightens around the answer. "I don't think it is anymore. Or maybe it never was? I don't even know." I wrap my arms around my knees, hugging them to my chest. "I think I really screwed it up. He's so angry with me, he won't even talk to me, and I have no clue where we stand."

I give her a sad smile, which she returns with a smirk that holds an echo of our old friendship. "If anyone can force Thorne to listen, it's you."

"What are you going to do now?" I ask, "Do you think you and Ethan—"

She shakes her head emphatically. "I'm not ready to be his friend. Maybe not ever."

I nod. *More than understandable.*

We sit together as the last light bleeds from the sky, watching the stars appear one by one like scattered diamonds. The silence between us is different now—not comfortable exactly, but not hostile either. More like the quiet after a storm, taking inventory of the damage but grateful the house is still standing.

"Are we going to be okay?" I ask finally, the question I've been afraid to voice.

Destiny considers this. "I think so. Eventually. But I need some time, okay? This whole thing is a lot to process."

"Of course. Whatever you need."

She starts gathering up the blanket, and I help her shake out the sand. As we walk back toward the parking lot, she says, "June?"

"Yeah?"

"For what it's worth, I think you and Sebastian make sense. I just hope you both stop being so scared and actually try this time."

"Me too," I whisper.

We reach our cars, and Destiny pauses with her hand on the door handle. "Good luck. You're going to need it."

Her taillights disappear around the curved road, leaving me alone with the quieting ocean and the first stars prickling through the purple sky.

I pull out my phone, thumb hovering over Sebastian's name. I've started and deleted a dozen messages over the past two days, but none of them come close to what I really need to say.

The screen glows in the darkness, beckoning. I just hope it's not too late.

CHAPTER 41
Fault Line

MY PALMS STICK to the steering wheel as I stare up at the Thorne mansion. Sunlight turns the white columns amber and the windows molten gold. I ran from this place once because my childhood best friend broke my heart.

Now I'm back because I might've broken his.

Or at least pissed him off.

The path to the front door stretches ahead of me. Each step stirs wasps in my stomach. A breeze stirs the gardenias lining the walkway. The same sweet, heady scent that clung to my clothes after summer afternoons in Mrs. Thorne's garden.

Please let Marta, their housekeeper, answer the door. She always liked me, and I could use those extra seconds to compose myself while she fetches Sebastian.

My rehearsed apology dies on my tongue as I press the doorbell, listening to it ring through the house. Sorry feels inadequate after kissing Ethan, carelessly hurting Sebastian, and ignoring him all these years without giving him a chance to explain.

I've screwed up so royally, it's a wonder I think this is a good idea.

Marta answers in her usual tan shirt and black pants. One look tells me she knows exactly my role in Sebastian's expulsion. Whatever affection she once had for me has hardened into something protective.

"He's not home," she says, already closing the door.

I glance at Sebastian's black Range Rover in the drive. "Marta, please. I screwed up; I need to fix it."

She huffs but steps aside. The courtesy ends there as she leaves me in the foyer like an unwanted guest.

Exactly what I am.

The crystal chandelier catches the light and throws rainbows across the walls and banister. So many memories lived here—racing down those stairs, socks sliding on polished floors. Sebastian's rare laugh echoing off high ceilings.

Movement at the top of the stairs draws my attention.

Sebastian.

He stands perfectly still, one hand resting on the banister, watching me. He's wearing gray joggers and a white shirt, like he's been doing nothing more stressful than reading all morning. The casualness is more unnerving than if he'd been dressed to intimidate.

He starts down the stairs. Slowly. Each step deliberate, his eyes never leaving mine. The boy I grew up with is gone—replaced by someone who knows exactly what power he holds and isn't afraid to wield it.

"June," he says curtly, his shoulders tight. "Shouldn't you be in school?"

Heat creeps up my neck. I ditched hoping he'd have cooled off by now, but judging by his tone, that was optimistic. "Can we talk?" I ask, stepping closer. "Please."

He studies my face for so long I'm sure he'll say no, but then he sighs.

"Come on." He turns back up the stairs.

I follow, fingers trailing the same banister I used to dare him to slide down. He never did. Probably because he watched me fall off too many times.

At his door, he steps aside, waving me in. Ever the gentleman, even when angry. Once I'm through, he reaches for the door, but hesitates before finally deciding to close it. The soft click seems to seal us in—no going back now.

His room is the same but different. The academic green walls still showcase taxidermied bugs and his watercolor dinosaurs, but the twin bed has been replaced with a king, and he's ditched the constellations and spaceships comforter for a more sophisticated duvet.

The bookcases framing the window are fuller, spines crammed together, and stacked to capacity, but I spot some old favorites. The *Encyclopedia of Egyptian Hieroglyphics,* and *Folklore from Around the World.*

He waits by the door, arms crossed, tracking my movements with the stoicism he's so good at. An antique clock on his desk ticks into the silence.

I know he's waiting for me to speak, but now that I'm here, I want to delay the inevitable. I drift to his bookcase, fingers trailing over the titles.

"I always loved this one." I pull out the book on folklore, focusing on the worn cover and not his gaze boring into my back.

"I know." The way he says it raises goosebumps on my arms.

The floorboards creak softly as he crosses the room. I don't turn around, but I feel the moment he stops, close enough that I catch the lavender on his skin. He leans in to study the pages over my shoulder, his breath stirring the baby hairs at my neck.

I have to concentrate on breathing normally.

"So you punched Ethan." The words come out lighter than I feel. "Feel better?"

His mouth quirks as he adjusts a glass-encased dinosaur claw. His fingers linger as if he's reliving the moment, and I catch the scraped skin on his knuckles. Then his eyes cut to me, all amusement evaporating. "No."

I take a breath.

"*I don't want Ethan. If I could take it back, I would.*" I need him to understand that part. "I really thought you wouldn't care."

"*Wouldn't care,*" he repeats, aghast. He pushes both hands through his hair. "Why didn't you tell me when it happened? Why let me overhear in class?"

"That was cruel." I swallow against my dry throat. "I was angry with you."

"Glad to see you haven't changed. Still throwing spiteful tantrums, even now."

The words hit exactly where he aimed them. I want to defend myself, but he's not wrong.

I hold his gaze even as my throat tightens. "Ouch, but fair."

His shoulders drop, and when he speaks again, it's like I've knocked the wind out of him. "So it was to punish me? Because I wouldn't kiss you in front of the aquarium crew?"

"Yes." My voice comes out quieter. "And because of what happened when we were kids."

He searches my face, and I see all the questions he wants to ask, or maybe he's trying to figure out when I became so cruel. "How can you think I wouldn't care? I thought we were at least friends again."

"Because you never cared." My voice cracks, and I stop, pressing my fingers to my lips.

"How can you say that? *I only care.*" He grabs a fistful of his shirt, right over his heart. "When you left, it broke my heart. And you never even told me why."

His forehead creases. "Tell me, Juniper, *please.* What did I do wrong?"

"It was what you told Sophie." I watch confusion slide over his features.

"Sophie," he repeats, testing the word.

"I was hiding behind the kitchen island." My chest tightens with the same ache I felt then—small, invisible, unwanted. "You told Sophie you'd never like someone like me, that it was disgusting. That you only played with me because your mom made you."

He blinks, understanding hitting him all at once. "June..."

I can't look at him anymore. Those words still hurt. Even after all this time, *they hurt.*

I swipe angrily at a tear that escapes, biting my lip to stop more from coming.

"Sophie said a lot of things. She teased me about everything, especially you."

"Why'd you say it?"

"I—" He looks stricken. "I was eleven, *June.* I was embarrassed, and I wanted her to stop. I never would have said that if I'd known you were there..." Understanding settles over his features. "I didn't mean any of it."

The silence pulls taut between us. When I finally risk looking up, he's staring at me like he's seeing everything for the first time—why I ran, why I stayed away, why I built walls he could never scale.

He closes the distance between us, and his hand cups my chin gently, holding me steady.

"I never wanted to hurt you. I loved you—" He catches himself, voice dropping. "I was terrified that if you knew, you'd stop coming over. It was never about you. *Never.* You were perfect. You are perfect. You were my best friend."

"Why didn't you ever…"

"Try harder?" His hand slides away from my face. "Every time your mom came without you, it crushed me. I came to the boutique, but you stopped going. When we started at Palm Vista, you ignored me. Nothing could change that stubborn mind of yours. Then you were always with Cole, and I…" He swallows hard. "I convinced myself it was better this way."

The weight of all those missed chances, all those years, crashes over me. He tried. All this time, I thought he didn't care, but he tried.

"I'm sorry." The words come out choked. "I'm sorry for never coming back. I'm sorry I kissed Ethan."

Sebastian's arms come around me, pulling me to his chest. He smooths a hand down my hair, and I let myself sink into him.

"I'm sorry too," he murmurs. "For yesterday. I was hurt and angry and scared I'd lose you again."

I pull back enough to look at him.

"Yesterday, when you said you thought you were imagining everything between us…" He pauses, eyes searching mine. "You weren't imagining it."

"Why didn't you kiss me then?" I step back. When he says nothing, I continue, "You still pulled away. So what am I supposed to think? Do you want me, or don't you? Are you not attracted to me?"

"It's not that," he says, but he looks miserable. "I am very attracted to you."

"Clearly." I eye him. "You totally can't keep your hands off me."

He makes a frustrated sound before he admits, "I've never kissed anyone."

I blink. "What?"

"Don't look at me like that," Sebastian practically groans, defensive.

"I'm not—"

"You totally are."

"But girls fawn over you at school. I'm sure it's the same at your parents' country club," I cross my arms. "You've never? How?"

"I've had opportunities." He crosses his arms, uncomfortable. "But whenever I'd think, *maybe this girl...*" He stops, looks away. "Something would stop me."

"Like what?"

"Like knowing it wouldn't be real. That it would be another part of the game everyone's playing. The same game my parents are trying to play with Avery and me."

I see him in a new light. The walls weren't about superiority or disinterest—they were about being genuine, and protecting his heart. How he pulled away when someone got too close. How he so ardently avoided his parents' setups, his reservation during our practice at the beach and his reaction at the preserve. *Because I wouldn't kiss you in front of the aquarium crew?* He was uncomfortable. Not uninterested.

"So you would have kissed me?" My heart hammers in my chest. "You wanted to; that's what you're saying?"

Sebastian stares, something stormy and electric gathering in his gaze—it drops to my mouth, and he swallows hard.

"June..." My name is a warning, rough, and scraped raw from his lips. But he steps closer.

I don't move.

He runs his hands down his face, fingers dragging over his jaw, and makes a sound somewhere between a growl and a groan.

His control shatters.

I don't have time to breathe before his hand circles my back, pulling me to him. His other hand cups my jaw, tilting my face up as if I wasn't already turning to him like a sunflower to the sun. The touch is reverent and possessive all at once.

My body reacts before my mind catches up, melting against him like we're made for each other.

His mouth meets mine, and everything that's been building between us finally breaks free. He's not tentative, like I expected. The kiss is urgent, confident, devastating—like he's been mapping this moment in his mind for years.

This isn't the careful Sebastian who measures every word, every movement. This Sebastian is unraveled, tempestuous—all the control he keeps locked away finally let loose.

And *it is nice*—no, better than nice. It's everything.

My back hits the wall, though I don't remember moving. The cool plaster is a shock until his knee slides between mine, and we're impossibly closer, every inch of him against every inch of me.

My hands find their way under his shirt, fingertips skating over the warm skin of his abdomen. The muscles jump and contract under my touch. Muscles I've been sneaking glances at during swim class for weeks.

My fingers tangle in his hair, pulling him closer, and he makes a sound that vibrates through both of us. I pull, not gently, and his hips press harder against mine, pinning me completely to the wall.

But it's not close enough. Never enough. I want to be consumed by this, by him.

My phone rings, and I've never wanted to toss it out the window more because it breaks whatever spell he was under.

"If that's Ethan," he mumbles against my lips. "I'm going to punch him again."

We're both breathing hard, both trembling, both desperately trying to remember how to function. His thumb traces my lower lip, swollen and sensitive, and I watch his eyes track the movement with an intensity that makes me shiver.

I laugh breathlessly, hands still tangled in his hair. "For never kissing anyone before, that was... wow."

He laughs too, the sound rumbling through his chest into mine, but then he goes still. Pulls back slowly. "Sorry," he says, eyes searching mine. "I didn't ask first."

I shake my head. "I don't care."

I pull him to my mouth and kiss him like I never plan on letting him go.

CHAPTER 42
Cause and Effect

WE END UP on his bed, staring at the ceiling. My leg drapes over his, his hand warm on my knee. The rhythmic thrum of his heartbeat pulses under my palm where it rests on his chest. My lips still tingle from finally kissing him.

After years of avoiding each other, this moment feels surreal, like I might wake up any moment to find it was all a dream.

"You broke your no-kissing rule," I tease.

"It was a stupid rule. I should've broken it immediately." He sighs, fingers gliding over my leg in a way that sends shivers racing across my skin. "I've wanted to do that for a while."

"When did you first want to?" I press, unable to hide my smirk.

His gaze shifts to me, then back to the ceiling. His throat work as he swallows, hands clasping loosely on his chest.

"Hmm." The sound rumbles in his throat. "I could say the obvious—Bryce's party. *That* was a lesson in *restraint*."

I make a noise of agreement, waiting for more.

"There's also after dinner with my parents, for obvious reasons."

"Obviously." I smile.

"There's the time in my car. When you were propositioning me, bossy as hell, and you smelled like summer sunshine, and cinnamon..." His mouth quirks up at the corner.

"I knew it," I say triumphantly. "I knew you wanted to kiss me then."

He eyes me again, lips twitching at the corners. "Do you remember sophomore year? When Destiny arranged that beach cleanup? And you went around bullying people to join?"

"I wouldn't call it that..."

"You stopped me in the halls, shoved a flyer into my hand, and launched into a speech about endangered sea life and how we're stewards of the planet and we all need to do our part." His eyes gleam with amusement. "You basically told me that if I didn't show up, I'd be single-handedly responsible for the destruction of all marine ecosystems."

I squirm beside him. "I don't think I was *that* aggressive..."

"You were." He smirks. "I wanted to kiss you then. Actually, that's why I started volunteering at the aquarium."

I prop myself up on one elbow, looking down at him in surprise. "What? You're kidding."

"Not at all." His gaze meets mine, steady and sincere. "You were so passionate about those turtles and the reef system, talking about how the trash was killing them... I went home and looked up local conservation efforts that night. Two weeks later, I was filling out the volunteer application."

Something warm and bright unfurls in my chest. "You never told me that."

"We weren't exactly on speaking terms," he reminds me gently as his knuckles brush up my arm. "But every time I helped clean a tank or with a turtle release, I thought about your face in that hallway—how your eyes got all stormy when you told me about microplastics." His fingers trace lazy patterns on my arm, leaving sparks in their wake. "I actually owe you for that. I much prefer marine biology to business economics or law."

"You are a strange boy." I laugh, shaking my head. "But I like it. You should let me boss you around more often."

He shifts onto his side, propping his head on his hand. "Does this mean you're my actual girlfriend now? No more pretending?"

"Yeah. No more pretending." I gaze into those impossible green eyes, letting myself get lost in them. Our childish feud feels ridiculous now. All the years wasted being too afraid to confront the truth. My fingers find the collar of his shirt, curling into it like an anchor. "I'm definitely your girlfriend now."

His thumb traces my bottom lip, and my breath catches. "In case this needs to be said..." he hedges, "no kissing anyone else, Pip. You're mine now, and you know how much I hate to share." His gaze flashes with something possessive and playful, and it stops my heart just enough for it to come raging back.

"Yours!" I grab a pillow and swat him. He deflects easily, laughing. "You barbarian."

He bats away the next pillow I throw, then pins my hand down on the bed. I look up at him, heart racing.

"It's only fair, after all." His voice softens. "Since I'm yours, Juniper Blake."

"Even when I'm being bossy and rearranging your rock collection?"

He pretends to mull it over. "Especially then."

"What if I rebuild your Lego sets?"

He pulls back with mock horror. "First, I dismantled them years ago. And second, absolutely not. Do you know how long it took me to build that pirate village? And then you started knocking the whole thing down?"

"Okay, okay," I laugh, remembering eight-year-old Sebastian's serious dedication to his elaborate pirate port. "Still a sore subject, I see."

My laughter fades as a lingering question rises to the surface. "What about Avery? Your parents' plans for you?"

His playfulness drains away. "I'm done living their version of my life." His hand slides into mine, where it rests in the narrow space between us. His lips brush my knuckles reverently. "I spent so long trying to be what everyone wanted. The perfect son, the future businessman, someone who'd make all the right connections."

"And now?"

"I want to live life how I make it." His voice drops lower. "And the only time I feel truly myself is when I'm with you."

The words settle over me, warm and real and terrifying.

"Do we tell everyone it started out as fake?"

His fingers absently play with a strand of my hair. "Do you want to?" He studies my face, waiting.

I shake my head. "I told Destiny already. I owed her the truth."

"It's no one's business but ours, anyway." He says it simply, like it's the most obvious solution in the world. "Who cares how we started, just that we're here."

"Really?"

"Of course." He tucks the strand of hair behind my ear. "I'm not going anywhere, June. Whatever happens."

The words settle around me like a blanket, warm and safe. After so many years of running, this—Sebastian's arms around me, his heart beating steady under my palm—feels like coming home.

"I like that." I snuggle into his side, feeling all warm and impossibly content.

He presses a kiss to my forehead. "Maybe years from now, it'll be our origin story we share at dinner parties or on our anniversary."

I lift my head to look at him, surprised by the casual way he's talking about a future—our future. "Years from now?"

His eyes lock with mine, something vulnerable there. "If... if that's what you want."

I search his face—he's been in my life since we were small. First as my friend, then as a memory I tried to forget, then as a pretend boyfriend, and now as something terrifying in the best possible way.

"I do want that."

The smile that breaks across his face is like the sun coming out from behind clouds.

He kisses me again, and this time it's slower, deeper, like we have all the time in the world.

Maybe we do.

EPILOGUE
In Good Faith

*H*AIRSPRAY BURNS MY nose as I push through the crowded dressing room at the Oceanic Grand Hotel. I dodge a makeup artist wielding false lashes and weave past models making last-minute adjustments to their champagne gowns. The space buzzes with controlled chaos—assistants rushing with clipboards, Mrs. Thorne's voice cutting through the noise as she directs the final arrangements.

Mom catches my attention from near the jewelry displays. She's still in jeans and a tank top, though her makeup is done, and the slight crease between her brows tells me something needs immediate attention.

"June, can you check these earrings? The clasp seems loose."

She places delicate silver and aquamarine earrings in my palm. "These are for Isabella. If they fall off while she's walking..."

"Got it." I dig into her kit for the special needle-nose pliers that won't scratch the finish.

Mom sweeps to the next model, as Mrs. Thorne appears beside me, resplendent in red silk.

"All fixed." I set them carefully in their velvet-lined box.

"What would we do without you?" Her eyes soften. "I've always wondered why you don't shadow your mother more often. You clearly have her eye for detail."

Before I can respond, she's swept away to address some new crisis.

I cross to where Mom works with Tori and Destiny, their hair partially pinned as she positions delicate silver combs designed to look like sea foam cresting a wave.

"These will catch the light beautifully when you walk," Mom says as she secures a comb in Tori's fiery hair. "Remember that when you walk so the photographers can capture the sparkles."

"I got it, Mrs. B." Tori practices the pose with dramatic flair. "Head tilted, eyes smoldering, thinking about how fabulous I am."

"You both look gorgeous," I say as I approach.

Destiny beams, touching the delicate silver strand woven through her blond hair. "Your mom is a magician." Our eyes meet in the mirror, and her smile is genuine. We've come a long way in the past few weeks—coffee dates and movie nights with Tori where the awkwardness finally melted into something like our old friendship. Not quite the same, but moving forward.

Mom's smile is warm as she adjusts the final piece. "It's not the jewelry, dear. These pieces don't *create* beauty—they only help us see what's already there." She steps back, admiring her work. "The right piece just lets your light shine through."

Her words hit differently tonight than they might have a few months ago. For so long, I've been hiding—pretending I didn't care about Sebastian, pretending I was fine being on the outside of this world that's actually been part of my life all along.

"Speaking of gorgeous," Tori says with a smirk, "have you seen Sebastian yet? The men's tuxes are..." She makes an appreciative sound.

"Not yet." I try to sound casual. "We've barely seen each other all week."

Between school, his volunteer work, and my round-the-clock preparation for the gala, we've barely had time together. The thought of seeing him in formal wear makes my heart race in a way that has nothing to do with pre-show jitters.

Tori and Destiny share a conspiratorial look. "You poor thing," Tori says with a sarcastic eye-roll.

Mom finishes with Destiny's hair and turns to me. "Honey, why don't you take a quick break? Check on Sebastian before we get you into your dress. The madness doesn't start for another hour."

"Are you sure?" I glance at the barely contained chaos.

"Go. That's an order from your boss and your mother."

Marta appears beside me with a small tray of appetizers—miniature crab cakes, prosciutto-wrapped asparagus. "For the boy," she says in her flat tone, but her eyes are warm. "He looked ready to crawl out of his skin earlier."

I take the tray gratefully. "You're amazing, Marta."

"Oh, and June? Tell Sebastian I said hello. And try not to mess up your makeup."

The knowing look she gives me makes my cheeks burn as Tori dissolves into laughter behind me.

THE HALLWAY IS BLISSFULLY QUIET as I make my way to the smaller conference room repurposed as the staging area for the men. My heart picks up speed from anticipation. After weeks of stolen kisses between classes, movie nights on his couch, and late-night phone calls, I still get butterflies every time I'm about to see him.

Laughter and conversation drift through the partially open door. I knock lightly, balancing the plate in one hand.

The door swings and Bryce appears, half-dressed—white shirt unbuttoned, his tie hanging loose.

"Blake." He grins, leaning against the frame with practiced ease. "Ah, bribing him with food. Thorne's a lucky man." He calls over his shoulder, "Thorne! Your girl's here with contraband!"

Before I can respond, Sebastian appears behind him, and my breath catches. He's dressed in a dark navy suit, his hair rumpled like he's been running his hands through it for the past hour.

He looks perfect. And when his gaze lands on me, they light up in that way that still makes my stomach flip.

"I'll leave you two alone," Bryce plucks the plate from my hand. "Payment for doorman services." He winks, disappearing back into the room and pulling the door closed.

"Hi," I say, suddenly shy.

"Hi yourself." His voice warms as he steps closer, hands immediately finding my waist. "I was just thinking about you."

"Good things, I hope?"

"The best things," he says, pulling me closer. "Though I'm looking forward to seeing you in that dress."

"I could say the same about you in this suit." I lean into his touch."How's it going in there?"

He grimaces. "Chaotic. Chelsea couldn't find the ties, and someone got mustard on their shirt. I'm actually looking forward to standing on stage, if it means a break from Cole and Mitchel arguing over spots." He rolls his eyes, before taking my hand. "The only good part is knowing you'll be up there with me."

He pulls me into a small alcove where the hallway widens. "I've been sitting in there for the past hour thinking about doing this."

"Is that so?" I loop my arms around his neck. "What kind of thoughts, Thorne?"

His smile turns playful. "The kind that would make your mother revoke my backstage privileges."

When his lips meet mine, it's with a gentle urgency that steals my breath. His hands cradle my face like I'm something precious, something he can't believe he's allowed to hold. I melt into him, fingers curling into the fabric of his jacket, and for a moment the gala and the chaos and everything else fades away.

"I've missed you," I whisper against his lips when we part.

"I missed you too." He leans his forehead against mine. "These past few weeks have been..."

"Busy?" I supply.

"I was going to say surreal." His thumb traces my cheekbone. "Sometimes I still can't believe this is real. That you're mine."

"Very real. Very yours." I press another quick kiss to his mouth. The wall clock in the hallway reveals I'm out of time. I sigh reluctantly. "I should go. Your mother's schedule is precise. If I'm late getting dressed, the whole show will be thrown off."

He groans, but releases me. "Fine. Responsibility wins again."

"I'll see you on stage." I squeeze his hand. "Try not to look too terrified."

Anxiety crosses his face before melting into something warmer. "I'll be fine as long as I'm with you."

"Focus on me, then."

"As if I could look at anyone else," he calls after me, and the warmth of his words carries me all the way back to the women's dressing room.

"THERE YOU ARE." MOM'S RELIEF is evident when I slip back inside. The frantic energy has settled into focused determination. Models in champagne gowns stand in formation, receiving final touch-ups. "I was about to send out the cavalry."

"Sorry. I got sidetracked."

"Bonnie has your dress." She nudges me with a gentle squeeze toward the small room with the clothes racks. "I'll be right there."

Mrs. Thorne and Sophie are already in the small room with the clothes racks when I enter. The midnight blue gown hangs like a slice of night sky brought to earth, silver beading cascading across the fabric.

"Well?" Mrs. Thorne watches my reaction. "What do you think?"

"It's beautiful." My fingers trace the delicate beading. The fabric feels lightweight and airy.

"Isn't it stunning? Straight from Paris," Mrs. Thorne says, her eyes bright with an almost girlish excitement. "When I found out you'd be in the show, I knew this had to be yours."

Her warmth eases something in my chest. We'd had a difficult conversation weeks ago—me owning my mistake with Ethan. Mrs. Thorne hadn't been angry, just protective of Sebastian in that quietly fierce way of hers. But once she saw I understood what I'd risked, what he means to me, she'd softened. Having her approval now means more than I expected.

"Thank you." My throat tightens as I smooth a hand down the beading once more. Bonnie's smile softens as if she understands what this means—not only the dress but everything it represents.

"Come on, June. Let's get you into this masterpiece." Sophie gives her mother a wry look before helping me undress.

I step into the gown, and Sophie moves behind me to zip it up. The fabric flows around me perfectly, the silver beading catching every flicker of light.

I step in front of the mirror as Mom enters, carrying a wooden box.

"Your crown," Mom says.

Inside is a creation more breathtaking than words—delicate silver webbing embedded with sapphires and tiny diamonds that sparkle when it moves. She places it on my head; it's surprisingly light, despite the complex design.

The room goes quiet.

"I feel like I stepped into a fairy tale," I whisper. "All I need is a talking animal sidekick."

Mom laughs, adjusting the tiara. "There. Now you truly are the Starlit Jewel."

Sophie lets out a low whistle. "June, you look absolutely—"

"Stunning," Mom says, her voice hoarse with emotion. "Oh, June. I'm so glad you're wearing this tonight."

"Mom—" I take a breath and try again. "It was never about you. I just didn't feel like I deserved them."

She abandons the pretense of fixing my hair, her eyes searching my face. "June, they were always made for you."

I swallow the lump in my throat as Mrs. Thorne turns to my mother with genuine awe. "Marianne, you've truly outdone yourself."

Mom nods, her eyes suspiciously bright. "This dress is perfect for June, Bonnie."

"We make quite the team, don't we?" Mrs. Thorne's smile carries a lifetime of friendship.

"Always have," Mom agrees.

Mrs. Thorne turns to me. "And June... you are absolutely beautiful. I've had the pleasure of watching you grow up alongside Sebastian."

"...almost like one of my own daughters." She catches herself with a laugh, glancing at Sophie. "Well, perhaps not exactly like my daughter, given the circumstances..."

Sophie rolls her eyes good-naturedly. "Mom's already planning the wedding. Just ignore her." She stage-whispers to me, but her smile is almost hopeful. "Though I wouldn't mind having you as a sister someday."

"Easy there," Mom interjects with a laugh. "Let's give them time to enjoy being young before we plan any weddings."

Mrs. Thorne claps her hands, commanding immediate attention. "Alright, everyone! Places!"

The room transforms into an orderly procession. Tori and Destiny merge into the group, their champagne dresses shimmering under the lights. We file out of the dressing room, heels clicking against polished floors as Mrs. Thorne leads us through the hallway toward the ballroom entrance.

Sebastian appears at the entrance, his tall frame impossible to miss. The midnight blue suit makes him look carved from the night sky, the subtle silver threading catching the light like distant stars. He weaves between rushing staff with single-minded purpose until he reaches me.

For a moment he just stares.

"You're beautiful," he says finally, the words carrying absolute certainty. Not just the dress or jewelry—he's looking at me with such reverence that I blush.

"Thank you," I manage, my heart racing under his gaze.

Mrs. Thorne beckons us to the line forming at the ballroom entrance. "June, Sebastian, you'll be last. The finale—when the music changes, that's your cue." She adjusts Sebastian's tie with motherly precision. "You both look perfect. Sebastian, remember—chin up, shoulders back, and for heaven's sake try to look like you're enjoying yourself."

"I am enjoying myself, Mother," he says with surprising patience.

"Buck up, baby brother," Sophie teases, giving his arm a squeeze. "At least you have June by your side."

"I'm sure Mother could find you someone," he says. Sophie's answering snort is loud as she slips in line.

Through the crack in the double doors, I catch glimpses of elegantly dressed guests rippling beneath blue and ivory light.

The orchestra strikes up a new melody—flowing and elegant, reminiscent of waves against a shore. One by one, models begin their walk onto the stage. Sebastian offers me his arm, and I place my hand in the crook of his elbow.

"Ready?" His voice is steady despite the tension in his shoulders.

"Focus on me." I squeeze his arm. "Pretend it's only us."

"That's easy," he murmurs. "It always feels like just us."

We step forward together. The ballroom unfolds before us—an underwater fantasy brought to life. Soaring Art Deco ceilings ripple with projected light, crystal chandeliers catch and refract illumination like sun through waves, and display cases shaped like coral formations showcase my mother's art.

A collective murmur rises from the crowd as hundreds of faces turn toward us. Sebastian relaxes as we move onto the stage, his natural grace taking over.

Mrs. Thorne's voice rises above the hushed assembly. "I present to you the centerpiece of our collection—the 'Ocean's Heart,' worn tonight by the daughter of our creative genius, Marianne Blake."

We descend the staircase to the ballroom floor. Mrs. Thorne continues as we walk, the spotlight following our progress. "This collection represents the culmination of decades of collaboration between two visionaries who saw beauty where others saw only darkness—the mysterious depths of the ocean, the power of midnight tides, the magic of stormy seas."

We reach the dance floor as the speech concludes, standing in a circle of light as guests form a ring around us, faces turned in anticipation.

The orchestra strikes up a modern waltz, and Sebastian turns to me, extending his hand with formal grace. "May I have this dance?"

I place my hand in his, unable to keep from smiling. "You may."

His arm encircles my waist as he guides me into the opening steps. We move together, and despite the hundreds of eyes on us, the world narrows to this singular point in time.

"Remember those awful dance lessons your mother made you take?" I whisper.

"How could I forget?" His eyes dance with amusement. "Though I have to admit, they're coming in handy now."

"You hated every minute."

"Not that I could admit it then, but there was one thing I liked about it," he admits, pulling me a fraction closer.

Around us, other couples begin to fill the floor—our parents, the other models with their escorts—but they blur into the background. The music swells as Sebastian spins me outward, then draws me back into his arms with practiced ease.

The melody winds down, and we finish with a smooth final turn that feels effortless, two halves moving as one.

The crowd applauds politely, and we make our way off the floor as the orchestra strikes up the next song. A familiar voice stops us at the edge.

"Mind if I cut in?"

Sebastian's arm tightens reflexively as we both turn to see Ethan standing beside us in his dark suit.

It's the first time the three of us have been in the same space since... well, since Sebastian punched him. Ethan and I have texted a few times since then—mostly him apologizing, me accepting, both of us trying to figure out how to be friends again.

Sebastian looks at me, the question clear. It's my choice.

Despite everything, we've all moved forward. Maybe this is the final piece of that.

I nod.

Sebastian steps back gracefully to allow Ethan to take his place. His smile doesn't quite reach his eyes as he walks off.

Ethan nods his thanks. He waits until Sebastian is off the floor before he says, "You look beautiful, June. Really beautiful."

"Thank you." I study his face. Some of the weight has lifted, even if he hasn't quite found solid ground yet.

"I wanted to say I'm sorry again. For everything. For making things so complicated, for putting you in that position, for—" He shakes his head. "For a lot of things."

"Ethan, we've already—"

"I know. But I needed to say it in person." He spins me carefully. "But I'm not sorry I kissed you."

I stiffen, and he hurries on, his gaze never leaving mine. "I needed to know June, and I do. You and Thorne... I see the way you look at him. The way he looks at you. It's different than I thought."

I glance over to where Sebastian stands at the edge of the dance floor. When our gazes meet, he gives me a small smile.

"But if he ever hurts you..."

"I know," I agree softly.

"What about you? Are you okay?"

He considers this. "I'm getting there. It's weird, you know? Being friends after... but I think we can do it. Eventually."

"I'd like that."

The music winds down, our time together almost over.

My eyes dance over his. "Ethan..."

"It's okay, Juniper." He squeezes my hand once before releasing it. "Thanks for the last dance."

He parts with a bow, melting into the crowd.

Sebastian is beside me, and we watch Ethan as he joins Jordan and Bryce as they gladly welcome him back into their fold.

"You okay?" Sebastian asks.

"Yeah." I turn to face him, hands coming up to rest on his chest.

"Good." He pulls me back into his arms as the orchestra begins another piece. "Because I'd really like to stop sharing you now."

"Possessive much?"

"When it comes to you? Absolutely." But his smile is teasing, warm.

"So how long do we have to be eye candy before we can sneak off?"

"Another hour, I'm afraid," Sebastian says with a resigned sigh.

"Should we mingle? Join our friends?"

His smile is radiant, private and just for me. "Dance with me."

I take his hand without hesitation and let him pull me close.

And as we move together across the dance floor, surrounded by swirling colors and music but lost in our own world, I realize that this—us, together—is exactly what we were missing all along. Not a deal, not a fake relationship to solve other people's problems, but something real and true and entirely ours.

As Sebastian spins me beneath the chandelier's light, I catch a glimpse of my reflection in one of the tall windows—I barely recognize this girl who stopped running from what she wants.

"What are you thinking about?" Sebastian murmurs against my ear.

I smile up at him. "That some storms are worth getting caught in."

His gaze shifts, going tender and hungry at once. He pulls me closer, and I can feel his heart beating against mine.

"I love you," I whisper, the words breaking free before I can catch them.

Sebastian's eyes search mine. Then his smile—the one that undoes me every time—spreads across his face.

"I love you too, Juniper Blake."

When he kisses me there on the dance floor, the ballroom fades—the guests, the cameras, the performance we came here to give. I don't think about the hundreds of eyes watching. I think about the boy who decorated his cave with glow-in-the-dark bats because I loved them. The boy who remembered every word I wrote, even when I thought he'd forgotten me. The boy who became my storm—and my shelter.

The gala was meant to fulfill a deal, to put on one last show. But somewhere between the fake dates and the no-kissing contract, we found something neither of us expected.

This was supposed to be where it ended.

But I know with absolute certainty: it's only the beginning.

ACKNOWLEDGMENTS

A BOOK IS NEVER JUST a book. It's a trail of late-night decisions, half-finished coffees, whispered ideas that refused to leave me alone, and the people who kept nudging me toward the finish line even when I tripped over every insecurity on the way.

To my family—you've been the quiet engine behind this story. Thank you for letting me ramble, meltdown, dream too big, dream too small, and circle back again. You never flinched.

Reece, thank you for diving into the early pages with the kind of honesty only a brave soul offers a writer. And Avalon—thank you for keeping the chaos contained so I could disappear into the world of this book without losing my mind or my children. To my boys: thank you for treating my writing time like it meant something. That mattered more than you know.

Daniel... you get the wild ideas, the "I swear this is the last revision" lies. Thank you for believing in all of it anyway—and in me. Every time I wanted to quit, you kept telling me to keep going.

Lace, thank you for the sharp feedback, the gut checks, and for calling out the weak spots with love and fire. You helped shape this book's spine.

To my early readers, beta readers, and every set of eyes that touched this story before it grew into the version you're holding now—your insight made it stronger, braver, and better.

And finally, to you, reader: thank you for turning the first page. Thank you for trusting me to lead you somewhere worth going. Stories only come alive when someone chooses to step inside. You did that. You made this real.

Author Bio

NICOLE LIGHTWOOD writes books the same way she collects them—obsessively, chaotically, and with her whole heart. A Florida native turned Kentucky homesteader, she builds stories steeped in coastal magic, messy emotions, and characters who will burn down the world for the people they love.

When she's not writing, she's spending time with her husband and five kids, wrangling three overly affectionate Dobermans, sketching her characters in Procreate or Photoshop, designing book interiors for other authors, or wandering bookstores under the guise of "research."

You can also find her here:
www.nicolelightwood.com

Subscribe for updates and upcoming releases.

www.ingramcontent.com/pod-product-compliance
Lightning Source LLC
LaVergne TN
LVHW091618070526
838199LV00044B/846